Cover Design: John Simoudis
Cover Production: Nick Zelinger/NZGraphics.com
Front Cover Design: Original Portrait of Marguerite de Valois, Age 16, by François Clouet ~ public domain
Author's Photo: Juliette Lauber

ISBN: 978-1-64456-464-6 [Hardcover]
ISBN: 978-1-64456-465-3 [Paperback]
ISBN: 978-1-64456-466-0 [Mobi]
ISBN: 978-1-64456-467-7 [ePub]

Library of Congress Control Number: 2022936249

INDIES UNITED PUBLISHING HOUSE, LLC
P.O. BOX 3071
QUINCY, IL 62305-3071
indiesunited.net

Praise for The French Queen's Curse

"A thrilling and mysterious fantasy saga filled with action and drama" - *Literary Titan*

"Cunningly plotted, filled with suspense and unexpected moments. Masterfully written" - *The Book Commentary*

"Juliette Lauber has fashioned a heady, passionate novel, both complex and illuminating. She carries us back in time to ancient matriarchal origins and tracks how they have been covered over repeatedly by the violence of the patriarchy. Importantly, she shows how the struggle continues in our times, how events of today might well be manipulated by these dark forces of the past. Kikki is a canny and sympathetic heroine striving to utilize her High Priestess powers for the good. Her partner, Torres, grounded in this world, is a perfect foil. And beautiful, innocent Queen Margot! Was ever a monarch more ill-served? It's thrilling to read how Kikki works to restore her to her proper place and set the world aright. I was swept away by *The French Queen's Curse.*" *NC Heikin, award winning filmmaker and playwright*

"Historical mystical fiction fanatics will devour this novel. A feminist DaVinci Code." *Lola Lorber, writer and doula*

For the Mother Goddess, and for Sarah Lovett, who embodies her, whose wisdom and support brought this novel to the light.

And for Paris, one of the great loves of my life. She has always enriched me.

The Kikki Trieste Trilogy
Book Two

THE
FRENCH QUEEN'S
CURSE

In Queen Margot's Gardens

JULIETTE LAUBER

INDIES UNITED PUBLISHING HOUSE, LLC

Pour moi, l'on ne me disait rien de tout ceci.
Marguerite de Valois, *Memoires*

-On the Saint-Bartholomew's Day Massacre
They told me nothing about it.

PROLOGUE

Outside Paris Winter 1572

In a small clearing deep in a wintry forest, a veiled figure knelt near the embers of a dying campfire. The last remnants of orange flames flickered and leapt like fingers of fire reaching for her dark robes. The woman leaned towards the flame, her young beautiful face drawn taut by determination. A strong hint of defiance showed through the flush in her cheeks. Her hands pressed together in a gesture of prayer or perhaps hope, and then she backed away. The fire hissed and crackled in answer.

With swift movement of long delicate fingers, Marguerite de Valois swept back her veil and lifted her face to the stormy moonlit sky, revealing the regal profile and porcelain skin of a young woman of royal lineage. A great beauty. She took a deep breath exhaling ghostly vapors and then reached inside her cloak.

Through luminous yet fiery dark eyes, tears streamed down her pale cheeks as she drew out a long-stemmed red rose. Her lips softened as she kissed velvety petals. She raised her head towards the sky and gazed fervently upon the moon and then cast the rose into the flames. An offering to the Twin Moon Goddesses of Greek mythology, Artemis and Hecate.

She whispered a prayer to invoke the ancient déesses who protected women like her. An homage to the fierce Sumerian Inanna, Goddess and Queen of Heaven and Earth and Mother Goddess—worshipped by the great ancient civilization of Mesopotamia millennia ago. All one in the Goddess.

Marguerite uttered a final prayer to her secret protectors. For though she was "Catholic" for appearances, for religious correctness at the French Court, her true loyalties were with the Goddess.

She rose and bowed low, pressing her hands together again. She whispered a last litany. As she backed away, she crossed her arms across her belly. Once more she lifted her face heavenward and threw both arms high, reaching for the moon. She hesitated, unsteady on her feet, yet sure of her path, sure as she was that she was one with the Greek Goddess Aphrodite—the one the Romans called Venus.

"Come, then, Your Grace," her companion whispered, "Cover yourself. We must go. It will soon be dawn." In the near distance, the awaiting horses neighed and snorted.

At last, Marguerite wrapped her hooded robe around herself and turned from the fire. Linking arms with her friend, she hurried through the forest to the carriage. Away from love, from Paris. Though it pained her greatly to part with her newborn daughter, she had to take her to safety. Away from her Mother and the King, the grave dangers at the royal court of France.

She wrapped the tiny infant more tightly in her blanketed arms and knew her heart would break once more at losing her. She steeled herself. She had no choice. To stay was certain death for her daughter. She shuddered with terror.

"Hurry!" her friend whispered. "Do not worry, we will get to the Convent of the Daughters. Their friends and yours will help us along the way."

The soldier crouched in the forest at the edge of the clearing, watching in silence. He did not move until they had gone and he heard the sure sound of the horses' hooves clattering on the hardened icy road that led through the forest. Then he mounted his horse and followed the carriage, keeping a safe distance. He *rode out of sight, skirting the trees, hidden.*

He stopped and pulled the reins up short for a moment and looked upwards. Fast-moving dark clouds scudded across the face of the moon. The night was fading to a slate gray dawn sky. He glanced back, towards home, the great city of Paris, peering down the narrow road, watching out for unwanted company. He saw no one. Tant mieux.

In the very far distance, he could make out the twin Gothic towers of the great Cathedral of Notre-Dame de Paris, just barely visible, silhouetting the predawn sky by divine ordinance. No other landmark penetrated the city's permanent layer of smoke from ever-burning winter fires.

Seeing no other soul on the road, he clicked his tongue against his teeth and urged his horse silently ahead, following the carriage just as it disappeared around a bend.

Thunder rumbled in the distance, and large drops of freezing rain pelted the rider. The heavens opened, and it poured.

He smiled. Snow had been predicted. But it was too warm yet. God was with him. It would be easier to follow the heretical whore and her accompanying witches in the downpour that muffled sounds. Though he wouldn't mind a good blizzard. That would slow the carriage down—but not him.

He whipped his stallion sharply, kept his keen blue eyes on the carriage and began to count the ways he would spend the gold promised by his King and his other benefactor, Queen Mother Catherine de Medici.

For he was confident that he would find her, though his brethren in God would also lay chase, for the bounty offered by the queen was generous. He would win this dangerous game and bring her and her damned child back in chains. God was on the side of the righteous.

"Long live King Charles IX of Valois, who serves by divine right for the One and Only True Catholic God!" He thrust his sword high and shouted into the rain. "In the name of the Knights of the Holy Sword of God!"

Chapter 1

Paris, December 2015

Véronique "Kikki" Trieste stood at the French paned door and stared down at the River Seine, chilled to the bone even in her long white robe. The staccato of a barge hitting the fast-running water under the nearby bridge, the Pont Royal, had awakened her at three a.m. from a haunting yet familiar nightmare of a bloody massacre centuries ago.

Paris's beloved River Seine was a peculiar gray-green dotted with golden halos from the overhanging soft yellow lights on Quai Voltaire. On the bridge, they glowed only dimly in the thick fog—lanterns hanging midair.

From the floor-to-ceiling windows that fronted her penthouse apartment on Quai Voltaire, Kikki had a perfect view of this ancient center of the City of Light—just like Voltaire, who had lived and died in this very building. Directly across from the Louvre and the early seventh-century Pavillon de Flore, an inspiring, majestic building at the end of the Louvre's long main gallery. Once part of the Palais des Tuileries, it was named for Flora, Roman Goddess of

Flowers and Spring. The pavilion had been burned and rebuilt—it, too, was rife with ghosts.

She parted further the heavy red velvet curtains, fingering their luxuriant softness as she opened the terrace door a crack and peered up at the sky. The waxing moon shone bright and insistent, breaking through dense clouds and fog. She smiled. Still in her vigil, she whispered thanks to the twin Greek Moon Goddesses, Hecate and Artemis.

She sniffed the cold damp air and sensed the oncoming snow. That would be a welcome change from the perpetual *grisaille* (a flat damp gray) that hung over the Île de France from late fall to early spring. Paris's dirty little secret.

Kikki knew that, Gaia—Mother Earth and Nature, would have her way. Weather changed rapidly as she spewed forth her wrath onto those who violated her planet.

Still, she thought, a snowy Winter Solstice and a full moon aligned perfectly for this important week to come. The prehistoric *Minoan Snake Goddess* that she and her lover Pepe Torres had uncovered on a deadly weekend in Santorini in August was to be exhibited at the Louvre on Friday, the very day of the Solstice— December 21, five days from now.

The Snake Goddess was sacred to the beliefs of the great matriarchal Minoans of Crete, and as early as 1600 BCE, the precious treasure was carried to their sister colony on Santorini—or Thera as it was known in ancient times—where Kikki had discovered her four thousand years later.

The Snake Goddess remained the sacred icon of the Mother Goddess from whom all were birthed—the Holy Grail of the Divine Feminine, revered by scholars and historians alike—entrusted to keepers of the Goddess lineage, like Kikki.

On the longest night of the year, the Wheel of Life would turn once more as Light and Darkness—matriarchal lineage pitted against patriarchy—battled beneath the full power of the Moon Goddesses. Timing the priceless Snake Goddess Premier Gala Exhibition on that very same night, at the world's most illustrious museum, would magnify her invincible power. The convergent alchemy would blast open an immense energetic portal just as battle was pitched—in the Goddess's favor, surely.

But nothing could be certain, and Kikki's psychic antennae were on high alert. Was she ready? Were they all?

She glanced at the table next to her *récamier*, eyes fixed on the small replica of the Snake Goddess. She remembered the first time she held the dusty ceramic goddess in her hands. *Déjà vu.* She smelled the damp stench of the cave, and her hands became warm, as though holding ancient earth. She struggled not to go back to that moment.

The statue on her table began to glow so that Kikki saw her features and felt her power: Our Lady of the Beasts—tiny, a mere eight inches in height—radiating a path of light through ancient earth. Strong arms extended clutching vipers. A tiny waist and beehive skirt of the Queen Bee Cult worshipped by the Minoans and ancient peoples of the Aegean. On her head, a mythical beast, both cat and owl. The vipers—symbols of retribution and warning. More importantly, she was a symbol of fertility and rebirth.

Kikki felt drawn to pick up the statue, but as she stepped towards it, she lost her footing on her long robe and bumped against the table. The Snake Goddess tumbled to the carpet, scattering books and papers.

Kikki cried out—then became silent. Her gaze shifted towards the bedroom at the back of the apartment where Torres lay sleeping. Had she disturbed her lover? She could just see his tousled black hair through the partially open door. She waited, holding her breath, willing him not to awake. In solitude, she could gather her energy and ground herself.

When she was satisfied that he still slept, she leaned to pick up the goddess and began to straighten the scattered papers. Her cold hands scooped up a film script she'd been studying for a new client, a challenging project that she had begun working on when she returned only a few weeks ago to her legal and business affairs practice after a break. No coincidence in Kikki's mind, the film was also the subject of the book she'd been reading even before the project crossed her desk.

Now, she put the script aside and studied that novel—the source of her nightmares and recent visions. *La Reine Margot* by Alexandre Dumas, its colorful cover depicting the young queen on her *récamier*, dressed in a white satin nightdress. She held close in her arms a man, Joseph de Boniface, Seigneur de la Mole, a dashing, dark-haired, blue-eyed young man from Provence dressed in black velvet with a purple cape, grasping a leather pouch with an urgent message from Huguenot leaders for Henri, King of Navarre. A soldier bearing a musket loomed over them, threatening death, while Margot held him off. She sheltered La Mole, the gravely wounded Huguenot seeking refuge on that murderous night. A man who would become Margot's lover.

Kikki shivered and a spike of pain hit her left temple as her eyes took in the images.

Her pupils dilated as she watched the beautiful young queen, Marguerite de Valois, lift in *bas relief* from the book cover. As the image hovered, blood from the wounded man began to stain the white robe Kikki wore.

Damnit, she swore silently. Not now. Please the Goddess, not now.

Light-headed, she hurried to the window and opened it an inch. Her temple throbbed, and she took a deep breath of biting cold air, hoping to ward off one of the otherworldly visions that she so often experienced.

Predictably, her present efforts were in vain. She felt deep in her soul the magnetic pull of the waxing moon and approaching portal of darkness of the Wheel of the Year that came with the Winter Solstice. An irresistible pull to other worlds in the darkest time of the entire year.

Dark brown eyes wide and pupils round black moons, she watched the Seine transform to a scarlet river rushing towards the sea. Mangled bodies, severed heads and limbs floated and bobbed as ravens cawed and pecked at human remains. Screams of the dying and mortally wounded filled the night. The potent chemical scent of blood invaded her nostrils. She gagged and gripped the curtains.

The nightmare that had awakened her returned as a vision, a force greater than her strong but fast-fading will to prevent it.

She smelled the stench of filthy, sewer ridden streets of sixteenth-century Paris and saw with crystal clarity the Seine, all filled with the blood of slaughtered Huguenot Protestants and other unfortunate souls caught in the massacre that began that eve of Saint-Bartholomew's Day, 24 August 1572—during the wedding feast of Marguerite de Valois to her Protestant cousin, Henri de Bourbon, King of Navarre.

An apocalyptic horror born of a singularly duplicitous and nefarious plot of Marguerite's mother, the Queen Regent, Catherine de Medici—widely known as Madame la Serpente, the Black Queen.

By the time the scourge was over, some seventy thousand souls had been slaughtered throughout the whole of France. That was Kikki's last conscious thought before she succumbed to the vision and shifted to otherworldly realities in time, space and dimension. She was drawn, as in her nightmare, but more real in vision where she literally entered that past life and that terrifying night.

Even while the bloody images flashed in Technicolor, Kikki looked down upon her long ivory silk peignoir as it transformed into that royal white nightdress now stained with darkest red blood.

Kikki became Marguerite de Valois, sister of Charles IX, King of France. She was trapped inside her apartments in the Louvre— once a fortress with moat and keeps—a prison and an impenetrable citadel to defend the great city. Converted by her father King Henri II to a Renaissance palace home of kings in the sixteenth century. Still a cold and dark place.

Her hated and treacherous mother—the mother who had forced her to marry for political power—for the dynasty and for her mother's insatiable need to control. Unholy and demonic was such a mother.

A twisted attempt to reconcile religious enemies. Or so her mère had said. To foil Margot's true love for the son of the Duc de Guise —a powerful enemy to the throne and the House of Valois of which Margot was born. And to bring the Protestant kingdom of Navarre into the bosom of France.

How Margot missed her father, Henri II. He would have told Margot about the impending horror and not left her to defend herself. He might have taken control to prevent it. Tears filled her eyes.

Her own mother had used her as a pawn in a hideous plot. She, the smartest, most educated and gifted of ten children born to provide an heir. Her mother would make sure she, Margot, had no voice.

She stood peering out through a heavy velvet draped window, helpless and horrified. Her own mother had put her in mortal danger and not warned her.

At eleven that night, the tocsin (warning bell) rang out in the royal parish church, Saint-Germain l'Auxerrois, signaling a frenzy of killing. Men carrying white flags bearing the Catholic cross and brandishing flaming torches of death stormed the streets below.

They shouted her brother, the king's orders—Kill them all! "*Tue! Tue! Tuez-les tous!*"

Hearing each bell resound with growing dread. Eternally damned on the eve of her wedding. Dark eyes wide with terror and tears. She was only nineteen years old and forever cursed by blood.

As quickly as she had experienced the vision, Kikki slammed back to the present. She sat abruptly on the edge of the powder blue velvet *récamier* a few feet from the windows.

Kikki focused on the Snake Goddess and took deep breaths to ground herself after experiencing moments of Margot and her complicated life—now recalling the image lifting from the book cover, Margot literally stained by the blood of La Mole that night.

Margot became his protectress, and theirs became a legendary love affair—until the evil Medici queen ordered his death and made Margot witness.

Kikki reached for Dumas's book, *La Reine Margot,* and she let her mind skim through Margot's story like the lawyer and historian that she was: Marguerite de Valois, Queen of Navarre and of France, nicknamed Margot, was a woman known at once as rebel queen and depraved whore. She was undoubtedly one of the most brilliant queens of France. Historians called her implacably perspicacious and one of the great minds of the sixteenth century.

She lived in one of the most turbulent and deadly centuries of the Renaissance. One of both extreme luxury and great poverty, marked by seven deadly religious wars that took the lives of more than three million people. A century in which ten queens ruled France. Among them, Margot was one of the most formidable. Her story fascinated Kikki.

Margot was ever tenacious in the face of impossible obstacles. A strong woman in a family of hypocrites. More educated than any of her sickly royal brothers, she was cultured—an advocate—like Kikki —a diplomat, a poet, fluent in multiple languages. She was a *devotée* of Plutarch, the Greek philosopher who spent his last thirty years as a priest at Delphi.

Throughout her life, she ceaselessly battled for her rightful place and voice as queen of France. She outlived her arch enemies, prime among them her mother, Catherine de Medici, the Black Queen. Margot was sixty-two when she died.

A passionate woman always looking for love. Only love could cleanse the blood that had cursed her. The *sang real* of a family that had betrayed her repeatedly throughout her life.

Kikki understood Margot's dilemma, though her own quest came in a very different context. She glanced at Torres. Could she make herself vulnerable to his love and still walk her own path as a strong, independent woman, fight for the return of the matriarchy and the Goddess? Would it really work, or would it divide her loyalties?

Kikki wasn't worried about family betrayal or royal blood. She was a modern American woman. The times were very different. Instinctively, she knew that the undeniable depth of their love created a mixing of blood. An alchemy. Would she too lose her voice and power?

Kikki and Torres had a new home in Paris in an early eighteenth-century building on the Rive Gauche, just where Margot had finally built her sumptuous palace and gardens upon her triumphant return to the capitol after eighteen years in exile. With calculated pleasure, Margot had chosen land on the Rive Gauche, directly across the Seine from the Louvre, home of Henri IV and his new queen, Marie de Medici.

Her one-time husband had banished her to a lonely mountain fortress in desolate Usson, deep provincial France, for the better part of her life. The king who had silenced her voice as queen of France and who plotted with her family and sent assassins to hunt her.

Margot's luxurious gardens had extended as far as the Quai Voltaire and rue de Beaune, an area known now as the Carré des

Antiquaires where Kikki and Torres lived.

What fated irony, Kikki thought, that they had chosen to make a home in one of Paris's oldest *quartiers*, center of a richly woven piece of antiquity and history.

The cruel turn of events on Santorini had cursed her Hotel Atlantis. Kikki fled what was to be an island haven from her busy Paris life, and returned to Paris for solace and peace. Only to be dogged by yet another curse—that of an ancient queen—the ghost of Margot, on the four-hundredth anniversary of her death.

How eerily connected. Kikki shivered.

Suddenly, a gust of wind blowing through old radiator pipes startled her. She cried out and then quickly covered her mouth.

She made herself still. A curtain rustled and dim light drifted from the front window to their bedroom at the back of the large apartment. Through the open door, she studied her lover, sprawled on their bed. Stretched naked the full length of his lean, muscled, six-foot-three frame, one olive skinned arm trailed off the sheets. His black hair shaded his face and those piercing ebony eyes she so loved. She thought him asleep.

The curtain settled. Kikki watched a trail of dust rise along the rose-colored flocked wallpaper and then vanish into the rococo ceiling molding. Was it the ghost of Voltaire, who occasionally visited or a spirit less welcome? A shapeshifter from the patriarchy— the ghost of the Black Queen, Catherine de Medici, *peut-être*?

Kikki quivered. The *quartier* was rife with ghosts, lost souls trapped in darkness. The eighteenth-century building on the Quai stood over an underground maze of tunnels that headquartered the Northern Resistance during World War II, in use during Margot's time and long before. They had served as the wine caves of the king and the *caserne* (barracks) of the Royal Guard. D'Artagnan, the famed musketeer, had lived a block away on the Quai with easy access to the Louvre when the Sun King, Louis XIV, summoned.

Paris was riddled with a spider's web of tunnels. By far the most gruesome—the Catacombes, burial ground and mass grave of bones for millions of Parisians—some six million in all. Since the late 1700s, when some long-forgotten quarries had collapsed taking buildings and people with them. The efficient city fathers had combined the quarries with the remains of a stinking cemetery

11

nearby—and *voilà*—the ghostly Catacombes.

The curious could wander that macabre labyrinth through alleys stacked with wall-to-wall skeletons. Hundreds of thousands of hollow-socketed skulls kept vigil over the living—drawing them to darkness in silent cacophony. Beware lost souls.

Chapter 2

Kikki rose from the *récamier* and glided across the soft Aubusson carpet to the fireplace in the front salon. Seeking warmth from the dying embers of a fire, she leaned her slim frame against the marble mantelpiece.

Staring into the glowing logs, she prodded the embers with a poker. The ghostly nightmares and visions from Margot's life had begun to invade her psyche around French Toussaint, the 1st of November, Pagan New Year or Samhain—a cross-quarter day in the Wheel of the Year, between the Autumn Equinox and Winter Solstice.

Why was Margot so ever-present, and what did she want? She'd yet to come to form in Kikki's 3D world, yet to use her voice. She was a shadowy light of ephemeral energy hovering, mostly at liminal times or in the depth of night. But Kikki had no doubt Margot's appearance was imminent.

In the dim light of the room, Kikki searched for answers. She peered into the darkness beyond the Snake Goddess, casting her eyes at last upon a long narrow table against the wall—her altar of goddesses—Athena and Aphrodite—asking guidance from the wise

Greek goddesses whom Margot, too, had worshipped.

Kikki's keen intuition told her that Margot brought warning that Kikki was about to be catapulted into very dangerous events. More difficult trials on her life's journey to serve the Goddess and all she stood for. Could she do it and still keep Torres? Or would it tear them apart?

At last living in relative domestic bliss with Torres, she was afraid. Even madly in love, that *détente* had required serious negotiation and more than a few shouting matches. It hadn't been easy for either of them to fully trust. Both were fiercely independent with big lives. Each trying to protect the other. Afraid to be vulnerable and afraid for the other's safety. A delicate balance.

The Snake Goddess's private premier at the Louvre would surely lure the powers of darkness, the male power structure and its unquenchable lust for power. What new form of terror would be unleashed this time?

Margot was key—and she was sure to be drawn to the gala given her love of Greek goddesses and her own secret battle for the Goddess and the Matriarchy—for humanism and enlightened rule in the midst of that warring high and righteous patriarchal century in which Margot had lived.

Margot would have a vital mission—and one for Kikki, herself, and for the twenty-first century, chaotic, still highly patriarchal world. That was how it worked when Kikki experienced visions and dreams of past lives. Margot would charge Kikki with a karmic lesson to be played out in the now—the present time—for resolution. Some called this dance between past and present "time travel."

She was so ineffably linked to Margot and her story, she wondered if she had she been her in a past life? Or one of her intimates? A scary thought. It wouldn't be the first time.

Kikki's eyes settled on her ceramic statue of the fierce Sumerian Goddess Inanna that glowed in the dark. Known also as Ishtar, she shared the marriage bed with her lover, Dumuzi. A bed Inanna had to leave, to descend to the mythological Underworld—or in Margot's case, exiled and marked for assassin's blades. Leaving love behind.

Kikki glanced again at her own sleeping lover. She was afraid for him like Margot had been for La Mole. Torres was a highly placed Interpol cop running a covert op from Paris, for the City of Light harbored a thriving and very dark underbelly—and that underbelly attracted the worst criminals and terrorists from all corners of the world. Torres was in constant danger. She hoped Margot would provide some guidance about how Kikki could keep herself and Torres safe.

If she were living in Margot's time, Kikki might have visited the friendly, if frightening, seer and astrologer, Nostradamus, or gone to see the dark Florentine magician, Cosmo Ruggieri, in his strange little house on the Île de la Cité. She'd have a wax figure of Torres molded to keep him protected. That's what Margot had done for the Huguenot, La Mole—in an attempt to protect and save his love and life.

The fire crackled. Her eyes were drawn to the marble mantelpiece, to the blue deck of Tarot cards wrapped in a filmy lavender silk scarf. Since moving into the apartment on Quai Voltaire with Torres, she had not touched the cards on which she had relied ever since she could remember. Well, hardly.

Now, she reached and unwrapped the cards, her favorite Mythic Tarot, from the protective silk. Eyes closed, she shuffled the deck, clearing her mind, calling upon her powers and the Goddess.

She drew a card and turned it over—Death.

Hades, the High Priest and King of the Underworld, replete with imposing steel helmet and long black robes. Hand beckoning to the innocents to cross over the River Styx to his dark kingdom.

Kikki's stomach knotted. Though usually she read this card as one transformation, positive and necessary change in life's journey, she knew that this time, it would come through physical death.

Her eyes turned to her sleeping lover. She wanted to keep her promise to him, her promise to give up being High Priestess. But she knew she would break it to save his life—just as Margot had done for La Mole.

She'd need more than Tarot cards. This week promised to be the fight of her life. With grim resolution, Kikki whispered a prayer to the Goddess and threw the cards towards the fire. They fell short, but a bright red-orange flame in the shape of a woman danced from the embers. The fire crackled. Kikki thought she heard a baby's cry.

15

Chapter 3

Torres wasn't asleep, merely feigning it. His worry for Kikki kept him awake and ready to go to her at the slightest sign. With the door open, he had a perfect view.

It had been nearly 02:00 when he returned to their apartment and found Kikki deep in sleep. Quietly, he'd eased into bed next to her. Not long afterwards, she slipped from his arms, leaving the bedroom to take up vigil at the front of their salon.

Now, he felt the clenching in his jaw. That's where his tension and concern went. She hadn't been herself lately. Tormented by nightmares that she refused to talk about—but he knew they had to do with that ill-treated French queen and a new film project about the very same subject. His gut told him she should have refused the client.

He also knew that, at heart, she was worried about the premier gala and exhibition at the Louvre on Friday evening. A first private showing that would draw a lot of attention from international power players to a coveted treasure—one that was very personal to Kikki.

He was sorry he had to leave her alone tonight but cancelling his plans had not been an option. Not only was he one of the hosts of the swanky diplomatic dinner at the Hotel de Ville, but the event was key to the first operation in his new position.

The soirée was held to celebrate a new committee he formed under the auspices of the Interpol division he headed. The International Art & Antiquities Anti-Fraud Council was his public façade and cover.

It was an unofficial group of mostly official people, with civilians mixed in, as was so often the case in these murky political waters. Even though he had long learned to tolerate politics, the cop in him hated the ambiguity.

Torres's new Interpol division spearheaded a global multiagency special tactics team aimed at dismantling an international network of traffickers in blood antiquities, artwork and archeological artifacts looted from war-torn regions. It was led by the International Criminal Court (ICC) in the Hague, in cooperation with the World Customs Organization, Europol and the OCB—French police experts in trafficking cultural treasures—part of the French *Police Judiciare*—of *Quai des Orfèvres* fame.

Hand-selected by Torres, his highly classified covert team was based at Interpol's Paris Bureau. Fortunately, his long time and loyal boss at Interpol, Florence Delattre, managed the tricky political coordinating and reporting functions, especially with the French ministries, leaving Torres autonomous and responsible only to the ICC.

They had been working and analyzing intel 24/7 for four months. His Operation Sphinx was a go, but he only had the next few days to reel in his asset, turn her and put her in play to execute the final plan this week. Which is why its opening soirée was critical.

A well-known cultural archeologist-cum-cop, Torres was in his element working the social strata of which his committee was made. He chaired it as a liaison/attaché from the French Ministry of Culture and Communication. It worked perfectly with his other cover job—an adjunct professor of archaeology at the Louvre's École de Conservation. If he weren't a man on a mission that he took quite seriously, he might have had fun with this group.

Yes, Torres, and if you weren't completely gone over the love of your life, Véronique, as he liked to call Kikki in certain moments, you would absolutely have a hot affair with the principal mark—and it would be wise to do so to ensure her loyalties.

He told himself to put the idea out of his mind.

The elaborate ten-course dinner had been held in one of many ornate gilded ballrooms at the Hotel de Ville. His mark was a beautiful young woman, high up in their target—a ring of internationally renowned art and antiquities traffickers that had been operating out of Florence for decades, if not centuries. They had recently expanded to blood antiquities to fund terrorist war chests funneled to a secret organization.

He replayed the evening again—his first face-to-face encounter with Natalia Becchina. He had flirted and seduced without restraint. He had always been good at the chase, being a Latin male after all—stereotype fulfilled in that respect, at least. Natalia had come on to him hard and fast, matching his passion.

She caught him in the corridor with a kiss—a real one, not the hello-goodbye *bises* on each cheek. Rather, a demanding kiss that whispered, I want you and soon.

Better for the op—and more difficult because of how deeply he felt about Kikki.

He couldn't deny the immediate sexual attraction between himself and Natalia. The French called it a *coup de foudre*. He called it trouble.

In the past, he would have had no qualms taking Natalia straight to his bed. But now—*joder!* A dilemma. His work, his career and so much more depended upon turning Natalia into an asset.

Despite their mutual chemistry, even as the kiss went deep with Natalia, Torres felt himself holding back. He had hardly looked at other women since he and Kikki had reunited several months ago. That was new for him.

At the dinner, he had backed away, much to Natalia's apparent surprise.

Now, he brushed his hair from his forehead so he could watch Kikki more easily. She knew he had an op in play but not what it was—that was information he couldn't possibly share. But that might help explain why she was overly worried about the exhibition —she picked up energy. Kikki had the sight, as his dear departed mother would have said, for she'd had it too.

Torres groaned inwardly—his life was filled with maddeningly intelligent and independent women! And that made it much harder for Torres to keep his worlds separate.

But Kikki couldn't know the truth: Operation Sphinx was multilayered, but at its core was a sting at the gala designed to lure their biggest targets out of the shadows. The biggest prize would be the elusive head of the Swords.

Torres felt it in his gut—he would get his target. His mother insisted that he, too, was blessed with a well-developed sixth sense. Maybe. But he was a cop, a rational man of science, an archeologist. He preferred to look at it as good instincts—intuition. His hunches always played out. He relied on his gut and it rarely failed him. Except when it came to Kikki.

He had great respect for Kikki's abilities, except when they meant she put herself in danger. She had been walking the razor's edge the past few days. To reassure himself, he reminded himself how strong she was.

After a lot of dancing around the subject, mostly on her part, he and Kikki were finally living together. His lips curved in a smile, a battle he'd won.

She would say that the Fates had ordained it. That it was their karma. Torres didn't care how she characterized it. She was his.

Paris could have been the perfect honeymoon, where they could play out their game of hot sex and slow love, but instead, it was now a proving ground.

His successful Greek Operation Minos had netted this choice appointment, and with it came an identity change. Carefully chosen to place him so he would be able to move in the right social and political circles.

No longer Commandante Pepe Torres, he was le Commissaire Divisionnaire and le Comte Jean Michel Beauregard de Torres. From an old aristocratic French family with certain roots in a Spanish branch on one side.

Kikki insisted on just calling him Torres, which suited him perfectly. He was, she said, with a knowing wink, her tower, the meaning of his last name, in more ways than one. If she really wanted her own tower with all the frills, she should relent and marry him. He wanted her all in. Impossibly stubborn woman, he thought, watching her stir the fire.

His genealogy was a dense old vine that he could barely follow. This was Europe, the Old World. The aristocracy and royal blood counted. It opened doors otherwise closed. Even if you could, as of old, buy your own title.

But his cover was more real and royal than anyone knew.

Given Kikki's present obsession with Marguerite de Valois, a woman as royal as one could be, descended from the original House of France, Charlemagne and the Capetian dynasty founded in the tenth century, he didn't want Kikki to know more about his "new" identity.

His family tree dated back to the Middle Ages when boundaries between Italy, France and Spain were quite different and bloodlines crossed. In patriarchal tradition, marriages were arranged between royal dynasties to gain land, title and power. All in a continent dominated by Spain, France and the Holy Roman Empire, by the Pope and his army of devotées. The House of France and the Hapsburg dynasty had ruled Europe for centuries.

The only person who knew all was his maternal Great-Aunt Isabela—fondly called just "Tía." She was now the matriarch of his family, after his mother and his beloved Nana Elena had passed. Tía was tough and vigorous at a mere ninety years of age, a good thing since she was holding down the family base in Granada, running her own secret operation.

After studying the family tree as far back as 1300, she had helped him put together a realistic lineage—realistic but not quite complete.

Just yesterday, Tía had told him that there was one more piece —a branch of the family story that she had kept secret. Now it was time for him know. But she would only reveal it to him in person.

He thought they had covered everything that needed to be coordinated between them. Somehow in the midst of this high-wire week, he had to get to Granada to see her. But what was it? And why had she kept it from him?

His eyes stayed on his lover as these thoughts rumbled around in his mind. At the moment, she stood in front of the fire, poking at it idly but not fully present. He saw that her face was pale and taut. He frowned but didn't stir.

Suddenly, she crumbled and collapsed onto the sofa near the

fire.

In seconds, he was at her side and had wrapped her in his arms. "*Diga!* What is it, Kikki?" he asked. "Nightmares and visions again?"

She nodded and finally said, "Look at the card closest to the fire."

"Death." He said evenly, trying to catch her eyes. "Transformation, right?"

"Not this time. You're in acute danger." She fixed an intent gaze upon him. Was the ill-fated rebel queen choosing the cards?

He watched silently as her dark chocolate eyes took on a luminous glow.

"I know it," she said. "I have been feeling it, and now it is confirmed."

"I'm a cop. That's my job. I am trained for that."

She focused on her lover. She saw his eyes and heart full of love. Yes, she thought, taking in his strong masculine form, she had to stop fighting him, stop pulling away and let him in. It was the only way to protect him and all that she held dear.

He brushed a lock of fine blonde hair from her face and put an arm around her slender waist. She leaned into him, drawing from his strength.

With a sideways glance, he saw her eyes soften. She was coming back to him. To the now.

She let him lead her to their bedroom. He told himself to be gentle and hold his desire for her in check. Now was not the time. She needed soothing.

Chapter 4

Torres settled Kikki softly into their antique bronze four poster bed. She slid quickly under the duvet, and he joined her. He placed his arm around her so her blonde head nestled in the crook of his elbow.

"You're freezing." He began to caress her slight shoulders.

Her teeth chattered.

He held her closer, gently massaging her.

"Let me help get your blood circulating. It will warm—" He kissed her on the forehead. "Let me comfort you, *mi amor*. Let go of it all, Kikki. Just be here with me now."

She lifted her gaze and caught his. And then sighed deeply, releasing the last vestiges of bloody visions from her mind. Glad to be free of nightmares and Margot and safe in his arms. She reached up and ran her hand lightly along his face, catching his eyes, sure of his love.

His lips touched her lightly at the curve of her neck, and then he kissed her tenderly. "I love you so much. Know that, Kikki."

"I do. It's just—"

"Then let me help you. Stop trying to protect me."

"I—I don't."

He silenced her with his lips, and she began to come to life, returning the kiss with need and surrender.

She searched for his tongue and closed the distance between them, letting him hold her tightly.

At last, she felt fully present with her lover. A gift of life.

He broke the kiss. "We can face this danger, Kikki, whatever it is. But only if we do it together. Trust me."

"I do. I want to—" She whispered. "But it's dark and big—and I'm afraid it will tear us apart."

"Only if we let it. If we don't trust each other." He waited for her promise.

She inched back, hesitant. Then she took his hand.

"I do trust you," she began. "But the darkness—a threat so enormous this time. You know I love you." She held his dark eyes and saw a smile and more.

When she said those words, which was rare enough, he felt a glow inside, as if his heart were bigger and brighter. As always, it came with passion—a deep desire for her.

He felt his want grow. He kissed her deeply, and she met his passion, tongues touching. Love entwined.

At just that moment, his private cell phone played out a riff of flamenco guitar. The moment broken.

Was this a sign she wondered. The beginning?

He felt her pull away from him emotionally.

"I'm sorry, *mi amor*. I have to answer it. It's my private phone and the caller is *granadino*," he said in a throaty voice. "The only people who have this number are you and Tía." He kept her in his arms and reached for it on the *table de nuit*.

"*Diga, Tía. Que te pasa?*" The line crackled, so he heard and felt acutely a distance between them.

"They've been here again," Tía whispered hoarsely. "I hid in the cellar."

"Are you hurt?" he asked alarmed, releasing Kikki. He sat on the edge of the bed.

"*Yo? Nada!*" she said indignantly. "There were four of them in the sedan. They emptied their automatic rifles—shattered the front portal and windows."

"Tía—*véte*! Get out. *Ya sabes*. They are extremely dangerous people."

"It was just a threat," she scoffed. "*Escúchame*! No one—*nadie* —will drive me from my home!"

"*Joder*!" So stubborn. She had always been this way. Torres clenched his jaw, fearful for Tía, but he'd been expecting something like this. Tía had probably egged them on, drawn them to her. Another impossible, feisty woman.

Kikki sat up, just behind him, careful to give him space but close enough to hear. She knew enough Granadino dialect to follow most of what was said. He was in supercop mode, eyes narrowed, thigh muscles taut, fingers drumming onto the night table.

"Tía, I beg you." His voice tight and urgent, he continued, "It's not safe. Time to go."

"I got their license plate, make of car," she said proudly.

"You must leave, Tía," he snapped, wanting to strangle her. "They'll be back to check for bodies—yours. And it's not safe to talk on the phone."

"I'm using that *como tu lo dice*, 'burn phone' you gave me."

"Good—throw it out. I'll have someone bring you a new one."

"*Que ridículo*! Who do you think you're speaking to?"

"Tía, you know how much I love and respect you, but these people are seriously dangerous. We've discussed it. *Por favor*."

"Not as dangerous as me," she hissed. "My mother, your Great, Great Tía, and your own *abuela* fought off La Guardia during the Civil War." She clicked her tongue against her teeth. "Our lineage has always fought for justice against corrupt patriarchal oppressors. I have a vast network, nephew—"

"Listen to me, damnit. We need to get you to safety." He could hear her moving and a crackle of static—then her breathing but not even a whispered word. "*Tía*! Are you still there?"

"I am not going into hiding—like before," she said with defiance. "*Joven*, we've got enough intel now. Their rear window had that coat of arms with the sword and the cross—that confirms it, no? And I have a part to play. The Daughters—"

"The same insignia you saw before?"

Kikki watched her lover's eyes go darker. She moved closer and touched his tense shoulder. She opened her mouth to speak, intending quiet words of reassurance. But froze.

Through the phone came an ear-splitting sound. A thunderous blast of noise and shattering metal.

"*Tía!*" Torres yelled, dropping the phone.

When he picked it up less than a second later, the line was dead.

Chapter 5

All silent fury and fear, Torres hit redial, but the call went straight to voice mail.

He jumped from the bed, hurrying into the salon. He stopped in front of the dwindling fire, mind racing. Deftly, he scooped up Kikki's Tarot cards and placed them onto the mantle, barely registering the scorch marks on the Death card.

Kikki watched from the bedroom as he rescued her cards. The small act touched her heart, but her stomach knotted with fear.

She studied him as he threw fresh logs on the fire and poked it violently so it flamed with a roar.

She rose and wrapped herself in her red shawl, breathing through a wave of dizziness. Be strong, she whispered to herself.

Now, her lover paced in front of the fire, phone to his ear, desperate to reach his aunt.

Kikki closed her eyes and tuned in psychically. Nothing. Tía was either dead or surrounded by so much ethereal protection that Kikki couldn't find her on the earthly plane—a distinct possibility with Tía. She had formidable powers, Kikki knew.

Even though they'd met only once, it had been a very enlightening afternoon. As they sat together in the Tuileries

Gardens, they had instantly connected, as though they knew each other.

It had been heartening for Kikki to talk to Tía about the Goddess, to rail with her against the patriarchy and the need for a new order for Mother Earth. Tía had felt far more like her older sister than a great-aunt.

Silently, Kikki padded barefoot to the salon and sat on one of two red velvet sofas in front of the fire. She tucked her legs underneath herself and waited for Torres to speak to her.

He stood with his back to her, still on the phone, but talking urgently now to a colleague. Mere moments before, he had been fully hers. Now, he belonged only to himself, and he emanated a strange yet familiar brew of rage, determination and, deeper still, a heavily masked fear.

Emotions tightly reined in—more than ever because his beloved Tía might have been ruthlessly assassinated.

By whom, Kikki wondered? And why? Were they Torres's enemies? Or were they Tía's? What the hell was going on? That gnawing feeling she had been having for weeks—the visions—Margot.

This was it—the beginning. Kikki was filled with dread for her lover and Tía. They had suddenly stepped off into the abyss.

He barked an order. "Get my jeans, will you!"

She ignored his sharpness, knowing it came from fear. When she returned with his pants, he was speaking in dialect again. Issuing more orders. Planning and plotting.

Thoughts of Margot and her aptitude and wont for plotting flew through Kikki's mind. Margot's message was starting to take form.

He finished his calls and came to sit on the sofa facing her, his expression stormy and tense.

"Talk to me, *mi amor*," she said quietly.

"I don't know what to—" he began in a tight voice, his cop wall. "Goddamnit, I told her to get out. She's more obstinate than you."

Kikki forced herself not to smile and asked evenly, "Who did you call?"

"My cousin in Malaga—she can get there fastest."

"Sara who works for Interpol and the Spanish feds?" Sara and

27

her husband, Manuel, one of Torres's oldest friends, were both federal cops. "What will you do?"

"I'm getting on a plane."

"Are you sure that's wise?" Her stomach churned. "There won't be a flight for hours."

"Private, military," he said, watching her closely. "And you're not coming with me. It's police business."

"Of course." She stood up. She knew it would be no use to argue. "Fine. It's better if I stay here. I have work to do. But you've got to tell me what's going on." She had to find out what she could. "Is this connected to your op?"

"It's Tía I'm concerned about."

"Me too!" And suddenly she remembered. A letter delivered by courier for Torres from Tía the day before. He had whisked it away. What was in it?

He was silent while he searched the pockets of a jacket he'd left by the couch and pulled out a red and white pack of Marlboros. He lit one and took a deep drag.

After a few seconds she asked, "So—your cousin is calling you with a plan?"

"*Claro* ..." The rest of what he said was drowned out by a loud chiming of bells.

They rang out four times. Four o'clock in the morning. From Saint-Thomas d'Acquin, just south of Boulevard Saint-Germain. Unless the wind blew a certain way, they were usually too far away to hear.

A shiver ran up Kikki's spine. She flashed on the bells at Saint-Germain l'Auxerrois that Margot had heard. The signal to kill on that fateful Saint-Bartholomew's Eve of August 23, 1572.

Kikki was right to sense terrible danger. She saw the Death card loom over Torres and gulped. Despite the heat of the fire and her cashmere shawl, Kikki felt bone-chilling cold creep into her.

And then a tap on her shoulder and the whispered voice of a young woman speaking arcane French surprised her. "*I am here. I will help you.*"

Margot! At last. A sharp pain in her left temple took Kikki's breath away. And now she welcomed a vision for it would bring needed information—access to other realms. She dearly hoped so for her lover, for Tía.

Margot and Goddess Athena, come to my aid!

Chapter 6

Torres's phone rang, abruptly bringing Kikki back into present time. He listened for a moment and said, "Call me back with details."

She watched her lover gathering his things—go-bag, weapons, laptop and cell phones.

They both dressed in silence, tension palpable in their bedroom.

A few minutes later, in the salon, they sat across from each other, studiously avoiding eye contact.

His left thigh pumping up and down, he tried Tía again with no luck. Deep lines furrowed his forehead. Long black lashes covered eyes that Kikki knew were filled with pain. Of course he knew how likely it was that Tía had been kidnapped or killed. She ached for them both.

"Goddamnit, why hasn't Sara called back?"

"It's only been a few minutes, love," she said gently. She wanted to go to him, but he was closed off, arms tightly wrapped around his chest. She wasn't the only one pulling away.

He finally caught her eyes, and his own softened. She saw an opening and took it.

"Why are they after your Tía? And who are *they*?"

He frowned. "I told you, it's police business."

"If that's true, then this attack on Tía has to do with your op. Is Tía part of it?" That made sense to Kikki. And maybe Tía instigated the attack intentionally. She was fierce and stubborn and fearless.

"Tía is not a cop and both of you—she should have—" He reached for another cigarette, lit it and took a drag. He blew a fine stream of smoke through flared nostrils.

Her lover was pissed at Tía, not just worried. So Kikki's theory made sense.

She closed her eyes to better bring the picture into clarity. The first thing that flashed was the Snake Goddess. And then Tía and a group of women surrounding it. Kikki had caught Tía's mention of the words "daughters" and "network" on the call.

Joder, he watched her going into trance—looking for information however she could. She had promised to back off with this High Priestess work. He intended to make her stick to it.

"Kikki, leave it alone." He shot her a pained look. He was afraid that one day they'd go too far and drive an insurmountable wedge between them. And that would be a real pity, when he'd finally found the love of his life.

She slit her eyes, studying him. Suddenly, the picture came to focus in her third eye, anger flared, and she held his look. "Damn you, Torres! You're using the Snake Goddess as bait to lure your targets! The gala exhibition—that's your bloody op, isn't it? You're running a sting!"

Chapter 7

"I have a right to protect what's mine, Torres."

"The Snake Goddess is not yours." He glared at the open tracking app on his phone.

"Not literally. But she is a powerful symbol for the Goddess and the Matriarchy. Your Tía would agree."

"Lay off," he repeated, voice tight, once more checking his phone. Why wasn't the car here yet? Why hadn't Sara called him back?

"Well, who attacked your Tía? The patriarchal power structure, that's who."

He held his ground silently, remembering Tía's description of the coat of arms with the sword and the cross. The Knights of the Holy Sword of God—his targets.

Kikki's eyes narrowed. "We wouldn't be in such a world mess if the patriarchal values—or lack of them—hadn't been running our sacred Gaia for so long! And now we're in yet another—or should I say *still*—war of religion or ideology, terrorism in the name of Allah —or Christ—or the Holy Land. War is the Patriarchy!" She was ranting but couldn't stop herself. "A grab for power and money under the latest guise of the alpha male. France calls itself a Catholic country. Does that mean it has the right to worship war?"

He stood and stoked the fire in frustration.

"Let's not get started on that. You know I agree." In fact, if she only knew how central that subject was to his team and the present op—blood antiquities funding war—powers he vowed to bring down. He looked over his shoulder and shot her a warning look. "Back off, Kikki."

"Fine," she said quietly, shifting her position on the couch. "But look at me, Torres."

"What now?"

"I don't want to argue with you, but you're shutting me out," she said, rising to stand in front of him. "Remember that you told me not a half an hour ago when I was spooked that we would face the darkness—a very big force this time—together."

"And we will, each in our own way." He reached for her hands.

She held his for a moment and then released them, decision made. "You're right. I'd like to go with you, but my time will be better served here. I've got a lot of work to do." She turned from him and walked back to her table in the front salon.

His eyes followed her, but he didn't move towards her.

She picked up the script. "I've got that film client to see this morning. It's a very complicated production, and I need to prepare. I'm meeting Monique before we see the client." She was relieved to have her longtime friend and partner, Monique Dubois, at her side. A welcome ally and vital to Cabinet Trieste et Dubois.

He glanced at his watch and stood up, "The film about Henri IV and Margot, right? I don't like this new client, Kikki. I told you before, I have a bad feeling."

"That's my business, Torres. As yours is police business, even if my Snake Goddess is part of your op. Monique and I can handle it." Parallel battles. His with the op and hers with the film.

"Are you sure it isn't too soon after your hiatus? You've barely —."

"No. My playing field, my battle. You'll just have to trust me."

"Do I have a choice? There's a real reason that cops can't tell their—" He searched for the word, "Spouse or partner about the work."

"Not again! Torres, I get that it's your work. An ancient tune.

Men continue to silence women—especially strong women who have intelligent voices—who want to contribute. Shutting us in, keeping us outside the power circle. Not telling us what's going on, no matter how strong we are. In the name of keeping us safe."

Kikki thought of Margot. She hadn't been told about the massacre. Kikki heard a ruffling sound, like taffeta, and then another whisper from Margot, this time her voice strong and angry:

"Pour moi, on ne me disait rien de tout ceci."

They told me nothing about it.

But I knew something horrible was about to happen that night in my mother's chambers. I was with my mother and my sister before bedtime. I could tell from the familiar conniving, sinister look on my mother's face and the fear in the eyes of my elder sister. My evil mother silenced my sister and sent me to my rooms. She told me to lock the door.

They left me alone on that horrible night, alone and terrified, in danger for my life. On a night that changed my destiny forever."

Margot's last words rung in Kikki's ears. She struggled to come back to the present, and so she walked back to Torres.

He pulled her into his arms. "I love you, Kikki. *Te quiero.* I have to keep you safe."

"Huh! My neomacho man!" she huffed. "And what about me trying to keep *you* safe?" If they were after Tía, they were going for his closest allies, his family—and most importantly, Torres himself. Take him down and the whole op would fall apart.

He frowned.

"If the Snake Goddess is bait, I assume your targets must be archeological or antiquities thieves. Are they one of these fanatical secret organizations?"

"Just drop it, Kikki. You know I can't tell you."

So that was it.

Torres's phone rang. He listened intently.

"*Vale.*" He turned and then said gently, "The car is almost here."

"Go then." She stepped up to him, letting go of anger and the need to know now. "But come back to me."

He pulled her into his arms again and kissed her hard.

When they released each other, fire and passion mirrored in

their eyes.

"*Va-t-on*," Kikki said. "Go. But call me."

He grabbed his bag. "Be careful. I love you. *Te quiero.*"

"Me too. Be careful, my love." As the phrase left her lips, her heart dropped to her stomach.

She had been so focused on the diabolic male power structure that she had missed a vital point. She ran to him as he reached for the door, her eyes wide with fear. She grabbed his shoulder, "Wait! What if it's a trap?"

"I have it covered." He stepped out the door.

"But—it might be more dangerous to leave me here. That might be part of the trap." Surely *he* knew he was a target. But what about *her*?

"I have you covered too. Remember, no one is who they seem. Friends and colleagues may be enemies."

As the door closed, Margot whispered again. "*You are both right. The forces of darkness are mounting. They come.*"

Kikki knew that *they* were already here in her beloved Paris. And she was alone.

Chapter 8

Kikki shivered, listening to the sound of her lover's fading footsteps as he hurried down the marble spiral stairway at the back of the building to leave. With each step, her heartbeat quickened.

She slipped her phone from the pocket of her robe. 04:14. Still quiet on the streets outside and deathly still in her now very lonely penthouse.

She wrapped her arms tightly around herself and took a deep breath, listening for the sound of their building's big entrance gate opening and closing on rue de Beaune. From the kitchen window of her sixth-floor perch overlooking the street, she made out Torres's familiar gait and figure hurrying to an awaiting car on Quai Voltaire, but just dimly. Since she'd last looked outside, a thick fog had descended on the city as it often did at this time of the year in the dark, humid, early morning hours.

She hurried to the French paned windows fronting the apartment, her place of vigil, where earlier she had seen visions of a bloody Seine. She parted the red velvet curtains and peered down at the street. The thick dark *brume* that rose from the river all but blocked her view.

But she heard her lover's voice just as he slammed the car door.

"Hurry! *Vite!*" And then a squeal of tires sliding as the car made a sharp right turn onto Pont Royal.

A sudden attack on Tía by a patriarchal secret society. The stakes were high and becoming clear. She hoped Torres's plan was a good one, and that Tía, too, had been ready for the attack.

She opened the window onto the terrace a crack and sniffed the air. It still smelled of snow. As she watched tiny snowflakes floated, and for a moment, lifted her mood.

But then a dark cloud descended, and she heard the distant violent wind of an approaching storm.

She closed the window and let the curtain fall. She sat and closed her eyes, sensing her lover across the Quai now, in a black sedan sliding on the icy road as it raced past the Louvre.

She could see in her third eye as though she were in the car with him. Looming on the Rive Droite, the magnificent Louvre complex—a stone building Kikki knew well—enormous worn ivory brick with embedded classic sculptures facing the river. Its Southern Galleries—La Grande Galerie—pet project of Henri IV, Margot's husband, ran the length of the Quai from the Pont Royal to the Pont Neuf.

Her spirit traveled still with her lover as the car flew east along the Right Bank of the Seine on a deserted Quai over the Pont Neuf. Past the Palais de Justice on Place Dauphine, the oldest part of Paris, the Île de la Cité—an island in the river once named Lutèce by the Roman Emperor Julian. And long before, home to the Goddess and peaceful and agrarian matriarchal tribes that tilled the fertile river land.

The church of Saint-Germain l'Auxerrois came into view, bloody ground of the massacre, and Kikki's throat closed.

Margot interrupted the journey, her tone familiar, but clear and insistent this time: "*You are not alone. But you cannot travel with your lover. Bring your spirit back. You must guard your own castle.*"

Margot was right. Kikki rose, determined. She had to find out exactly what was unfolding. It was the only way to save herself and those she loved. Kikki was not trained for police work, but she was a kick ass lawyer with a warrior's heart and the soul of Athena.

Since awakening from her nightmare, many elements had

become clear, and they were all connected: Margot's presence, the Snake Goddess Premier Gala Exhibition at the Louvre, Torres's op and the attack on Tía by a secret patriarchal society. The enemy had attacked Tía to get to Torres and those closest to him. And they'd be coming for Kikki too.

Their ultimate goal would be to defeat the matriarchy and those, like her, like Margot, who worshipped the Goddess and her ways.

And they would use the highly charged week leading up to the full moon and Winter Solstice. A time when the forces of darkness, human and otherworldly, were legion, lusting for power, fighting to defeat those of the light at all costs.

What was Margot's message? And when would she provide Kikki the specific information needed to fight this battle?

She checked the time again. Only minutes had passed. It was far too early to call Monique, who she would see in a few hours. She stared at her phone screen, willing Torres to call and knowing he wouldn't. Could he fly in this weather?

The adrenaline rush was fading. She closed her eyes for a moment, weary of battles, yet knowing she couldn't sleep and had no time to waste. The gauntlet had been thrown down.

She returned to the kitchen. A strong coffee would clear her mind. Minutes later, double expresso in hand, she sipped the hot nectar as she paced the front room.

Her eyes were drawn to the script. She reached for it and started towards her own writing desk on the far side of the front salon. She stopped when she saw a flash of Margot. Her writing table was already occupied.

Margot was seated with her back to Kikki. She wore a long red dressing grown. Raven hair floated down her back. She dipped a feather quill pen into an inkwell. A worn black leather journal lay open at her side. She turned her head to glance at it and wrote on a single sheet of fine parchment.

And then Kikki heard Margot say, "*Look in his study.*"

Her brain kicked in, and she remembered the letter delivered to her lover yesterday. She knew where to begin.

She picked up the small bronze Snake Goddess statue, as protection and weapon, and headed to Torres's study, just off their bedroom. Sinking into his leather desk chair, she allowed herself a moment to relax. She inhaled deeply. It smelled of him—tobacco and his Givenchy Gentleman cologne. She felt her heart connecting with his. "Trust yourself and him," Kikki said aloud. "It's the only way."

She placed the powerful goddess directly in front of her, in the middle of the leather blotter pad, and slid open the middle drawer of the mahogany desk. Hand-carved in Spain in the seventeenth century, it was a very special piece of furniture that Kikki knew well. She'd purchased it for Torres when they'd moved into the penthouse. She got a good deal and more from her friend Gabrielle Laroche, an antique dealer in the neighborhood.

Another dot connected. Gabrielle served with Kikki on the Louvre's special Greek/French committee for the exhibition. She made a mental note to check with Gabrielle to verify that the genuine Snake Goddess awaited the exhibition from the safety of one of the Louvre's high-security vaults.

Kikki sorted through papers in the drawer, all neatly organized, but her search netted nothing—yet. She knew she would not find any details on his operation. He was meticulous.

But she also knew the desk had a secret compartment. Almost as if Torres were daring her to use it, she found a tiny skeleton key taped under the brass desk lamp. Feeling only slightly guilty for invading his privacy, she unlocked the panel under the drawer. All for a higher good.

Et voila! An envelope addressed to Torres in Tía's distinctive scrawl. Enclosed with Tía's letterhead was a separate sheet of paper:

To the Daughters of Inanna

"Hear us, you decrepit heretical witch and those who follow you and your group of whores and witches! Woman's original sin shall be purged from God's Kingdom on Earth. We shall wreak death and fiery vengeance against you and yours. One by one. We shall scorch the Earth to annihilate you. Rivers of your blood shall flow to cleanse and purify the Kingdom of God. It is time. We come for you before the light turns."

The Knights of the Holy Sword of God

Their seal was a sword and crucifix elaborately entwined.

Kikki's hands burned. She thrust the letter at the feet of the

Snake Goddess and whispered, "Holy Mother Goddess!"

Chapter 9

Her hands burned and a fist slammed into her stomach. A psychic attack from the darkness. But now they had a name. The Knights of the Holy Sword of God!

Searing pain engulfed her, and she gasped for air. She reached for the Snake Goddess, now glowing, vipers writhing and hissing. Kikki gripped the statue in her left hand and cool relief flooded through her veins. She bowed her head and evened out her breath.

Her right ear caught a high frequency sound wave. She winced. And then she heard an unintelligible whisper in French. But was it Margot? Or the enemy? Was it Margot's evil patriarchal mother, the Black Queen? For surely, she would have been one of the Knights of the Holy Sword of God.

Kikki lifted her head and caught her own image in the mirror on the wall across from the desk. She was ghostly pale and her eyes were dilated, pupils huge. Long hair flew straight out, not blonde, but singed gray like an old crone.

"Damn you in the name of the Goddess!" she shouted. "You will not win this fight!"

She blasted herself with white light of pure love from the Goddess and looked again. She was once more herself, though her

41

dark eyes were still haunted.

Still gripping the Snake Goddess, she shoved the letter into her pocket and stood. Just before she left the room, she paused and quickly glanced back. Her eyes caught a framed ceramic sculpture on the wall above Torres's desk. Her lover, the archaeologist. She smiled.

It was a museum replica of a clay plaque from Mesopotamia—a god and goddess embracing each other in their marriage bed: Inanna and Dumuzi.

Inanna, Goddess of Heaven and Earth, Goddess of Love and Wisdom.

Kikki closed the door to the study knowing that Inanna would protect her.

She returned to the kitchen, wide awake, preparing for battle. As she waited for the spew of coffee from the expresso machine, she plotted. Who were the Knights of the Holy Sword of God? Or more accurately, who were the men who sought more power for the Patriarchy? This went far beyond antiquities theft and a sting operation that targeted her treasure—of course, she knew that. This was a time of war, a fight for Light and for the Goddess.

Torres had tried to hide this from her. She understood why, but he should have known his pretense would fail. Did another bloodbath await—a repeat of the Saint-Bartholomew Day's Massacre? Not on her watch!

And who were the Daughters of Inanna? Why didn't she know of them? Tía was their elder, their leader. That was certain. The threat was sent to her.

One more time into the fray with layers upon layers and mirrors reflecting an impossible labyrinth.

Torres had kept all of this from her, but she had her own secrets. And now she was more certain than ever that this new client and his film about Henry, King of Navarre and France, were central to the imminent threat.

She returned to the salon and picked up the file. After stoking the fire, she began to read from a single sheet of notes in her invaluable partner, Monique's, fluid calligraphy:

To: Kikki
From: Monique

Project: Working Title: *Henry IV—King of Navarre and France*
- *This is a remake of a remake. Focusing on Henri and his rise to power to become known as Henri the Great, from king of the small but independent nation of Navarre in the south of France. A Bourbon prince of the blood, a long-time threat to a Valois throne and a Huguenot.*

- *The maniacal and manipulative Catherine de Medici, Queen Mother to Charles IX, arranged the marriage to end the Bourbon's claim. Hoping that her remaining male children, Henri, Duc d'Orleans et Anjou and François, Duc d'Alençon would rule in turn and breed male heirs.*

- *The script portrays Catherine's move as clever political strategy to unite and reconcile Huguenots and Catholics. An alliance for the good of the Valois and the great Kingdom of France.*

- *She married her least favorite child, the rebellious and scandalous Margot, to the young king of Navarre. Henri is portrayed as beatific because he got saddled with the difficult Margot.*

- *Margot depicted as a young scandalous princess with many lovers who needed to be forced to toe the line. A rival and threat to politically savvy Catherine.*

- *Rumors abound—Margot had already had a child out of wedlock from her lover, Henri, Duc de Guise, of the extremist Catholic family that headed "La Ligue," enemies to the Valois, and that her mother put a large bounty on the child.*

- *Margot was the great beauty of the Valois court, but she needed to be contained.*

- *Margot POV in this film is from male historians who called her a whore and a nymphomaniac, not fit to rule. Should have been sent to a nunnery or locked up.*

Kikki smiled at Monique's emphatic comment in the margin:

WTF! Where is Margot's true POV?

Catherine de Medici plotted the slaughter of thousands of French subjects from beginning to end, all while pretending to forge an alliance with Margot's marriage to Henri de Navarre. She hated Henri. She cursed Margot.

So why is Catherine de Medici portrayed as a sympathetic woman whose only crime was to save and protect her family? They claim she was victimized because she had to live in the same household with her husband, Henri II's mistress, Diane de Poitier for decades. WTF!

I think Dumas called C. de Medici one of the great monsters of history. I agree!

The Black Queen was a ruthless murderer! She hated her beautiful daughter and sought revenge and craved power, whatever the cost.

Kikki closed her eyes, and Monique's notes floated to the floor.

Sleepy, she began to drift. She heard the sound of horses' hooves on cobblestones and the present world disappeared.

She was there, in that time after the massacre, many months after the marriage, watching through Margot's eyes. Kikki became Margot:

The carriage bumping over the cobblestones jostled her insides. The driver cracked the whip and the horses galloped faster.

The four of them, Margot, her dear confidante, Gillonne, a wet nurse, and Margot's baby, were all wrapped in blankets. She draped an anonymous looking carriage with heavy layers of dark wool curtains to keep out the cold and hide herself from those who would do her harm.

She was terrified. The horses galloped at full speed, and she could not see out. The world was closing in on her.

She was taking her newborn daughter to safety. She had to be brave. She drew on the anger at what they had done to her, those who should have loved and protected her and her child.

She had to take her child far away, far from the grasp of her treacherous mother and once loved, now mortal enemy, her elder brother, Henri d'Anjou, next in line to the throne, and her brother Charles IX, King of the greatest Catholic country in Christendom.

Peering out from behind the curtains she finally breathed a sigh of relief. They were far from the crumbling old walls of the city, on the other side of Porte Saint-Jacques and heading to the forest of Rambouillet. The snow had stopped, and the fog cleared a bit.

The baby stirred in her lap.

This would be the last time they would spend together. Mother and daughter. Her heart ached unbearably. Why did it have to be so? Bitter tears froze on her cheeks.

Oddly, now she remembered the only kind words her mother ever spoke to her: "Ma fille—vous êtes née dans un misérable temps."

In a moment of weakness and motherly affection, her mother had felt sympathy for her daughter, Marguerite, the last of the great Valois dynasty. Sympathetic because she was born in a miserable, wretched era.

What lapse had caused that brief moment of affection from her mère?

What she remembered more clearly, as if she could feel the pain once more, were the beatings, the plots and her mère's hatred. She knew it was because she, Marguerite, of all the ten children her mère had borne from her beloved father, Henri II, was the most beautiful, the healthiest and certainly the most brilliant. Her mother was a jealous viper. And she was her dear father's favorite, and her mother saw her as rival.

Anger increased. She rocked her daughter, who was curled up in her lap, swaddled in a blanket Gillonne had knitted for her.

Deep inside her heart she was hollow and sad.

Her mère was a powerful force in a man's world. And yet, did nothing to aid and protect her daughter Margot. Non, au contraire. She used her.

A bitter taste filled her mouth. Why did she have no rights, no voice, no position of dignity? Did she have no right to love? And to one day, in her own right, become the queen of France? She was a Valois! Descended from the original royal dynasty of her great and beloved France.

Why did her own daughter have no right to the throne? Her mother would make sure of that. She would conveniently use the law and the papacy. Women were not fit to be queens in this patriarchal Catholic country.

The carriage hurt her womb, still tender from childbirth, as it rumbled on the frozen highway. She wished the pain would stop.

She recalled the most recent betrayal. Her marriage. What vicious act! Treated like a pawn for twisted political gain—conspired against by her mère.

Her true love married off in haste to another at the order of her mère and her frère, the King.

Mais, non, that was not enough for her mère. She led the call to massacre thousands of Huguenots on that bloody night.

Her mère had planned this duplicitous twist all along, brought all the Huguenots to Paris to better be able to annihilate, to slaughter all of them—her own French people—she had engineered the murder of the Huguenot leader Admiral Coligny so she could convince the King he was in danger—that Huguenots would seek vengeance.

A wedding gift of atrocities from the Devil. Betrayal most heinous.

Les noces vermeilles. Scarlet wedding!

And now she, Margot, was forever cursed.

The baby stirred and gurgled.

She had to be strong. Get the baby to safety to the Daughters' Convent in Tuscany.

For if discovered, what fate awaited her? Her brother King Charles IX would charge her with treason. Her mère, the Queen Mother, would surely kill her child. She, Margot, would face certain death.

Her mère would make sure no mercy was shown. They would both be silenced.

She shivered, not with cold but with terror.

She kissed gently her daughter's forehead and whispered, "I vow to avenge this betrayal and swear to save you, my daughter, perhaps the last of the Valois line, from such evil times when women were treated as objects to further dynasties if they had the good—bad luck to be born into one. When women had no rights.

"This will not be your destiny my sweet daughter, nor that of your Valois descendants."

Chapter 10

The porcelain coffee cup Kikki held dropped from her hand. It caught the edge of the glass table and shattered. Her arm jerked and her eyes fluttered open. She remembered a frightening image of Margot fleeing. She closed her eyes and tried to bring it to consciousness. Another important message from Margot.

It helped Kikki to piece together the clues she needed. Her visions often revealed Kikki's past lives, but not always. And their meaning wasn't always clear.

And then, Kikki realized she had actually been Margot in the vision. So perhaps, she had been the French queen in a past life and was carrying Margot's karma. Frightening thought.

On the sofa, she stretched out her cramped legs, allowing the lingering remnants of the vision to envelop her. Fear knotted in her stomach, and she broke a sweat at the sudden wave of claustrophobia. She was traveling in a carriage. It jostled her insides. A heaviness—a form—rested on her stomach. She was bitterly cold.

Kikki's mind clouded with distant thoughts, as if they did not belong to her. She listened for morning sounds to tune into present time. The shrill shrieks of seagulls startled her and then soothed her. A familiar tune.

They were on a predawn flight that began at the great round pool of the Luxembourg Gardens to their perches on the banks of the River Seine.

She stood, careful not to step on the broken pieces of a favorite cup. She sighed and walked to the dying fire. Gently, she moved the screen aside and began to stoke the embers. As she was about to place a new log onto the fire, she heard one last loud squawk. A bird separated from the flock. A lone gull crying like a lost child.

Another detail of the vision—a knowing—flew through her third eye. There had been a baby in the carriage. That had been the weight on her lap—on Margot's lap.

Trapped. Margot and the baby were trapped.

Kikki knew this was vital information, part of the picture that would play out this week. But why? And how?

She picked up the script and began to read.

The chirping of her phone startled Kikki a couple of hours later. A text from Monique to meet her at the Voltaire café to discuss the film client meeting that morning.

She made herself a *tartine* from a day-old baguette. She toasted it and slathered it in rich sweet butter and fig jam. Fuel.

She was weak from lack of sleep and the high-wire dramatic events of the short night. She popped a capsule into the expresso machine on the kitchen counter and watched the coffee spill into the cup. While she crunched down on the *tartine*, she thought about Torres.

She wondered how bad the storm was and how he'd made it out. He might be in Spain by now on the ground, but she didn't pick that up. Not yet. But soon.

His voice echoed in her ears and she heard again his last words —"*Te quiero.*" I love you. She was frightened for him. Scared that they might never see each other again.

She slipped her phone out of her jean pocket and stared at it, willing it to ring. Finally, she hit the button to call him. All she got was voice mail.

"Get moving, Véronique!" she scolded.

She sat at the round oak kitchen table and forced herself to finish the *tartine* and coffee. She had to get out of the apartment, where she was starting to suffocate.

Fear would not hold her back. The only way out was through.

But first, she needed some real battle armor for the outside world.

In her bedroom, she opened a small wooden box that she had hidden in a drawer. Reverently, she removed its contents—the rose crystal necklace dating from prehistoric Santorini, recovered from the archeological digs at Ancient Akrotiri.

She ran her fingers over the ancient magical stones, caressing the necklace until it began to emit warmth and a strong scent of roses.

Her fingers tingled, and energy shot through her. She clasped the necklace carefully around her neck. "May it please the Goddess, let Torres, Tía and his cousins all be safe."

She donned her heavy coat, red cashmere scarf and boots to protect her from the impending storm. She stepped out the door of her building onto a large courtyard. She crossed diagonally to the gate on rue de Beaune. It wasn't snowing at the moment, but a dusting of snow lay on top of icy cobblestones. She tread carefully.

When she was nearly to the gate, an enormous gust of wind blew up out of nowhere. It buffeted and howled into the courtyard. She wrapped her scarf more tightly around herself.

As she watched, the wind and swirling fog formed into the shape of a wolf—large, hungry yellow eyes fixed on her.

Her heartbeat quickened. They—the Swords—were already here in Paris, mounting the battle. She clutched her bag, remembering the words of the threat, then she hit the *porte* button to open the immense gate, once meant for horses and carriages. It didn't open. She was trapped, like Margot.

She reached for the rose beads, and then she surrounded herself with white light and marble pillars of Athena. When she hit the button again, it released the latch. She breathed a sigh of relief and let herself out of the courtyard.

Before the gate closed, she glanced back. The wind and wolf had disappeared. But a plume of black smoke streaked the stormy gray sky, leaving a bolt of black lightening. And a putrid odor. The smell of death, blood and the chthonic bowels of darkness—like the portal that had spewed up evil in Santorini.

She gulped and hurried the short distance to the corner café. Her eyes fixed on the gold light that shone from the old-fashioned lantern outside Le Voltaire Restaurant—a beacon in the fog to a haven of safety.

Chapter 11

When she reached the corner of Quai Voltaire and rue de Beaune, she felt safe but still wary. In the glow of light from the lantern, she breathed a sigh of relief. Inside the café, the lights were at half power, and they would stay low until the café opened for business.

She slipped her phone out of her pocket, glancing at the time. It was near 06:30. Few souls were out and about. Monique wouldn't be there for a while.

Still quite dark outside, as it would be until nearly 08:30 during the height of long, dark winter nights. Light traffic was picking up on Quai Voltaire, a three-lane-wide boulevard that ran west along the Seine in the Seventh Arrondissement. No snow, but she knew it was coming. Stormy clouds she'd seen in the night had gathered in full force. The city was socked in.

Kikki took the crosswalk across Quai Voltaire to the Seine to connect with living water and the French River Goddess Mélusine—a shapeshifting water fairy mermaid. She leaned on a worn green wooden bookseller's box. The *bouquiniste* was closed at this hour.

Watching her breath join the fog, she looked out over the gray-greenish cast of the fast-running Seine. Choppy white caps churned the stormy waters. She could barely make out the Pavillon de Flore and Louvre galleries just across, only shadowy lights of street lanterns trying to break through the *brume*.

She glanced to her left at Pont Royal just adjacent and still bathed in darkness. It was dotted with quaint lantern streetlights glowing eerily in a foggy predawn sky, before the sun came up and the day began. Liminal time. She shivered and pulled up the hood of her warm shearling coat.

The fleet of municipal garbage trucks was on the prowl, engines revved to pick up the green-lidded gray plastic bins lining the Quai and rue de Beaune.

Just behind Kikki, one tank like truck ground to a halt at the stoplight to turn off the Quai. Undaunted by fog or black ice, the behemoth would round the corner and traverse the Pont Royal towards the Tuileries.

She shivered from the cold as she turned to walk back across the street. She was rewarded. As if by magic, the door opened and the soft yellow lights of the Voltaire shone cheerfully.

Bon! Kikki smiled, coming fully down to earth. Thankfully, the beloved neighborhood café and restaurant on the ground floor of her building was open today, a Monday. They must be having a private event, Kikki thought.

They were in the midst of setup. Kikki knew she could convince her friend Catherine, who mothered the café from behind the bar—rather reigned the *domaine*—to make her a double expresso. Kikki would enjoy ordinary *conversations de comptoir*.

"Catherine! *Bonjour*!" Kikki called as the auburn-headed Catherine bustled outside in her *bleu-marine* Voltaire *tablier* carrying a round, heavy marble café table. Catherine nodded at Kikki.

"Let me help you," Kikki said quickly.

"No. Moussa is here." One of the tall black African men who kept the classic café of *La Vieille France* running smoothly.

"Is Monsieur P here?" Kikki asked, referring to the owner, watching as Moussa came out a door, weighted down with a large stack of quintessential rattan bistro chairs.

"Not yet. If you wait a couple of minutes I'll make you a coffee." Catherine shoved a table into place. Catherine studied Kikki in the dim light, frowning, "You look like you could use one."

"I could use a vat—and I've already had nearly a gallon!"

"What are you doing about so early?" Catherine teased as she hurried in and out, leaving the rest of the task to Moussa. "Come inside. You'll catch *la crève*."

"I thought I could help you open—for the price of a cup of coffee."

"Hah!" snipped, Catherine. "You're not strong enough to lift these tables. And you know they don't like it." She referred to the owners.

Obediently, Kikki followed her inside. "*Oui*, Catherine."

"You look like *le diable*! Did you get any sleep?"

"Not much." Kikki took her usual place, standing at the counter facing Catherine.

Anybody who knew anything about Paris, France, in general, but especially haughty Parisians, knew that the woman behind the counter was the most important person in any cafe. Piss her off, show her disrespect and you paid. Considering how hard Catherine worked, Kikki thought it fair enough.

Catherine filled the grinder at the side of the industrial-sized highly polished steel expresso machine with aromatic coffee beans. She waited, breathing in the heady aroma of freshly ground coffee, allowing it to renew and ground her.

Kikki watched her friend expertly grind out a double portion and shove the metal container into place, her movements graceful and strong at the same time, a choreography ever mesmerizing to Kikki. The machine ran hot water in its own syncopated rhythm, streaming it into the dainty white and blue flowered porcelain cup.

Catherine interrupted Kikki's reverie, calling out over her shoulder, "*Qu'est-ce qui s'est passé?* A spat with your lover again—or too much fun! *Quelle chance!*"

Kikki hesitated. "He left in the wee hours for Spain—family emergency. His Tía was attacked by intruders."

"*Ç'est grave?*" Catherine shot Kikki a serious glance over her shoulder.

"*Très*. We don't know if she's alive or dead." It soothed Kikki to share the disturbing news with Catherine. The French enjoyed sharing bad news.

"I'm surprised you didn't go with him but glad you stayed,"

Catherine said, checking her hair and makeup in the mirror above the bar.

"Why? I might have been able to help."

"Hah!" Catherine said, placing a steaming hot cup on the shiny bronze bar counter in front of Kikki. "Stay here, do your own work and keep your nose out of his. I'm telling you—" She pursed her lips and shook her head. A familiar Gallic gesture of disapproval.

Kikki nodded, acknowledging the advice, and then raised the cup to her nostrils, breathing in the intoxicating smell. Heaven in a cup. With a tiny silver spoon, she selected a small chunk of raw brown sugar and dropped it in with a splash. She stirred and stared unseeing at Catherine's back. She was now moving with great purpose into her day, making a *café crème* for Moussa, preparing for the early arrivals, Monsieur Picot and Chef Hervé.

After a sip, Kikki said, "I needed this, thanks. Actually, *mon associée* Monique should be here soon. We have to prepare for a meeting with a new client. It's for a film about Henri IV, but I think there's something fishy about the client and his film."

"You sound paranoid." But Catherine's tone was of curiosity. "It's good you'll have a sensible French woman like Monique to bring you down to earth! Even if she is half Greek!" Catherine chuckled.

Kikki smiled. "You're right. I'm lucky to have Monique at my side."

"More nightmares?" Over her shoulder, Catherine once again shot her a concerned look.

Kikki took a bigger sip and this time scalded the roof of her mouth. "*Eh, merde!*" She sipped cold water from a tall glass, waiting for the burning sensation to cool. That, hearing voices, having visions, she thought to herself—but that was way too much information for Catherine.

"Too much wine last night?"

"No, just the right amount! I had a dream about La Reine Margot. A caped man was climbing a silk rope into her window."

"She had a lot of men climbing in her window." Catherine laughed.

"It makes me think about someone crawling in through my own terrace window—and I don't mean a lover." She spoke slowly, voicing for the first time a fear that had been hidden in her subconscious. With Torres's absence, it was becoming more real. She involuntarily shuddered.

Catherine regarded her thoughtfully. "You know they say that this building is haunted, and particularly that penthouse apartment you live in."

"*Sans doute*. Given the number of souls that have died in this dense part of the old city, I am sure that all buildings are haunted."

"*Peut-être*," Catherine said, lining up dainty white demi-tasse cups in front of the expresso machine. She came out from behind the bar to set up the dozen some tables in the small café and said, "I've seen ghosts here in the café."

"*Vraiment?*"

"Sometimes early in the morning when it's still dark out. Usually in winter, like now, near the holidays. Once, someone tapped me on my shoulder as I was unlocking the metal *store*. I thought it was Monsieur P. When I turned, no one was there. I nearly had a heart attack."

"I can imagine." And Kikki knew exactly what it must have been like. She'd love to talk to the owner of the restaurant, *Maison Picot*, about his experiences. The Voltaire had been in his family for three generations. "Center of the Northern Resistance during World War II because of easy access to the tunnels through the café and under the building and river, right? So many souls," Kikki murmured.

"There's a plaque on the building," Catherine said. "M Picot won't talk about it."

Kikki sipped her coffee, suddenly wary. If the male order was assembling, she knew what side M Picot would be on.

The owner wore his restaurant and heritage as a badge of honor of *La Vieille France*. And he made sure that everyone knew. He indulged Kikki as *l'américaine*, while constantly assaulting her with the ruinous politics and nonexistent culture of her nation of birth. A morning entertainment ritual for snobby French clients. *Les américains* had ruined the world and knew nothing. A young nation *sans culture*—unaccustomed to suffering like the old cultures of Europe, especially the proud and noble French.

"Well, as for the ghost of Margot—" Kikki began.

"Here comes Monsieur now. Shh!" Catherine rechecked her

makeup in one of the many mirrors and hurried to her station behind the counter, straightening her apron.

"Oh, he's probably seen his share," Kikki whispered with a smirk.

Monsieur Picot was a handsome, youthful man in his seventies. A classic Frenchman of good breeding, a notable hint of aristocracy in the fine features of his face, classic Gallic nose. Sparkling blue eyes that held mischief, high cheekbones, cheeks rosy now from the cold.

"*Bonjour*," Kikki greeted him, kissing him on both cheeks. "*Ça caille, non?*"

"It's winter. What did you expect?" he teased, taking off his cap and running slender chef's fingers through his thinning hair. "*Vous êtes tombée du lit?*" Why are you up so early?

"I guess you could say that—" She tried not to take offense at the implied jab with the *tacinage* (the tease). "Couldn't sleep," she murmured. She caught a vibe from him that she had never noticed before. A sharp glint in his eyes that was more than teasing. As if he were hiding behind a mask. Torres had warned her about people not being whom they seemed. She backed away with a polite smile and narrowed eyes.

Was she in the lair of the Swords already? Had she been there all along and never known?

Chapter 12

Kikki turned her head just as Monique Dubois walked in. She breathed a sigh of relief, happy to see her dear friend and in sore need of moral support. She could hardly download all that had happened with Catherine.

"*Bonjour, ma belle!*" Monique called out to Kikki.

The light of the café danced in Monique's green eyes and shimmered off her shoulder length, thick honey-golden hair. She was tall, slim and chic—a quintessential Parisian woman. Still, her straight nose and large heavily lashed eyes revealed her paternal Greek heritage.

Kikki crossed the short distance, and the two friends kissed affectionately.

"You're freezing, Monique!"

"*Eh—bien sûr*! It's so cold and damp outside! I walked from the metro at rue du Bac." She shook out her white fur coat but didn't take it off. Under her coat, she wore black leather pencil pants and over-the-knee suede boots with a stylish three-inch stiletto heel. "I hate this weather. I'm dying to go to Greece to bask in the sun and swim in the sea."

"Me too." Kikki nodded. "It'll be awhile. Let's take this booth by the door so we can have some privacy." Though no other customers had arrived, Kikki knew it wouldn't be long. The strategic booth was in a nook just behind the front end of the café's bar and tucked to the left of the narrow entrance. "And we'll have some room to spread out. *Merde*! I forgot my file!"

Monique laughed. "No worries. I have mine. Glad you have that Vuitton red vintage *sac* I love."

"For good luck!" The large market-basket-shaped red bag was Kikki's favorite.

They scooted into the booth, one on each side of the banquette —a polished wooden table flanked with classic red leather banquette seats.

"How are you, Monique? I love your new haircut. *Très chic.* Shows off your gorgeous eyes." Kikki watched Monique settle in and unwind the long emerald green scarf that matched her irises.

"Thanks. And you've lost weight. Are you going for the very French boyish look? I hope not. It doesn't suit you. Or me." Monique squared her shoulders and spine.

"Hah. I wish. But no, the Goddess gave me this body, and I like it just fine."

"Torres driving you crazy? Is he pressuring you to—uh—marry him? Hold out. Take my word for it!" Monique laughed, but she was concerned for her friend. She was evidently very stressed— hollowed cheeks and circles under her eyes.

"I haven't been sleeping well. That's all. But let's get to the work. It's important."

Monique nodded. "Sure."

"And thanks, I loved your notes!"

Catherine appeared and gave them both a smile that rose all the way to her bespectacled eyes. "*Bonjour, Madame Dubois!*"

"*Bonjour*, Catherine, and call me Monique, *s'il vous plait!*"

" *Très bien.* I'm glad you're here. Kikki could use some sensible company."

"*Ça va*, Catherine!" Kikki quipped.

They both ordered double expresso and *pain au chocolate*.

Catherine hurried away, and Monique looked Kikki in the eyes. "You look like hell! Are you okay?"

"You should have seen me earlier!" Kikki mocked, doing her

best to make light.

"What happened? Are you having those nightmares about Queen Margot again? This film may not be a good thing for you— or us, however tempting the promised large retainer."

Kikki paused before answering, nodding to an *habitué* who had also come in early from the cold, drawn to morning rituals, conversation, newspapers and coffee.

How much should she tell Monique without worrying her too much? They were very close, but Kikki was protective. Monique accused her of mothering her too much.

"Kikki, *dis*! And don't sugarcoat it, as you Americans say."

"Yes, still having nightmares. Margot seems to have taken over my life. Visions, and now whispers of advice and warning." But there was so much more.

"*Vraiment*? What has she said?" Monique leaned across the table conspiratorially.

"I'll get to it. But the main reason I look like—as you so kindly put it, hell, is because it feels like I've been through it. Torres got a call. His great-aunt, Tía, was attacked."

Monique shuddered at the news before she could fully compose herself. She must not show Kikki more than she should. For Monique knew Tía very well. Kikki wasn't aware they were longtime sisters in the Daughters of Inanna. It wasn't the time to reveal that to Kikki, not yet.

"Holy Goddess! Is she alright? Is Torres?" Monique whispered. Her voice was steady, but she was shaking inside.

Kikki's eyes started to well with tears, and she turned away, swiping them with the back of her hand. "I don't know, Monique. She might have been killed. There was an attack and then an explosion."

Kikki gave Monique a quick sketch: from Tía's phone call to Kikki's realization that Torres was using the Snake Goddess to bring down a secret patriarchal society. The attack on Tía was the first blow.

"*Putain de merde*! That's intense. Torres has gone to battle in Spain."

"Fucking hell is right!" Kikki broke off, breathing deeply.

"It's terrifying—but remember he's a warrior. He'll be okay, and Tía is tough as nails from what you've told me." Monique reached across the table and laid her hand on Kikki's.

At that moment, Catherine arrived with a basket of *pains au chocolate* and two double expressos. "*Et voici, mesdemoiselles. Bon appétit.*"

Both women caught each other's eyes for a moment, each needing to let go of her private worries and concerns.

Catherine hovered a moment. "Everything all right? Anything else?"

Kikki smiled, "*Merci*, Catherine. *Parfait!*"

"*Très bien.*" Catherine bustled away.

Kikki selected a *pâtisserie*, inspecting the flaking buttery layers with dark chocolate peeking out the side. With her first bite, the sweet and savory flavors nudged her back to earth and Paris's delights, to the pleasures of life in the moment. "*Miam!*

"Hmm, they have the best here!"

Kikki took another tiny bite and rolled her eyes. "Heaven!" Knowing they had to get back to business, she took a sip of expresso. "So—I wanted to go with Torres, but you know how he is —"

"And in this case, he's right—I'm glad you didn't go."

Kikki frowned. "Torres and those close to him are in grave danger. And so, I think, are we all."

Monique sat back and crossed her arms in front of her. "The patriarchy—*encore!*"

Kikki thought about showing Monique the threat to Tía. It was tucked in her coat pocket. It wasn't time. Not yet.

"Wow, what an intense morning." Monique sipped coffee. Forcing her thoughts to stay focused. She prayed that Tía had made it out alive, and that she had a plan because they needed her this week. She picked up the dossier to shift gears. "Let's talk about the film. It must be key to the whole conspiracy."

"I agree. I have a bad vibe. Someone is using it to get to us, Monique. This client has PATRIARCH written in bold black letters. But we can turn the tables on whomever is behind it. Use it to defeat our enemies. Are you up for it?"

"I love the way you think. I'm with you." Monique was scared, but Kikki was her mentor and she wasn't going to show fear.

"Are you sure? Because I can deal with this client on my own and get what I need." Kikki didn't want to push Monique. "It's your choice, really."

"No! I am absolutely helping you. It's my cause too." Monique grabbed a stack of papers. "I've got all my notes, the treatment, the script," Monique said, taking a deep breath. She was up for the battle this week. So much was at stake.

"Okay. Let's get started." Kikki began, "First of all, let's talk about the film in general. Not the legal issues. I'm confident we know what we're doing on that front. Although, if this guy is as shady as my instinct and your research indicate, we'll want to be very careful. Our reputation is at stake."

"Damn right!" Monique said, agreeing. "Not to mention our livelihood."

"So, at this first meeting—10:15 this morning at our office, right, Monique?"

"Yes."

"First, let's talk story. I sure as hell am not going to work on such a sexist representation featuring only Henri de Navarre, Madame la Serpente de Medici and the rest of the patriarchy of the House of France. Margot has only a minor supporting role and is painted in a totally negative light."

Monique smiled. "Let's hope they will be open to our superior feminine knowledge about Margot's power and brilliance. Her plight and her fight. It will make for a much more interesting film. Otherwise—"

"One more remake for the good old boys."

And at that moment, as if they had conjured him with their words, Monsieur Picot appeared at their table and inclined his head, smiling. "*Bonjour, Madame Dubois. Comment t'allez vous?* Is your family well?"

Monique extended her hand, and he bent and brushed it with his lips.

She winked. "Yes, my daughter is in the capable hands of my husband this morning. His turn to get her to the *école maternelle*." She lied intentionally to annoy the very conservative owner.

He made a *tisk tisk* sound with his tongue. "Such modern women." As he spoke, he glanced at the file open on the table. "An interesting case?"

"Quite," Kikki said. "A film about Henri the Great. I'm sure you would love the way they've put the film together."

M Picot flung his arms enthusiastically, speaking proudly, "He was a great king who built modern France—even if a Protestant from the back of nowhere, in Navarre. But American filmmakers, I suppose? They won't know the most interesting parts."

"Such as—" Kikki caught his eyes with a challenge.

Monique gave Picot a shrewd smile and said, "The most interesting part about Henri IV is La Reine Margot!" She baited.

"*Oh, mais non*! She was a *putain*. A depraved whore. She deserved her banishment from court. There were rules that she ignored." He frowned in disgust. And batted his serviette at the table, as if to fend off the spirit of Margot.

"Oh, right, double standard. A queen's body was sacred and divine, only for breeding male heirs in service to the king and God. But the king could have lovers, whores and an official mistress," Kikki sparred, barely suppressing her anger. She felt M Picot watching her through narrowed eyes.

"Monsieur Picot!" Catherine interrupted. "*Téléphone!*"

He scuttled away. Kikki was thoughtful, turning to watch him go. Was he one of the Knights of the Holy Sword of God?"

"Well, there's a good place to start!" Monique said. "Henri de Navarre, a Bourbon prince of the blood was some match! Margot was far superior in every way to her cousin. But the Valois throne was at stake, and Margot's brothers were not good candidates. Nostradamus's famous prediction that three Henries would rule terrified Catherine de Medici. Francois II succeeded his father and Catherine's husband, Henri II, but died young. When the Black Queen arranged Margot's marriage, his successor, Charles IX, was ill. He was violent and unstable with a strange blood disease that caused rages. He would not live much longer and had no heir. Then came Henri, Duc d'Anjou. Well to make a long story short, her brothers were sickly—if it wasn't syphilis it was tuberculosis, or both. Not one produced a male heir—just what the Black Queen was worried about. She never wanted Henri de Navarre to be King of France—the third Henri. In fact, she hated him."

"But better he be king and carry on the lineage through the

House of Bourbon than Margot." Kikki finished off her *pain au chocolate* and licked her lips. "Sinfully good." She picked up the treatment and script and scanned. "So, all because of Salic law excluding women from dynastic succession, Margot could never rule on her own. If her husband, the king, predeceased her—which he in fact did—*any* female children would not have a right to the throne. Fucking outrageous!"

Monique set her cup of coffee down and said, "True. Totally absurd. During the same time period, Elizabeth Tudor took the throne, and she was considered by Catholics to be Henry VIII's illegitimate child. She ruled alone and had no children. And proved a power to be reckoned with."

"It makes me furious," Kikki said. She finished the rest of her coffee and set it down sharply. "The POV of this film supports patriarchal laws—a woman could not and should not rule a kingdom without a man at her side."

"Original sin and tainted blood of women. The old Adam and Eve story that carries through Judeo-Christian and other cultures, and certainly Catholics and Protestants of that era."

"Greek mythology, too, Monique," Kikki added. "The Classical period, not prehistoric Minoan, in which the matriarchy and Mother Goddess were supreme, and woman was honored."

"True, but the pantheon of gods and goddesses were much more well-rounded," Monique said with a grin. "Not that I'm biased by my ancestry."

"Margot worshipped the Greek goddesses and strove to be as just and strategic as Athena. She wanted to look like Aphrodite." Kikki agreed

"The famous French sculptor of the sixteenth century, Gujon, honored Margot with a statute that is still in the Louvre—*Les Trois Graces*. Marguerite de Valois was one of three Marguerites who were revered French royalty." Monique glanced at her watch.

The café was bustling with customers lined up at the bar now. She had to take her seven-year-old daughter to school, though she'd intentionally told the owner otherwise.

"Yes, in fact, it's one of my favorites," Kikki agreed. "After the *Winged Victory of Samothrace,* the Goddess Nike."

"*Moi aussi,*" Monique agreed, peering into her now-empty

coffee cup.

"Shall we have one more expresso, Monique?"

"Why not! Life is too short and precious to deprive ourselves. And we've got a lot of work today—" She eased off, not wanting to further stress Kikki.

Kikki signaled to Catherine, who was nearby at the moment, serving *tartine*, butter and homemade plum jam to a customer at a small table near the front. She nodded and then rushed off.

"What were we saying. Oh, right, Margot's beauty. She was the pearl of the Valois court. Her name even means 'pearl' in Latin. And she favored pearls, naturally."

"And 'daisy' in Greek," Monique added with a sparkle in her eye. "I've got a photo of a portrait of her. Isn't it in the file?"

"No—I didn't see it," Kikki said, thumbing through the pages spread out on the table. "Oh, wait! Here it is. It's the commissioned portrait of her when she was sixteen."

Monique slipped the shiny photograph of the old portrait from a plastic sleeve and held it under the light on the wall over their table.

Kikki admired the portrait, peering closely. "Quaint. Proper dress, hair up in braids as was the formal custom, emphasizing her high cheekbones. A demure but elaborate dress with the ruffled lace collar up to her ears. She was a beauty. Look at her eyes—they show her wit and charm, with a *soupçon* of cunning."

"She had perfect facial features, black almost iridescent eyes, luxuriant dark hair and a porcelain complexion—an elegant long neck and good figure." Monique added.

"Plus, although she was slightly taller than average, her feet were fashionably small!" Kikki laughed. "Her gowns, hairstyle and jewels were the epitome of chic."

"She was a trendsetter and very beautiful, Kikki. Even at sixteen. So full of vitality that her enemies tried to stifle her."

"In vain, thankfully."

"Listen, I have to go soon. Have to take Michele to school. I don't get to spend enough time with her. I don't want her growing up thinking the *au pair* is her mother."

"How could she ever think that? You are such a presence, and she takes after you. She has your eyes and your laugh, not to mention your intelligence."

Monique grinned, pleased, a proud mother.

"But before you have to go, speaking of daughters, before it slips my mind, what about the scene in the film in which her evil mother puts a bounty on Margot's newly born daughter? Easily believable of the Black Queen. King Charles IX might have gone along with it even though he was fond of Margot, but the prevailing patriarchal historical view holds that Margot was sterile. So why do they highlight this in the film? It doesn't fit."

Monique nodded. "I wondered about that story line as well. Her fecundity has been a subject of debate. We've both read the history, including Margot's *Mémoires*, written when she was in prison. From that reading, Margot wasn't sterile, but her wicked mother told her she was."

Kikki chimed in, "And that was only because it suited her Machiavellian political purposes when Margot was sexually active and not yet married. And when she did marry, she was expected to produce a male heir? Or not? I don't get that either," Kikki said, drumming her fingers on the table in annoyance. "I believe Catherine hoped it wouldn't ever be necessary and that the Valois could carry on the throne through her favorite son, Henri III."

"Yes, that's twisted isn't it, Kikki? I read that one of the Black Queen's seers had a vision that Margot was sterile, so Catherine passed that information on to her daughter."

"Right." Kikki nodded. "And Margot took all manner of herbal concoctions to ensure she wouldn't get pregnant. But other well-respected historians say she did have two or three children. Though never from her husband and no male heirs. Daughters from lovers."

As she said the words, Kikki flashed on the vision. Margot, in a carriage with her daughter and her lady-in-waiting and *confidante* Gillonne, fleeing Paris on a wintry night to take her child to safety. She wanted to tell Monique about the vision, but she hesitated.

"Since you have to leave, let's wrap up," Kikki said finally. "The script paints Margot as a depraved whore—those words exactly. Just what Picot said!" That gave her pause. "Bottom line—why would they come to us with such an anti-feminist film? It's a trap. They're playing us."

"It sure feels that way. The background information is very

sketchy. I can't trace the financing. It's there, but where did it come from? A lot of money. Millions! Layers of nestled shell companies. I've also discovered a French partner linked to the shells that has a limited company set up in Lichtenstein. The listed principal is an *aristo*—a count from the Berry region—and pretty far to the right— a Bourbon and in line for the French throne. Long live King Louis XX!"

"I wonder who referred them to us? I keep trying to figure it out," Kikki said.

"Doesn't say." Monique studied the file. "In my initial conversation with this guy, the Executive Producer, Robert Moreno, he said he read about you on LinkedIn."

"Unlikely. I worked for a long time in New York. Know a lot of people in the business." Could it be her old boss who made the connection? Kikki wondered but didn't say. The script angle would be just the kind of thing he would throw her way to piss her off.

"So it is a trap," Monique said, arching a brow. "Clearly, the film is key to the whole conspiracy. They're using it to get to you."

"They know I can't resist any chance to set the record straight about Margot and iconic women in history. It's a ploy—a war strategy, Monique," Kikki whispered, concerned about being overheard. "Keep your enemies close—the tactics of Sun Tzu."

"So, Kikki, *fais gaffe*. We'll be very careful. What's our game plan?"

"Take the meeting, of course."

And what was Margot's agenda? Kikki wondered.

Retribution at least.

Chapter 13

❧ ——•—— ❧

Torres checked his watch—08:33. After a three hour and fifteen minute flight, they had just landed at a private airport in Granada. In Paris, hours earlier, on the way to the airport, he had tried in vain to reach Tía.

Just as he was boarding the plane at Le Bourget, the private airport near Roissy CDG, his phone rang. It was Tía's number, but it wasn't Tía. The connection crackled and finally broke up. It had been a male voice, a young man speaking in what Torres recognized as the *patois Andaluz* of Tía's region. But Torres only made out the words "*mensaje*" (message) and "Tía" before the connection failed.

Once they had cleared the stormy winter skies, in the air, Torres used his sat phone and called again around 05:30.

"*Dígame!*" The young man said, clearly audible this time. "*Mira*, is that you, Tía's nephew, Torres?"

"*Claro*. Who's this?"

"A friend of Tía's. I live across from her. She gave me the phone and asked me to call you."

"You mean she's alive? Is she hurt?" Torres breathed a sigh of relief. "Where did she go?"

"She was alive. Not sure if she's wounded. I heard the shooting

67

and the explosion. I was up anyway," the young man said and then hesitated.

"*Que! Dígame!*" Torres fired off.

"Well, someone picked her up at the corner but that car, the one that had come by earlier with the shooters—*pues*—they followed. After—I don't know what happened to her. But I checked her house, after she left like she asked. The place was ransacked, and the portal destroyed by an explosion."

"You shouldn't have. These people are very dangerous."

"*Yo sé.*" I know, the young man had agreed. "We know all about them."

Torres was furious at Tía and her network of spies. At the same time, he was grateful that they had been there.

Then the young man said proudly, "There was one of those guys in there. Wore a white cloth hood and a big crucifix. Covered with blood. Dead, I think, but I didn't get very close. Caught in the explosion. Tía had it rigged to go—I helped her."

Torres had smiled, despite a growing anger, mixed with concern and something like dread. Tía had it all figured out—as usual.

"I won't call *la poli* then. Tía told me not to."

Torres assured him that Tía was right, adding, "I'll be there soon with backup, and we'll handle it." He didn't want his crime scene compromised. The last thing he needed was the locals involved. In fact, the local cops were probably rife with Swords, maybe one or two of them in this attack. That's what his gut told him.

"*Claro,*" the man said. "We'll keep watch until you are here."

The first attack by the Swords. Damn Tía! He knew she'd drawn them to her, probably taunting them to attack. Now in addition to retaliation for this first strike, he had a crime scene to contain, evidence to sift through, a body to deal with—not to mention a missing Tía.

Tía had intentionally drawn out the enemy, and yet, she had also urged him to come down to speak to her about some vital secret. Well, he was here. But was *she* still alive?

He sure as hell hadn't expected Operation Sphinx to kick off in Spain with the opening blow to his team. It hit Torres where it hurt, leaving him exposed and his beloved Tía in jeopardy. That hadn't been *his* plan.

The target of his sting, the Knights of the Holy Sword of God, was a secret society, as Kikki had figured. But so much more. The global umbrella organization overarched the Florentine antiquities dealer's operations that financed the Swords' weapons, bribes and political favors, all to carry out an unholy secret war.

The latest intel he had gotten was from Florence Delattre "Flo," once more his boss and colleague though higher up the Interpol command chain. It pointed to a fanatic Spanish branch of the Swords—Catholic terrorists. Thank God he trusted Flo completely to come through because right now he couldn't trust anyone else.

As wheels finally touched down, he'd reviewed his plan for the best approach. He'd been able to get a secure line and a good connection to go over it with Sara and Manu by the time the plane taxied to a stop.

Now, he hurried through the familiar chill of December in his hometown, Granada, to their awaiting armored SUV at the small private airport. He got in, more than glad to see Sara, Tía's youngest great-granddaughter and her husband, Manu, Torres's childhood friend. Both were elite and highly skilled operatives with the Spanish Feds, Cuerpo National de Police (CNP), Europol and Interpol—and now part of his covert team.

With Sara behind the wheel, they sped off into Granada. Tía lived in a villa in the Albaicín, a rambling medieval *barrio* on the hillside across from the Alhambra. She also had a *finca* in the foothills of the Sierra Nevada, far enough away but not completely isolated. Torres wondered if she had gone there.

The large inner courtyard hidden from the street had a small stable where she kept one or two horses. Because she lived alone, she said that having a horse nearby kept her active and gave her empowering horse energy for company. Torres's lips curved in a half smile. Kikki would have said the same thing.

Lorca was Tía's favorite stallion. She had always joked that she knew she could get away anytime she needed on horseback and hide in the hills, as Féderico García Lorca had done during the Spanish Civil War.

But the young man hadn't mentioned her horse, Lorca, and Tía had left on foot to a car.

Tía had always been mysterious and enigmatic. At ninety, the family matriarch, one of a long line of powerful women in Torres's family culture, Tía was fiercer than ever. As a boy, he remembered overhearing hushed conversations between her and his grandmother Elena. They had secrets and mysterious visitors. She had irons in a lot of fires and had always been an activist.

The young man had been a big help. Tía was smart, and with her network, chances were good that she'd already made it to safety, but he wouldn't know until he laid eyes on her.

Fear would not serve him, so he let it fuel his righteous anger. Those *cabróns* would pay if anything happened to either Tía or Kikki. He honed his focus on what was right in front of him.

Torres had convinced his cousins that they should go in together through the back and not split up. He would have heard from Tía's spies if the Swords had shown themselves.

They would be back, Torres knew. And right now, they might be lying in wait nearby. Tactically, it made sense for the enemy to wait until Torres arrived. His death would serve as retribution for the death of one of their own.

Now, with Torres on point, the three approached Tía's *carmen* (a freestanding house) in the heart of the Albaicín on one of many narrow donkey paths. They were silent and cautious as they approached. And each well-armed.

The three of them were going in without backup. He was counting on the element of surprise. Because he didn't know what or how many they were up against.

The radical Spanish branch had a lot of supporters, according to Flo, Tía and Torres's intel. But the Albaicín was not the kind of *barrio* where an army would work. Maybe a small squad, like Torres and his cousins.

As they approached, Manu spoke in a low voice, "Do you think she's still alive?" When Torres didn't answer, Manu said what he knew they were all thinking. "*Joder*, I hope they didn't get her as she escaped!"

Torres said, "She's wily." He chuckled softly.

Manuel and Sara glared at him. Torres replied, "Just trying to steady myself with a little levity."

Reining in emotions, he became calm, cool and aware of every movement, each stone on the path. The azure of the sky deepened and the sun's warmth intensified. He was ready. He caught the homey smell of woodburning fires. And the unique dry chill of his hometown, tucked into the mountains. So unlike the damp, cold blanket of Paris.

Torres led the way as they moved silently and in single file along the narrow path, once perfectly covered with cobblestones. Now, more were missing than not. The approach had them winding their way around the back towards Tía's property on a narrow path for about one klick.

"*Cuídense* at the next corner," he whispered, signing with his finger.

They crept carefully, hugging a high stone wall that curved around a bend about five hundred meters ahead, almost to the entrance to Tía's courtyard.

Suddenly, an old man appeared from behind a wooden fence that was covered, even in mid-December, with lush bougainvillea. He walked with purpose straight towards them. Torres narrowed his eyes at the man's shotgun. A wide-brimmed black Cordobés hat hid his angular face. Torres signaled to stop.

The man raised the shotgun, sighted and lifted his chin. "*No te mueven!*" Don't move.

Was he friend or foe? Part of Tía's network? Torres held his Beretta ready, flush against his side. He signaled to the others to lower their weapons.

"Are we trespassing on your property? *Lo siento,*" Torres said with calm assertion. Sara and Manuel took up position on either side of him. Three abreast.

Torres relaxed his stance and motioned to his companions to stand at ease. "We mean no harm," he said in dialect.

The man didn't answer, didn't lower his weapon. They were still in the crosshairs, but Torres's gut told him they were not in danger.

Torres took a deep breath, "*Mi tía*—she lives around the corner. She showed me this path when I was a boy."

The man kept the shotgun level and advanced a few paces. "*No te conozco.*" I don't recognize you, he said.

His voice was familiar to Torres, as were his bright black eyes. If

Kikki had been there, she would have said it was a good sign. Tía also had dark eyes that glistened. And then it struck him.

"*Papito*? Is that you? *Soy yo*, Pepe." The old man had been abroad for a long time, but apparently, he was back. Torres had known him since childhood. A dear friend of the family. Papito had all but raised him when he was a boy, after his father died.

The man eyed him suspiciously but lowered the gun. Back ramrod straight, he took two long strides that put him only inches away from Torres. They locked eyes.

Silence. No one stirred. And then the man exclaimed. "*Hombre! Tanto tiempo!*" He clapped Torres on the back and lowered the gun. Torres let out a long breath.

The old man grinned widely. "*Tan viejo.* I don't see so well."

Torres smiled with relief. "You're not old at all. *Hombre!*"

"Tía asked me to keep an eye out for our enemies. They shot up her house pretty good, but she was ready for them. She said you'd be coming."

Quickly, Torres filled Papito in on what the boy had relayed. Torres was glad to hear that the local cops hadn't been spotted and neither had the Swords, neither by Papito nor by Tía and Papito's extended network.

"One of them went in the back—I watched him walk into the trap she laid." He laughed. "*Cabrón* didn't come out."

"*Vale.*" Torres reached out to clasp Papito's hand in a gesture of solidarity. "*Muchísimas gracias.* Wait here. Watch our backs as we go in."

Just around the bend in the path, hidden from view by the old stone wall and the overhanging branches of a pomegranate tree, they waited. The old man was an impotent lookout. But he had been the perfect distraction. God was on their side, as always. Long live those who served the one true, righteous Catholic God! They made the sign of the cross simultaneously.

While the heretic rattled on with the old man, they walked quietly towards their enemy, in single file, AK-47 rifles at their sides, faces hooded, masked in white cloths.

Chapter 14

Just as Torres arrived in Granada, at 08:30, the sun rose in Paris behind darkly clouded skies. The icy fog clung to Kikki as she stood on the sidewalk in front of the café. Traffic had picked up on Quai Voltaire.

She wrapped her scarf more tightly, securing the hood of her long black shearling coat. She was on her way to see her dear friend Liam at the Hotel Regina on the Right Bank, just behind the Louvre.

She crossed diagonally to the bridge at the end of rue du Bac, a busy street that led to river's edge where centuries ago, before the Pont Royal was built in 1685 by Louis XIV a *bac* (small boat) ferried passengers across the Seine.

Kikki's boot heels clicked smartly as she walked along Pont Royal to the Rive Droite. She shifted her fears for her lover and Tía by focusing on her conversation with Monique, mentally preparing herself to enter the busy world that was Paris on a wintry Monday morning.

After the very early morning she'd had, she felt as if she were literally crossing over to another time and dimension.

Midway across the bridge, she looked out at the layer of white fog hovering above the river. The Seine appeared like a magical long green serpent cloaked in a white fur coat winding its way through the city.

The feathery branches of a Spanish moss tree hanging low over the river glistened with heavy dew. Hints of light filtered through its branches, and the fog shroud parted with the first rays of sun. Kikki whispered a prayer of thanks to the River Goddess Mélusine.

Finally, she picked up her pace heading north, weaving through the other Parisians on their way to work.

Kikki needed loyal allies like Monique. And preferably physically embodied and alive in the present. Her savvy friend Liam was the Tarot's Magician—highly psychic. She hoped he could intuit more about what was going on and help her form a strategy.

At the far end of the bridge, she stopped in front of the Louvre on the busy Quai François Mitterrand, once the more appropriate Quai des Tuileries. A blast of frigid wind blew her hood off, startling her. She amped her invisible crystalline protection.

Traffic lights turned green, cars and buses moved, and pedestrians heading north and south across the River Seine scurried to unknown destinations. Kikki followed a well-traveled route across the street to the Jardin de Tuileries. Fondly called the *Tuiles*, as the gardens were built in 1564 on the site of an old *tuile* (tile) factory. Ironically, Kikki's favorite playground was a royal garden commissioned by none other than the Black Medici Queen.

A prickle crept up her spine, a reminder to be on guard against shapeshifters and dark energy. Margot's mortal enemy would make a stand with the patriarchy this week, as she had done four hundred years ago, most infamously with the Saint-Bartholomew's Day Massacre.

It was only a matter of time before she materialized.

At the stone Sphinx statue atop the wall on the southwest corner of the Tuileries, Kikki stopped and looked through the fence that bordered the gardens, its wrought iron bars tipped with golden arrows.

In the near distance, the undisturbed, well-ordered garden grounds wore a blanket of snow, as did the green bronze lion in the center of the round pond across the way. She cast her gaze beyond to the stately rows of chestnut trees, barren in winter, their branches laden with a few inches of fresh snow.

She was startled by a sharp pain in her left ear. A whisper of a voice that sounded like Margot's, "*Beware, danger is near!*" The rest was muffled by the repeating screech of a police siren.

Startled, Kikki blinked, and abruptly, the golden tips of the iron fence transformed into sharp blades of silver—swords dripping with poisonous tips. The air smelled no more of snow but almonds—like arsenic.

Feeling a presence, she spun around to face the ancient sculptured stone buildings of the Louvre that opened onto the gardens. Although she saw no one, she whispered, "Who are you?"

She wanted confirmation that it was Margot speaking—even if it meant doubting a queen of France.

She heard the voice again clearly.

"*I am Queen Marguerite de Valois. You know me well. I have appeared to you before, have I not? I have shown myself covered in blood on the night of the massacre.*"

The words seemed to come from nowhere and everywhere at once.

Kikki said, "Times are perilous. How can I be certain that your voice is not being used by the Black Queen, your antagonist and hated mother? There is much darkness, and my vision is not clear. I fear someone is blocking my psychic abilities."

"*You are wise to be wary. Ma mère is here, and indeed, we will both face her scorched soul in battle. She wears a mask as the face of the enemy.*"

"*Then show yourself. Prove you are Margot, and I will see you and recognize your true self.*"

The temperature plunged, and a frigid wind blew suddenly from the west, rustling the barren chestnut trees in the alleyway along the gardens. In a swirling cloud of snowflakes, Margot came to life.

She wore a red taffeta ball gown with voluminous skirts over fine lace petticoats and a tight bodice that lifted her breasts. Her raven black hair rested on bare shoulders and décolletage. A row of pearls encircled her delicate long neck. Atop her head, she wore a bonnet woven with pearls and rubies. Her porcelain skin was radiant, and her regard determined. She was more beautiful than her portrait.

Her flashing black eyes caught Kikki's. *"Do you now believe it is I?"* She spoke in a high-pitched arcane French.

"Yes, I see you clearly and feel your luminous presence. The goodness of your heart—"

A golden light emanated from Margot's bosom, and Kikki felt a warmth in her own heart, as if she had been touched. Now, she was certain Margot's fierce and loving spirit stood before her.

Margot's deep ruby lips curved into a caring smile. *"I understand your doubt. You have been betrayed before, many times, as was I. You, most recently, in Santorini."*

"I was betrayed," Kikki said slowly, surprised that Margot knew her history. *"You are right. I came back to Paris for haven."*

"Yes," Margot said kindly, *"But now, sadly, Paris, your beloved City of Light, a place you thought safe for you and all women like you, is threatened by more darkness and betrayal. I have always been a strong voice for love, justice and all that you fight for. For the Goddess and our way of life. Paris was once a peaceful fertile river land, and native tribes lived by the rules of nature and respected Gaia, our Mother Earth. We must fight for our ways, or we will be annihilated. This will take all your cunning and mine together. For everything is at risk."*

Kikki's heart quickened, skipping beats. *"What do you need from me?"*

Margot's sweet voice trembled with anger. *"Revenge— retribution—a righting of wrongs. Justice."*

In awe and slightly fearful, Kikki took a step back, feeling the heat of Margot's passion. *"I'm here."*

"I need your help. The time is now, as is written in the stars. Go as the Goddess Athena, with your battle armor and sword of finest steel. Fight to reveal the truth, and let justice be meted out to those who seek to violate us. You must save our beloved city, Paris, and the precious Snake Goddess from those who would destroy all that she symbolizes. You must be brave and your sword sharpest. They call themselves the Knights of the Holy Sword of God, but they have long been darkness and evil itself."

"I've heard of them," Kikki said. *"But how will we know them? How will I recognize them?"*

"You will know our enemies though they hide behind masks," Margot whispered. *"Your lover fights them as a warrior, but you can defeat them with your wisdom and knowing, as Athena. My own mother colluded with the darkness, with those who sought power above all else. She joined the Patriarchy. She joined the Swords."*

Kikki suppressed a shudder of fear. *"How can I alone defeat such formidable forces?*

"You will not be alone. We, who are of the Goddess, have been readying for battle and will be at your side, but you must lead the fight."

"Do you mean the Daughters of Inanna?" Kikki whispered, fingering the threat letter in her coat pocket. *"Are you one of them?"*

"Of course. As will you be soon."

"Please, I beg you, what is to come?"

"This is all I can tell you now."

"Why can't you tell me more? For surely it would help me, help us all."

"You know it is not that simple. You will have choices to make along the way. I come to you now to tell you this. It is time to choose to fight."

"But I've already chosen, I'm here—when is the first battle?"

Margot raised one hand, as if to calm Kikki. She said, *"We cannot seek to influence the Goddess's divine unfolding of events. All will be known in its rightful timing. Hurry through the gardens to see your friend, but take time to truly know your own heart. If you freely choose battle, I will send you a sign."*

In a sudden gust of wind, Margot vanished.

Kikki looked around, her attention instantly drawn to a bright yellow light in an upper floor of the Pavillon de Flore. Her eyes followed its path through the *brume*. It spotlighted a raven sitting atop the sphinx.

The raven, one of Kikki's animal protectors, signified crossing time and dimension, as Margot had just done. Ravens were magic to Kikki—real magic was at hand. It would be needed. They were harbingers of news, bearing messages.

But if this was the sign from Margot, it could also foretell evil.

The highly superstitious people of that era believed the raven to be a harbinger of death.

The raven squawked loudly. Kikki took off along the edge of the Tuileries, eager to see Liam.

As she reached the northern edge of the gardens, she slowed, experiencing a sense of stillness that seemed to stop time. She heard the echo of Margot's admonition: "*Hurry through the royal gardens —but take time to truly know your own heart.*"

She found herself seated on a stone bench. She slipped her hand inside her coat and ran fingers over the rose crystal stones at her throat. She asked for clarity to see the entire picture.

The darkness of the Winter Solstice and the waxing December moon, the last of the lunar calendar year, were building magnetic pressure from within the Universe and Mother Earth. Soon the portal would open.

The Patriarchy, in the form of the Knights of the Holy Sword of God, were bringing war. Kikki fingered their ominous letter, folded now in her coat pocket. "When the light turns—"

On the Solstice. The same evening as the Snake Goddess gala.

Margot had said that they were prepared, but Kikki must lead the battle. Holy Goddesses! The Daughters of Inanna with Tía as their leader. Tía would be readying for this if she wasn't already dead.

So much for a retreat and an attempt at domestic bliss with her lover. She would have to be High Priestess and Athena, Our Lady of Justice, at once.

Could Torres accept that? Or would it break them?

Kikki leaned over, cradling her head in her hands. How she detested this ever-present struggle to overcome injustice and malevolent forces. The amount of energy that it would demand overwhelmed her. She wanted to run. But she knew that she was about to cross over the threshold, and once she consciously made the choice, there would be no turning back.

Tears of anguish froze on her cheeks. Anguish turned to rage, and a tumult of emotions swirled inside her heart, her soul. Again, she sensed time slowing, almost stopping. Would her rage ease to anger—and finally to acceptance? The strong scent of roses emanated from her necklace.

Finally, she stood, knowing she had made her choice. Willingly, she would take the next step in her journey. The Goddess called. Paris, her beloved city, her home and refuge, was threatened, and in days would be under siege.

She turned her gaze towards I. M. Pei's glass *Pyramid*, rising in the middle of the Louvre's principal courtyard. The bizarre juxtaposition of old and new—a geometrical wonder of light and glass. Now it served as a focal point that activated and cleared her mind, like a dancer spotting to execute a perfect pirouette.

Kikki experienced a kind of fusion. High Priestess became one with Athena.

She began to walk with purpose, imagining her hood as a helmet. Athena's sword grasped firmly in her right hand. In the still foggy light, she peered with the owl's eyes that saw all for Athena—and for Kikki.

She walked from the end of the Tuileries, crossed the rue de Rivoli and stepped into the Place des Pyramides. There, she passed Sainte-Jeanne d'Arc mounted on her stallion. The maiden from Orleans waving proudly her banner.

Jeanne, France's savior—a brave young woman who had visions of God that called her to save her beloved country. Later—a threat to the ruling powers, she was burned at the stake as a witch by men in the name of their so-called One True Catholic God.

Kikki felt the full weight of her decision. But she did not falter. She stood taller as she hurried to Liam. He waited with a welcoming smile under the eaves of the Regina—the Queen's Hotel.

Chapter 15

"You look like you've been to Hades and back!" Liam teased, linking her arm as she stepped onto the curb. In his early thirties, he was tall and lanky with black hair swept from a Saturnine forehead, emphasizing a handsome face with a proud nose and easy smile. A gold Bulgari watch peeked out from his bespoke Italian suit and cuffed shirt. Behind fashionable eyeglasses, his gray eyes showed worry as he and Kikki kissed in greeting.

"More like late sixteenth-century Paris. Literally a burning Hell of a time and place. You won't believe what my morning has been like. High melodrama even for Greeks. Or the likes of you and me, Monsieur Magicién."

"But you look different. Your energy has shifted." He studied his friend, reading her. She looked like she was in shock, as though she had been through a transformation since he'd last seen her. Almost a rebirth, despite her wan physical appearance.

"You can thank La Reine Margot for that." Kikki looked up at him and smiled. "Wait until you hear about what's happened. Time to consult the Tarot."

He ran his free hand through his well-coiffed locks. "I told you to be careful what you ask for."

"Like Greeks bearing gifts?" she said affectionately. "But what do you mean?" she asked more seriously as they walked across the marble-floored hotel lobby.

"When you first came to Paris you chose to live in that *quartier*, her neighborhood, the gardens of her palace. And that was even before you moved into the fabulous penthouse on Quai Voltaire with Torres."

"Huh, perhaps," she allowed.

"And, I don't think the irony—or karmic destiny—has escaped you—that you conveniently found office space on rue de Valois."

"*Mais oui*, you're right, as always." A long one-block street bordering the Palais Royal. "Margot's stomping grounds. You're saying I asked for all of this—consciously or unconsciously manifested this conflict."

"With a little help. More like you were called. But you know that." He shot her an enigmatic look. "Come, have a cup of hot tea —perhaps a little brandy to warm you. You look like you've been up all night. It's freezing out." Despite a new manner of confidence, she looked as pale as the ghost that stalked her. "Calvados? I have a very good one—aged twenty-five years. Very smooth. It will take you right to Normandy and soothe your troubled mind."

"That would be very welcome." She felt her mood shift, allowing herself to release the tension she held, relieved to be with Liam. High Priest to her High Priestess.

He escorted her through the lobby, signaling one of his minions to take her coat and another to follow.

"*Après toi, mademoiselle*," he said, ushering her into the classic bar, red velvet banquettes and deep, comfortable armchairs in an intimate setting. Cool, quiet, dark.

"Let's enjoy our favorite room of mirrors, eh," he chuckled. "In your state, you'll be more comfortable in that Alice and Wonderland crossed with Louis XV Rococo decor." That caused her to laugh, as he had intended. "I'm glad you still have a sense of humor."

"Because we'll need it," they said in Greek chorus.

He opened a padded door off the bar and ushered her into the small side room replete with flowery wallpaper and wall-to-wall mirrors, gilded glass tables and dainty chairs. They settled into a more comfortable velour bench and table at the back of the room, side-by-side.

A *garçon* appeared. Liam whispered in his ear in rapid Italian, and with a nod, the handsome young waiter vanished.

"Your language abilities never cease to amaze me," Kikki said, wanting to stay off hot topics until she had tea and Calva.

"I come by it naturally with my gene mix of Greek, Irish, Italian and French."

"But mostly Greek, though raised in New York from the age of sixteen. How is it your accent is so perfect?"

"What can I say, darling. I have a knack for languages."

"And lovers who speak them. How is your Belgian boyfriend?"

"He's history. He was, well—not refined enough for my taste."

"Few are."

"You should talk. And your live-in lover, would-be fiancé? Have you agreed to marry him or at least become engaged?" He placed his long, elegant fingers gently on her wrist. "You need an anchor, Kikki. You've definitely got hot sex—enough with the slow love."

Her throat began to close, fearful for Torres. But before she could ask Liam what he was picking up, the waiter reappeared. He laid out a spread onto the finest bone china by Villeroy & Boch, a highly polished silver teapot steeping with Kikki's favorite smoky Chinese tea, Lapsang Souchong, a basket of Paris's best *pâtisseries* in delicate mini version, *bien croustillants*, as she loved them, rich with butter.

Her friend was taking very good care of her, as always. And he had managed to distract her. She reached for a mini-croissant. "I seem to be ravenous this morning."

"I gathered—" Liam arched one well-shaped brow. "Please. They are all for you."

"*Bon*, but I have to watch my girlish figure."

"Keep watching as you eat. I'm sure you won't see it move." He laughed at his joke.

"Cute."

He studied her intently. She was a courageous, vibrant woman who possessed bountiful inner strength. But she would need help in all dimensions. He hoped she was ready, and that he was as well.

When she had sipped enough fortifying tea and taken a couple of large swallows of the Calva, aged and as smooth as promised, she let out a sigh of relief and almost contentment.

"Now—enough about my love life," he said holding her gaze. "Tell me what's happened. And I don't have to be a psychic to get that—though luckily, I am and perhaps I can help you."

"I hope you can because so much has happened in the last few, very few hours," she began, and then, with trembling hand, she set her cup onto the saucer on the glass table. "Honestly, I don't know where to start. I'm completely blown away."

"Well, let me help you, darling," he said with reassurance. "Monique called me after you had breakfast and she filled me in." He lay a hand on hers to calm her. "I am so sorry to hear about the attack on Tía. It's good that Torres went to her."

Like Monique, Liam knew Tía well though Kikki had no idea. In truth, he had been tuning in to events all morning. He'd awakened at 03:30 with a jolt, knowing something catastrophic had happened. And though he often had tea with Kikki before she went to her office, this morning was no ordinary day. The gauntlet had been thrown down.

"Before I get into it, please Liam, what are you getting about Torres? Is he alive? Safe? I haven't heard from him." She caught his eyes, searching for answers. "Are your psychic antennae picking up any intel? Something world changing is going down—a huge battle with the darkness. We have known it was upon us. This is only the start."

"*Pas de panic*," Liam murmured, pouring her more tea. "Torres is okay—for the moment. Stop worrying. He's in Granada, *n'est pas?*"

She nodded, tears welling up in her eyes, and she turned from him to compose herself.

He said softly, "It's going to be okay. I'm here for you. But first, tell me everything while I prepare the card reading."

Kikki took a sip of water and then gave him a rundown. Her voice was fierce and determined, masking fear, he knew. He nodded solemnly once or twice but didn't interrupt.

She could nearly see the psychic wheels turning in his brain, like some kind of kaleidoscope putting events in order. It comforted her.

"And then there's Margot. She appeared to me just now in the

Tuileries in full court dress. An apparition as real as you and I sitting here now." Kikki peered into the brandy snifter at the few remaining drops of Calva, swirled it, sniffing its heady apple perfume. "She'd been whispering to me this morning, and I've had even more lucid nightmares and terrifying visions.

"As we approach this week it is understandable. There is much darkness—and I'm not talking about the weather."

"No, I've been dogged by it all morning. As though I am being hunted by some great black creature."

"I know what you mean," he said quietly. "But the dreams and visions—tell me. The Saint-Bartholomew Day's Massacre again?"

"Yes, but there was more this time—I actually became Margot in a carriage. She was fleeing Paris with a baby girl."

"Hmm. Only you—Margot incarnated. What exactly did she say to you in the Tuileries?"

"She told me that all was at stake, that Paris must be defended and that I must make a choice, a conscious decision, to fight this battle for the Goddess—to be Athena—again—and soon—as in now. They would stand by me, ready, but I was to be her emissary and lead the charge." She eyed him watching his reaction, as she finished off the Calva.

"So much for small talk! Marching orders from a queen, even if a four hundred-year-old disembodied spirit."

"Do you know of the Daughters of Inanna? Margot said they would support me, and I would soon be one of them."

"Yes, I've heard of them. A very old secret society that worships the Mother Goddess and her ways. Inanna was the formidable Sumerian Goddess of Heaven and Earth, named for the Evening Star, Aphrodite, thousands of years ago—" he began but stopped short, waiting for Kikki.

She rifled through her handbag and pulled out the envelope.

"Monique told you that Tía was attacked by a secret patriarchal society, *non?*"

"*Oui.* Not surprising. We have been expecting something like this."

"True, but I found this in Torres's desk after he left."

"Snooping again."

"Don't get righteous on me. Read this. It's addressed to Tía. It's a threat letter, the old-fashioned melodramatic kind. Now we know who represents the forces of the Patriarchy and darkness."

Liam took the letter out of the envelope, adjusted his glasses and read.

"Clearly Tía must be the leader of the Daughters of Inanna. And that's why the battle began in Spain. She drew them there, *non?*"

Liam kept his eyes on the letter, taking it in.

Rivers of blood shall flow to cleanse and purify the Kingdom of God. We come for you before the light turns.

"This gives me goosebumps, Kikki," Liam said. "The picture is forming. We know who and when. On the Winter Solstice."

"Help me, Liam. We need a strategy."

"You've made the choice to fight this battle. I saw that the minute you walked in the door." He placed the letter on the table and laid a comforting hand across her shoulder. "Margot's right. Remember that you're not alone and you won't be alone. I'm here for you. We all are."

"I sure as hell hope so. And I hope that I will have the courage. I feel like Sainte-Geneviève against Attila the Hun. Jeanne d'Arc's job was nothing compared to Geneviève's."

"Now you're the patron saint of Paris in addition to your other duties?" Liam laughed. "Always dramatic." He signaled to the *garçon*, who had just appeared at the door, for replenishments.

"Well?"

"*Éla!* Listen to me, Kikki. Slow down. I promise the cards will help us. But your mind and spirit are spinning. Please, take a deep breath."

"I'm so glad you're here," she smiled up at him, eyes glistening. "It's a lot to take in. We've both been feeling it, with the darkness of winter and the nightmares and visions. The upcoming Snake Goddess Premier Gala Exhibition. Solstice is a difficult time. The energy has been building. Lost souls come up from the bowels. And I don't mean Margot."

Liam shot her a grim look.

"And I could feel Torres's op ramping up. I knew I was on some kind of threshold. But this? I did not see something this big."

She took a sip of lukewarm tea. Liam eyed the door as if he

could will the waiter to appear. And indeed, just as he turned back to Kikki, the door opened and the *garçon* hurried to their table.

They both waited silently for him to clear the debris and serve the tea and Calvados.

Then Liam changed gears to shift the energies. "Nice of Margot to recruit you—or volunteer you, eh?"

"She was a queen of France, and she fought for her life and for what she believed in. She pitted herself against her family, her diabolic monster of a mother and the rest of the ruling patriarchy. Yet she never was able to achieve what she really wanted."

"Those were very different times, Kikki. I have some ideas, but they're not fully formed."

"Yes, me too. But there's not much time to figure this out. I feel an internal clock ticking faster and faster. As though time has speeded up." She looked up at the intricate carved crown ceiling mold studding the mirrored ceiling. "Oh, I nearly forgot. Margot also assured me that you would be able to tell me more."

"Did she? Well it's time to let the cards reveal the truth." Liam reached into the pocket of his suit jacket and slipped out a shiny black deck. Like Kikki's, *The Mythic Tarot*, based on Greek mythology.

"I'm afraid to see—"

"I won't throw too many. Don't worry, Sainte-Geneviève." He winked to reassure her. But, in fact, he was very concerned for his friend. She was in grave danger.

"Goddesses, I hope you're right." She sipped hot tea and followed it with Calva and felt better. "I drew Hades—this morning and then almost threw my deck into the fire. Maybe it is cursed."

"Please! Leave the melodrama to me," he shook his head. "But fire is one way to clean it. You rescued them, didn't you?"

"Torres did. He knows me too well. I think I should get a new deck."

He searched her dark eyes, concerned that she was in over her head. "Cards have to be a gift."

"Well then, I'd love one of yours. Are they out yet?"

"No, but soon. Shall we?" He had cleared a space on the table and held the deck in his hands, poised to begin.

"Wait." She checked her phone. No messages. She shot Liam a

pained look. "Why haven't I heard?"

"We're here for messages, are we not? Tech and spirit. Either way, I predict you'll get a message very soon, though not from your lover. Focus and clear your mind. Eyes closed."

He shuffled expertly, split the deck and drew four cards laying them face down.

"Ready?"

Chapter 16

Kikki opened her eyes. "Go ahead, turn them over—"

Liam studied her. Her eyes were deep, pupils dilated, and she was almost luminous. He turned the cards over one at a time:

The Hierophant: A Centaur—half man, half horse, in a dark cave, holding sacred scrolls in one hand. With the other, he makes a secret sign with two fingers.

The Three of Swords: A king slaughtered in his bath by his queen and her lover, three swords pierce his heart, with black brooding sky over mountains.

Justice: The Goddess Athena in silver helmet and battle armor, sword in one hand and scales of justice in the other. An owl perched on her head.

Judgment: The God Hermes in a white tunic under a red cloak, with a winged helmet and sandals. He holds a caduceus, a magic staff entwined with two snakes. Coffins lie at his feet, and from sarcophagi the dead rise. The sun rises behind him.

Her voice caught in her throat, but she forced herself to speak. "The Hierophant is the High Priest. And in more traditional decks, the Pope himself, representing the traditional male power structure. Placed next to the Three of Swords—not good. The death of King

Agamemnon: literally a bloodbath."

"I'm reading, so let me do that, please, oh Madame High Priestess."

"*Desolée.*"

"Agamemnon was killed by his Queen Clytemnestra as revenge for sacrificing their daughter Iphigenia." Liam picked up the card. "Poor Iphigenia had worse karma than Margot, hee hee!"

"Yes, she did, and why do you find it funny?"

"Being Greek, I really have to keep my sense of humor. Or go crazy."

She smirked. "To continue—daughter and mother were both victims of male treachery. Agamemnon was a cruel, vengeful warlord. Sending his innocent daughter to her death on her wedding." Kikki sucked in air. "Bloody weddings!"

Liam eyed her over the rim of his glasses, "You've never been fond of weddings, my dear. But listen. In the myth, he offended the Goddess Artemis by boasting in her sacred grove. The Twin Moon Goddesses Artemis and Hecate manifested a deadly storm that trapped the king's fleet."

"Stopping him from heading straight to Troy to head the war party to find Helen, another high-spirited woman."

"Indeed. No one could say no to the Moon Goddesses, especially Hecate, Invincible Queen of the Underworld. The king sacrificed his daughter to lift the curse," Liam said knowingly. "Typical Greek tragedy—one as bad as the other."

"So because the cards show the horrible warlord Agamemnon and his bloody sacrifice of Iphigenia, you think this week's battle will be a patriarchal bloodbath by the Knights of the Holy Sword of God? And if so, who is their leader according to the cards? The Hierophant?"

"Patience, *ma belle*—let me finish. The deaths were all bloody. That's just the way it was—French history or Greek mythology, take your pick."

"*Pour changer!*" she said with vehemence.

"True, but not the point. Necessary for healing. The other cards bear that out."

"If you say so," she said grudgingly. "But if Margot is Clytemnestra in this story, she's seeking revenge, against her mother in this case. But there's something here I can't pull together —how is this all going down?"

"Don't get so emotional. It's clouding your psychic abilities. Use the images."

She nodded, calming herself with a deep breath. "Okay, the Three of Swords is a healing after bloodshed. And then, Justice."

"All will be revealed, Kikki."

"Do you know how many times I've heard that?" Kikki bared her teeth and growled melodramatically.

When Liam started to laugh, she held up a palm. "I'm not really joking, you know."

"I do know—it's frustrating. I get it." Liam sighed. "But you understand all too well that destiny is never set in stone. Each action you take or fail to take will result in an outcome that in turn sparks new choices—which, in turn, result in a new outcome, which—and so on and so on—" Seeing Kikki's acquiescence, Liam said, "Consider the last card: Judgment brings epiphany and resurrection. We could also call it Light."

"It better be soon. And I hope the blood that is shed isn't Tía's or Torres's."

Liam focused at a point in the middle distance. "You'd better hope it isn't yours, my dear. I think the Three of Swords is more about you effecting a healing as part of this battle."

"So not Torres and Tía now," Kikki said, frowning. "But the future then?"

"The near future. Very near. And perhaps you, rather than Margot, can be seen as Clytemnestra—though we know that you are Lady Justice incarnate. The next card is Justice. Look at her, Kikki, the cards don't lie."

She picked up the card reluctantly. Athena, a severely beautiful young woman on a throne between two ivory columns, dressed in her armor, sword grasped firmly in her right hand, scales of justice in her left. Her all-seeing owl giving her clarity. Her white robe suggesting her purity. The black and white patterned floor symbolizes the ability to integrate dark and light into order.

"Margot told me she would guide me, along with the mysterious Daughters of Inanna and her ghostly self. And that I had to fight for and be Athena."

"Except for the reputed chastity of Athena." Liam chuckled.

"Very funny. Not in the mood for jokes. And honestly, I'm tired of being Athena. I'd rather be, say, Atalanta, Amazon Warrior Goddess—or Wonder Woman, the way things are shaping up."

"Get over it. That's your karma, Athena. And you are a lawyer, if not a judge, if I haven't lost the plot of your life," he said with finality. "The Tarot cards are clear that there will be Judgment and a burden lifted. Someone raised from the dead. By the act of Justice, the balancing of karma—by bringing the truth to light. Interesting —"

"That's what Margot said she wants—justice. Along with retribution and revenge!"

"Does she? Well, let me see what else I pick up—" He adjusted his glasses and stared out into the mirrored room again.

Kikki focused on keeping her mind clear so she, too, could receive necessary information. One psychic reading for another psychic was always a bit touchy.

Finally, Liam caught her eyes with a serious look. His deep voice sounded as if it came from the other side of the room. "Another meaning of the Three of Swords is literally a curse. As was on the House of Atreus, the House of Swords. That's it. A curse must be cleared."

When she heard the word 'curse,' she got goosebumps. "Margot was certainly cursed. Are you saying I'm cursed?"

"Not necessarily. There is a curse at work. It makes sense with what we know."

"The threat on Tía is a kind of curse. But it's not about Tía, or Tía alone. It's because she is the leader of the Daughters of Inanna."

Liam agreed. "She is a symbolic figure. Representative of the Goddess and all that they want to destroy."

"Just like the Snake Goddess, *non?*" Her temples were beginning to throb with too much psychic input—between her and Liam and coming from other realms as well.

"Take a breath, *chèrie.*"

"So we're all cursed, and we've got to lift it. Torres is on the frontlines at the moment." Her heart sunk to her stomach.

"I don't know what will happen. That's just what I heard, Kikki. But you already know his life is at risk. Leave the police work to him. Trust him. He's a pro."

"You sound just like him."

"Well, I'm right, aren't I? And while you're at it, trust yourself and your wisdom. That's how Athena was able to strategize and save Athens."

"Or?"

"Or the only way to lift a curse is to burn cloves, honey, but there aren't enough cloves in Paris for this one."

"You're right." Get a grip, she told herself.

He was pensive, staring at the cards. Then he looked up and turned to her.

"What? You're frightening me!"

"Sip some more brandy."

She finished the small snifter and let it warm her. "Let's have it."

"When does your *expo* open at the Louvre? Saturday?"

"Yes," she said carefully, "Though, as you know, there's a special gala on Friday. Very exclusive—"

"Stop there," he said. "The Three of Swords is a first battle that you have to win. These cards will play out by or before Friday night's gala—and there won't be a Snake Goddess to exhibit unless you can change the outcome, effect that healing. The Snake Goddess will be the least of your worries."

"I understand," she said *sotto voce*, more to herself. "But after Santorini. Oh Liam, I just want a quiet, normal life in the City of Light."

"Stop with the whining and get out your broom! Hee hee!" His eyes twinkled. "And don't talk to me about a normal, quiet life! No way, Kikki. You had better get ready, or you'll be the next victim. Death might be quiet enough for you, *naï?*"

Chapter 17

They were startled when someone knocked on the door to the salon.

"What is it?" Liam asked sharply.

Timidly, the young man opened the door and entered carrying a silver tray with an envelope.

"A man delivered it to reception a moment ago. Said it was urgent. My sincere apologies for interrupting." He bowed.

Liam slipped the ivory envelope from the tray. "You may go."

"It's for me, isn't it, Liam?" She reached for it with shaking hands.

He pushed her hand away. "Patience, darling. I need to make sure it isn't poisoned and from Catherine de Medici, given what's going on."

Kikki's breath hitched at the mention of the Black Queen. "You're right. You know, she sent her *nans* (dwarf companions) to spy and do her dirty work. Or her infamous *escadron volant* (the flying squadron)—her personal court. Her *parfumeur*, Maître René, was feared for the efficacy of his potions and powders. She murdered Jeanne d'Albret, Henri IV's mother, the Huguenot leader, with poisoned gloves.

"Yes—" Liam nodded. "Her reputation for poison and dark magic is legendary—a poisoner and intriguer of the same stamp as Lucrezia Borgia. But you, really, *chérie*, are you sure you have no Greek blood?"

"Only in my heart and my past lives, but since you are Greek, I trust that your evil eye protection holds for us both. You did mention a curse," she said.

He paused with the envelope midair, pondering. "Here, take it. It's fine."

She slit the envelope open with a letter opener. The single page was from Torres's trusted archeologist friend Jean Marc Montalembert, director of the Musée d'Homme in Paris.

"He will call you on the Hotel Regina line in a few minutes, from his usual mobile phone. Not the secure phone. Play the part. He is fine. Managed to get shot, but not seriously."

Just as she finished reading, she heard a discreet sound, and Liam deftly reached inside his coat for his iPhone. "Hotel Regina, how may we be of service?"

"It's for you." He handed the phone to Kikki.

She took it and stood up quickly, nearly toppling the table, and crossed the room to stand near the window that overlooked the Louvre.

"*Mi amor*—" She hesitated. What did that mean, play the part? This elaborate subterfuge meant their conversation was being monitored. "Are you okay? I've been so worried!"

"*Lo siento, mi cielo.* So much has happened. I have to make this quick."

"But are you hurt?"

"Flesh wound. But fine."

"Tía?"

"She survived the explosion—" he said, his voice filled with pain —"but, ultimately, she didn't make it. We were too late."

Tears filled her eyes. "I am so horribly sorry," she said in a shaky voice, feeling a lump of pain in her stomach. "And your cousin and her husband?"

"Thankfully, they are fine."

"But you are wounded and Tía's dead. Oh my Goddesses! How tragic! Are you sure you're all right? Don't lie to me."

"I'm fine. Tía lived a long and happy life—" His voice hitched. "We will take care of arrangements for Tía. I'll be back as soon as I can." He paused and said, "You're with your friend, *mi cielo*. It's better."

"I feel so helpless." She struggled to keep her voice steady. "I want to come to you—"

"Too dangerous. I have to go. *Te quiero*."

"*Je t'aime*. Come home soon. Please be extremely careful."

"I always am, *mi amor*."

Slowly, Kikki walked back to the banquette. She sat heavily and caught Liam's eyes with a stunned and bewildered look, turning over what Torres had said, searching for truth.

"What? He is okay, *non*? I told you he would be."

"No. He's not all right. He's been shot, and Tía is dead, Goddesses rest her soul."

"Oh honey, I'm so very sorry about Tía." He took her hand.

"I can't believe it. He says he is okay, but—I don't know."

"Did he tell you what happened?"

"No. Jean Marc said to 'play the part,' warning me that the call would be tapped. I guess."

"So you won't be going to Spain?"

"He says it is too dangerous. Funny, a part of me didn't believe him when he said Tía had been killed."

"Why?"

"It was the way he said it. And my own inner radio was nearly shouting at me that he's covering up something. But he always does. And it was a staged call, *non*?"

"Maybe you don't want it to be true. You were quite fond of her?"

"Well, yes. She comes from a long line of—"

"Witches?"

Her lips curved into a slight smile. "Yes, wise women. Surely, she would have been able to protect herself, to shield herself."

"Maybe it was her karma and her time." Liam sat next to her and put his arm gently around her shoulder. "Perhaps it was her you saw in the Death card."

Liam remained silent. His psychic senses told him that Tía hadn't been killed. Tía was meant to come to Paris this week for the

Snake Goddess Gala and the Winter Solstice celebration. And, as every year, the Daughters of Inanna would hold their annual meeting of the Council of Eight. Tía's formidable powers were needed.

Without her, Kikki really would be alone on the front lines. For not sharing that insight with her, he felt guilty, but he knew he couldn't interfere with the unfolding of events.

She ignored him and went on, "Torres was very emotional. His voice broke up and he sounded teary. It was bizarre."

"He was faking it for whomever was listening? Men cry, too, even macho Spanish cops!" His quip met with Kikki's arched eyebrow.

"There's nothing we can do now." Liam deftly shifted gears. "Speaking of Justice, *maître*, maybe you should start by getting to your office. Real world duties must—even for worn out supergoddesses." He winked. "And me too. Time to don my cloak of good manners and make sure all is running smoothly and that cranky high-handed guests are having all of their needs met—the ones I can take care of anyway—"

"*Eh, merde!* Meeting with that potential film client. So what do you think? He couldn't be the head of the Swords?"

"I don't get that."

"Why am I not getting a clear read? Someone behind the film?"

Liam closed his eyes for a moment and then said, "There is very strong incoming energy that is masking the leader. He's going to be very hard to track. I can't get at him or her. But the person you're meeting is connected."

"Shapeshifters, Catherine de Medici—" Kikki's mouth quivered.

"The enemy will take different guises. Like the hydra with many heads. The Knights of the Holy Sword of God is one brutal patriarchal society. There are also others. The Order of the Golden Fleece on the surface may seem perfectly innocent, Hapsburg aristocrats protecting their heritage, but underneath—" He raised his eyebrows.

"True. And then there's the Opus Dei, the Priory of Sion, the Order of the Holy Spirit in France—and on and on."

"Yes, but the Knights of the Holy Sword of God are at the top of the world game now." Liam shot her an earnest look. "Maybe you should cancel. I get that the timing is not right for today."

"No. Remember Athena. We need to engage with the client and turn the tables. Know thy enemy and keep him or her close. It could be a woman, *n'est pas?*"

"Pay attention. Keep your protection up," Liam said sternly.

"I have to go, Liam," she said abruptly, gathering her things. She was starting to feel nauseous and smelled something faintly like sewage, odd in this elegant establishment.

"Can you smell anything, Liam?"

"Like—you're wearing too much *J'adore Dior?*"

She shot him an annoyed look. "You don't smell it? It's a strong stench."

The lights grew dim, and her eyelids became heavy. The walls closed in on her.

"Get me out of here, Liam. I don't know what's going on, but I don't feel safe here anymore."

"Calm down, Kikki." But he could feel something off too. He surrounded both of them in white light. "It's risky for you to go when you're so upset. You look green. *Katse.*" Sitting down, he picked up the deck still on the table. "One more card?"

She shook her head grimly, something still not right. Feeling danger.

He turned the card over slowly—the Devil, a Satyr, a dark creature, half man and half goat, dangling a man and a woman from chains held by the monster, enslaved to darkness.

Liam whispered. "A betrayal—you will be tempted and tested by someone from your past, someone who chose their path long ago. It's their karma and the curse I told you about."

She stared at the Devil image. Tyranny and madness. Evil and enormous power.

Chapter 18

Kikki clutched Liam's arm.

He let out a slow breath, taking Kikki's hand, afraid for her.

Kikki rose from the banquette. She had goosebumps from head to toe.

Liam stood, arm around her shoulder. "I'm frightened for you, and it takes a lot to scare me. It's as if you will be—*comment on dire* —terrorized. And the dark force can move from one person to another, hiding."

"*Je sais,*" I know, she said, voice trembling. She took deep breaths as they crossed the room. "*Ouff*—can you not smell it now? It's sulfurous."

Liam's hand had closed around the bronze door handle when he caught a whiff. "You're right. It smells like sewage. Ack! I promise it's not the ancient plumbing. We just had it redone." He buttoned his suit jacket. "It's coming from that dark Devil force!"

He opened the door quietly and motioned for her to go ahead of him. She shot him a weak smile.

"We always do it in style, *non?*" His voice was light, but his eyes steel gray clouds.

The reek and smoke nearly overcame her. When Liam opened

the door wide into the adjoining bar, she gasped.

A congregation of Orthodox priests in long black robes, beards and tall hats flocked around long tables set for breakfast with white china and crystal. They stood *en masse* for their Bishop, who had just entered the room, striding in his handwoven golden silk robes.

Kikki's knees buckled, a large, invisible hand was crushing her chest. "What are they doing here?" she whispered hoarsely. "Do you see them too? Or am I having a vision?"

He stopped in the doorway, one arm protecting Kikki. Then shook his head, mystified. "I thought I had cancelled them—"

"Orthodox priests. Liam, someone in this room is the Devil incarnate—or living in his body, someone possessed absolutely, enchained. Just like the card."

"*Naí.*" Liam whispered yes.

"Is there a back door?"

"Not that we can reach from here. I'll walk you out."

Kikki commanded herself to be strong, carry her power as Athena. She touched her fingertips to her rose crystal necklace. Immediately, the sacred talisman activated.

When the Bishop turned to her, she held his disapproving gaze. Her eyes were drawn to the large ruby ring set in fine gold bedecking his left hand. It blew off black smoke, a warning.

Shielding her face with one hand, she pulled up the fur-lined hood of her coat. "I don't know what is worse. For *it* to see me or me to see *it.*"

Then time stopped. She stood frozen at the door with Liam at her back.

The black robed men metamorphosed from present day Orthodox priests to sixteenth-century soldiers bearing flaming arrows and swords. Their soldiers' hats bore white crosses made of cloth, marking them as Catholics, the advance division of the Saint-Bartholomew Day's Massacre.

As Kikki watched mesmerized, the soldiers were sucked into a sinkhole in the floor—a portal—along with the tables, chairs and china.

Left behind was a river of blood snaking its way out of the open door of the bar through the lobby to the hotel's exit and into the Place des Pyramides.

The Bishop was still present. But then he rose, hovering a second above the scarlet river.

Kikki blinked. When she opened her eyes, the Bishop was gone, and in his place, she beheld a woman dressed in an austere black gown, collar high at the neck, head veiled in black.

The unmistakable hostile countenance of Catherine de Medici.

Behind the Black Queen's left shoulder, another figure took form.

Kikki recognized her young daughter, Marguerite de Valois, an ephemeral porcelain beauty. Her piercing black eyes filled with terror.

The stench filled Kikki's nostrils. The Black Queen's lips moved, but Kikki couldn't hear the words. Rushing water reverberated in her ears. And then her hearing cleared.

A hollow sepulchral voice bellowed in French, "I forever curse thee, *sorcière maudite!*"

Kikki looked at Liam wild-eyed. "Holy Goddess!"

"Go! Now!" He had seen it too. As she started for the door, he called out a warning, "Kikki, don't be alone with this client!"

A last cry from the Black Queen echoed—*Malédiction!*

An evil curse. Kikki fled, wading in a blood river—cursed forever like Margot.

Chapter 19

At about the same moment that Kikki fled the Regina, on the Left Bank, a tall, beautiful young woman wearing a stylish camel cashmere coat sauntered into the Voltaire café. She stopped short of the café's bar and flipped her shoulder length chestnut red hair from under her coat. From heavily lashed, expertly made-up hazel eyes, a look of indifference on her heart-shaped face, she studied the *habitués*—mostly men and a few women in suits and overcoats, fashionable scarves carefully arranged.

Were French men vainer than their Italian counterparts, she wondered idly? A running debate for Natalia Becchina.

Her full, deep scarlet lips curved slightly as she stepped further into the cozy café. She eyed an unoccupied booth right in the middle. As she unbuttoned her coat, she turned for a moment facing the bar and posed—someone who was accustomed to being admired. And then she slid gracefully into the banquette, facing the door. She held her head high, nostrils of her finely shaped nose flared, waiting imperiously to be attended to.

She knew of this venerable institution of *La Vieille France*. Many of the most important antique dealers in Paris had boutiques in the neighborhood and frequented the Voltaire before going to their nearby businesses or the auction houses—Drouot, Sotheby's, Christies—just across the river on the Rive Droite. She hoped she would overhear something useful.

Still reeling from the night before—and a nearly sleepless night —she couldn't get that gorgeous man out of her head, or more precisely, her now hungry body. That Torres had swept her off her feet. She could fall hard for him, and she bet he'd be hot. He was just old enough to know what a woman wanted, she figured early forties. More than ten years older than she. Their exchange of tongues and liquids in the corridor had shot straight to her sex.

When he finally released her, she had hurried back to her table and ordered a double whiskey, neat. Either add to the fire or build it, she figured. She smiled to herself, now, feeling a pleasant arousal.

She'd have to be careful and stay on point. She'd been briefed on him, but no one had mentioned how handsome and charismatic he was. That was wicked of Uncle Franco. He knew her taste in men. She and Torres were a good match. If they hadn't been working opposite sides.

"*Mademoiselle?*"

Natalia looked up, startled from her reverie. "*Café espress serré, très serré, et un pain au chocolate,*" she said in perfect Parisian French to the short, harried woman who had come from behind the bar to wait on her.

All smiles and *politesse*, but a bundle of nerves, Natalia thought. She prided herself on her knack for reading people. She supposed it was in her genes. Thinking about parents she had barely known, she frowned.

She had a mission to carry out for her only family, Uncle Franco Becchina Pelligrini, who had made his riches trading in antiquities, many of which were either looted or of questionable origin. The latter he considered "appropriated" for the good of historical and archeological preservation.

She knew that many of the artifacts were forgeries. It was so easy these days. Either way, she had no moral issues with the business. People would buy anything. Even if they knew the truth, they wouldn't care, as long as they could further advance their social status. She and her uncle and his cohorts were mere facilitators for their greed and power. So-called illegal trafficking was just semantics. Natalia was a very practical woman.

Better they should be taken care of by a museum or collector with a sense of appreciation than left in the hands of pious diggers who kept them from the light of day as long as possible, tied up in academic red tape and posturing, each trying to outdo the other.

Natalia raised one perfect eyebrow, musing on her uncle's Machiavellian philosophy.

"Let them live and breathe so they are appreciated. They should be taken out of hiding so we can enjoy the life in such precious ancient beauty. And if I profit from it, *molto bene*. And all the better for you, Natalia, so do not forget—you are my only family."

It was he who had gotten her involved at an early age. Now, just twenty-seven, she had every advantage—rich, beautiful, multilingual, highly cultured—*très cultivée*. She was well-traveled and lived between New York and Florence. She had attended a very exclusive boarding school in Switzerland before going on to Columbia, where she received a master's degree, and then Harvard, where she got her MBA.

Along the way, she made it a point to meet all the right people. Throughout her childhood, she had been spoon-fed the art, antique and archeological artifact business by her dear uncle. She could handle the best of them. She should have been a spy.

In fact, she had been approached by the American government while at Colombia but had turned them down. The family business appealed to her more. It certainly was more lucrative. And Natalia had a taste for luxury.

And in a way, she was a spy at the moment because she had a dangerous double-agenda. She'd been appointed to this committee with no real teeth, to assist in protecting Europe and the world's heritage from thieves and forgers. A cross-border committee she knew existed for show, while its real core was made up of very experienced cops, covert operatives like Torres.

Momentarily, her coffee was delivered to her along with the *pain au chocolate* by an older man with blue eyes and silver hair wearing a worn but well starched apron. He smiled demurely at her. "*Mademoiselle, ici voilà.*"

"*Merci,*" she said smiling politely, tucking her hair behind her ear.

His eyes sparkled. She pegged him as the owner. She'd come again and use her full radiant charm on him. He might be very useful.

She narrowed her eyes at the coffee as she plunked a lump of brown sugar into the *demi-tasse* and stirred slowly. Before she took her first sip, she could tell that it was not strong enough. The French, unlike the Italians, had not nailed the art of a heart-jolting expresso. And she needed to be alert today. She had a lot to accomplish. As she sipped, she scolded herself silently, "You are too spoiled. Be careful."

Her thoughts strayed to her Italian lover, Marco. Her heart beat faster. She took a bite of the *pain au chocolate* and her juices flowed.

Chapter 20

Tía recited quietly in Spanish lines of Féderico García Lorca's poem:
Sevilla para nacer. Granada para morir.
Malaga de mis amores, como me acuerdo de tí.
Cadiz es un blanco pañuelo y un suspiro en la
bahía.
Esta es mi tierra—y se llama Andalucía.
Lorca had wanted to die in Granada. And so he did. Did she too want to die there in her homeland, she asked herself? Lorca was a romantic and a poet but undoubtedly more romantic—though not more Andaluz—than Tía.

She sat in the dark at the back of the dining room in a straight-backed chair that supported her old spine. She was exhausted from the trip and the preceding events. A lot had happened in one short night and part of a day. She smiled to herself, pleased that she had succeeded in her plan to draw them into the light and seize the offensive. Her nephew had been furious. Menos mal. It had to be done.

And now she could do her work in Paris under the best cover there was—death.

Judging by the dim light filtering through gaps in the closed

105

curtains, she thought it must be around 10:00. She longed to sleep, a short siesta to refresh. But she couldn't. She was keeping vigil. Drinking strong coffee. Anything could happen. The time was upon them.

She thought about death, being ninety, though she felt she could go on for twenty more years. She had important work to accomplish. And she was reluctant to turn over the reins of the Daughters of Inanna. Her grand-nephew would have been ideal, or his companion, Véronique Trieste. *No podía ser.*

Torres was already in way over his head with this new position, and Kikki was, despite her long years in Europe, an *extranjera*, an American expat, a foreigner.

It wasn't as if their group excluded those outside the roots of the old European world. All of the Daughters' societies were linked and united when it came to their goals. Unified worldwide, they had grown over the centuries—in service to Gaia and her ways, their precious Mother Goddess, Mother Earth.

But Kikki belonged neither to Europe nor her country of birth. She was unique. American by birth but not by lifestyle. She was an important ally and shared their truths. Tía's grand-nephew had finally picked someone worthy of him and his matriarchal heritage. She was smart, with the heart of a warrior. A truth seeker— demanding truth, justice and equality. And she was a powerful intuitive.

They needed Kikki. She would fight the battle this week against the Swords on her own terms, on her own highly principled grounds that aligned perfectly with the Daughters.

No, it would have to be her Sara who would take the reins. And soon. Tía had begun the discussion with her, and although supportive, Sara had insisted that it wasn't Tía's time to step down, that Tía had much to teach and give yet. It was not her time to die.

Sara had been definite. They would review the matter later. But later was now. Oh, how Tía wished her sister Elena was still alive. What would she do next? How would she orchestrate victory in the most humanistic manner and with the least bloodshed? So many wars littered their history, perpetrated by male tyrants conquering in the name of civilization. It was not the way. Of that Tía was certain.

Although there were factions of their centuries' old secret society that advocated violence to finally vanquish the dark forces. That was not what the Daughters of Inanna stood for!

"*Que no!*" Tía shook her head vehemently, and her waist length coal black braid flew—a trademark—appropriate for an old white *bruja*. She smiled slightly, waiting unseen, hidden from all.

Chapter 21

Kikki stopped just outside the entrance to the hotel. She stood still, facing the back of the golden statue of Jeanne d'Arc in the middle of the Place des Pyramides. The river of blood had disappeared as she crossed the hotel's threshold. She was relieved to return to reality, but her heart was still pounding and her vision blurry.

Outside, it was light, or rather gray. The snow flurries that had begun earlier with Margot's appearance in the Tuileries had stopped, but the skies hadn't cleared. They were socked in with the usual *grisaille*, low-hanging clouds heavy with freezing rain ready to fall. Alone, she wanted to sit down for a moment and sort through the dizzying array of information she'd received. The final curse from the wicked shapeshifting energy of the Medici Queen had sent her spinning.

Her knees trembled, but she straightened her back and slowly began to walk the short distance to the corner of rue de Rivoli. There, she leaned against the inner wall under the stone arches of the square, her mind and heart racing in rhythm.

The card reading promised justice and rebirth at a high cost—a bloody battle, sacrifice, patriarchal high priests—and a curse! It would take far more than cloves, she thought grimly.

Especially if the Devil was concerned, a satanic madman at the center of a betrayal. That spoke of vengeance. Carnal enslavement was another interpretation. Would she be chained to a monster? Who?

What horrors did the vision of the dreaded Black Queen and her terrified daughter Margot portend? A modern repeat of the barbaric massacre?

Torres was safe but wounded, and Tía was dead. Kikki's heart sank. She had a knot of fear in her belly. Her lover was not out of danger, and neither was she.

Suddenly, she felt the panic rise along with a profound loneliness. Rather desperately she wanted Torres by her side. His reassuring male presence would ground her. He always did, however much they were sometimes at odds. She knew he was more wounded than he let on. When would he come home?

She stood shivering under the old stone arches of the rue de Rivoli, built by Henri de Navarre, cold to the depths of her soul.

What was her next step? She took a breath and, with red gloved hands, pulled her phone from her coat pocket to check the time. It was 09:45. Her meeting was at 10:15, and she was only five minutes away. She hadn't been thinking about the client when she dressed to leave her apartment earlier. Still in jeans and black cashmere turtleneck with over-the-knee suede boots. With most film clients, casual worked. But this was different.

Did she have time to go home and change into something more business-like—more commanding of respect, she wondered, shoving the phone back into the pocket of her coat.

Liam had counseled against meeting the client, and she took his counsel seriously. But Kikki refused to hide out in her city. If she did, she certainly couldn't save it as Margot demanded. Liam's last warning was, *don't be alone with him.* Monique would be there, thankfully. Kikki wanted hand-holding and home-cooked French scolding, tossed with the Greek philosophical approach to life that was dear Monique.

But her savvy colleague wouldn't be at the office yet. Kikki had time to kill.

"Bella," she heard her friend Cleo's voice whispering. "Breathe. Call in your guides for protection, and let the Goddess lead you."

She was glad to hear Cleo's friendly voice, even if on the ethers. She and Cleo had built Hotel Atlantis together. Her beautiful and talented belly-dancer soul sister was keeping their dream alive in Santorini. It made her realize how much she wanted the company of a friend—a living, breathing human connection. Her closest Paris girlfriend, NC, was in New York for the premiere of her latest feature film. And now Liam was busy. With a shiver, she circled back to her longing for Torres.

"Stop it!" Cleo whispered. "Don't feed the fear."

Kikki's thoughts turned to Greece, a strong heart-yearning. She missed Santorini and Hotel Atlantis. The sapphire sea, endless cerulean blue sky and a dome of stars. The moon on a clear night. And she missed Cleo and music, dancing and the joy of life on the island.

It was a bit early, but Cleo might be up. Kikki fingered the phone and wondered where she could go for privacy. A warm café. There wasn't time to cross the river and come back. And besides, he was a film client so he would expect the meeting to be casual.

Under the most benign of circumstances, she had the sense that Paris was like a large animal, a rhinoceros with the Seine at its center, the spine. There was a constant pull from one side of the river or another. Right Bank, Left Bank.

She felt it more acutely now, a high-wire tension, as if hovering over the Seine—half of her body on the Right Bank and half on the Left.

She lifted her head and closed her eyes. Her mind cleared. She would follow her intuition and trust to be guided.

Just as she stepped out from under the arches onto the Place des Pyramides, a murder of crows flew over, flying south towards the Tuileries and Quai Voltaire, looking for prey.

With a gasp, she stepped back. Not that way. Her favorite gardens forbidden for now.

She turned left, leaving the square, walking carefully along the slippery sidewalk, under the lovely colonnades bordering rue de Rivoli, making her way slowly east towards her office.

The ceiling of clouds suddenly lowered, shrouding the Louvre opposite her. The old stone buildings had a menacing surreal look, as if they were floating.

Dim yellow headlights of cars and motorcycles flew by heading towards the Champs-Élysées. A steady rhythm of horns klaxoned like a swarm of angry wasps.

A day that had begun in the wee hours with her nightmare about Margot had turned deadly. It promised to be a very long day with very little light.

Chapter 22

She picked up her pace, more sure-footed, walking briskly along rue de Rivoli. The long boulevard traced La Grande Axe that ran from east to west through Paris, changing names as it did arrondissements. It began at the eastern edge of Porte de Vincennes near Place de la Nation, where throne-topped pillars marked a regal entrance to the city for the Hapsburg Princess Anne of Austria to marry Louis XIII, son of Henri IV.

On rue de Rivoli, despite the inclement weather, the traffic was heavy now with all manner of vehicle, cars, French city bicycles (*Velibs*), buses and pedestrians.

Head down, eyes alert, Kikki hovered at the far edge of the throng of people, walking with greater determination as she passed the Northern Galleries of the Louvre to her right.

But she misstepped and slipped off the sidewalk, nearly colliding with a pushy man with a very Parisian scowl. He swore angrily at her, as though he owned the sidewalk rights.

"*Putain de merde!*" Fucking hell!

A tall slim man wearing a navy overcoat and black Borsalino sprinkled with snow stopped to help her.

"*Est-ce que ça va? Il vous a fait de mal?*" Was she all right? Had he hurt her?

She looked up surprised at his concern. "*Non, ça va, merci. Très gentil.*"

He hooked his arm firmly into hers to help her back up the sidewalk. She looked up to catch his eyes but couldn't see them under the wide brim. Funny, she thought, I have the same hat.

"*Encore merci.*" She drew free from him, hurrying along the sidewalk again.

This time, she moved directly to the center of the crowd of people. She felt tiny pinpricks at the back of her neck. There had been something about him that gave her pause. When she turned around to look for him all she saw was a Borsalino bobbing up and down at a constant pace several feet behind her.

Somebody who had been kind but out of place. Most Parisians would have ignored her mishap. Stop it, Véronique, you're overreacting. It's the fear. He's probably a foreigner going about his business who doesn't know the city's unspoken code.

To be safe, she increased her protection, adding a thick layer of certainty blue. Then she shot a strong gold grounding firmly to the center of the earth.

She also picked up her pace towards the Palais Royal a few blocks away. As she strode along, very faintly she heard Cleo's voice.

"*Prothesis!*" Be careful. Confirming Kikki's concern.

There *had* been something off about that man. And now she was sure that he was following her. Who was he? Had the Swords found her? How?

Chapter 23

The tall man adjusted the brim of his hat and turned up his coat collar. Not that anyone would recognize him. These souls were going about their business heads down, like automatons, barely aware of the world around them.

How did they live in this beautiful city that had been blessed by the One True God and not see its beauty? He was glad he had been chosen by the Grand Master for this important task, and he was well-prepared.

When he had finished with her, all would be easier. He knew by her reputation that she was a fighter, the heretical witch. But he had right on his side and a Holy Sword.

He clenched his fists, impatient to overcome her. Then he shoved them into his coat pockets and took a deep breath. When he let it out, he couldn't help himself from hissing. A short woman next to him carrying a heavy briefcase looked up, a scowl on her face.

Calm down, he said to himself in his native Slavic language. Blend in. He smiled and tipped his hat, apologizing in stilted French, "*Veuillez m'excuser, madame.*"

Silently, he recited the rosary, clasping the holy beads in his pocket. And then he narrowed his eyes and sought out his prey. She had taken refuge in the crowd. No matter. The heathen whore had nowhere to go where he couldn't find her. She would not escape him.

And her gypsy cop boyfriend, along with the Most-Heretical Tía, would be dealt with by his brothers in the Knights of the Holy Sword of God. The brethren in Spain were particularly vicious. He knew they would succeed. The tall man's thin lips curved into a smile of cruel pleasure.

Chapter 24

Kikki hurried, moving like a dancer, weaving past the tacky tourist shops setting up their wares on the long block of Rivoli. She was tired, pushing herself to go faster, operating on pure adrenaline now in short supply. She buried herself further in the crowd and set her sights on the Place du Palais Royal.

She kept her focus on the stoplight at the next corner. A multi-street intersection fed into the Carrousel du Louvre, one of the museum's entrances and an upscale shopping mall under Pei's *Pyramid.* Four vaulted archways stood sentinel over the two-way road for vehicles.

With a glance over her shoulder, she caught sight of the Borsalino still tailing her and gaining ground. The light turned red on Rivoli, and traffic surged into the intersection. She walked faster, using her rush of panic to advantage.

If she crossed the intersection, she only had one long block to the Place du Palais Royal. If there were a free table in the café, she could stop for a *chocolate chaud* and call Cleo. The man wouldn't attack her in such a public place, surely. And then she would go on to her office on rue de Valois. If the signs were right. Timing was everything.

But she had the distinct feeling that someone—the Devil or the High Priest—was blocking her abilities to know.

On the corner, just ahead in front of the Benelux Perfume store, a large group of Asian tourists were gathering behind a young man with blue spiked hair. He waved a long metal pole topped with a tiny flag that bore the number ten.

Jostling a few people sideways, Kikki hurried to the far side of the crowd so she was flush with the fronts of the tourist shops. At the corner, she darted left onto the street that flowed into the Louvre.

She pressed against the perfume store's vitrine, willing herself to become part of a large ad that covered the entire window, featuring Dolce & Gabbana's latest scent worn by a scantily dressed Penélope Cruz.

Kikki waited for the man to pass by so she could get a better look at him.

She reinforced her shield, making herself invisible and hoped her powers were greater than those that opposed her. Paris was her city. She was sure it was not his.

Chapter 25

Impatient pedestrians jammed the corner sidewalk waiting for a green light, tourists vying with Parisians for space. Kikki used them as cover.

Seconds later, the man joined the crowd. Covertly, she watched him. He looked right and left, hatted head high, hunting her.

Kikki caught a good look. He had a large head, too big for his lanky body. Her now very keen vision bore through the crowd and caught the glint of a gold crucifix at his throat, barely visible at the collar opening of his dark overcoat.

In a flash, Kikki recognized the dark shapeshifting energy of Catherine de Medici. She hurled a ball of white light, hoping to send that energy to another galaxy. When she looked again, the man was still there, and so was the Black Queen's force. He turned in her direction, and she pressed flat against the window, yanking a woman in front of her as a shield.

The woman looked at her indignantly, and the man stared long enough for her to memorize his face.

Suddenly, the light turned to blinking yellow. Out of order. The crowd took advantage and rushed the crosswalk. He followed, crossing the street with the wave of people, searching for her, spotting in each direction.

Bon. Her protection had held so far.

Now she was certain the timing for the meeting with this client was not right.

Her coat pocket buzzed, startling her—her phone. She ducked into the doorway of a shop that had just opened and pulled it out.

"Monique! I was just about to call you. What's up?"

"You first," Monique answered.

Kikki glanced out furtively, head protected by her hood. "Can't make the meeting. Can you call and reschedule?"

"Witchy woman! Exactly what I was going to say. I have more details on the backers for you, but Kikki, the timing isn't right to meet the client today. We need to refine our strategy, *non?*"

"You're right. Can't talk now, Monique. A sinister man is following me—one of our enemies. I'm not going to the office and neither should you."

"*D'accord.* Are you sure you're all right, Kikki?"

"I will be. Call you later. You be careful, too, please. Our enemies are here and on the move. I have a lot to tell you. *Ciao, bella!*"

Monique disconnected the call, swallowing hard. She was very frightened for Kikki. Monique stared at the photo of Kikki on her phone's screen, whispering a silent prayer. And then, she dropped the phone into her bag and hurried towards the Chapelle des Louanges in the Palais des Beaux-Arts on an errand for Tía.

Chapter 26

Kikki backed up further into the tourist shop after her call with Monique. The shop owner gave her a look, but she smiled at him and began to turn the racks of hooded sweatshirts bearing proudly her city's name—*Paris*. Surreptitiously she watched the sidewalk. A few seconds later, in a throng of people, the man in the Borsalino passed by, moving steadily. He kept walking towards the Place du Palais Royal, head popping up and down searching for her.

Keeping her head down but feeling as though she'd achieved a victory, she donned the virtual mantle of Nike from Samothrace and zigzagged across rue de Rivoli, threading through honking cars and *motos*.

She ducked into the Louvre at Passage Richelieu and made her way under the high vaulted ceiling into the main courtyard. She emerged at the heart of the Louvre's main court, Napoleon's Courtyard, with its controversial centerpiece—the *Pyramid*.

She stopped to catch her breath near the now frozen fountains and one of three miniature pyramids in front of Café Marly, on the terrace of the Louvre. It was already open for breakfast for the hearty and privileged. Despite the weather, patrons sat outside in booths in heavy coats under electric heaters, fashionable scarves and haughty noses to the sky.

She scanned the people entering around her. No sign of her pursuer. She checked the ethers but picked up no energetic signature.

Now what? If only, like any good witch, she actually had a broom. She smiled to herself.

The energetic rhinoceros beckoned towards the Left Bank and home. She swiftly pivoted, passing beneath the gallery above, the Pavillon Sully, and through the magnificent portal flanked by pink marble columns.

Kikki came out in what was once the center of the Medieval Louvre, the Cour Carrée, now a square courtyard that integrated with the whole museum. Imagining it as it once was, Kikki shuddered, sensing a dark presence closing in. Ghosts from long-ago whispered secrets. Swords clashed. Jailed prisoners wailed from dungeons. Impotent kings screamed at servants and queens.

Quickly, she crisscrossed the courtyard, skirting the large round fountain in the center on her way to the much beloved footbridge, Pont des Arts, to her side of the river. She stopped for a moment to ground herself. She looked to the sky. Still a heavy *brume* and the gray wet clouds were spitting freezing rain, not gentle flurries. She secured her hood.

To her right through the windows, Kikki caught the interior spotlights on the Greek Goddesses in the music room, the Salle des Caryatides, a recreation of six Greek maidens who served the Goddess Artemis and supported the *Caryatids Portico* of the *Acropolis* in Athens. Archaic and mystical, the maidens' familiar presence was ordinarily a welcome sight for Kikki, but now she thought of Margot and betrayal and cruel predators.

In that very room, at sixteen years of age, a maiden, Margot celebrated her debut ball. Her possessive brother Henri pried her from the arms of her love, Henri, Duc de Guise, in front of all the court and took her to his hideaway nearby.

In the tortured interior of the Louvre Palace long ago, lovers met in secret in personally decorated hidden niches called *cachettes*.

And it was there, too, that years earlier Margot had her first sexual experiences at a young age with the Black Queen's favorite son, Henri. A future king of France, Margot was his privilege to have when he wanted. He repeatedly raped her, considering Margot his own, obsessed. Margot's mother did nothing to protect her.

Rage surged through Kikki. Now, she felt acutely the Black Queen's near presence in the Cour Carrée. She summoned Athena's sword, furious at such betrayal—seeking vengeance for Margot and others like her.

She hurried, passing the exterior of the Louvre's Southern Gallery of important collections that bordered the Seine, checking the high windows for the *Venus de Milo*, ordinarily a great joy to behold in the inky blue reflection of twilight on a clear evening. Today, the room was dark.

Just before she stepped into the vaulted passage that led onto the Quai de la Rive Droite, she glanced over her shoulder for her ominous pursuer. When she didn't see him, she felt relieved but wary as she moved through the shadows to the wintry light and open protection of the Quai.

Traffic was heavy. Kikki waited for the light to change, longing for home. Just opposite, the great golden dome of the celebrated Institut de France stood in perfect alignment. Kikki had to hand it to that feisty queen. On the precise spot across from the old Louvre fortress, her home and sometime prison, Margot built her own palace twenty-five years later where the Institut now stood— claiming her reward and a certain retribution by living well, and as she chose, exactly facing the Louvre where resided King Henri IV and his new family. And she made him pay for it as settlement for a "royal divorce"—a church sanctioned annulment.

Margot, ever the forerunner of fashion, out of exile after nearly twenty years, finally back in Paris, made of the Left Bank a chic, artsy place to live. It could be said that she started the famous and infamous salons that became the rage. *Brava*, Margot!

Kikki's phone vibrated, jolting her from reverie. She snatched it from her pocket and checked the caller ID.

"*Kalimera*, Cleo!"

"Kikki! Thank the Goddess I got you at last!" Cleo said in a tight voice. "I'm worried. What is going on? I keep picking up that you're in danger. I haven't been able to sleep, and the damn phones on this island—"

"Cleo! So happy to hear from you," Kikki said, forcing a steady voice. "And you're right about the danger. I was going to a quiet café to call you, but then I—"

"Someone's following you, right?"

"*Naí.*" Kikki whispered yes. "You saw it—I mean him?"

"Yes. He intends to kill you."

Kikki's stomach curdled. "I know. Can't talk. Send me protection. I'm on my way home, and I'll call you from there."

"Turn back! Don't go home!"

But Kikki didn't hear her friend. "What?" The line crackled and went dead. "Cleo?"

"*Eh merde!*" She shoved the phone in her pocket, increasing her pace, anxious to get home now.

A dense thick fog hung low over the river, long wispy tentacles reaching up towards the bridge. Panic rose from her chest, closing her throat.

The traffic light turned green, and she sprinted across the boulevard and up the stairs to the Pont des Arts footbridge. Booted feet hitting wood steadied her, although she felt as if she were floating above the river, above the earth without anchor.

Focus on what is ordinary and every day, she told herself. Blend with Parisians on their way to work and walk with them. A few paces ahead, she caught up with a small cluster of scruffy students on their way to the Palais des Beaux-Arts just across the Seine on rue Bonaparte. Kikki nodded and smiled. They barely saw her, bleary-eyed at that hour of the morning. Probably stoned. She remembered those days. Her stormy and fearful mood lifted some. Almost home.

Chapter 27

Kikki walked several yards onto the bridge, and the clump of students separated, dawdling mid-river, a favorite romantic spot, in no apparent hurry to get to their art. A broody looking young man with greasy black hair stopped to light a joint. A puff of smoke merged with the fog as Kikki passed. The heady aroma, more pungent with the dense humidity, tickled her nose. Two lovers leaned against the railing in a fervent kiss, hands searching for warm bare skin under coats.

Kikki passed them and found herself abruptly isolated, the only pedestrian on this part of the bridge. She'd kept up her guard this whole journey, but now she became even more vigilant.

The wrought iron railings had been freed from wall-to-wall padlocks—lovers swearing forever true in the most romantic city in the world. Not long ago, the locks had been pried off and thrown into the Seine and the iron railings encased in Plexiglass. So much love had weighted down the bridge.

Kikki hadn't liked the locks because they blocked light and disfigured the bridge's whimsical nature. The glass casings were an improvement, and the play of light through the pattern of iron railings was far more enchanting for this quintessential wooden footbridge across the Seine.

Everything changes. Especially in Paris.

Thinking of love, she worried about Torres. She slowed slightly and reached to touch the rose quartz necklace. Protection and ancient love. It was radiating heat. She kept walking.

Still near the middle of the bridge, the fog rose from the river veiling shadowy figures. The somber baroque sounds of a lone viola wafted towards her. Someone playing a solemn dirge by Marais. She knew it from the soundtrack from the film *Tout les Matins du Monde. All the Mornings in the World.* Appropriately ominous for a morning such as this.

The river rushed beneath Kikki. Why was she thinking about such horrors? She felt completely alone at that moment. She pulled her coat closer, head down, cold to the bone and spooked.

Just then, a gust of north wind whipped across the bridge and lifted the fog. Kikki's eyes were drawn to the Seine, a dark green stormy river rushing fast like a coming storm beneath her. The waters were high and both banks were nearly submerged. As the fog lifted, a sole intrepid Bateau Mouche, the *Catherine Deneuve*, made its plodding way upriver under the bridge, the loudspeaker blasting badly amplified Italian—the history of the Institut de France and Le Vert-Galant, the eastern tip of the Île de La Cité, long ago formed by joining two smaller islets and the Pont Neuf, a bridge that sported Henri IV on horseback ruling over his city, Henri the Great. Kikki grimaced.

The boat's blinding spotlights made it easier to see the other bank and her way home. Energized, she walked faster, passing the viola player, a rotund man clad as a French Renaissance court musician wearing a blue tunic, worn leather vest and black cape over black tights, and a floppy oversized beret with sequined feathers. She glanced at him and he smiled. His bare fingers were raw, yet stalwartly he played on. She stopped and fished in her pocket for change and threw a couple of euros into the battered leather case at his feet.

When she looked up, a woman sat next to him. Appearing out of nowhere. Kikki was sure she had not been on the bridge before. Where had she come from? Seated on an ornate gilded stool, she wore an elegant ermine coat and a Marie Antoinette wig of bright red hair that set off her ivory skin. Her long slender throat was encircled with a delicate string of pearls. She picked up a bow and plucked her violin in accompaniment.

She turned her wooden stool towards Kikki. The plaintive strings of the violin hit a high note that pierced Kikki's left ear. It signaled other realities. Pay attention, Véronique.

She cringed in pain and looked more closely at the woman. Margot! A real live woman dressed as Margot? Hallucination or a vision? What missive did she have? Mesmerized, Kikki watched as Margot lowered her lashes and set her bow and violin down. The man with the viola continued playing its mournful notes.

Margot put a finger to her lips and beckoned Kikki closer. Obeying, Kikki took a step towards her.

"What do you want?" Kikki pled, voice trembling.

"Attention! Partez! I came to warn you. Get off the bridge. Now!" Margot whispered sternly. As Kikki watched, a pristine puff of white cloud snaked around Margot. Kikki blinked, and Margot vanished along with the cloud.

Kikki slid her eyes to the right and found herself looking directly at her stalker. How had he found her? Holy Goddess! Planted in front of a bench, he blocked exit from the bridge. He was poised to attack. They locked eyes. And then he came for her. She turned to run back the way she'd come but instantly she saw an apparition appear—a statue of Catherine de Medici cloaked in black gossamer.

Kikki held fast to the railing, scanning the houseboats lining the river's cobbled pathway along the Left Bank. Just before the man reached her, the court musician lunged out and blocked him.

Just long enough for Kikki to make her move.

Without further thought, she climbed the freezing rail, took a deep breath, held her nose and jumped into the Seine's swirling icy waters. She hit the frigid water in the wake of the *Bateau Mouche.* Just before she submerged, she summoned an unearthly scream that echoed back to her in duet. Margot's high soprano joined hers.

Chapter 28

Kikki plunged down into dark waters, dragged below by mass and velocity and the weight of her heavy coat and boots. Within seconds, the force of deep, conflicting currents pushed and pulled her body, sucking her downriver even as she continued to sink to the depths. Blinded, and her body numbed by the cold, murky waters, she still heard echoes of the viola. Real or a hallucination, or music from the netherworld? Fractured thoughts flashed, and one held: she may not have all the mornings in the world.

Not unless you fight! She heard the voice without knowing if it came from inside or from without.

Lungs on fire from holding her breath, she swirled and tumbled downward, somehow understanding that she would be pulled downriver in the undertow before she ever reached bottom or managed to surface again.

So fight she did. Hair clasping to her face, arms and legs twisting wildly against the river's forces. But she seemed to be held in place, almost in slow motion as oxygen pressed out of her lungs. A desperate urge pushed her to gasp for breath, but her brain still functioned enough so she knew one watery "breath" would be the end of her.

Involuntarily, she opened her eyes. Muddy turbulent water and sand stung. Had she somehow sunk thirty feet to the bottom? That wasn't possible, unless some otherworldly force had come to her aid. Fighting to right herself, she began to pray for help.

Mutely, she called for the sea priestesses and sirènes of the Seine and Mélusine, River Goddess. And if Margot was her ally, where was she?

This time the message came without a voice, and it commanded: *"Swim, push off, climb to the surface!"*

But now she had no bearings. Which way was up? Which way was down? Still, Kikki wouldn't give up, she couldn't give in, not without a fight! Legs scissoring and hands clawing, she began to move—but was she simply tumbling, rolling in circles even as her feet and hands smacked against invisible things solid enough to hurt her.

And then miraculously, she found purchase on something, a rusted-out bicycle maybe? She shoved off with an unworldly strength and began to rise. And then, as if she were being lifted, floated to surface.

Head barely above water, she gasped for air and let out a long, hard wheeze along with a good amount of putrid river water and sand. She coughed violently and swallowed more water. Struggling to take in air, she went under again, popping quickly back up, spitting out water.

She opened her eyes and could only see inches in front of her face. Had anyone heard her scream? They must have seen her jump. Someone on the bridge. Or one of the many *péniches*, the houseboats nearby that lined the Rive Gauche.

She opened her mouth to call for help, but no sound came out. Instead, she swallowed even more filthy river water. Galaxies of stars surrounded her. She was close to passing out, both burning and numb from the frigid water.

The Seine wound its way through Paris under thirty-seven different bridges and had always been a favorite spot for suicides or dumping bodies.

But it wouldn't be hers!

That was her last conscious vow before her spirit left her body and she was whisked off to another universe. Was she dead? There was no white tunnel. Her mind, hovering between worlds, knew she was seconds away from fully leaving her body and never returning. Not in this life.

In that last fleeting moment, her only thought was of him—Torres and how much she loved him. She didn't want to die. Not now. Not after all she had fought for.

Unconscious and fading fast, she heard a voice. *"Then you will fight for us? For him? For love?"*

Was it Margot?

Where was she? Santorini? It didn't feel like the silky volcanic waters of the caldera or the Goddess energy of her island. The energy was too dense and too sinister. Margot was not of that world. Margot, who wanted her to bargain with death. And then Kikki knew she was in Paris, dying or dead in the Seine.

"You chose to fight for us, for me, for Paris, for what is true and right—the Light of the Goddess, for Inanna, and the Divine Feminine. For love. Now that you have seen the face of our enemy, one of the soldiers of the Swords, are you still willing? For he is but a hollow shadow of the powerful forces coming. You fear for your life and rightfully so. It hangs in the balance. And so does your lover's. Are you willing to lose him?

Margot spoke urgently, demanding: "I fought my entire life for love. As punishment because I was a threat, I was banished to a feudal military fortress perched on a volcano. It was like being buried alive for twenty years. They tried to kill my daughter, and they hunted me with brutal assassins—my power-mad mother and vile brother, Henri d'Anjou. My husband, who swore to be my ally. This same patriarchal madness now threatens you and your city.

"All I wanted was a voice as a Queen, as the last of the Valois line, my fair due. The right to love and have children. I was repeatedly betrayed as were so many women, my sisters, in the name of the One True God. Burned at the stake as witches and worse.

Only love can cleanse and lift the curse of blood brought by warring societies bent on greed and power. Kikki, you have an opportunity to do this. Yet, your unconscious spirit is reluctant still. Your heart, mind and soul must be one in the fight. You tried to run, and the darkness found you anyway. You must be stronger than them. Promise me again that you will don the cloak of valiant Goddess Athena and for the Daughters of Inanna and wear it until we have won. We will be with you. Continue this fight. The battle is upon us. If you hesitate, you will lose all, your lover and all else, and so will we. Do it in the name of love."

Kikki found herself in that tunnel of light, spirit hovering above her limp body. Both moving swiftly, but surely towards Margot, who demanded an oath once more.

"Yes. I promise. I vow," Kikki said gravely.

And then she felt the snap of being back in her body, coming into consciousness in time and place. Strong arms encircled her. She felt herself lifted and heard a din of white static noise. And then that cleared and was replaced by a cacophony of human voices and seagulls screeching—like babies wailing.

Finally, a man with a deep voice shouted, "*Madame, pouvez-vous m'entendre?*" Can you hear me?

She felt a hard slap to her ribs and a sharp pain in her chest. She gasped, mouth wide open, but she could not take a breath. She tried to open her eyes, but they were frozen shut. And then, she felt her heart stirring and her sluggish heartbeat quickening.

"She's coming around!" Muffled voices.

She spewed up foul water and choked. A man's muscled body lifted her, supporting her head and back. She wheezed and coughed. Her eyes were heavy, still closed, and she was not yet conscious.

A man! Who was he? And was she safe?

Her mind formed disparate thoughts. With a surge of adrenaline, she remembered the man who had been hunting her. She could see him clearly in her third eye.

Her eyes flew open.

Chapter 29

She was in a rescue boat. Her stomach churned, and she vomited up more putrid river water. She flashed on Santorini—captured in the sea by her onetime husband in that past life four thousand years ago.

Her mind raced, and she doubled over in pain. The word repeated itself—Paris. It was where she lived, wasn't it? And didn't she hear through a long tunnel the lyrical sound of French voices?

She shook violently from the frozen waters, her lips swollen shut. Tears stung bitter cold.

"*Madame, est-çe que vous nous entendre? Vous êtes saine et sauve.*" A French woman's gentle voice. You are safe and sound, she said.

A veil had been lifted, giving Kikki a moment of clarity. Les Sapeurs et Pompiers, the fire and rescue team, had a station in the Seine wedged between houseboats, only a short distance from the Pont des Arts. She walked by it daily. One of the reasons she had risked the leap into the frozen river.

Her first waking thought was of Torres.

"Torres—my mobile?" She tried to speak, but those words were only in her mind.

When she was safely inside the floating *caserne*, wrapped in blankets, she tried to speak again, but her throat was raw and tight. No voice.

Over the ethers, she cried out silently to her lover, desperate to connect with him.

"Torres, call me! Someone tried to kill me!"

Chapter 30

Many hours later, Kikki stirred. Feeling drugged. Scattered thoughts and hazy images flew through her weary brain.

She opened her eyes just enough to see that it was already dark outside, though the light had never really had a chance that snowy foggy day. She wondered about the time and the darkness. Where was she? Her heart raced searching for the answer. An inner voice told her to trust. She was protected and had survived an ordeal.

Every bone and muscle in her body ached. She moaned and turned over. Floating on soft goose down, she drifted back to sleep.

In her dreams she saw women in long white ermine-hooded robes. They were in the Tuileries. The ground was a white blanket, and it was snowing softly. The familiar large pool and fountain near the eastern end wasn't there. Instead, a large bonfire spread warmth—orange flames and the aroma of cedar mixed with heady scents of frankincense and myrrh.

The women stood in a circle, and each held a white candle. Their eyes and most of their faces were covered with shiny gold cat half masks.

When she looked more closely, she saw a lone figure standing in the middle.

133

The women began to sing in an ancient tongue, and they danced around the central figure, paying homage.

As they twirled and pivoted closer, Kikki saw the woman in the center more clearly. She was wearing a golden bejeweled crown and holding a sword pointed to the heavens. The Goddess Athena.

The song picked up tempo and jumped an octave. High-pitched and yet harmonious. The women whirled like dervishes.

They were thirteen in number. When they finished their ritual dance and song, they blew out their candles and lowered them to the ground ceremoniously.

Now, they raised delicate silver and lapis lazuli wands with their left hands and waved them to the beat of an unseen drum. They sang in low alto, breathless, twirling faster, robes soaring, waist length hair flying and sparkling with gold.

Wands spread golden pink-hued fairy dust that mixed with softly falling snowflakes.

Finally, they slipped out of their robes and stood for a moment naked and at one with Mother Earth.

The Goddess Athena in the center remained still as the women broke the circle and snaked closer to her.

Her silver sword shone, as though it was lit from within.

A cold wind began to howl and snow fell faster. The women closed the circle at her feet and bowed.

The Goddess rose above them, floating off into the snowy skies heading towards the Palace of the Louvre that stood out in bas relief to the east.

And then, Kikki saw herself with the women. They led her to the center of the circle. She was afraid and exhilarated.

When she peered up at the Goddess in the sky, she saw her face clearly: Margot as Athena. Accompanying her was a Goddess wearing a horned crown riding the backs of two lions with a lapis lazuli wand in one hand—Inanna.

And then, abruptly, Kikki stood in Athena's place in the middle of the circle. She picked up the silver sword that lay at her feet and raised it to the heavens.

The next time Kikki swam to consciousness, she heard a voice, *Kikki! Wake up! I need to speak to you.* Cleo?

She uncurled slowly from the fetal position. Every muscle in her body screamed in pain, and she had a splitting headache. Her mouth was dry, tasting of chemicals, and oddly, thyme and honey. Her head swam, dizzy. She lay back down on her side.

But she knew now where she was. In her apartment in Paris. And mercifully not at the bottom of the caldera or the Seine.

A jumble of vivid memories flooded her mind. She sat up in her bed.

The light in her bedroom glowed dim and shadowy. The door was ajar, and she made out the soft light of a lamp in the front salon. A slow-burning fire emanated warmth.

Was Torres here? Was she alone? Her psychic sensitivities were but a steady buzz. She couldn't pick up anything.

She swung her legs over the edge of the bed. It was then that she discovered that she was dressed in her silk *peignoir* and a warm robe. She wasn't alone—or someone had been here to take care of her.

Pressing her hand to her forehead, she felt warm beads of sweat. She had a fever.

Goddesses, it was no wonder. She had jumped into the Seine in dead of winter.

"*Allô?*" She eked out a hoarse whisper. "*Il y a quelqu'un?*" Is anyone here?

No answer. Her mind came into a blurry focus. She remembered the kindness of the Sapeurs et Pompiers and a vague memory of a woman undressing her and putting her to bed.

She had felt then as though she were floating on a cotton cloud, blissful. They had probably given her drugs and a sedative to sleep.

She tried to stand and saw stars. Abruptly, she sat on the edge of the bed. In a flash through her third eye, she saw the man in the Borsalino who had stalked her. And Margot appearing on the bridge to warn her. Her throat closed in pain and she tasted bile.

Stop, you are strong, she told herself. With sheer force of will she stood on shaky legs. Tentatively at first, she wobbled out the bedroom towards the warmth of the fire.

A crystal pitcher of cool water resting on a silver tray had been placed on the table by one of the bordeaux-colored velvet sofas. She sat on the edge, careful not to sink too far. It was time to return to the living.

With shaking hands, she poured water into a glass and drank slowly. It soothed her throat. A bar of her favorite Lindt dark chocolate had been placed on a small plate. She broke off a small square and chewed slowly.

Moving very carefully, she crossed the room. She found her bag, still soaking wet, with its contents spread out on the table to dry. And there was her phone—in working order and fully charged.

She picked it up and checked the time. Four o'clock in the morning—but what day?

She returned to the fireplace and slumped onto the sofa. With unsure fingers she began to scroll through the call journal.

No call to or from Torres. She remembered that he had told her not to call him.

Was he all right? Remembered fragments of their brief call at the Regina—he was wounded, but how badly? Tía had been killed in the explosion. Her heart sunk. That all seemed a lifetime ago.

A text from Monique: *Are you okay? Client impatient. Call me! xo.*

Several calls from Cleo. She listened to the first voicemail, which brought back a hazy recollection that Cleo and she had been talking and then cut off—before she nearly drowned. She played the message again.

"Turn back. Don't go home!" Cleo's voice was stern and fearful.

Chapter 31

She set the phone on the coffee table and sipped more water. Chilled, she had to warm up and get her blood flowing.

Her phone chirped, and she stared at it. FaceTime from Cleo. Kikki took the phone in hand and pressed accept.

Cleo's beautiful familiar face came into focus, tousled red hair, smeared makeup. Wearing a red silk kimono, one that Kikki had given her.

"Kikki! Finally!" It sounded like Cleo was yelling. "Are you okay?"

"Softer, please," Kikki whispered. "I have a hell of a headache."

Cleo brushed her hair out of her eyes, "I'm sorry, *bella*. I have been worried sick about you. I have been trying to call for hours. What happened to you? You look like a ghost."

"I feel like one. Luckily, I'm not. But for the grace of the Goddess."

And then, she sketched quickly the recent events. The connection went in and out. "What are you picking up psychically, Cleo, right now. I need to know."

Cleo closed her eyes, and her face went soft, head cocked, as if listening.

"You told me to turn back. But why did you tell me not to go home, Cleo?"

"I saw this dark energy filling your apartment, and you—let me think—" Cleo opened her eyes and clipped her hair on top of her head like a rooster's red top notch.

Kikki stood up and started to pace, trying to tune in. She called up the smell from the Hotel Regina. Foul and dark. Catherine de Medici's apparition. Her stalker on the bridge.

"I have it!" Cleo cried. "I saw someone climbing into your window. A horrible man—"

Kikki swallowed hard, fighting to stay calm.

"The man following you. He wore a Borsalino?"

"Yes." Kikki shuddered, cold from deep inside.

"He morphed into that dark energy that I saw in your house."

Kikki's heartbeat picked up. "Holy shit, Cleo!"

"Get out of there. Go anywhere. Right now!"

The line went dead. Black-gloved hands encircled Kikki's neck and squeezed. She choked. Her arms flailed, and she squirmed, trying to slip out of his grip. She kicked out and tried to twist, desperate to fight back. But she had little force against his strength.

"Save her!" Kikki heard Margot's voice call as his grip tightened and her breath was cut off. She slipped into near unconsciousness and collapsed.

And then a burst of fire exploded before her eyes. A deafening sound, like thunder, resounded in the apartment. And then everything went black.

Chapter 32

The next day, Tuesday morning, bright sunlight flooded through the windows that fronted the penthouse. The heavy red velvet drapes had been drawn. Tía tended the fire, coaxing it into blazing flames. She smiled, pleased. Her patient was resting comfortably on a sofa in front of the fire. A cozy down duvet wrapped her in warmth. Only the top of Kikki's blonde head peeped through.

The young woman was still fast asleep. Soon, she would be awake. She was breathing easily. Tía longed to wake her so she could talk to her. Should she? Time pressed. Torres was on his way.

Kikki's eyes fluttered, and she began to rise to consciousness. She held on to the images in her last dream—a tall woman with fiery red hair. Young, she saw her kissing Torres and tossing back her head with laughter. They were in a corridor hung with beautiful luminous paintings by the masters in ornate golden frames.

In a corner where no one could see them—where? Was it Margot? She tried in vain to capture the essence of the woman. The vision faded as she wondered if it was real. And then, suddenly, she was fully awake.

Her eyes flew open and through hazy vision she saw an old woman with a finely wrinkled face and a long black braid. She hovered over Kikki smiling. Kikki didn't recognize her at first.

"You're awake!" Black eyes sparkled.

Kikki tried to raise herself up onto one arm, and she felt every ache and pain in her weary body. Memories of what had happened flooded back, and with them, a knowledge that her caretaker was Tía. How?

"Tía? But—"

"Yes, it is me. I'm so glad to see you back with us." Kikki felt Tía's scrutiny and a golden glow of healing flooding into her body.

"Torres told me you had been killed in the explosion—"

"I'm sorry, *querida,* we had to. It was the only way."

Kikki raised herself slowly to a semi-sitting position and rubbed her eyes. Her throat was raw, and her neck hurt. She reached automatically for her crystal beads, still miraculously, if not magically, intact.

At the same moment, she flashed on the black gloved hands around her throat and the loud noise—a gunshot! She sat straight up.

"It was you who saved me!" Her stomach knotted. "Wait, you've been here—"

"Yes. I was on guard, but in the kitchen, when he climbed onto the balcony in the middle of the night and came in through the window. I was ready for him—although I'm sorry I let him get close enough to hurt you."

Just like in Kikki's nightmares and visions. "So then it was you who watched over me after I nearly drowned—the pitcher of water and chocolate."

Tía nodded and passed her a full glass. "Drink. You are still very fragile and dehydrated."

Kikki winced in pain. She took the tall glass and raised it to her lips. She gulped and choked. Then she burst into a coughing fit. She threw off the duvet and stood up.

Tía set a firm hand on her back. "That's it. Get it out. Your throat needs to be healed so you may speak and know the truth. We are on the eve of great and powerful change. Your fifth chakra must be in full working order. To speak and be heard, to hear and understand."

Still coughing, Kikki shot her a mystified look.

Tía passed her water. "Sip. Take it in slowly, gently. We need you."

After a few minutes, as Kikki drank, she began to feel better. She sat down again.

She had known Tía was powerful. Kikki was not surprised that she had saved her life—twice it seemed. Nor that Tía was, indeed, alive. It had been a ruse, as Kikki had suspected. Keep Tía safe. And Torres had used her and Jean Marc to pass on the message to those who sought to kill her.

But now—now was time for truth. Kikki looked squarely at Tía, seated on the edge of the coffee table in front of her.

"Tía, what happened in Granada? Torres—is he okay? Where is he?"

"He's safe and he's here," Tía said carefully. "*Pero*, he's at an important meeting."

"Here! Paris?" Kikki was suddenly fully alert. "Where's my phone? I have to hear his voice."

"Not yet. Trust me, Verónica." Tía took Kikki's hand in hers, dry and calloused from age, a deep brown from the sun and, yet, soft. "You're still vulnerable. It would slow your healing."

"I don't care. I have to speak to him," Kikki said. "But he's hurt —"

"He'll be fine," Tía said reassuringly.

Kikki flashed on her near-death at the bottom of the river, recalling Margot's words, her plea for a promise that Kikki fight for her love. Fully conscious, now, Kikki was hit with the realization that life without Torres was not something she wanted to contemplate. She had come a long way from hot sex and slow love. She let out a long slow breath.

"*Crée-lo.* He's seen a good doctor, one of our allies. And he comes from tough stock, like me." Tía smiled. "He was lucky. He always has been."

"Well, thank the Goddess for that!" Kikki rejoined. She was thoughtful, for a moment conceding to Tía's wisdom.

Kikki looked up at Tía. "When will he be here?"

"Soon. *Patiencia.*"

Kikki nodded, though she did not feel at all patient. "And the man who you killed in my apartment? Some save, and I see no trace of it."

"I had a little help. He's been taken care of." Her withered lips curved into a proud smile.

"The man following me on the bridge, the same one?"

She nodded. "Yes, him."

"Well at least *he's* out of the way—"

"There will be others, as you must know, *querida*." Tía frowned, her black eyes severe.

"Yes. Inevitably." Tears filled Kikki's eyes. "Tía, I hope I can handle it. I am not as strong—nor as wise—as you."

"But you are, Verónica."

She changed the subject. "What day is it?" Kikki felt herself ground completely into the present.

"*Martes*—Tuesday early morning," Tía said offhandedly, as though the hour didn't matter.

"Really? An entire day has passed! Wow!"

"You needed rest. You've been sleeping for quite a while."

"I guess." And then Kikki remembered talking to Cleo earlier. Before the evil man had tried to kill her. Cleo had warned her, and Tía had her back. Kikki was silent, chewing her chocolate slowly, inhaling with all senses the medicine of bittersweet cocoa.

Kikki stood up, unsteady but mobile. She walked slowly from the warm salon towards the adjacent kitchen.

"I've got to have some strong coffee, get my head on straight. I'm a little loopy." Tía must have given her something to sleep that long and maybe the *sapeurs* had too—the woman rescuer had been worried.

She eyed Tía intently. "Before you tell me the rest—you're going to *verdad*?"

"*Seguro que sí.*"

"I have to know it all." Kikki reached the far corner of the apartment where the cozy kitchen was tucked beneath the eaves. Windows facing the Seine and onto rue de Beaune and the Quai. Light and cheery. When there was sun, as there was today, at least for the moment.

Tía followed Kikki, the fall of her footsteps barely discernable on the parquet. "I will make you café."

"No. I have to reenter the real world. Really, I'd rather—"

Tía's firm alto voice cut her off. "I know how you like your coffee—dark, strong, *sketo.*"

"Okay. You make it, Tía. I am not going to fight with you."

Kikki watched while Tía took a porcelain cup from a cupboard above the coffee machine and prepared her coffee using Kikki's classic Bialeti steel stovetop Italian expresso maker. She knew exactly where everything was. How long had Tía been here?

Tía raised her thick black brows, exactly like Kikki's lover would have done. She motioned for Kikki to sit with her at the round oak table and placed two steaming breakfast cups in front of them.

"It's time we talk. I have much to tell you."

Kikki held Tía's eyes as the perfect dark nectar slid down her throat, burning hot on her raw esophagus.

"Let's hear it. I'm ready." Caffeine kicked in.

As Kikki opened herself to Tía, ready to hear the truth, Margot appeared in blue silk court dress just behind Tía. She wore a benign smile, and her black eyes sparkled, just like Tía's.

Chapter 33

Torres grit his teeth. He stood erect despite the excruciating pain under the left side of his rib cage where he'd taken a bullet. He reached with his right arm to lower the black beret he wore over his high forehead, black hair tucked underneath. He sported a two-day stubble on his olive-skinned face—paler than usual from pain and lack of sleep. His lips were tight, fixed into a frown, as he trudged up the steep hill of Avenue des Nations-Unies that skirted the gardens beneath Palais de Chaillot on the Place du Trocadero.

But the more constant pain in his chest was not from a gunshot. It was about Kikki. He had left her alone, and they had almost killed her. He forced himself to put guilt and worry aside and focus on his mission.

He hurried to meet his longtime friend, Jean Marc Montalembert, fondly JM, director of the recently reopened Musée d'Homme in Chaillot's complex of stately neoclassical buildings. The museum was once one of the world's premiere anthropological museums, now less so, due to the creation of Musée Quai Branly-Chirac and France's political reorganization.

They had agreed to a face-to-face meeting to fine-tune strategy, review the latest *humint*, human intelligence, and so he could brief

JM on the Spanish skirmish. Plus, special delivery of an artifact. Then, he would head straight to Kikki. Her soft smiling face and all-knowing dark brown eyes filled his head. And then, abruptly, he winced when someone jostled his wounded left side.

The streets were crowded. It was that time of the year. Almost Christmas. Lots of tourists, some in pairs and others in groups. Any of them could easily be an enemy dressed as a tourist.

Had the bump been accidental or intentional? Scanning discreetly from under the brim of his beret, he saw no one suspicious. But he remained vigilant. He would take a circuitous route. SOP.

He'd been watching for a tail since they'd dropped him off on the Left Bank in front of the Eiffel Tower. Directly across the river from Chaillot.

The last couple of days had been grueling. He worked anger and pain to patiently clear a path through the crowded sidewalk, dodging tall thin black men hawking miniature Eiffel Towers and a young American couple with a toddler in a backpack and bundled up against the cold. The child was not happy. His wailing pierced Torres's cop armor. Poor kid.

The longer he walked, the worse the pain was. He clenched his jaw tightly. Focus, Torres, he scolded—silently still worried about the pedestrian who had jostled him.

He took a moment to gaze around at the sights. He scanned the crowd, an idle look on his face. Tightening his wool scarf and zipping higher his leather bomber jacket, checking the taped cracked ribs and the hidden package.

When he finally crested the steep hill, he turned southwest—away from his ultimate destination—to Avenue Paul Doumer, a lovely tree-lined residential street and one of the six spokes on the wheel of the Troc traffic circle. Adrenaline fueled his inner radar. No one caught his eye or looked the least bit interested in him.

He continued his deviated course, heading south on rue de la Tour, towards the Seine and Place de Costa Rica. He reached into his pocket and slipped a foil package out, popping a couple of high dose *Doliprane*—Tylenol without the codeine.

He needed a clear head now.

Chapter 34

———•———

Torres walked slowly on a residential side street before heading to the meeting point. The short street was quiet but for a young dark-haired woman in a well-cut cashmere coat walking a Jack Russell terrier that strained on its leash.

Even as he kept watch, his mind turned back to Granada. He was reliving each beat—double- and triple-checking that they had covered all the bases. He hoped their tactics had accomplished more than the killing of three foot soldiers from the Swords' organization.

He hoped they had reinforced the message to the Swords' principle leaders that they had indeed killed Tía.

The cold seeped through his leather fur lined jacket—bone aching pain.

He had survived the turbulent flight back to Paris on a military transport. That, thanks to Flo, who had his back and was a fiercely loyal ally and critical in hierarchal organizations like Interpol—especially with the multiagency operation. She had arranged transport to Beauvais, a small airport south of Paris.

Thanks to the Kevlar vests, he hadn't been killed, but it had been a firefight, and they had faced heavy artillery—Russian AK-47s. One bullet hit his left side, through-and-through just below the vest, missing his vital organs by millimeters, but he had lost blood. The entry and exit wounds were stitched and dressed and his cracked ribs bound. The doctor sent him away with a stash of antibiotics the size of horse pills to ward off sepsis.

Torres took a last drag of the cigarette and coughed. He had been lucky, but breathing was not easy. He stared at the cigarette, and then sighed heavily. One more long drag burned his throat. He exhaled through his nostrils, using the nicotine to pump him up.

He crossed the sidewalk to the neoclassic complex of buildings of the Palais de Chaillot, heading for the Musée d'Homme, his thoughts still on Granada. He stopped on the wide-open square dedicated to human rights, a favorite spot for tourists and skateboarders. He lifted his phone to capture the perfect view of the Seine and the Eiffel Tower, playing tourist.

After they encountered old Papito, they turned the corner in the path behind Tía's home where they were hit with a barrage of gunfire. Torres expected a trap—Tía had upped the stakes when she went on the offensive with an IED—and the Swords had lost one of their soldiers in the explosion.

Torres, Sara and Manu were ready for the Swords' tactical squad when they hit, bent on revenge. But, as point, he'd been forced to expose more than a shoulder.

They'd taken out two of the Swords, who dressed in masked hoods and tunics marked with crucifixes. The third escaped on foot, and Sara gave chase. At the back gates of Tía's, she dropped him with a shot that turned his white hood blood red.

Torres and Manu arrived on her heels. When they pulled the hood up, they discovered "he" was a young woman, a mere teenager in a hijab, wearing worn jeans and a sweater—and a vest loaded with explosives. Prayer beads encircled her wrist.

It happened fast. Sara spotted the detonator that the woman had dropped when she was hit. A veteran of EOD, explosive ordnance disposal, Sara quickly defused the bomb.

After wrapping Torres's bleeding gut with a shirt, they moved the three bodies into Tía's compound: the dead girl and the two male Swords.

The front portal was destroyed, a mess of debris between Tía's rigged explosion and the mafia-style hit when the Swords in the car had emptied their rifles.

They found body parts of the Sword who had triggered Tía's IED.

Tía—and her missing stallion, Lorca—had fooled them all and led the charge, even after she made her escape. It had worked. But when the firefight was over, Torres had a dead jihadist wearing enough C-4 to blow up most of Tía's house. So that's exactly what they did.

They set off the second explosion, watching from a safe distance. The blast destroyed what was left of Tía's *carmen* adobe. In the midst of the rubble were multiple bodies.

When the local cops "officially" arrived, they would find charred and shattered remains. Torres hoped the locals would believe Tía was dead, taken out by the Swords. That's what they'd report to their contacts in the organization. Torres might even buy himself a bit of time if they thought *he* was the other body.

And that was almost exactly what happened, as reported to Torres later that day by a reliable source. Killing Tía was a win for the Swords, even if a few soldiers were sacrificed. They thought they'd won the battle—although they weren't sure about Torres.

Tía had orchestrated the whole thing. And now she had a perfect cover, just as she had planned. *Que bruja!*

Chapter 35

Torres tossed the butt of his cigarette onto damp cobblestones, grinding it into dust, still pissed at Tía about her elaborate and dangerous ploy.

The Knights of the Holy Sword of God were a threat to Tía's society, the Daughters of Inanna, and all they stood for. A common enemy. He knew that was why she'd drawn them out. Still, he was angry she'd carried out a preemptive strike. *Joder!* That was for the cops, for his team.

For months, Torres and his team had studied the Swords and the Florentine racket's activities, their players and their movements. The Swords had long used Torres's *cause célèbre*—the heart of his op—looting of archeological antiquities, history and art—to achieve their goals. To Torres, they were one and the same—Becchina & Fratello—Becky Bros.—and the Swords.

He stretched a painful left arm to keep it from getting stiff. And he was counting on turning his mark for the final play—if he could. But he had to be careful with Natalia Becchina. An emergency trip to Spain hadn't helped. He was meant to reel her in today in Paris. Now, he'd have less time, and he was injured on top of it.

Tía! Afterwards, on his way out of a village in the foothills of the

Sierra Nevada's a black SUV with military hardware and heavily tinted windows pulled up. He heard the whoosh of an electric window lowering and then the distinctive "psst" of Tía.

"*Ven, sobrino!*" He shook his head, thinking back on their recent meetings, a little bit in awe of her abilities. *General Tía!*

He had agreed some weeks ago to let Tía in on his plans for Operation Sphinx because he knew she had been receiving death threats from the Swords. He had wanted to protect her.

She had scoffed, not worried about threats. But had insisted it was critical that they coordinate their activities for the week of the gala exhibition in order to protect the Snake Goddess. But he had only given her bare bones about his sting and his plan to lure the head of the Swords into the open, along with their highly placed criminal allies. They'd all be on the Louvre's guest list for the gala.

He chuckled quietly, gazing off at the Eiffel Tower in the misty distance. What a crafty matriarch she was. He hoped the Daughters hadn't bitten off more than they could chew.

When Torres climbed into the SUV, Tía gave him the package and told him to guard it with his life. It was the Swords' coveted ancient coat of arms.

A precious and powerful object kept hidden by Torres's family for centuries. A priceless piece of history and archaeology, yes, but more than that, Tía warned him. A talisman to the Swords that—in their hands—could stoke their powers. Tía cautioned him to be careful because, though she had energetically cleansed it, it inherently carried darkness and evil.

Now it was taped to his chest, and he would gladly turn it over to Jean Marc, the obvious choice.

But that hadn't been the secret.

No, the secret was about Natalia Becchina, his mark. He had been genuinely stunned. And it made for a surprising twist. Required rethinking strategy. Now he fully understood why Tía had insisted on coordinating with him. His mark was his distant cousin—which created a conflict of interest between his op and the Daughters' goals.

He started across the Avenue Franklin D. Roosevelt, heading for the meet at Musée d'Homme. He shook his head. Things always had a way of getting screwed up. Chaos theory of crime. Still, his team had gone over the possible twists and turns. All the ways it could go wrong. They'd be prepared for all eventualities—he sincerely hoped, vowing on his Abuelita Elena's grave.

Joder! As always, Kikki had known his op's endgame—the sting at the Louvre gala. The risk was justified to meet necessary ends. And, ironically, it would also serve to preserve the precious Snake Goddess, along with everything the ancient relic stood for.

Over the past four months, since Kikki discovered the Snake Goddess on Santorini, his new highly secret team at Interpol had been picking up *humint* that a half dozen of the wealthiest and most powerful men in the world of blood antiquities wanted to get their hands on the ancient statuette. Literally.

Torres was betting that the absolute leader of the Holy Sword of God would be unable to resist the chance to steal and exchange her with a forgery at the gala. Torres and his team had been gathering and documenting mounting evidence as they allowed the Swords to infect the Louvre's world-renowned security system.

As the symbol of the Mother Goddess and matriarchal power, the Snake Goddess was the ultimate prize for the patriarchal elite. What better way to befoul the sacred symbol of the Matriarchy than to use the Snake Goddess to fund patriarchal terrorism. Once they had her, they could auction her off to the Swords' highest bidders from every continent—among them, a prime minister, an emir, a prince, a cardinal who may well become the next Pope.

He couldn't afford to fail. If there were justice, a point on which he was more than skeptical, and ever fighting for, the sting would expose a centuries' old network of crooks and greedy men and women of power—politicians, religious leaders, their icons, aristocrats and more. Most important of all, he would finally flush out the head of the Swords—cut the head off the hydra—and eviscerate their well-entrenched global network.

It all came down to Paris this weekend. Kikki said Paris was the center of the world—and had been since ancient times, one of the gateways of Planet Earth protected by ancient ley lines—a portal—magical energetic line. Once open allowing instant travel from one point to another.

She was once again correct. He could debate the mystical theories, but as an archeologist and cultural anthropologist, he tended to believe her. He'd certainly experienced electromagnetic energy surges at ancient and sacred sites worldwide. The play for world power this weekend was Paris—the center of the wheel from which all would unfold—or unravel.

He studied Place du Trocadero, one of many similar traffic axes in Paris, the scientific—or in Kikki's world, mystical—principle in action. Five boulevards came together, not a perfect circle, more like a pentagon with a garden at the center and five unmarked lanes of traffic that drivers theoretically knew how to navigate. Chaos again.

Trocadero was named for an important historical battle that involved patriarchal French Royalists and Spanish rebels in Andalucía—the Battle of Trocadero.

Torres shook his head at the thought that the very same French Duke who had rescued a Spanish island in Andalucía from rebels, also a onetime king, was probably a distant relation of Torres's. A very confusing historical time. Right after Napoleon had lost the Battle of Waterloo.

Patriarchal predators all—birds of prey pillaging spoils of war.

Who were the rebels this time?

It was apt, Torres thought, that he was here now, gathering close his allies and ensuring protection of his own. Jean Marc being primary, part of the power base that ruled Paris and, most certainly, a rebel in disguise.

JM was not only well-connected behind the scenes, he was popular and had entrée into the highest levels of Paris society. He was as *haut* French as anyone. Enough of a well-turned-out chameleon to slip in and out of the establishment of *La Vieille France.*

JM was critical to Torres—a member of his international council and also part of Interpol's covert squad. He wasn't a cop, but he had been military. Torres had deputized him.

Torres was nearly to the museum when it began to sleet. *Coño!* Pain surged and he used it to still his thoughts, moving into that Zen space that served him so well. Deepening his awareness, solidifying his confidence.

And then he lost his concentration. Kikki popped into his thoughts. Damn the woman! She had thoroughly invaded his heart and mind. He wondered if she was trying to connect with him now in that psychic way of hers.

What he wouldn't do for the love of her. He had been torn because the minute the cargo plane hit the ground, he wanted to run to her side. A lifetime of discipline kept him on course.

How he wished they could leave her out of the coming events. He allowed himself a small smile. She was right: he would like to lock her up in a fairytale tower. But he knew she played a key role, one way or another. And he couldn't stop her even if he wanted.

Hours ago, after the battle in Granada, his cousin Sara had counseled him to think of Kikki as one of the team. He didn't like it. And he was worried about this new client of hers. But he couldn't stop her from doing her work, even if it was connected—not short of arresting the guy. He'd have to cover that some other way. JM was on it.

Kikki would be part of Tía's action plan on the front lines. His heart tightened with fear for his love. Kikki had nearly drowned in the Seine, only to be attacked in their home.

What kind of partner did that make him? What kind of cop? How could he protect her? How could he do his job and let her do hers? She had to fight for justice as he did—but in her own way.

Dilemmas—and they tore him in two.

This constant push and pull were too damn hard.

Fiercely independent and stubborn woman! Still, Kikki was part of him. He couldn't lose her. But soon, she would have to make a choice. If she wanted independence so much that she couldn't commit to marry him, to be his life partner, she could have all the freedom she wanted. But he'd be gone.

He wanted more. Life was too damn short.

Chapter 36

Intent on his thoughts, Torres still sensed someone invading his space. He pivoted, drawing his Beretta but keeping it flush against his jeans. Bad business to open fire in this crowd of holiday tourists.

"Jesus, Torres! I'm glad you didn't shoot first and look later." Jean Marc blew out a cold breath that vanished in the sleet. He gestured with slender fingers registering Gallic displeasure. He swiped at a curly lock of sandy hair that had escaped his narrow-brimmed hat. Clear plastic-framed spectacles perched on the end of his patrician French nose that almost masked Eastern European Jewish origins. Green eyes flashed momentary shock and then quickly scrutinized Torres.

Torres holstered his weapon. "You really should have said something, JM. I have a bad case of trigger fever."

"*Tranquille*, man. Be cool." Jean Marc unfurled an immense British umbrella that seemed incongruent to his wiry frame. Still, it protected his classic Burberry cashmere coat, carefully arranged navy scarf and charcoal wool slacks. "Let's get out of here. Follow me."

Torres was taller and had to duck under the proffered protection from the steady sleet.

"Not secure at the museum?"

"Can't be positive. Might be paranoid. It's reopened but there are still too many workers coming and going. There's a bench not far up Avenue Woodrow Wilson."

"Pretty sure I don't have a tail," Torres said. "Doesn't mean there isn't one, keeping distance."

"Right. Now you have my eyes too. Well done! Tía got back here safely."

"Thanks to her connections. Neighbors in the Sierra Nevada, everything lined up. She flew off in her cohorts' awaiting private plane from a nearby field at the base of the Sierras, not far from her *finca*." Torres shook his head. "Nice of her to let us know beforehand."

JM laughed quietly. "Très Tía. My people delivered her to your apartment, escorted her upstairs. Kikki is fine, by the way. They are plotting, *sans doute*."

Torres shot JM a pained smile.

"Kikki's tough, like Tía. Don't worry. And it's not your fault, you know."

Torres grunted. "*Seguro—*"

"Christ, Torres, I can see you are in terrible pain. Your normally handsome and youthful face is showing strain and age."

They sat on a wet cement bench partially protected by the bare branches of a large tree. Not far from the museum, but it gave them a better opportunity to observe the surroundings.

JM pulled out a newspaper and held it open under the umbrella. Next to him, Torres toyed with a cigarette pack. He lit one and stood. Everywhere he looked, he saw a sea of umbrellas and enormous tourist buses lining the Troc and side streets, with heavy traffic weaving around the spokes of the traffic circle.

JM glanced at Torres sideways and spoke in a low voice, muffled by the sleet and wind.

"Let's do this, and I'll send you back to your women."

Torres took a hit off the cigarette, ground it out, and sat again.

Both men leaned together over the open pages of *Le Monde*, and in seconds, the package passed from Torres to the inside of JM's coat.

Once secure, Torres briefed JM on Granada and what Tía had

told him, leaving JM as stunned as Torres. For a few minutes, the two men sat in silence—but the damp and sleet made contemplation uncomfortable, to say the least.

JM slipped an iPad from inside his coat and several open files filled the screen. The two reviewed the updates quickly.

Torres cleared his throat and said, "Looks good, JM. The new security hire at the Louvre—the Swords' slick embed—any sense he's spooked?"

"No. He's been very busy, and we've been enjoying the show through our 'keyhole.' He's infected the system with bots, and we've caught his texts and a phone call when he reported to his handler at the Swords. The conversation was cryptic, but with our security footage, it all creates a very prosecutable picture."

Torres grunted his satisfaction, and then the two men discussed plans for the next couple of days leading up to the gala. JM confirmed he would send all workers in his museum packing, do a sweep for bugs, keep it rotating. They'd set up there as base. Today.

"Appropriate to use it as our HQ, *non*, Torres? The Musée's basement was an important center of the Northern Resistance during Nazi occupation—*putains d'enfoirés!*"

Torres shook his head.

Again, they fell into a silence, broken awkwardly by JM. "So—when are you seeing her again, the gorgeous and fascinating Natalia Becchina?"

"Tonight. An intimate dinner. That had better be enough to reel her in. No more time."

"Good luck. Even with your wounds, I trust your charm will win her over. Just don't let her suck you in too far, my friend. Women!"

"Yeah, complicated isn't it?" Torres said.

"Complexity—that's what you've always gone for in life, and in women, especially. It's your *forté*."

Torres finally laughed. "I hope we've got enough people—it's lean on manpower, JM."

"*T'en fais pas.* Don't worry. By Thursday—two days—all will be in place. Our people are the best. You can trust them. Less is more. No leaks. Flo and I are on high alert to maintain the team's secrecy. Brilliant to keep us hidden under her own division."

"Let's keep it that way. No fuck-ups!" Torres barked. "I'm out of here."

Chapter 37

On Quai Voltaire, Kikki sipped her third cup of expresso. She munched on dark chocolate and Greek yoghurt with honey and walnuts. Fortification.

The coffee coursed through her veins, and she felt much clearer. She set her cup on the saucer with a loud clatter.

Tía rose calmly. "Come, let's go back to the salon and sit in front of the fire. We don't have much time."

Kikki followed, watching the old woman who tossed her head so her long braid swung back and forth. The full black velvet skirt of her dress swished as she crossed the short distance into the salon. A picture of confidence.

"*Siéntete.*" Tía sat on the sofa with its back to the windows.

Kikki took the other, shoving the duvet aside. She sat upright, spine against the cushions to support her lungs and kidneys where a dull ache had settled. The fire burned brightly.

Tía slipped a slim silver case and matching lighter from a pocket in the folds of her skirt. She lit a pungent cigarillo and drew it into her lungs, savoring the moment.

The distinctly sweet odor of the miniature Cuban Cohiba smelled good to Kikki. Mixed with the cedar and pine scent of the fire, it awakened all of her senses.

She didn't wait for Tía.

"Time for all of the truth," Kikki said sharply. "I had a near death experience and was almost killed in my own house. Your nephew has been evasive. Classified mission: his sting aimed at the Snake Goddess—he's opening the gates of Hell. Hades himself!"

"Take a breath, Verónica. You are one of us, and I will tell you what I can, what you need to know." Tía smiled and took another dainty, yet—Kikki thought—masculine, perhaps hermaphroditic, drag of her Cohiba.

"What you *can*? And I suppose when you say 'us,' you refer to the Daughters of Inanna about whom I know next to nothing. So far, I see you, me and the ghost of Marguerite de Valois. This is very big. I *need* to know everything, Tía. And we will need reinforcements. I'm ready to help, even lead the battle. But I have to know who the players are and what is planned. Even Jeanne d'Arc didn't do it alone! I have the feeling everyone is keeping secrets from me, and I'd like to know why? It has to stop!"

Tía leaned her head back and let out a rich laugh.

"You laugh, Tía. I don't find it funny, though I'm glad you still have a sense of humor. I gather we'll all need one. A fight to the death against the Knights of the Holy Sword of God, a powerful secret patriarchal society, a dark and dangerous group with far-reaching, sinister tentacles. It is so familiar to me. And not only because of what happened on Santorini, but as if I've lived this battle before. If I could recall everything from that past life, it would help, but I cannot. So unless you want to do a past life regression here and now, you need to get real. By which I mean full disclosure. Maybe Torres can claim classified police work. But not you too."

"Listen to me carefully, Verónica. I am the Elder Sister of the Daughters of Goddess Inanna, of whom you are already aware. It is an ancient secret society, light holders of the Goddess and her ways, respectful of Gaia, matriarchal, humanistic, peaceful and nourishing. Like the prehistoric Minoans and Therans to whom you are so connected. We trace our lineage to them and others of like thinking—the Celts, the Sumerians, the Babylonians, ancient Egyptians who worshipped Isis, the Moon and Mother Goddess."

Kikki smiled and pointed to the two altars that displayed her collection of goddesses.

Tía turned and nodded approvingly. "They are beautiful and keep clear energy in your home."

"Thank you. So tell me more about the Daughters of Inanna. Margot said she was one of them and that the Daughters would help me fight the battle. Thank the Goddess you are alive to guide me."

Tía nodded slowly. "We are not all women, though our numbers have always counted more women than men. We are great in membership and cover the globe. We are growing in these turbulent, violent times. Which means we are more than ever a threat to the patriarchal enemies—those who attacked me and whom Torres seeks to bring down—the Knights—"

"Of the Holy Sword of God. Yes, as I said, I know about them."

"We are at a crossroads that, by divine order of the Goddess, will reach climax at Winter Solstice. Darkness seeks to prevail. Our enemies have thrown down the gauntlet. And you, *querida*, have manifested the perfect battleground with the Snake Goddess exhibit."

"Played right into it, as if it were predestined," Kikki said with what she hoped came across as irony because though she was angry, she did not want to take it out on Tía.

"By no coincidence, here in Paris where we hold our yearly Winter Solstice Celebration and our Council of Eight meets."

Kikki heard a high-pitched buzz and the tiny hairs stood up on her arms, almost as though she were at the beginning of some kind of initiation. She pinched her wrist to stay present. She wanted more information from Tía before she entered those other realms.

Tía said proudly, "The society is named for Inanna, the Sumerian Goddess of Heaven and Earth, Love, Wisdom and so much more. I know you're familiar with her from your collection and because of who you are, in addition to being a fierce advocate and savvy lawyer."

Kikki blushed. "Thank you. Yes. I know her. Also known as Ishtar."

"Indeed. She was chosen by those who formed this secret group hundreds of years ago as one whose qualities most completely represented the Mother Goddess—of Gaia, and both Heaven and Earth. As Goddess of Love, Innana uses love as a weapon to vanquish the power and greed in which our enemies revel."

"And one of her symbols is the star, the evening star, the planet in the night sky." Kikki heard Liam's voice echoing her own as she spoke. "And Aphrodite was the Goddess of Love—and the planet that is generally known by the Roman Venus."

Kikki leaned across the coffee table holding Tía's gaze, excited now and feeling the support of the Daughters and Tía beckoning her into its arms. As Margot had said, soon Kikki would be one of them.

"Yes, an eight-pointed star, a rosette. As Goddess of fertility and plenty, she also carried a straw knot for the gate to the storehouse." Tía closed her eyes, almost in reverie, and took a slow drag of her Cohiba. When she exhaled, the smoke formed the pattern of Inanna's straw reed.

Kikki smiled and sat back. "She was a protectress, too, like Artemis or Diana." And now Kikki remembered she'd seen Inanna riding lions in the sky in her dream earlier.

Tía opened her eyes and placed her cigarillo in the crystal ashtray on the coffee table. "She also carries the energy of Athena. Inanna had her holy sword and lapis lazuli wand."

"A true pioneer for the Great Mother Goddess. A Light keeper for the planet."

"*Claro.* She rode on the back of two lions into battle for justice— like me, like Margot, and like you, Verónica."

As Tía spoke her name, Kikki flashed on a light at Tía's neck, her fifth chakra, just visible above the black velvet bodice. She wore a necklace set with emeralds and pearls from which hung a golden pendant, a ruby-studded eight-pointed star.

Tía smiled and held Kikki's eyes.

Kikki reached up to touch her own necklace. The ancient rose crystal beads were hot and a strong aroma of wild roses filled the air.

The two women smiled knowingly at each other as if making a pact.

Chapter 38

Tía broke the silence.

"So now you understand, Verónica."

"Yes, but who is the leader of the Swords? How will we stop them? We need a plan—"

Tía silenced her. "Shh. He is almost here, your lover, my nephew. I hear him."

Kikki let out a long breath, knowing her lover was safe. But that only made it more urgent that Tía finish.

"But why the secrecy? He knows all about this, doesn't he?"

"Of course, and he is a member of the Daughters."

Kikki thought about the threat letter she found in Torres's desk.

"They sent you a threat. At least tell me about it. I expect there were others, and this has been going on for a long time."

Tía rose and moved to the back of the couch, pacing.

"Yes. I expected you to read it."

"You were ready for them, *que no?*" Kikki saw their words flash in front of her, and she said, "They plan to attack as the light turns —Winter Solstice. Three days from now. The same day and evening as the gala. They want to steal the Snake Goddess, right?"

"Yes, they do. Because of all that the Snake Goddess symbolizes," her strong Goddess energy. They want to destroy her, and by doing so, they believe they will destroy our power and weaken us. That is but one part of the plan—"

Kikki stood and picked up the iron poker, stirring the logs. "There's more—a curse to be lifted because if it is not, then Snake Goddess or not, we are doomed to live in the shadows under some new form of patriarchal tyranny."

Staring into the fire, willing it to take, a part of the vision Kikki had yesterday flew through her third eye.

Margot with her confidante Gillonne and a baby huddled in a carriage in the woods, stopped at a campsite.

Suddenly, the fire roared anew, orange flames filled the chimney. It crackled, and sparks flew out into the room frightening her.

She jumped back and then shot Tía a questioning look.

"What else, Tía?"

Margot appeared just behind Tía. She wore not her queenly dress of satins, silks and pearls. She was wrapped in a rough-hewn black hooded cape. Tears streamed down her face.

"You must not let them take my baby daughter."

Margot floated up and hovered between the two women. She looked directly at Kikki, pleading, "I beg of you. Protect her from the curse of blood. Le sang real."

Kikki swallowed hard and nodded.

"Did you see Margot or hear her just now, Tía?"

Tía said quietly, "I didn't hear her, Verónica. And I cannot see her. She is your muse. Your protectress and your guide. But I know what she wants."

"She asked me—"

Tía put a finger to her lips to stop Kikki from talking further. And then she spoke gravely.

"We have been protecting someone for a long time and will continue to do so. *She* is our hope. *She* is our secret weapon."

"But who is *she*? Because we need her now!" Questions rang in Kikki's ears. Tía couldn't be talking about Kikki herself, surely not. Incoming information was beginning to jumble between past and present lives in Kikki's mind, swirling. Her head throbbed in pain.

Tía parted her lips to speak and just as quickly closed them.

"Tía! Tell me!"

At that moment, a key turned the lock in the door to the apartment.

Chapter 39

Torres set his go bag down quietly by the door just inside his office, wincing as he leaned over. He sighed with relief to be home. You were damn lucky, he told himself. And so were Kikki and Tía.

The next moment, Kikki flung herself at him and wrapped her arms around him. The pain increased but he didn't care.

"Oh my Goddesses," she said, holding him tightly. "I was so scared I wouldn't see you again."

"Me too," he whispered.

She released her grip, suddenly remembering he was wounded, and stepped back.

"You look like hell," she said with spirit. Knowing he wouldn't want to dwell on his wound. Not now, anyway, her neomacho man.

"Thanks a lot. I could say the same, but I am a gentleman." He drew her close again, kissing her hard and deep.

She met him with equal fervor, slipping his beret off and letting her hands roam his thick black hair. Head to head.

When they finally broke their embrace, Kikki said quickly, "I love you so much. You know that don't you? I nearly—" she paused, editing her words. "So much has happened and yet, none of it matters, not without you."

He felt his heart smile. And then he kissed her again, tongues intertwined. His hands roved her body and he felt himself grow hard. Love was very sexy. He had been surprised she had so quickly met his need for her, spoken the words she was always frightened to speak. Maybe, just maybe—if they could survive this epic storm.

Suddenly, she broke away. Wait, she thought, where was Tía? She had disappeared.

"Okay, lover boy. Hang on. We have company. As much as I'd like to—"

He silenced her with another deep kiss and leaned against the office wall that separated them from the rest of the apartment. His hands under her sweater. Fingers found her breasts, full, nipples erect and inviting. He caressed and squeezed hard, wet mouths still locked together.

She reached into his jeans. One hand stroked his hard penis and the other cupped his ass. Then she took one of his hands from her breast and slid it into her jeans.

Swiftly, he had her out of her clothes and his fingers in her hot wet sex.

Breaking the kiss, she moaned. "Oh—Torres. Please—"

His eyes searched hers, relishing the moment. But he too was impatient. And ready.

With his left arm, gritting his teeth with pain, he reached for the office door, still keeping one hand where it belonged. He wouldn't let go of her. Not now, not ever, he knew.

He heard his Tía humming a familiar Andaluz love ballad, clattering china in the kitchen. Quietly, he closed the door.

Kikki pulled him onto the leather sofa, barely big enough for two. They were naked in seconds, clothes flying as they flung them in the direction of his desk. She grabbed a soft blanket on the edge of the sofa to protect their nakedness from the cold, drafty room.

He was less agile than usual. He grimaced when he flipped off his boots. He'd never admit how much pain he was in. She studied the bandaged ribs and felt a hitch of pain in her own ribcage.

Though maybe it was only her heart-stopping love for him. Get out of your head, Véronique.

He kissed her tenderly and gazed at her for a moment, feeling his own heart do flip-flops. And then her hands were on his hard cock, wanting.

"Now, Torres! We've had enough foreplay for a lifetime!"

He smiled at the *verité* of that *double entendre*. And then all thought and pain vanished as he plunged inside her very wet sex. They moved in synch as they always had—perfect fit.

She felt the wave build quickly inside and crest. He circled fingertips around and around her flower of love.

"Oh! More!"

He gripped her shoulders and pressed hard against her, moving rhythmically, relentlessly in and out. Wild with passion. Pain gone. Trying to hold on.

"Swear you will never leave me, Torres. Promise me!"

The whole of his strength and life moved in her, driving deep. He took what she gave as she came again and again, biting her lips to keep from screaming.

"Promise me," she moaned, barely intelligible.

He drew out of her and gathered her tightly into his arms. Her fingers traced his face, nose, lips. And then she drew him closer, encircling his waist, willing him to come back.

"Kikki—I would never leave you, not willingly. I love you too much. Don't you know that? My world is nothing without you. I am so very sorry I left you in danger. You were right."

"Shh." She put a finger to his lips. "I am fine. I know that you had to go to Tía and I had to stay here."

He let her guide him inside her one last time. Slowly, rhythmically they joined. They came at once with a shuddering climax.

Finally spent, though not sated, they lie wrapped together. Both breathing heavily, the rise and fall of chests and hearts united.

Neither wanting to break apart. To savor forever their sacred bond, a soul union.

Kikki closed her eyes. A oneness she had only experienced with him.

Chapter 40

In the afterglow, Kikki sat alone in the dim light of the small office. Torres had slipped out to tend to Tía. Kikki could hear them talking rapidly and quietly in Andaluz dialect. Arguing at the kitchen table over coffee and perhaps *Chinchón*, a high-proof Spanish anise liqueur.

Kikki was glad to be alone. She dressed quickly, dizzy with overpowering emotion and physically spent. And yet, quite clear about one thing. She knew what she had to do. Margot, who had loved fiercely and yet failed to enjoy true love, was right. And so was Liam.

If Liam's cards played out, the price would be high. Not Torres, she vowed!

She knew the way it worked. The path and the test of initiation would have twists and turns. Margot had recognized that and demanded total commitment.

She closed her eyes and slipped instantly into half trance, straddling worlds. Searching for more information.

The Tarot card she had first drawn in the witching hours of Monday, a long two days ago, loomed largest in her vision. Hades in black robes of death, face masked behind a steel helmet. Outreached hands with long claws extending over the treacherous River Styx, beckoning unwilling souls. Who was behind that mask? Who was the enemy?

Yes, she knew what she had to do to keep her lover alive. If she —if they—made it through the week.

The archetypal cards danced in front of her, alive with their potent energy.

Justice—Athena in white robes of peace, silver sword of truth thrust towards the heavens. Seeking peace through shrewd strategy. The great Greek city named for her as the one who offered the olive branch—chosen over Poseidon, powerful and violent God of the Sea.

Mistress of the smooth political maneuver and the minimalistic but clever tactic.

Through Athena's Justice, Revelation would come—Judgment and Rebirth—Hermes as the Psychopomp, the Guide of Souls. A young man with curling black hair wearing the white of the righteous messenger, but on his shoulders, a cloak soaked in blood.

An icy chill seized her heart.

The Three of Swords cast a malevolent shadow over the others. King Agamemnon, the cruel warlord, naked and vulnerable, slaughtered by Clytemnestra and her lover. A solemn ritual of revenge, a bath of blood set in marble under a black and brooding sky.

Just as similar dark storm clouds gathered over Paris.

Kikki drew in a quick deep breath and went deeper into trance.

The information flew through the ethers from the squawking mouths of a trio of ravens.

We curse thy lineage—House of Atreus for the evil deeds of King Tantalos! The arrogant King mocked the Gods. Butchered his own children, cooked the flesh and served it up as a banquet to the Olympian Gods.

Malédiction on the House of Valois! Vous sont tous maudits! You are all cursed. Margot's voice screamed at her mother and brothers through a raven's beak.

"Mother right versus father right. Matriarchy versus patriarchy," the raven cried in Kikki's own voice, flying so close that she felt the brush of its wings.

Kikki shivered. Her belly expanded. The pull of the waxing moon—the Moon Goddesses Artemis and Hecate demanding sacrifice. An innocent woman, like Iphigenia.

Curse and healing—but only through bloody death and the clash of Swords. WAR.

In trance, she spun in time and space. Astral body and mind overflowing with pieces of the puzzle. Ancient curses and secrets. A sizzle of lightening exposed the truth. Athena's justice would come with demands from the Hierophant—a High Priest coveting power in the name of the Pope—ultimate patriarchal symbol.

A dark cloud fragmented her soul's mind mirror.

Kikki shook her head sharply to bring herself out of trance.

Please, she cried. And with a snap, she was in her body, present in Torres's small office.

Insistent questions began to take shape as her mind cleared. Who was the High Priest? Who would be sacrificed? Kikki wrapped herself in the blanket, chilled to the bone.

She must know everything about her enemy if she was to save Torres, herself and fight for all the Daughters of Inanna stood for. She couldn't go in blind.

She closed her eyes and prayed for answers, pushing her limits. She took steady deep breaths, pulling energy up from the Mothers of the Earth and down from the Mothers of the Universe. She opened her channels and tuned in, asking for guidance and information. Nothing.

Let go of the struggle, she told herself.

Not yet, she heard. All will be revealed in the rightful timing.

But Kikki could feel that she was being blocked by Catherine de Medici, a sinister dark force that could move from one form to another—shapeshifter. In whose body?

She felt renewed after making love with Torres, but perhaps her inability to see was because she was still weak from her near-death experience. And vulnerable to the Devil.

It was suddenly very quiet in the apartment. Tía and Torres had stopped talking or moved so far away she couldn't hear them. In the silence, her channels were suddenly clear.

A familiar image of the High Priest as the Centaur Chiron—half man, half beast hidden in a cave. She heard herself gasp when the

Centaur morphed into a lion's head, burning red coal eyes, teeth bared to devour, hungry for flesh. Beneath the head, long black robes. And the putrid smell of the Devil.

The high-pitched sound pierced her left ear, and the sharp pain in her temple made her double over. When she came up for air, she heard one word—*betrayal.*

She stood up so abruptly she saw stars and gripped the desk to steady herself.

The threat was very close. Time for truth, for revelations. Torres and Tía knew much more than they were telling her.

But when she tried to open the door to the small office, it wouldn't budge. She turned the antique brass handle again. No luck. Now she was physically blocked!

A wave of cold damp air seeped under the door and around its frame. She shivered.

Just as Margot had been held captive by the Black Queen and her brother in the Louvre, Kikki was imprisoned in her home. She shoved at the door with her boot and shouted.

"Damnit, Torres! How dare you lock me in here!" Just as her boot hit the door a second time, it opened, and he stood in front of her.

He smiled ruefully. "It was stuck. Maybe it's your witchy antennae playing tricks."

"Not funny. Not to someone who nearly drowned yesterday." She stalked out of the room swearing, marched to the fire and shouted. "Torres, it's time to talk, now!"

Chapter 41

"*Voy.*"

She poked at the logs until they burned brightly. She breathed deeply trying to calm down.

He came and stood next to her. She edged him aside with her elbow.

"Give me a little space. I am—"

"I get it. Sit down, please. Let's not set the apartment on fire. Your temper—"

She steadied her trembling arm and placed the poker firmly in its holder. But she couldn't quite keep the anger out of her voice.

"Why is the door to the balcony wide open? It's freezing in here."

"Tía wanted some fresh air. Well, as fresh as you can get on Quai Voltaire at this time of the year."

"Really? What time is it, and where is Tía?"

"It's nearly 18:30. The sun we never saw has long since set." He spoke with a frown. He understood why she was angry. Because he was pissed at himself, too, and felt guilty—in spite of the safety detail he'd left to watch over her.

They sat down on the sofas, facing each other. Kikki picked up a large bottle of Volvic water and took a sip. It still hurt to swallow.

"Tía began to tell me about everything, but she didn't finish. I need to hear it from you, Torres." She wasn't going to mince words. "Information is power. I refuse to play the victim!"

"I'm so sorry, *mi amor*. It shouldn't have happened. I had people watching out for you."

"I know, but they failed because the enemy works on other dimensions. So talk."

"I'll do my best." He couldn't possibly tell her all, but she was going to push him hard.

"Do better than that! And you look like you're about to go somewhere, lover."

"Not yet. I'm not ready to leave you." Deftly, he crossed to sit next to her. He put his arm around her.

She pulled away. "You aren't getting off the hook that easily. And I hope Tía's not out on the balcony. It's not safe!"

"*Claro que no.* She's fine and close by. Don't worry."

"How can I not?" She took a sip of water, indignant now. She looked across at him, studying his black eyes, taking in the strain in them, worried about his wound and the very big job he had taken on. She knew his responsibilities were a weighty cloak—a heavy mail coat of armor. "What happened in Granada?"

He grimaced. Not from pain, but from knowing he had to let her in. He fished a cigarette out of a pack and lit it. He took a deep drag, using the nicotine for energy and savoring the burn. Then he quickly sketched the events for her.

"A jihadist! I am so grateful you are alive." She felt herself soften at the same time her fear ratcheted up.

He nodded grimly and took another drag.

She waited impatiently before she said, "This hit squad was a radical offshoot of your target. Look, I'll spare you the inner struggle with what you can and cannot divulge. I know who they are. The Knights of the Holy Sword of God."

He shot her a surprised look. "Did Tía tell you?"

"No—it doesn't matter how I know. I just do. Two secret societies pitted against each other this week. The Swords and the Daughters of Inanna. With me and Tía on the front lines."

"Kikki, you are not on the front lines." He stubbed out his

cigarette in the ashtray.

"YES I AM. And this patriarchal cabal is out to destroy everything I believe in. The Snake Goddess, right? And everything you hold dear. So don't tell me I'm not front and center too, police op or not."

He said quietly, "I want to protect you."

"I understand." She softened her voice. "Because I want to keep you safe too. But I'm afraid that this week there is nowhere to hide. It is all converging. Your work, my work. Our very lives."

"But, Kikki, *you* don't have to fight this battle. It makes it that much harder for me."

"I'm sorry, but I do. I'm on the Louvre exhibit committee and an international lawyer. I have the competence to fight in my own area of expertise. Do not leave me in the dark. I have a right to know because it's very clear that you and Tía have been sharing info for quite a while. You've coordinated the gala exhibit of the Snake Goddess with her."

"Against my fervent wishes." He started to reach for another cigarette and stopped himself. Instead, he reached across the table for Kikki's bottle of water. "May I?"

"Of course," She knew he was trying to appease her and that he was in a lot of pain.

"Tía just reamed me out. I said I couldn't expose you, and she let me have it. She told me you were a part of this. My cousin Sara said the same."

"Tía's right. And you need me. We'll figure out what has to be done. Whatever happens, we're not losing each other in this war— but we can only win united. Isn't that what we said not two days ago, before the attack on Tía? You said we'd fight whatever dark force there was together. Did you not mean that?"

Tension locked his shoulders and his wound started to throb. "Generally speaking."

"That's a cop-out. Sorry for the pun." She shot him a shrewd smile. "But you used me, lover, to pass on the information that Tía was dead. In my world, by doing that, you made me part of the bigger picture."

"It's a good cover, but it wasn't my idea. I'm still pissed at Tía for pulling this stunt."

"*Merde*, Torres, you used me as an operative. Maybe you should deputize me!"

He frowned and inched away from her. "Not going to happen. And you're exaggerating. I'm truly sorry for that, *mi cielo*. But I hoped you would get that it was a cover. JM's note was meant to convey that—*play the part.*"

"Elaborate subterfuge. I was genuinely upset. And imagining Tía dead and you wounded, Goddesses knew how badly—" She stopped, realizing she didn't want to go that far. She knew how guilty he felt. She could see it in the pain in his eyes and the lines in his forehead. "Look. We're both safe. I survived, and Tía's cover is in place. We need to move forward quickly. The Swords are funded by your usual crooks. And that's where the Snake Goddess exhibition comes in."

Torres edited the version he was willing to share. "It coincides with major moves the Swords plan. They've been planning this for years. And I've been working this intensely with my team for the last few months—had my eye on them for years."

"*Évidemment!*" She stretched her legs, propping them on the coffee table.

"Tía will make sure your Snake Goddess is safe."

"As much as I care about the precious relic, she's merely symbolic to them. The Swords are a threat to humanity. It's more than stealing pieces of time or history. A sort of patriarchal *coup de monde*! More like stealing Mother Earth—our precious planet."

"They're well financed, armed to the teeth."

"Through blood antiquities, right?" Kikki shot him a shrewd look.

"Yes. They're sitting on a massive loot. And could actually pull off a military coup, but they don't seem to want to play it that way—so far," he said gravely, not surprised that she understood perfectly. "But in time, who knows—secretly they have already amassed an army, and they number among the wealthiest in the world. They're just waiting to drop the net."

"Terrifying!" Kikki felt a familiar cold shiver as the picture began to come together, a quickening.

Kikki thought of Margot and her first love, Henri, Duc de Guise and *La Ligue*—the radical Catholic group that sought to destroy the

Valois dynasty and take the throne from Henri IV. Margot, while in exile, had conspired with the League for vengeance against her husband, her brother Henri and her mother. She'd even pulled off a military coup. Nostradamus spied for the League while still counseling the Black Queen.

Torres had stopped talking and was watching her carefully.

"And now I know why Margot has been urging me to take on this battle, one begun long ago," she said. But she wasn't going to tell him about Margot's charge to her in the Tuileries.

"Margot? I hope you didn't meet with your new client—the one with the film about Henri IV. It's too dangerous. They could be involved. You don't know who's behind them."

"Do you?"

"No." He cut her short intentionally because he knew far more than he could tell her.

"Monique and I have done our research. And it's my profession. I thought you got that."

"I get it. But that was before they went after you, me and Tía." Torres laced his fingers with hers, a gesture that he hoped would stop Kikki's questions.

"You have to trust me to do my business, as I will have to trust you."

"*Joder!*" She was painfully right. "Kikki—"

"Who heads the Swords, damnit? The antiquities racketeers? I doubt it. There's more."

Torres stood up abruptly. He couldn't give her intel.

"Kikki, it's too risky. I told you before. No one is what or who they seem. They wear many masks. The man who tried to kill you was obvious. Now they will be more careful. You can't afford to trust anyone this week."

"How can I fight a battle against unknown enemies, Torres? Surely you know exactly who their generals are?" Their High Priest, she thought with a shudder.

He dodged, checking his phone. "That's not your job—its mine."

She ignored his suggestion, driven to find out all she could. "Surely you don't think—after all that's happened—that the Swords will stop here. That they won't make a play before the gala. They'll try again." She remembered Liam's reading about a determinative battle—which she had to win, or there wouldn't be an exhibition. But she wasn't going to tell Torres it was in the cards. He had enough. "Look, I've got to check in with my team." He pulled out his phone and checked the screen. "I have a meeting." He stood up and headed for his office.

"And I've got to call Monique." She stood up and headed to the front of the salon.

When he was gone, Kikki focused on the power of the Snake Goddess, the matriarchy in Pre-Bronze Age Aegean times. And her Hotel Atlantis.

The ancient relic of the Goddess had saved her life. And now, this precious treasure was to be put on public display, fêted to by the elite powers—the Swords—on an evening that marked—and invited—the greatest darkness of the year.

Worse, it was Kikki herself who had brought her to them. Had she been tricked and manipulated from the start? Betrayal at her own unwitting hand?

Facing powerful, faceless enemies.

She was at a crossroads. Torres was stonewalling her. Tía was holding back. This was another test. What would be next?

In answer, the door to the terrace suddenly flew open, sending in a biting wind. And with it a stark image—almost a hologram—the Black Queen. A black veil shaded eyes of hate, long black gown stiff as her hostile regard.

Chapter 42

Outside, on Quai Voltaire, Natalia Becchina leaned against the wall overlooking the Seine between two booksellers closed at this hour. She peered up at the lights in the penthouse apartment where she knew Torres and his girlfriend lived. She'd never met her but had heard interesting things. She was a lawyer, Natalia knew. Which gave her pause, but more in the way of challenge.

She couldn't see any movement. But something told her they were home. She usually had good instincts, and she trusted them.

Natalia turned and leaned over to peer at the River Seine. She shivered. It was cold and quite foggy, that wet kind of fog she associated more with London or Milan. The Seine was churning and dark. Rather ghostly. No tourist boats. Cancelled because of the weather. A night like this one was romantic enough for films, but the ordinary tourist would not enjoy the magic of beautifully lit ancient monuments if they couldn't see them. Not to mention the danger of being on the river on such a night.

Across the Quai, the Voltaire Restaurant was in between services. It was both a fine restaurant that served lunch and dinner and a friendly café. The café service ended at 17:00. The café staff were finishing up their daily cleaning, and the restaurant's waiters and chef were eating in one corner of the restaurant. She could almost see them through the lace-curtained window.

Natalia was looking forward to intimate dining later with select members of the committee, more informal than the grand soirée at Hotel de Ville. More time to get her hooks into that gorgeous man, Torres, and find out precisely what he was after. Everyone had an agenda, especially cops like him. She wondered if he knew that she was a plant. Most likely. They would both wear their appropriate masks for as long as possible.

Whatever she found out, she had strict instructions to report immediately to her uncle.

She had just come from a meeting with the renowned *antiquaire*, also on Torres's anti-fraud council, Gabrielle Laroche. Such a lovely person and so knowledgeable.

Natalia would have a hard time getting anything past her, so she wouldn't try. Her uncle had insisted otherwise, but when Natalia brought up her uncle's name, Madame Laroche had been polite, but her smile cooled.

They had met on rue de Lille, in the smaller of Mme Laroche's two boutiques. She and Gabrielle had shared coffee sitting on benches at long solid wooden tables with an interesting provenance. Gabrielle said she had been able to acquire a few pieces, including high wooden choir stalls, benches and other community tables from the chapel of a convent in Tuscany. She hoped to obtain the rare collection in its entirety, but the rest of it was held by a private collector.

The magnificent furniture was similar to the large pieces that Natalia knew her uncle and his associate were about to sell—though she hadn't seen the pieces and knew little about them. Natalia didn't mention this coincidence to Gabrielle.

The convent was not far from where Natalia had been born and briefly lived before being whisked away as a toddler to New York by her mother. Natalia hadn't said then, but one version of her birth story was that she'd been born in the convent itself.

She had felt the familiar pit in her stomach at the lack of information, the missing pieces she had always sensed. Never whole, not complete as a person because she had lost her parents. Natalia was two when her mother left her father in Italy. Not long after they had settled in New York, during a trip to the Italian homeland, her mother had been killed in a private plane crash. Her father had died in the same accident.

Natalia had always felt as though she didn't really belong to this world because of this lack. Her emotional attachments were few, except for her Uncle Franco, who had brought her up.

She turned away from the stormy river and slipped her phone from the pocket of her long fur coat. Her uncle's associate, "Fitz", as she called him, was late. He was supposed to have called her as soon as his private jet landed at Bourget. It should have landed by now. Such an infuriating man.

Though she had only had brief contacts with him, and always by phone or email, she had quickly categorized him as a megalomaniac —a grade A narcissist. Still, she told herself that she would follow her uncle's instructions to the letter—she was to facilitate things— whatever that might mean.

Her uncle was also arriving in Paris by private jet tomorrow. Last minute preparations and strategy had to be discussed about their business. They had a number of items on their agenda this week before the holidays.

Normally, she was a mere messenger for these two men who seemed to believe themselves gods. Was she excluded from important discussions because she was a woman, or was it something else?

Yes, she thought, frowning, she would consider herself like the Goddess Iris, Messenger for the Gods. She did have her advantages. Messengers picked up valuable secret information. And you never knew when it might come in handy. In this case, she was glad she'd done enough eavesdropping and snooping to be on guard.

The partner, Fitz, was an antique dealer/collector of considerable standing through his family ties. And his partnership with her uncle expanded both of their operations, but Natalia wasn't sure it was Uncle Franco who benefited most.

The partner was the kind of man who used people—a ruthless man. Her uncle assured her that it was a good way to expand the business. And Fitz was a very important corporate attorney who acted for a number of Fortune 500 companies, some of them media conglomerates, though he considered himself above the fray. He called himself "a strategist who focused on global transactions." He was "in finance."

Uncle Franco was especially impressed that his partner was on the board of New York's prestigious Metropolitan Museum of Art. You didn't get much higher than that in their world. Except, of course, the Louvre.

Her uncle had intentionally avoided formal or public association with those kinds of well-respected institutions. Like the Uffizi Gallery in Florence. He preferred to work his contacts and his angles behind the scenes. That had been the way in their business for generations.

Until now, her uncle had warned her to keep her distance from Fitz. Though worried, Natalia was confident. She had youth on her side and was sure she could handle him.

Still, she felt uneasy about the agenda in Paris. She had a feeling that this was one part of her uncle's business she would prefer not to be involved in, and she had expressed concern to her uncle. He had said it was her family duty and that when the time was right, he would reveal what, why and where. For now, she was to do his bidding.

A heraldic call—he had said mysteriously—if not rather pompously. Natalia had not liked that. Not one bit. She had said nothing but had vowed to herself that she would stay informed, whatever the means.

Whatever they were planning must go beyond counterfeit and forgery, something which to her was not much more than a game at which she excelled. Her highly developed intuition told her that they were entering into more violent territory. A political power struggle of some kind. Her uncle had been nervous. Calm by nature, his blood pressure was up.

Italian by blood and fluent in the culture, Natalia considered herself savvy. Some things in the antique and art world, not to mention in general, couldn't be done without paying certain bribes. But this—this was much more. The world was a perilous and chaotic place in these times. One had to step carefully.

She shivered and turned her thoughts to Torres, smiling as she relived the sensual pleasure of feeling his muscled body against hers. Her mission was to use him and keep her uncle informed.

JULIETTE LAUBER

With pleasure!

Chapter 43

When she left the apartment, leaving Torres and Kikki to their privacy, Tía's small frame slipped easily into the narrow secret passageway behind the fireplace. She was *petite* and had just barely been able to reach the latch to the left of the gilded mirror that hung over the mantle. The heels of her riding boots gave her the extra boost. But the latch stuck. Apparently, it hadn't been used in a while.

It came unhooked just in time—as Kikki stormed into the salon. With the panel open a crack, she had caught her nephew's look. He had mouthed—*cuídate!* She nodded and disappeared from sight.

The narrow space ran along the entire east wall of their apartment, adjacent to the adjoining wall of the building next door. An *hotel particulier* in which the singular Rudolf Nureyev had lived in the high-flying manner of an artist of his talent. Hugely, wildly and with great passion. The thought encouraged her and strengthened her resolve.

Before starting for her destination, she squatted in the passage, listening to their conversation. The skirts of her long black velvet dress swished slightly when she swayed. She held them close, tucking them between her knees. Kikki not only had strong psychic powers but acute hearing. Tía swore to herself, sure she had been discovered.

She heard Kikki tell Torres to be quiet for a moment.

"I thought I heard something. Are you sure Tía is safe?"

"Quite. Why?"

"Oh, nothing, just thought I heard the sounds of skirts swishing in the corridor. Can't tell where the sound is coming from or if it's even real."

"Maybe it's your Margot."

"Maybe it's Tía. Margot's skirts are much more distinctive— heavy taffeta or satin silk. Whomever it is, it feels as though they are friendly."

Tía smiled and stood. She tiptoed noiselessly between old wooden structural walls to the back of the apartment and the secret staircase. It was exactly adjacent to the interior one for the apartment.

She circled all the way to the *sous-sol* (the first level below ground) and then crept towards the front of the building.

Tía had had no time since she arrived in Paris to ensure that the familiar underground passage was safe and hadn't been blocked because of construction—or for more sinister reasons. She prayed to Inanna that the way would be clear so she could go the whole length of the Quai using the old underground labyrinth.

She was headed to a secret meeting place. She was dead, so far as her enemies were concerned. Without a better disguise, she needed to move underground until she got to Margot's Chapelle des Louanges in what remained of her extravagant palace across from the Louvre. It was in the core of the L'École Nationale Supérieure des Beaux-Arts on rue Bonaparte, a bit of a distance. And she was running late, exhausted. A state for which she chided herself. She stopped and ran energy and light to restore herself.

Through a small crack in the buildings, she stole a glance at the Quai outside. Fog was heavy, but she could just make out the silhouette of a tall young woman in a long fur. The woman had long red hair that framed her pretty face. She was staring up at the penthouse—at Kikki and Torres's home. Why? There was something familiar about her. But if she was friendly, then why was she looking up at Torres's with a certain malevolence? And yet, she had a very bright lavender aura. Mixed messages.

Why had the Goddess shown her to Tía just at the moment she looked out? Not a coincidence, she was certain. And why couldn't she get more information about her? Was Tía being blocked by someone or something in the dank ancient labyrinth? Souls crying to be released from their purgatory. Was it the darkness coming from the young woman?

Tía fingered her necklace, and the information flew through her third eye. Instantly she knew. It was Natalia Becchina, the woman they were sworn to protect. Tía hadn't seen her in person for a few years, only in photos. A very beautiful woman and extremely complicated— high-spirited youth. Tía remembered her own and experienced a moment of envy.

She prayed they would succeed in their mission. Soon, they would approach Natalia to bring her into the flock. For now, the task was in her nephew's capable hands. How she had enjoyed sparring with him over this very woman in those few moments they had in Granada. He was being put to the ultimate test.

It was time for him to step into his rightful place. He was a great cop, part of the patriarchal hierarchy working for justice from within. But he, as one of the Daughters, owed a duty to them to keep Natalia safe.

Tía would know more about how they would proceed after the council meeting at the Chapelle des Louanges.

The small hexagonal-shaped chapel had been home to an old secret coven. Male historians claimed it had been home to a branch of the Augustine order, the Couvent des Petits-Augustins. Though, not coincidentally, their philosophy and cult resonated with Margot's own beliefs. Their true beliefs had been kept secret from most. Tía stifled a chuckle. And what ironic misdirection. The revered Saint-Augustin held strict beliefs about celibacy. But he had only turned to God and chastity after a life of sexual obsession and promiscuity.

In the small hexagonal chapel today remaining hidden symbols and secrets of old, paintings of saints and Italianate religious sculptures had been veiled by the Goddess's light and magic for the Daughters. That is where their council met each year at Winter Solstice. They would be discreetly admitted by their gatekeeper,

Monique Dubois, who had inherited the prestigious post through family ties going back generations. And also, Kikki's partner and friend.

One by one, the eight members of the council—one for each of the points of Inanna's eight-pointed star—would arrive at their Paris sanctuary. Now, also battle headquarters. Matters were coming quickly to a head. Solstice was in three days. It had begun.

Soon, Tía would bring Kikki.

Chapter 44

In their apartment, Torres reemerged from his office, business finished for the moment. Kikki sat on the *récamier* by the windows and gathered a bordeaux cashmere shawl around her shoulders. She studied her lover.

He sat in front of the fire working his finely sculpted jaw. The furrows in his brows deepened, and his eyes narrowed. Part of it was pain. The rest was moving into that zone to which she had no access.

She had to give him that. He was her partner, and he was also a cop and a very secretive person. She nearly laughed aloud at how alike they were.

Suddenly, Kikki was drawn to the window. She stood and drew aside the heavy velvet drapes, peering out through the sheer *voiles*.

Her gaze was drawn to a tall beautiful woman standing on the Quai opposite. And then the woman seemed to vanish, enveloped in the thick brume. Gulls flew from the Louvre across the river, shrieking.

A familiar piercing sound hit Kikki's ear. She flashed once more on the vision of them huddled in a carriage, Margot, Gillonne and the baby. This time, she saw more.

JULIETTE LAUBER

A soldier on a stallion riding in pursuit—brandishing a steel sword hilted with a lion's head and a crucifix.
A Knight of the Holy Sword of God!

Chapter 45

Torres watched Kikki too. He had told her what he could. The rest he'd leave to Tía. And some things could wait. There was still time. But not much. Their intel was that the leaders of the Swords weren't arriving until later in the week. Tomorrow, Wednesday at the earliest. They'd tracked one boss to Alexandria, Egypt. Poised to head to Paris when he'd finished his business there. Torres was counting on highly covert Greek/Egyptian operatives to stay on him and track nefarious dealings and movements.

It wasn't that he didn't trust Kikki, he told himself. If she knew, she'd jump the gun and blow the sting. Especially if she knew that Victor Fitz-Perkins, her boss from years ago, was possibly head of the Swords.

Best idea he had was to keep her from attending the gala. Though Tía had been vehement. Torres had a responsibility to the Daughters. They needed Kikki at the gala.

He reached for the red pack of Marlboro's on the coffee table. As he flicked the lighter, she came to join him in front of the fire. He lit the cigarette and took a drag.

He was apprehensive and feeling a little crazy too. The dynamic with Kikki had shifted.

She was stepping into this fight with a new level of her already considerable power. After weeks of semi-hibernation, she was back with a finely tuned force. And it was palpable. Like she'd been plugged into an electric socket.

But *joder*, he was a mere mortal with enormous responsibility— a lot riding on the sting.

"Aren't you going somewhere tonight, Torres?"

"*Sí.*"

"Are you sure you can manage, with your wound?" She stood up and looked him up and down. "You really should quit smoking, you know. I feel tons better since I finally quit."

He inhaled deeply. "I'm fine. Wasn't I in top form when we made love?"

"Definitely." She sat on the coffee table in front of him. "Are you going to tell me what you're doing tonight or do you want me to divine it?"

"I'm going to a small dinner—members of my committee. And, actually, it's downstairs at your beloved Voltaire." He stood and took her hand. "Gotta get ready."

"That sounds fun and important." Her voice was even, but she was delighted. She needed some time to herself. She had to get out, get some fresh air and a change of scenery. She felt claustrophobic. A glass or two of her favorite Saint-Émilion would be perfect. It would help her to soothe her mind so that she could plot her moves on this complex chessboard.

She was done trying to pry information out of him—for now. She'd find out herself. One way or the other. She always did.

She wanted to call Monique back to set up the meeting with the client for tomorrow, but she didn't want Torres listening in on the call.

It was nearly seven p.m. Though the Voltaire café was closed, she would probably be able to talk someone into letting her in. Antoine, one of the owners, Jacqui's son, would be amenable.

"Who's going to be at the dinner?" She kept her voice level, hoping to get names.

He squinted at her. "Just a few people, not the whole committee —" He wasn't going to tell her that Natalia Becchina would be there, though his level of frustration with Kikki was so high that he was sorely tempted to push her jealousy buttons, test her independent streak against the thought of him with another woman. But now was not the time.

Kikki smiled, accepting his evasive answer for the moment. She could easily find out who was at the dinner. As for his committee, she knew about Jean Marc and Gabrielle. But who were the others? Her memory was vague at the moment. Her concerns had been elsewhere, until now. Who was his mark? Her intuition told her there was a woman involved. She'd be at the dinner tonight.

"Well, you had better get ready then, Torres."

He knew she was up to something. He walked towards the bedroom and then stopped and shot her a knowing glance. "Where do you think *you're* going?"

"Just downstairs to have a glass of wine and talk to normal people."

"No. Absolutely not. *Joder!* Didn't you hear what I said? Damnit, Kikki! You can't trust anybody."

"*J'ai besoin de changer d'air.* I'm suffocating in this apartment."

"Wait. Tía will be back soon."

"I am just going to the Voltaire's café. It's only downstairs, and it's my local—practically another room in the apartment." Insufferable man, trying to curtail her movements. Damn him! "Don't be so controlling. They're closed, and I'll be there with the staff. No harm can come to me. They're as protective of me as you are!"

"I am arranging to—"

"Let me guess, have someone on me 24/7? Fine." She could deal with guards. "Do whatever makes you feel better, but I'm going to the café, and you'll have to tie me down to keep me here."

He laughed despite his displeasure and growing worry. "That might be fun."

"In your dreams, lover."

If she did meet up with someone from the Swords, who knew what she might unknowingly or intentionally, give away. "I mean it, Véronique."

"*Incroyable!*"

He caught her by the arm and looked straight into her eyes.

"You don't know what you might be interfering with, and if you run into the wrong people—"

"Screw you!" She held his eyes, her own all fire.

"Perhaps you should consider a career change, then?" She was furious, and he was running out of moves. "We can enroll you in the freshman class."

"Maybe I will!" She parried. And then she pulled away from him. She grabbed her coat and bag and headed for the door, slamming it on the way out.

Torres had a gut instinct to cancel his dinner.

Chapter 46

Waiting for the elevator, she got a text from Monique: *Meeting rescheduled with client for Wednesday at noon. Are you okay? Call me!*

Kikki answered: *Perfect on all counts. Call you later.*

Wrapped in a long black wool coat with a warm burgundy cashmere scarf, Kikki started up the short half block on rue de Beaune for the Voltaire, pleased to be out of the house and feeling strong.

She peered through the windows and the front door of the Voltaire café. It was officially closed, but the restaurant would reopen at seven-thirty p.m. Café tables had not yet been dressed for fine dining. Catherine and the café staff had gone, but she saw Antoine Picot at the back, coming from the kitchen.

She rapped on the door and signaled to him. He swiftly crossed the room, greeting her with a genuine smile that reached his bespectacled eyes.

"*Entre. Tu es toujours bienvenue. Il fait très mauvais dehors. Brhh!*" He took her coat, assuring her she was always welcome.

He settled her into the comfortable booth in the middle of the café. She sighed and began to let go of the tension.

Moments later, with grand flourish, he appeared and placed a decanter and a crystal wine glass before her. He bowed. "*Mademoseille, ça vous plait?*" He presented the bottle with its *étiquette*—Château Beycheville Saint-Julien Grand Cru 2010.

"*Tu me gâte! Quel plaisir!*" She caught his eyes and grinned widely, touched by his kindness and happy to be spoiled. A favorite wine she only drank on special occasions.

She waited reverently as he poured a taste into her glass. "I took the liberty of tasting it, but you be the judge."

Ceremoniously, she swirled the wine in the crystal, watching rich legs spindle. She sniffed delicately, taking in the heady aroma. Dizzy with anticipated pleasure, she sipped and swirled the nectar in her mouth to release its full flavor before allowing it to glide down her throat.

"*Antoine, c'est plus que divin.*" Divine.

He beamed and bowed again before filling her glass. "Compliments of us and your gorgeous *compagnon* who called to check on you. I assured him that you were here and not out storming the gates. I promised that we would take care of you."

She looked up at Antoine, "Seriously? Well the wine is the least he can do. *Les hommes!*"

Antoine shot her an enigmatic smile and then he tiptoed away.

She felt spoiled, privileged. And not a moment too soon. It was exactly what she needed to regain her strength and confidence. Small courtesies, easy friendship. And warm ambiance.

The best of *La Vieille France* was fast fading but still there if you knew where to look. A comfort to her. Paris living her long history. Struggling as she had done for millennia to make peace with change.

He returned shortly with a Damask serviette and a dainty plate of olives encircled by fine rounds of saucisson sec.

"I'm in the kitchen, Kikki, so if you want anything, just come and get me." He smiled fondly. "The café is yours until we send you home in another forty-five minutes."

"Wonderful! You are a dear! *Santé!* You have no idea what a couple of days I've had."

"*C'est nôtre plaisir.* Perhaps your luck has changed because I had just decanted that bottle for clients coming this evening. I know it's your *préféré*," he said with a sincere smile and warm glance. "I'll keep the decanter at hand for you."

Once he had left her alone, she recreated the ceremony in private communion. She swirled the velvety dark red wine and watched as it formed voluptuous legs. Her breath was one with the elixir. Its intoxicating bouquet floated up—a tangible living being. A ceremony of love.

The precious liquid snaked around her tongue. She tasted of the rich earth from whence it came. In her mind's eye, she saw rows of green vines plump with grapes ripening in the sun in the old vineyards of a sixteenth-century château. As it slipped down her throat, it soothed her wounds.

In moments it went right to her head. Greedily she drank again and then helped herself to a ripe green niçoise olive.

She had reached a level of peace that was badly needed. Her mind had settled. She was grounded and coming back to herself. Simple pleasures.

She was halfway through the first glass and knew she'd have another. But she would need some food. An *omelette mixte*, ham and cheese, with a bit of salad would be perfect. And definitely some bread and butter. Even though it was way past the hour that the French would butter their bread. *Çela, ne se fait pas!*

She laughed and felt a great release. Then she scooted out of the booth, careful not to knock over the glass, and went to the kitchen in search of Antoine.

Chapter 47

Natalia Becchina opened the door to the Voltaire café and crossed the threshold without hesitation. No one seemed to be there, though it looked like someone had been sitting at the middle booth where she had sat that morning—a nearly empty glass of wine and the remains of olives and *charcuteries*. Unfortunate, but not irremediable. Could be someone interesting. Snooping was one of the things for which she was on duty. One never knew who one may meet who could be useful. Machiavellian principles working at their best.

She had wearied of waiting outside in the cold for Fitz to call. A glass of wine would warm her. The Voltaire was the obvious and closest option. She could leave before the appointed hour for her formal dinner in the restaurant adjacent and make a late entrance. Revolving doors. Already dressed for seduction, she smiled mischievously and pulled her coat closer.

"*Il y a quelqu'un?*" She stepped into the room, asking if anyone was there.

Antoine and Kikki peered from the kitchen and answered in chorus. "*Oui. On est là.*"

The woman looked familiar to Kikki, but she couldn't

remember why. And she didn't care in the least. She was more interested in food, wine and gossiping with Antoine in the kitchen over a very buttery ham and cheese *omelette* with a bit of salad.

She had turned her phone off after the text from Monique. Her time, her space.

She discreetly leaned into Antoine and whispered, "Do you know her?"

"*La moindre idée—*" He studied her discreetly. "She looks interesting. Well dressed, poised and beautiful."

"True. Will you refill my glass? I am going to stake out my territory."

"Oh, come on, Kikki. Let's invite her in for a glass," he said as he left to greet Natalia.

Kikki's mouth turned down slightly as she returned to her booth. She watched as Antoine welcomed this woman who kept her coat on. Perhaps she was cold? It was a damp night out. Already dark and freezing.

Maybe Antoine was right. Frivolous conversation with this woman would take Kikki's mind off her troubles. She looked like she'd be fun and was maybe just thirty, slightly younger than Kikki. A charismatic stranger who had the sense to find the Voltaire and confidently walk in after hours.

Kikki silently chided herself for not being her usual curious and sociable self, though she had reason.

"*Veuillez me joindre?*" She looked up and finally offered her invitation.

"Thank you. I'd love to." Natalia beamed, curious about the pretty blonde who seemed to be part of the inner circle.

The woman spoke a perfect French, though she didn't look or seem French. Kikki's curiosity peaked.

Natalia extended a well-groomed, olive-skinned and perfectly manicured hand.

"Very kind of you. I am Natalia," she said in an unaccented American English as she slid gracefully into the booth.

"And I'm Véronique," Kikki responded—sticking to English and Véronique would be wise. She wanted to remain anonymous. Torres's advice to be careful rang in her ears. Americans were frequent visitors to the neighborhood, especially with the Musée d'Orsay and the Louvre close by.

Kikki wasn't sure about Natalia. She seemed more European. You never knew who you'd end up talking to in Paris, in the vortex of this Carré des Antiquaires and especially in the Voltaire.

Still, there was something about Natalia. Good or bad, Kikki didn't know. She had put herself on psychic holiday with Antoine's delicious attention. Pity. Now she'd have to amp up a bit.

In silent awkwardness, each studied the other, focusing on their hands, resting easily on the smooth polished wooden table. They looked up, eyes met and they burst out laughing.

"No, not married," Natalia said ruefully. "Far too young."

"I agree, and a very scary and antiquated institution."

"Right you are. Looks like some very nice wine," Natalia changed the subject.

"It is. Antoine, would you be so kind?"

He interrupted her, anticipating, "Shall I bring the decanter and another glass?" He smiled at both women. "I shall be right back."

"Are you visiting, Natalia?"

"Yes. Business and a great pleasure, too, of course."

Antoine was back quickly and poured Natalia a glass.

"*Santé!*" Kikki wondered what Natalia's business was. "May your trip be successful as well as fun, Natalia!" Her name rolled a bit hesitantly off Kikki's tongue. That signaled caution. She hadn't had that much wine.

"Thank you. And you?" Natalia was nearly certain Véronique lived in the neighborhood.

"I live here." She took a sip of wine and began to tune in, curiosity now fully aroused. "What brings you to Paris?"

"Business with the antique dealers," Natalia offered. "We have a company that deals in fine art and antiquities in Florence. The family, that is."

"So you speak Italian, as well. *Molto bene.* I only speak a bit. Do you live in Florence?"

Natalia took another sip and smiled. "Some of the time, though, I travel a great deal." This Véronique was interesting, she had potential to be useful. "Do you live near here? You seem to have— how shall I say, inner access. Aren't they normally closed at this hour?"

"Yes, but they often invite *les habitués* on off-hours. It's a family business. Been here for generations." Avoiding the question about where she lived.

"I had that impression. I've read about it." Natalia took a dainty sip.

She didn't want to give Véronique the wrong impression, though actually Natalia was in the mood to have quite a lot of wine. But she wanted to stay sober for dinner.

"Did you meet with some of the *antiquaires* in this *quartier?*"

"I had a delightful and informative meeting with Gabrielle Laroche. Also Alvaro Roquette and Pedro Aguiar Branco."

Kikki shot her a genuine smile. "They are wonderful people. Such fascinating works. They are very, *comment dire*—aware of the feminine aspect of antiques and art in history, as well as the female artist."

"Yes, I agree," Natalia said, pleasantly surprised. "Exactly what I thought about them. Makes sense in the City of Light, a very feminine place."

"True. Paris is a woman. And London and New York, definitely men rule," she said, forcing herself not to get on that soapbox. "Though, believe me, Paris has a distinct male ruling class, even in the twenty-first century."

"Italy, in general, is certainly very male," Natalia said with more vehemence than she meant to reveal. "But I was raised to deal with it." She thought best not to mention her uncle. Or her upbringing.

"I know what you mean. So what period of—" Kikki wondered about this woman's lineage. She had the olive skin of an Italian, but she spoke like a worldly American with European breeding.

"Mostly mid to late Renaissance in France and Italy."

Kikki thought about Margot. Natalia was dead-on with the time period. Coincidence?

"They were intertwined at that time. France and Italy." Kikki considered if she should mention the obvious players—Margot and the Black Queen.

Natalia drank her wine and simply nodded.

The two women clinked their glasses and enjoyed the stolen moment and the bonhomie.

In the silence that reigned, Kikki heard a swishing of satin skirts and got a waft of strong perfume—a pungent musky rose—Margot. Kikki set her glass down brusquely. Was there no respite?

She cocked her head to the left, waiting for that high-pitched French.

"*Talk to her about me, about my cruel mother—Madame la Serpente. It's time. I want you to get to know this woman better. She is someone you must know,*" Margot whispered urgently. "*I am counting on you.*"

"*Why?*" Kikki asked silently. Tuning in, she felt a jolt of masculine negativity from Natalia. Perhaps merely protection.

"Fascinating time period of history between France and Italy, or what we now know as Italy," Natalia said, placing her glass on the table.

Kikki cleared her throat. "Obviously, the marriage between Henri II de Valois and Catherine de Medici did much to advance that *mélange*. She brought Italy's Renaissance style, art and libertine lifestyle to France—macaroons too—not to mention her business acumen. And her knack with poison." Kikki looked directly into Natalia's heavily lashed hazel eyes and said, "Though I can't say that I am a fan of hers."

"No?" Natalia frowned into her glass. "She was an extremely powerful woman. Accomplished a great deal for France under very difficult circumstances. She had to put up with Henri II's dalliances, his long love affair with Diane de Poitiers. And, finally, his insanity. Not to mention all of those crazy sick sons of hers. She was an important political force in a turbulent time. I find it impressive that she was able to maneuver so successfully amongst all of those powerful men."

Natalia knew her subject. But how could she take the side of that cruel Machiavellian tyrant? Kikki wondered.

"Perhaps, but what about her brilliant and neglected daughter. The Queen Mother supported those ill-suited sons to rule, and all at the expense of Margot." Kikki savored the wine. "Marguerite de Valois has been recognized by such authorities as Voltaire and others as one of the greatest queens of France. And all despite the fact that her mother betrayed her, isolated her and continually plotted against her."

"Who was it, the poet Brantôme or Ronsard? Besotted with her, called her the Pearl of the Valois, a beauty, smart and high-spirited." Natalia laughed. "And a total nymphomaniac! Not sure I can blame her mother for that. Besides, I'm sure you know that Catherine de Medici herself did not have an easy upbringing—she was an orphan. The ruling Medicis in Florence were out of favor. Florence was at war. Her parents were both killed in ensuing violence against the rulers of the city-state. Her aunt placed her in a convent to keep her safe. And even then, she was in considerable danger. It was finally Pope Clement, a cousin, who rescued her from certain death."

"And the Pope used her marriage to Henri II to cement the papal alliance with France. Just like Catherine did with Margot. That should have made Catherine more sympathetic to her daughter. Respectfully, I don't agree with your view of her. And it's not fair, given that from a very young age, as young as ten, her brother, Henri d'Anjou, molested—well—raped her. Later as King Henri III, he continued to consider her his privilege to take when he wanted. Incest and abuse that her mother was aware of and tolerated. I call that unforgiveable. It also colored her viewpoint of sex and lovers."

"Pretty common in those days," Natalia remarked. "Sexual matters in families were different. And marriages were political alliances, not love stories."

"Concluding she was a depraved sex addict, as we'd call it now, is a male establishment historians' viewpoint—a stereotype and a hypocritical one at that. Can you imagine what it would have been like for a nineteen-year-old girl to be forced to marry and then have her wedding feast turn into a slaughter because of her mother's duplicitousness!" Calm down, Kikki told herself, not easy to do. "She was beaten to within an inch of her life by both her mother and brother Henri when they discovered she was sleeping with the young Duc de Guise."

Natalia drank a goodly amount of wine and gave Kikki a shrewd look. "Please, don't stop now. I love discussing the varying viewpoints of history. My uncle and his partner are totally obsessed with Catherine de Medici. They've acquired everything of hers they could get their hands on. So I guess I have had the benefit—or not

—of the other point of view. My uncle's partner is a total fanatic. She is one of his heroes. I've heard his rants about how admirable and powerful she was. She should have been king. She had the biggest balls in all of Europe, he said." Natalia laughed.

Kikki could feel her blood rise. "She was a total sellout to the patriarchy. Coopted at a young age. Collusion. But worse, if you ask me, in today's terms, we could correctly say she was born a full-on sociopath."

"I don't know about that. Pretty strong language. But who can blame her? There was no other way in those times. I have to say she was one of the great Queens of France, one of the most powerful women in history. She knew how to get what she wanted. The Italians excelled at that. Machiavelli dedicated his work *The Prince* to her father. It was Catherine's Bible." Natalia held Kikki's eyes with challenge. "And her daughter, Margot, well, you have to admit she was out of control. She refused to play the game either politically or personally."

Quietly Kikki said, "You mean the game where men could do what they wanted? Everything justifiable for the good of the political state. And, naturally, no one batted an eye that the men, and especially kings and royalty screwed anyone and everyone and were encouraged to do so! It proved their virility. Kings were entitled to have lovers and bastards who might someday take the throne, but female royalty who did the same were guilty of treason!"

"If you put it that way—" Natalia smiled, enjoying the debate.

"Well that was the way it was," Kikki said quietly. "And Margot had good reason to take lovers—not that she needed to give one. She sought out love to cleanse herself. She was cursed by the many bloody wars in the name of religion that went on for most of her life. She was used, tarnished, banished and hunted by assassins—led by her mother. No wonder they called her the Black Queen. Margot could never get enough love. Margot fought back at a high personal cost. In the end she prevailed. History or her-story should remember her wasted greatness rather than call her a whore." Kikki was very curious to see where this woman stood.

Natalia was silent, apparently studying her wine glass.

At last she said mildly, "Well opinions do vary. So, are you a historian then? Or just a Margot groupie?" Oh, she shouldn't have said that. "I'm just kidding. I can see her point of view. But really, are you a historian, a professor?"

Kikki was relieved at the change in subject, though alarmed at Natalia's evident admiration for Cruel Mother Medici. "Neither. But a bit passionate about that era. And how can one live in Paris and not be fascinated by its history?"

"True enough," Natalia said mildly. "I hope I haven't offended you."

"Of course not. I just think you might study Margot a bit more closely before you side with your business partners or your heritage."

Call it history or antiquities, Natalia had brought up the subject. And her family business focused on the very era in which Margot lived. Coincidence?

They sipped wine at the same time, avoiding eye contact. Simultaneously both smiled and offered a toast to the other.

Natalia broke the silence. "So then. What do you do?"

"I really don't like to talk about what I do, but as we have shared this moment together—I'm a writer and a lawyer, and a bit of a dilettante perhaps, in the true sense of the word."

"Really? How interesting!" Natalia's inner alert went off, and she had a wave of nausea, but she didn't know why.

"Are you all right?" Kikki suddenly felt the beginnings of a headache. She knew it came from Natalia and not the wine. The room seemed to close in on her, the lights dimmed. Very confusing vibes from this woman. Who was she? Why did Margot want Kikki to befriend her?

Kikki took a deep breath. What was going on? Damnit, Margot! Or was it Natalia?

Natalia interrupted Kikki's thoughts, saying, "I'm perfectly fine. Long day. Funny stomach. Probably shouldn't be having wine. Though I so love it!" She laughed. "A party girl in the guise of a businesswoman."

"I can relate to that." Kikki felt Natalia soften and was relieved.

Antoine signaled at the same moment that Kikki, herself, thought it time to leave.

"Still. I have to stay alert. Business tonight," Natalia said as she applied a coat of deep scarlet lipstick that set off her striking red hair. All accenting heavily mascaraed eyes rivaling Margot's. "Alas, I must stop—take a walk to clear my head."

"Me too. I've got to do some work. I've been negligent or distracted—"

"I know what that's like. So much distraction. So many yummy things in Paris. And the men! I met one—" Abruptly Natalia stopped herself.

The two women smiled at each other as if they shared a secret.

"Will you be here long?" Kikki asked, surprising herself. "Perhaps we'll meet again?"

"Yes, I will be here all week. Around the neighborhood."

"Maybe late coffee tomorrow—or a glass of wine?" Why had she said that? The words spilled out of her mouth unbidden. Margot was using her as a vessel to speak to Natalia, she realized with alarm.

"Would love to. You must know all the secrets."

"A few," Kikki said enigmatically. If you only knew, she thought to herself. "Antoine, *encore merci. Bon courage!*"

Kikki had been thinking of Torres, longing to see him before he left. She hoped she could catch him. She was happy and also rattled by Natalia. Torres was home—her safe harbor. And there you have it, Mademoiselle Véronique Trieste, she mused. Some independent woman!

And I shall see you later in another guise, Antoine, Natalia thought. Antoine and Véronique could be very useful, and now she was "in." It had been easy. This woman piqued her curiosity.

But there was someone she was more anxious to see again tonight. She'd make sure Antoine sat them next to each other. The women parted affectionately, kisses on both cheeks, each thinking about the same man.

Jean Michel Beauregard de Torres. *Dite*-Torres.

Chapter 48

Torres was standing in front of the fireplace checking his look in the mirror above the mantle and tying his latest gift from Kikki—an Hermes cravat. It was a soft sea-blue, almost like the Santorini sea, but not that bright. It had a contrasting pattern of powder blue and ruby in some fanciful shapes.

Paris was a somber, if chic, place favoring black and muted colors in the winter. He wanted to look conservative for the dinner. Neutral. The tie was set off nicely by his pale blue-cuffed shirt. This year's collar. His dark navy Armani suit was cut for comfort and style.

But he couldn't manage the cufflinks because of his injuries. He had chosen the hammered gold antique Greek coins that Kikki had gifted him, which bespoke taste and class. Suggesting old money. And also, his lucky charms. Nothing a cop would wear. Enigmatic.

He might have preferred a professor-like cashmere turtleneck but didn't think it fitting for tonight. It would be a turning point, if all worked as he had planned, both for Operation Sphinx and for what he was starting to think of as Operation Inanna.

He glanced at his watch, past 20:30. Where was Kikki? He felt a frisson of fear. But just as he thought it, she burst in the door.

"Hey gorgeous!" She threw her arms around him and caught him with a hot wet kiss. "You look good enough to eat, babe. Time for a little—"

"Regrettably not now, *mi amor.* No time. I was waiting for you to come back." She tasted of wine and her eyes were bright. "I'm glad you had a good time." And that you're home safe and sound, he thought but didn't say.

"I did. Divine wine. They spoiled me!" She winked at him. "Met the most interesting woman."

"Good." He wondered who but kept silent. "Can you help me with these cufflinks, *mi amor?*"

"Of course. How nice you're wearing my gift. I'll feel better about what you might get up to," she said as she fastened one and then the other.

When he had finished, he looked into her eyes. "You're staying in, right?"

"Yes."

He took her in his arms and kissed her, still worried about leaving her alone. He had arranged for a protection detail, but unfortunately, he wouldn't be on it.

"Not to worry." She read his mind and smirked. Protection detail. Ho hum.

He released her and shot her a skeptical look. "You need to rest. Tía should be back before long."

She walked him to the door. "Don't have too much fun yourself. You are not invincible, Torres. Be wise and careful!"

"I'm a cop, remember."

"You never let me forget. Now go and play your cover—the distinguished and very rich archeologist-cum-professor that you look! The women will be falling over you."

"How do you know there will be women there?"

"Oh, come on—" Kikki said. He kissed her hard and then let her go.

The door closed behind him and Kikki stared at it. And then immediately wondered if Natalia was going to his dinner. Could it be possible? That would be quite a coincidence. She found she didn't like the idea at all.

Chapter 49

Victor Fitz-Perkins, Esquire had checked into the Ritz on Paris's famous Place Vendôme under an assumed name. He locked the sacred objects, documents and money in the safe in his usual Suite Imperial on the top fourth floor, personally curated for him. He took a long hot bath in the pristine enormous marble bathtub—a tub fit for a king.

He had meticulously groomed and dressed for the evening. To be as invisible as someone as famous as himself could be. He walked through the elegant reception with the collar of his coat turned up and the brim of his black felt hat tipped over his eyes. He was sure no one at the Ritz, his second home in Paris, had recognized him. Not yet.

He hadn't uttered a word because his deep gravelly voice was very commanding and distinctive. He could silence a stadium with it. He really detested not being fawned over, but it was a necessary sacrifice.

Although it was pitch dark, biting cold and quite foggy, he wore sunglasses—like a rock star who'd been up all night. They were especially designed for him, so he could see as acutely as if it were broad daylight and then some—not quite thermal like soldiers wore, though he owned a pair of those. He thought the sunglasses disguised his otherwise supremely celebrated presence.

Then he'd returned to his waiting black Mercedes sedan. Nondescript, like every other one in Paris—though a stretch limo was more his style. But not tonight. He wanted to blend in.

Tomorrow would be different. He would make an entrance with great fanfare and appropriate entourage. Victor Fitz-Perkins was someone to be reckoned with and to whom homage was owed. It was his divine right.

Tonight, he wanted to be on his own. He'd been looking forward to it all the way across the Atlantic.

As he settled into the compact sedan, Victor reviewed his meticulous plans and looked back over the evening's preparations. As agreed, and handsomely paid for, the concierge who knew him best had arranged to be off duty. He was handling certain important and very private matters for Victor, including personally attending to final construction details on his subterranean private temple. The concierge would be back at his post tomorrow and the rest of the week. Victor would need his services for the next few days—until the mission had been accomplished, as he had no doubt that it would. He was running it wasn't he? The Emperor Napoleon I was a dwarf and incompetent general whose conquests were inconsequential compared to Victor and what he was about to achieve. He chuckled to himself.

It was time to seize the glory that God had willed. His true destiny.

And he had planned and orchestrated with meticulous attention. Victor always kept the important people in his life isolated. That was one of the principal ways he maintained his power over them. He parsed out meager information to each, enough to pique interest, create intrigue and admiration. No one person had the full picture.

No one knew his full agenda, especially not his partner, Frank Becchina Pelligrini.

Frank wasn't expected to arrive until the next day.

In the meantime, Victor had an important rendezvous. He couldn't wait. His reward—and more importantly— his revenge. She would never see it coming.

He replayed his earlier grooming ritual in his mind. As he dressed in his en suite dressing room, he had admired his tall, lanky form. Deceptively thin in appearance, he was all muscle under his perfectly cut Savile Row suit. He favored the British touch. Preening in front of the mirror, he had run a hand through his well-kept silver hair and admired his handsome, powerful figure.

In the three-sided full-length mirror, he had checked his profile from all angles—supremely pleased. For the third time, he swept a lint brush carefully over the shoulders and down the length of his suit jacket. He snarled with displeasure, regretting the lack of a valet.

"Fit to kill—and seduce," Victor had said aloud, stepping close to the center mirror to inspect his impeccably white teeth. They ought to be. He'd paid a fortune to the Central Park dentist. He had run long manicured fingers across his well-sculpted face—the creative work of the best plastic surgeon money could buy. His shave was close and perfect. He hadn't missed a hair. He had a phobia about facial hair.

Holding the crystal bottle in front of him, gaging the correct distance, just before leaving his suite, he had sprayed himself with his personal *eau de cologne.* Just the right amount. Manly.

This was going to be fun.

In the back seat of the sedan, he double-checked the glass divider between himself and the driver to make sure that it was properly sealed. Impatient for it to be time to make his call, he glanced at his gold Patek Phillipe watch. In the meantime, he was at home in the Mercedes parked on Place Vendôme. A spectacular monument to all that Victor revered. His Citadel.

Victor wasn't in the least jetlagged thanks to a special miracle drug. Not to mention luxurious attention and comfort on the flight across the Atlantic on his new Gulf Stream. He had also thoroughly enjoyed the attentions of a young blonde, very leggy and well-endowed masseuse on his plane. An excellent massage and a good ride on her afterwards.

She had gone all the way to Alexandria with him and kept him entertained, aroused and primed for his short business meeting. He'd dropped her there before heading to Paris.

She reminded him of Kikki. He frowned and narrowed his steel gray eyes, wondering if he should have worn the sapphire contact lenses. Fuck her! Thinking of her made his blood boil. He forced himself to hold in his rage, keep it contained in what he saw as his special place, fire energy in reserve for the fight.

He transformed into his super God self and flew to the top of the tall bronze column in the center of Place Vendôme. Shapeshifter. He became the Eagle. He shrieked and spread his massive wings, surveying his city—his kingdom.

And then he returned to the back of the sedan. Victor opened his eyes and felt calm and renewed.

He smiled, content with himself and with who and what he had become. Victor maintained both a high profile and a secret life that had to be kept separate. And Kikki was one of the few people who had actually understood that. Not that she knew everything—far from it.

Right out of Harvard Law, he had established his own Manhattan law firm, one bearing his name only: Fitz-Perkins Law. He had skyrocketed to the top of New York's legal heap, stepping on bigger and better competitors along the way. Kikki had come to work for him as a young associate, inexperienced and ripe for molding to his tastes and needs. About seven years ago now.

She had been the perfect seductress to his high-rolling New York film business, and she was savvy, smart and hot. He had taught her all she knew and given her *entrée* to his clients. And she had shown her gratitude, as was right. She understood the rules. It was easy to lure her to his bed. Young, gorgeous and high-spirited. No ties. Just the way Victor liked his women.

Victor's wife had not been pleased about the beautiful young associate who often shared his bed in his Manhattan apartment, but his wife was a practical woman who hated social engagements. She stayed on their immense estate in Greenwich and traveled a great deal for her interests. And really, Victor and his wife hated each other. It was now a marriage of pure convenience.

Victor had sought his wife out in college. He had targeted and courted her like the skilled predator he had become by then. Because of her connections, her pedigree, and not the least, the vast fortune she inherited. They had married right after graduation,

His wife had served him well. That was one reason he had risen so quickly, hobnobbing with the right people early in his career. Not that his wife deserved credit. He was equal to his reputation and his clients. Handsome, brilliant and charismatic, with Machiavellian skill, he had built his power base amongst the movers and shakers.

Still, she had garnered him New York's Metropolitan Museum of Art as a client through her earlier work as a curator and because of the massive donations that her family had made since the museum's early days.

Unwelcome, his thoughts returned to Kikki. He inspected once more his tanned and manicured hands. She had been perfect for him in so many ways. No messiness of romance. They each had independence, he dominated her and she liked that.

Until the end. He scowled, sheer rage searing through him. Fucking ungrateful cunt! She had him to thank for everything, but she'd run off to Paris because she liked it better. What a ridiculous romantic idea! She tried to appease him with flattery. She wanted to take what he had taught her and run her own similar kind of business from Paris.

He never should have introduced her to his French clients. She had a knack for languages that he didn't. Wasn't the universal language English?

That had been a few years ago—he had blocked out the actual date of her departure. Grudgingly, he had to admit that she had made a moderate success of it so far. It didn't make him proud. The more successful she became, the more infuriated he got.

But he made it a point to hide his displeasure and appear to be generous by sending her the occasional client. A way to keep tabs and a hold on her. He often saw her when he was in Paris. They had ended up on opposite sides of important negotiations a few times and had sparred, though naturally, he always got the best of her.

She always and obviously enjoyed their time in his suite at the Ritz afterwards. Of that he was certain. And why wouldn't she? A finer male specimen than himself did not exist on the planet. She should consider herself lucky.

Until this past spring. She had accepted his company and enjoyed their meeting. They had flirted. She had teased there would be more. But out of the blue, after she had downed half a

211

bottle of a fine Champagne Ruinart Millésimé 2010, the fucking cunt had said no. Turned him down, refused to go up to his suite. Her excuses, by god, were unconvincing and insulting.

She told him it had nothing to do with how she felt about him or her attraction to him, but she had met someone, and it was serious. She wouldn't tell him who the man was.

She actually walked out on him in public in the Ritz Bar, leaving him at a peak of sexual arousal and fury. That vile scenario had repeated on the next few occasions he was in Paris. On the surface, he had been careful to accept her wishes. It was all about the veneer, wasn't it?

But the cunt-whore had not only offended him, she had made the fatal mistake of underestimating him. Now she would pay dearly. No one treated Victor Fitz-Perkins that way. What impudence!

He knew everything there was to know about her cop-cum-archeologist boyfriend and then some. They would both find themselves way out of their league over the next few days, but especially Kikki. The fucking cop thought she was safe because his flimsy intel—intel that Victor had manufactured—placed Victor in Alexandria this very night. He'd paid off the right people, and the stupid asshole cop was none the wiser.

And now, Victor knew that right this minute, she was alone in her apartment. Not for long.

As he sat in the sedan's back seat, idling in front of the Ritz, he pulled down the vanity mirror and stared into eyes of fury. He felt the blood rise. He watched horrified as his otherwise perfect face became marred by scarlet marks. No surgeon had been able to cure that genetic defect. His whore mother's fault.

He closed his eyes and took a deep breath. He willed the marks to fade, reeling in violent thoughts of vengeance by reminding himself of his mission and his purpose.

And then he applied extra make up to cover the hateful splotchy red birthmarks. He was always careful to keep them hidden.

When he looked back in the mirror, his face was once more a refined, expressionless study in masculine power. A polished, slightly aloof demeanor at all times—a mask that hid his true agenda. It was of utmost importance now.

Mask in place, he tested himself. Intentionally, he turned his thoughts from Kikki to the other significant women in his life—his wife and his mother.

He had no father. Victor was a bastard and his mother was a whore. A filthy prostitute. She had abandoned him when he was only five years old—packed up and left without so much as a goodbye to her only child. He had bounced from foster home to foster home in the gritty social services system of Pittsburg.

A major driving force of Victor's life for as long as he could remember—his hatred for women. At the same time, he despised himself for his weakness for them. But he had that under control— the women in his life were there to be used and used up. He peered at his mask again. The veneer had not cracked, despite violent thoughts. He had passed the test. Indeed, he had great control.

His hatred for women fueled his true passion, second only to self-adulation—ensuring global male dominance and power, and the wealth and position that was theirs—and his, by right. And so it was that he targeted and then became Grand Master of one of the world's most ancient and powerful patriarchal societies—the Knights of the Holy Sword of God.

He shook back his silver lion's mane and envisioned himself thrusting the Holy Sword of God coldly into the hearts of his enemies.

Showtime!

Chapter 50

He lowered the divider and commanded. "Drive!"

Victor had intentionally forgone the scheduled call to Natalia, blowing her off. Frank had said she would facilitate things, and that was what Victor expected. Frank had also assured him that they could count on Natalia to do whatever was necessary to carry out their plan. She was firmly on their side. Victor expected no less, but he didn't trust anyone. Especially not a woman.

He'd known Natalia since she was a girl. In fact, he'd known her mother, though even Frank didn't know about that. He knew exactly who and what Natalia was. She would serve them nicely— whether she wanted to or not. Her mission was to seduce Torres and obtain all the information she could on the cops' plans. That's why she had been put on the anti-fraud committee.

Natalia was spoiled and she hated not getting what she wanted. Given her lineage, it was not in the least surprising. But good old Frank had raised her right. She was primed to be used as Victor's pawn. Frank would not be able to object.

But fuck Natalia!

Tonight was about pleasure, he thought, as they snaked through traffic at the brightly lit Place de La Concorde, complete with its Ferris wheel at the far end of the Tuileries Gardens, La Grande Roue de Paris. Lit up now with the colors of the Russian flag alternating with the French tricolor. The wheel was, indeed, turning.

As a young man whose goal was to become the richest person in the world, Victor had shrewdly realized that a lot of money could be made in art and antiques, particularly forged and stolen items on the black market. He had sought out Frank Becchina Pelligrini, who already had a long-established business and partnered with him in Becchina & Fratellos.

On his own turf, as a silent partner in another company, Victor had opened an antique store in the right neighborhood, just off Madison Avenue near 60th Street, not far from his own apartment on Fifth Avenue and 74th Street.

He selected a manager whom he could control to run the shop, someone recommended by Frank as experienced, knowledgeable and worldly. Victor kept iron control over his man through traditional means—blackmail. He covered the man's gambling debts and provided his drugs. And, of course, very tight and constant surveillance by Victor's private security team—a company he owned. The same company that watched Frank. Victor knew every move that Frank made.

Like Frank, Victor had a penchant for French and Italian Renaissance and a great admiration for that redoubtable Queen who had brought Italian Renaissance to France—Catherine de Medici. At any cost, Victor had acquired a very impressive collection of art and artifacts that connected to his heroine.

She was a superior example of a manly woman, first disciple of Machiavelli and supporter of all that brought about power—perfect manual for cruel autocrats. She stood behind her weak, ill and twisted sons and manipulated them to suit her needs to maintain, at all costs, power. At least her sons were men—of a sort.

She waged war against her daughter, the whore Marguerite de Valois, ensuring that she never ascended to the throne of France. The great Catherine chose a Bourbon Protestant to marry her depraved daughter, to carry on the Valois line through a related branch and prince of the blood. King Henry of Navarre became King Henry the Great at a time when France was at the height of its power, a force to be reckoned with. Victor intended to return the flailing country to its rightful place in the world. That bitch-cunt, heretical witch, Margot—she got exactly what she deserved.

Victor was surrounded by faithful soldiers and lieutenants, and victory was theirs for the taking. Among the spoils of war, they would steal the worthless *Minoan Snake Goddess* and pieces of the Louvre's invaluable collection—all highly personal to the whores. Everything that the Daughters of Inanna stood for would be destroyed. Natalia would become his slave. It would be a walk in the park.

Frank was due by tomorrow. They'd meet at the main temple before the other members of the council of the Knights of the Holy Sword of God arrived. The first tranche of the operation must be carried out discreetly.

He reflected on this as the driver circled the neighborhood between Place Vendôme and the Louvre. They had just crossed the Pont du Carrousel which spanned the Seine between the two majestic galleries of the Louvre's southern façade. The driver took a right and drove west along Quai Voltaire, where Kikki lived with her Spanish cop.

Kikki had been making bad choices. It was time to rectify that. He ordered himself to be disciplined, to think of her only as part of their op—what he thought of privately as Operation Lion. The lion would devour his enemies and roar by the end of the week.

Victor and his compatriots of the Knights of the Holy Sword of God would have their Holy Grail—and then some serious housekeeping was in order. Purification and purging—ethnic cleansing on a global scale. Like Catherine had done with the premeditated ethnic genocide of disloyal Huguenot Protestants by rounding them all up in Paris and arranging their slaughter on Saint-Bartholomew's Day. Brilliant strategy!

Like great men had always done: Milosevic, the Butcher of Belgrave; Nero; Julius Cesar; Caligula and Alexander the Great. They eliminated the weak, the old, the sick, and above all, the women.

Alexander the Great was a great role model to Victor. He, too, had hated his mother. And set out to conquer the world to get away from her.

Victor fingered the talisman he always kept with him, an authentic relic, symbolic of his worthy cause—a miniature lion's head from Ancient Thebe. A city Alexander the Great had destroyed to set an example to those who would not subjugate to his authority.

Political, military and economic dominance—the principal of hegemony. That is exactly what Victor intended to achieve this week. It was his time. And like Julius Cesar had done conquering the Galls—and unlike Attila the Hun who had failed—Victor would conquer Paris.

The limo came to a standstill in heavy traffic. "Drive around them you imbecile—idiot! Use the sidewalk!" Victor barked.

They circled the Musée d'Orsay and headed east along rue de Lille. They crossed the rue du Bac and turned left one block from the river onto rue de Beaune, where Kikki lived.

Victor felt his power coursing through his veins. He thought of the coming pleasure and grew quickly engorged. Calm yourself, Victor. But that was hard for him. He was a very impatient man.

He watched Torres walk through the large blue wooden gates of the eighteenth-century building on the corner of rue de Beaune and Quai Voltaire. The gate was adorned with lion's heads as doorknobs.

Ironic, considering Torres's Operation Sphinx, that two stone sphinxes sat under the lions.

Torres stopped and made a phone call. Victor had that covered: a tap into Torres's phones by his security. But if anything got fucked up, he was ready to fire the second security team. Torres had done a better job of backstopping his new identity in Paris than Victor had anticipated. Torres playing a fake French/Spanish count. He didn't believe for a moment that Torres had an ounce of *sang real*. Victor certainly did, making him far superior in all ways.

Victor knew that Torres was on his way to the dinner with the beautiful and very sexy Natalia. Victor himself would like to have her, but she was strictly reserved for Torres in this battle. One of the jobs Victor knew Natalia would enjoy better than others to which she hadn't yet been made privy.

Victor's private and very personal agenda was vengeance. First, destroy Kikki's relationship with Torres. He would make a good start tonight. She wouldn't be able to resist seeing him. Baiting the mouse in the trap, using her to his content. She would never know what hit her. And then, he would neutralize her. She was a loose end and he was feeling particularly vindictive.

Who in the fuck did she think she was? She was about to find out. Soon, he would have the pleasure of killing her. He hadn't decided when he would take his ultimate revenge. But not yet, not before he had punished her while she was alive. It was deeply personal for Victor.

He smoothed his perfectly arranged hair to calm himself. Tonight would be different—a charade for old time's sake. He knew just how to play her. Now Torres was gone, and she was alone and vulnerable.

Kikki, you have gone too far, he thought. Your flanks are exposed. And you no longer have that decrepit Spanish witch. The Daughters of Inanna are about to go up in flames like all other Goddess worshipping witches and sorcerers who refused to worship the One True God. They were weak and pathetic women and men who failed to understand the danger of women in power.

Victor dialed Kikki's number. She picked up on the first ring, as he had known she would with Torres gone. He smiled and thought —into the lion's lair, Véronique! On this very dark night, I am coming for you.

Chapter 51

Kikki was thinking about Torres when Victor called. She noticed the blocked call and answered, thinking it was her lover.

"Miss me already, babe?" she said seductively.

"Good evening!" Victor said in his distinctive gravelly voice, "It's been a long time, Kikki, too long. I've missed you too."

Abruptly, Kikki sat down. "Victor?" Her former New York boss. A very powerful man to whose charms she had succumbed, much to her shame and deep regret.

"You were expecting someone else?" He grinned with self-satisfaction. Got her!

"I'm—uh—surprised to hear from you." Her heart pounded, and anxiety closed her throat. "Are you in Paris?"

"Indeed I am, as are you. Fancy that."

What did he want? Why was he here? Now of all times.

A flood of thoughts about Victor raced through her mind. He had been dangerous, married, and that attracted her. They had chemistry. And Kikki enjoyed sex. She had been a very young and ambitious lawyer. But she was a woman in a man's world. She hadn't been part of the very closed New York club of power brokers. And Victor had opened doors for her, given her a place—

an opportunity. At the time, she hadn't thought it a big deal. In retrospect, very naïve.

And now Victor was here in Paris during this critical week. Coincidence? Not likely.

He had to be part of this whole conspiracy. Either way, he would know everything about it, given his hunger for power, background and *modus operandi.*

Her mind raced. He was most certainly one of the Swords. And he could well be their leader—the face of her unknown enemy.

She and Monique had to hone their strategy with the film client, and Victor could help. In fact, thinking about it now, he was probably backing the film. They knew the client they were to meet was essentially a front man.

He made it a point to know each important person's secrets. Could she get any information from him? Risky, but gutsy. That suited her.

"Are you still there, Kikki?" Victor coaxed.

"Yes. Sorry. I—my mind was elsewhere." She felt the rawness of her throat. Her temples throbbed. She ignored this and assuming her power, spoke confidently. "You're staying at the Ritz?"

"Where else? Let's have a drink!"

"Hmm. I don't know." Keep him wondering.

"Kikki. You need to relax. Stay in touch with old friends. It's good for business." He laughed. "A glass or two of champagne in the Ritz Bar. Life is too damn short."

She did feel stronger and clearer, in her own power ready for battle, especially after her talk with Tía—not to mention Margot.

"Uh—A lot of work to do and a late date already." She pretended to hesitate.

"What have you got to lose?" he asked.

Everything maybe, she thought. But Torres wasn't talking. This fit with her agenda.

She thought about her conversation with Tía, about the Goddess in all her faces—Inanna, Isis, Athena, Hecate. She knew that in these last hours she had crossed the threshold.

She could kill a couple of proverbial birds with one stone. Personal redemption for falling prey to Victor long ago, and she could sharpen her battle skills on Victor—take him by surprise.

And he was in her city. A woman's city where she had the advantage.

A vision of the Snake Goddess with her snakes danced in front of her. Snakes hissing. Retribution.

"So, are you in?" he said.

"Sure. I'm in. When?"

"Now. I happen to be in the neighborhood. I can pick you up."

"Fifteen minutes, Victor, at the restaurant on the corner of rue du Bac-La Frégate. Can't miss it. See you in a few—" She disconnected the call.

Minutes later, Kikki stood in front of the gilded framed mirror in her dressing room and applied another coat of crimson lipstick. She ran perfumed and freshly varnished fingertips through her blonde hair. Heightened color emphasized her cheekbones—or her fear.

Her neighborhood, not the Ritz where his suite was dangerously at hand. La Frégate was a popular corner café—on the Quai Voltaire at the intersection of rue du Bac, just across from the Pont Royal. It was a bit on the faded elegance side, but she liked that about it.

She was known, but not like the Voltaire where she was family. And she didn't want it to get back to Torres. Given the gossipy nature of the *quartier*, she thought she should be prudent. Plus, she knew Torres would have someone watching her.

That wouldn't be a problem, she mused, making a final inspection in the mirror—satisfied that she would be irresistible to Victor. Enough so he would let his guard down and share secrets, she hoped.

Torres didn't know a thing about her relationship with Victor, she realized. He only had a vague idea that she had worked for someone in New York. *Merde!* She had completely blocked it out. He had a thing about her keeping former lovers secret from him. As far as she was concerned, it was the past. He had one too.

Men—weren't they really all alike—possessive when it came down to it. She pulled on her over-the-knee black suede boots, wrapped herself in a black hooded cape and headed out of the apartment.

She still felt a bit nervous—or was that just a guise for her excitement? Battle armor, Athena, she said aloud as she closed the door and headed for the elevator. One careful and strategic step at a time.

Chapter 52

Jean Marc was staked out not far from the gate to Kikki's building. He was disguised as a sushi delivery boy on a motorcycle parked behind a large van on the far side of rue de Beaune, not far from the corner, just cross from the Voltaire.

He had caught Victor's black Mercedes sedan when it first passed by, even though they all looked alike, these elite cars with their distinguished passengers. When it circled back, he noted the license plate. He was on the phone running the plate when Kikki came out.

Kikki peered out the gate, saw Jean Marc and willed him to turn his head away. He did. She slipped out the gate and turned left. Jean Marc didn't see the black-caped figure hurry along rue de Beaune towards rue de Lille behind him.

She zigzagged between two oncoming cars, head down, throwing up a shield of protection that kept her safe and invisible. She hugged the right side of the buildings on rue de Lille, parallel to the Seine, heading west.

Halfway to rue du Bac and La Frégate, Tía appeared. She was walking quickly towards Kikki, arm in arm with Gabrielle Laroche.

"Tía!" Kikki stopped to greet them. Grateful to see Tía on the way to her dangerous mission. As she walked, she had asked the Goddess for a sign, and here it was. And very affirming. She knew intuitively that they were well cloaked, protected from their enemies.

"*Bonsoir*, Verónica. I see you've decided to go out," Tía said, exchanging a knowing look with Gabrielle. "You see, Gabrielle, I told you."

The two women walked arm and arm. Like many French women, Gabrielle was hatless, stray strands of her signature *coiff*—a chin length bob of shiny black hair—blew in the wind, catching streetlights, forming a halo. Tall and stately, almost a foot more than *petite* Tía, she swayed slightly like a tall tree. She was bundled in an elegant jacket over black slacks and matching black and silver patent leather sport shoes. Her dark eyes caught Kikki's, smiling warmly. Despite her aristocratic origins, Gabrielle Laroche was no snob.

"I'm glad to see you both. Torres wanted me to stay home, of course, but I had an unexpected opportunity that could help us. I think I am wisely guided, but if you have any—"

"Tell us."

The three women stood in the shadows on the dark side of rue de Lille away from a nearby restaurant, the Bistro de Paris and its bright lights. Kikki laid it out for them.

"I see," Tía said. "We have just come from an important meeting of the Daughters Council and made much progress. The timing of this man's call is no coincidence. Meeting with him will help us. Time presses."

"That's exactly what I thought," Kikki whispered. "Torres—"

"Never mind him," Tía said. "He has his work to do, and we have ours."

"And if it's a trap? Because I am certain this man is one of the Swords—maybe their leader."

"Follow your intuition. It is your journey and only you can know. We support you and will help you as we can. You have to follow your heart. Do not be afraid to engage with the dark side. It is part of the path. You are protected. Danger is everywhere, Verónica. But we cannot become paralyzed by fear."

"What if I'm wrong?"

"We all make what we think are mistakes. But there are no mistakes, Verónica. And we must take the risks for the sake of Mother Earth."

"*Elle a raison*, Kikki," Gabrielle affirmed Tía's choice. "*T'inquiet pas.*" Don't worry.

The women embraced, and Kikki continued alone, steps more certain.

She turned onto rue du Bac and hurried north towards the Quai, feeling confident and in charge. She made a quiet entrance to La Frégate through the side door on rue du Bac and looked for her favorite table in the bar area, facing a window with a spectacular view and very private. She willed it to be empty.

But he was already there, sitting smugly at her table. She was instantly on high alert. Her heart skipped a beat taking in the familiar line of his strong swimmer's back and silver hair. She could smell, even amongst all the odors of the restaurant's bar, his distinct, personal cologne.

Merde! A quiver of danger tingled her spine. Victor was an immutable force. Could she really handle him?

At the same moment that Kikki reached to touch her rose crystal necklace for protection, Victor turned and shot her an inviting smile.

Without the least hesitation, she crossed the short distance to the table.

"My god, Kikki! It's been too long." He stood and extended an arm, beckoning her. "You look ravishing as ever. Paris agrees with you, kid."

She stopped short of the tiny round café table and loosened her cape. Taking him in, an unexpected rage surged inside her—one she had blocked for a long time. It felt old and urgent.

Steady, she told herself. This is your city and he is a guest. She pushed the rage back down and greeted him, keeping the edge out of her voice. "You don't look half bad yourself, old man."

He reached to take her hand and lift it to his mouth. When his lips brushed her hand, she felt heat. As though he had burned her.

He pulled out the café chair for her, "Sit, my dear. I've ordered a bottle of their best bubbly, Ruinart, of course, and two dozen of your favorite oysters—*Fine de Claire No. 4.*"

She took a deep breath and sat down. "Perfect! You always did know my mind. I'm famished."

"I'm surprised at your choice of venue, Véronique." He frowned. "It's a bit dowdy for you. Are you sure you wouldn't rather —"

"No. The view is magnificent. Take a look across the Pont Royal."

"Can't take my eyes from you. I'm—I'm—"

"At a loss for words?" she laughed. "Hard to believe. So what business brings you to Paris?"

"Let's not talk about it. Too boring."

"Your business is never boring, Victor." She smiled. "I must say you do look dashing. Have you been pampering yourself somewhere?" Flattery usually worked.

"Thank you. I did have a certain 'cure' and I feel ten years younger."

"So are you here on business for the Met?" And then, the obvious occurred to her. "I thought, perhaps, you were invited to the gala event at the Louvre this week?"

She watched his left eye flicker. One of his tells. He was about to lie to her.

"No."

"An exhibition of a *Minoan Snake Goddess*. I helped organize it." Surely, he knew. So why lie about it?

"That's excellent. Good for you." He couldn't give her the satisfaction. Her tiny fucking Minoan Goddess. He couldn't wait to smash it. "Oh, of course. Sorry. Must be jet lag. I hope to go."

"Glad to hear it." She glanced out at the lights of the Pavillon de Flore across the Seine and had a flash of insight. "Are you meeting with someone from the Louvre—the Directeur Général or the Président himself? I wouldn't be the least bit surprised. Do you have something for his collection? Private—or?"

His eyes lit up and he laid his hand on top of hers. "You always could smell a deal in the making, Kikki. I taught you well."

"Indeed." She allowed his hand to cover hers on the zinc table despite the scorching sensation—and flashes of women burning flew through her third eye. Careful, Kikki. Go slowly. She lifted her hand.

"So give, Victor? You know you can trust me."

He certainly couldn't trust her, but he could dangle the bitch, he thought. "Okay. Yes, meeting with the Louvre. Business for the Met. And may need their help with a new film project. And I have a deal to close with my partner. He's flying in from Italy."

An Italian antique dealer and a meeting with the Louvre about a film—her intuition had been right. He was backing her client's film. And part of the Italian antiques racket. It all fit Torres's op perfectly. Victor was definitely a highly placed Sword. She was scared but exhilarated.

"Sounds very important. But I expect no less," she said mildly. He had thrown out a few clues, intentionally mixed up. She needed more concrete information. "Lawyer business or antiques?" Kikki asked lightly. She held his gray eyes, willing him to reveal more.

"Uh," Victor felt his face begin to flush, and he worried that his marks might begin to show through his makeup. He was seething inside and overtaken by an obsessive need for her. How did she manage to so quickly get her claws into him? She would pay. He did his best to keep defiance and anger out of his voice and spoke briskly. "The latter. Less interested these days in the law."

"I get that."

"My partner has some invaluable pieces. Met and Louvre. You know. Should be an interesting week." His voice was staccato, a tactic he used to tilt the table in negotiations, to threaten even.

She watched him squirm in his chair, uncomfortable with what he had said. Usually that meant he had given away more than he wanted. Good, her plan was working.

"Tell me about it, Victor?"

But he deflected. He raised a hand to beckon and growled loudly. "Where is the damn waiter with the champagne?" He was going to dangle the cunt and watch her try to win her pathetic play of gleaning his endgame.

"Ah, Victor, you never were patient. I wonder you can do business at all with the French." She laughed.

He scooted his chair closer to her, affecting to be relaxed, she thought, just as the waiter arrived with the champagne.

They were quiet as the waiter opened the bottle with a flourish and filled their flutes. She felt Victor's thigh against hers. All male energy. Holy Mother Goddess! It was still there, that chemistry. And it was primal. She inched away.

He raised his glass. "To us!" They clinked glasses.

She took a large gulp of champagne. "Indeed." She caught his eyes and saw a glimmer of lust. Holy shit! She suddenly got a strong hit that they were on completely different planes of reality. Of and from, two separate worlds with no bridge between them. How would she get to him?

And then that look vanished. His face became a mask. She couldn't read him at all. She reminded herself that she was in control of her fate and that the Goddess had her back. Stay in your power, she told herself.

She toasted him, "Well, here's to your deals closing and to you. Thank you for all that you taught me." She felt her throat close up on her lies and hoped that her strategy was working to elicit information because she was in extremely dangerous territory.

She took another large swallow of champagne and set the flute on the zinc café table with a loud clunk.

"Are you all right? You look a bit pale." He leaned in closer to catch her eyes.

"I'm fine. Just tired and hungry." She strained to focus. Something was going on with him. His moods were shifting quickly. Why? She couldn't get it. Dark forces blocking? The Black Queen again? She spoke as evenly as she could, though she was trembling inside. Her mind was making a fuzzy connection which she couldn't grasp—like gossamer. "So, your partner is an Italian antique dealer?"

"Hmm." He studied her. "Yeah—"

"And you're meeting with the Louvre."

"I already told you that, Véronique. Are you losing you edge?" His voice was gruff. Fucking bitch! She thought she could pump him for info.

"Of course not. I learned from the best, Victor," she parried. Careful, she told herself. "I'm curious. You know me. I like details. You don't have to get pissed off. Men are so touchy."

"Just teasing. Don't get uppity! Have some more champagne. I think you need it." He smiled cheerfully and poured more champagne. Anger abruptly gone.

What the hell? What were the Swords plotting? Who was the Italian antiques dealer? Was Natalia involved? All of these questions swirled in confusion.

Suddenly, the champagne went straight to her head, exploding in her brain—mind spinning.

"You do look a bit tired, poor dear. Working too hard. Or playing even harder?" His voice sounded far away, but angry with an edge of familiar jealousy.

She felt dizzy. She looked away from him and focused on the softly lit beauty of the Pavillon de Flore, trying to get it to stop moving. She needed food.

"Are you sure you're okay?" he leaned closer into her, lust back in his eyes. "Let me get the waiter. *Garçon!*"

She blinked and saw stars. She tried to stand but couldn't. Realization hit too late. His endgame was seduction and revenge. He hated women. And she had walked into his trap.

He was darkness itself, possessed by evil. And he must be the leader of the Swords.

Silently, she begged, "*Margot! Help me!*"

In answer, she heard a woman's voice speaking French with a harsh Italian accent. *"Die! Heretic! Whore! I curse you in the name of the One True Catholic God!"*

Kikki blinked and looked at Victor. In his place, she saw the apparition of Catherine de Medici in her *de rigueur* black veil and gown.

Kikki tried to scream, but her mouth barely opened, and she heard no sound.

And then, Victor was speaking very quietly in her ear, his voice as if underwater.

She rose compliant as he bundled her into her cloak, covered her head and whisked her out the door and into his waiting limo. She was too weak to resist.

In the back of the sedan, she felt hot salty tears roll down her cheeks and a sharp pain of fear as her heartbeat slowed. She fell unconscious, her head resting on Victor's shoulder.

Chapter 53

Torres and Natalia sipped champagne in the Voltaire, settled into a table near the window in the second dining room. When he had arrived, some twenty minutes ago, she was already seated on the rose velour banquet whispering conspiratorially with Antoine.

Torres was shown to the table by Thierry, one of the long-time waiters. He took his coat and smiled, raising his well-shaped eyebrows as he checked out Torres's suit. And, Torres thought, possibly his ass. Though Torres was more concerned about the women in his own life than Thierry's attentions.

He ushered Torres to the table, and just as they arrived, Natalia threw her head back in laughter. Torres felt the heat rise as he watched her, unseen. He signaled to Thierry to wait in the small corridor between the two cozy dining rooms. Thierry nodded solemnly and stopped in concert with Torres. Thierry's lips were pursed, as if he wanted to say something, but he understood the need for discretion.

Torres stood back, wanting to study Natalia and check his phone for messages. He had a gut feeling that the evening was not going as planned. No messages from Kikki. He hit speed dial. No answer. Torres hoped she had fallen asleep.

A tall handsome waiter approached Thierry and said quietly, "*Alors?*"

Thierry turned his head slightly, showing disapproval. "*Attends,* Pascal."

Torres looked up and caught Pascal's eye. He smiled broadly at Torres, and the next moment his smile disappeared, replaced by the professional Parisian waiter's stern frown.

"He's calling Kikki, Pascal," Thierry whispered. "We have to help protect her. And not from him—he's the best man she's been with in a long time."

Pascal joked, "The woman waiting for him *est canon* and dressed to kill. Looks like she wants to eat Torres alive."

"We'll see about that—" In a choreographed move, Thierry accompanied Torres the short distance to the table.

"Jean Michel Beauregard de Torres," he announced quietly to Antoine. "Monsieur Le Comte."

Torres and Natalia locked eyes. She wore a sheer silk dress that showed off her *décolleté*.

She oozed sensuality and sex—and he responded. It was what he had to do, he told himself. Want was written all over Natalia. *Menos mal.* It would make his work easier. She might be a distant relation, but what did it matter in this century?

He enjoyed the warm feeling of pure lust for a moment and then took her proffered slender hand and brushed his lips across it. Discreetly, he admired her breasts and erect nipples.

Thierry cleared his throat and interrupted him. Antoine held out his chair.

He took a seat across from her and said, "*Bonsoir.*"

"Where are the others?" she asked coyly.

Torres had taken the precaution of making sure no one joined them. His secretary had contacted the other committee members." "Unfortunately, they had to cancel at the last minute. It will just be the two of us."

"Well, that's good." She winked and then flipped her long red hair aside. "Don't you think?" She reached casually across the table and placed her beautifully manicured hand on his.

Their connection was electric—just as it had been at the Hotel de Ville. He pressed her fingers and felt his blood rise.

Thierry, who was still hovering, disapproval apparent from raised eyebrows, backed away when Antoine returned with a *coupe de champagne* for Torres.

Chapter 54

Three hours later, Torres palmed Thierry a large tip and followed Natalia out the revolving door of the Voltaire. A bitter cold wind whipped his scarf across his face—like a dark shadow. Natalia huddled in the corner of the terrace, flush against the wood-paned terrace panel. Torres crossed to the opposite side of the terrace, out of hearing.

He tucked the scarf into his coat and gestured that he'd be a minute. And then he slipped his phone out of his pocket.

"Checking up on your girlfriend?" Natalia smirked.

Torres couldn't hear what she said, though he had a good idea. She had been very insistent in the restaurant as they finished their intimate meal with a very old Armagnac. Pressing him—seducing was more like it—to act on their mutual attraction.

Still no answer from Kikki. Straight to voice mail. And no text either.

He did have one from Jean Marc that said all was well. Something reassuring—maybe. He didn't like it. He wanted to touch in with JM, but he was occupied with Natalia. She had to be his priority at the moment.

Torres turned it over quickly in his mind and decided he had to trust JM to do what he was supposed to do. Time to reel in Natalia.

He crossed the short distance and found her lips. Truthfully, he'd been wanting to kiss her for the last hours as they both pretended to enjoy the superb meal. He drew her into his arms, and they both surrendered to the attraction. Tongues meeting, mouths eager to possess.

There was a sexy urgency in her kiss and a need in his that was real. *Joder*, how had he gotten himself into this? It was supposed to be an act. But it wasn't. The man in his primal state knew.

When they at last broke their embrace, Natalia pointedly sucked on a slender forefinger and said, "If your girlfriend isn't at home, let's go to your place. You live upstairs, right?"

He didn't answer. Instead, he kissed her again and allowed his hands to roam over her breasts. She arched her back and moved in close.

"Come on, Torres. It's bloody freezing out here. People are watching—your waiter friend Thierry is making a meal—or a movie —of us. I hope your tip was big enough to keep him from talking."

"Assuredly, Natalia. Your nipples are hard and inviting—" He circled one with his index finger, raising the stakes. "Don't worry— he can't see. My back is blocking his view."

She opened her coat and stepped back, as if to wrap it more tightly around herself, and threatened to expose him dipping into her breasts. Over Torres's shoulder, she winked at Thierry, whose eyes were glued to them, brows now uberarched. Having fun, she stepped slightly to one side, giving him an angle to see more.

"You are very naughty." Torres tweaked her nipple hard, and then with both arms spun Natalia further into the corner, affecting to keep her warm.

She laughed. He held her gaze, drawing her to him. Her pupils were dilated, and her eyes were all sex. He kissed her again with meaning. She moaned with pleasure.

"You are as hot for me as I am for you. It's just sex. Who cares about your girlfriend? I can't believe a man like you would give it a second thought. Why fight it?"

His lips curved up slightly in the dim light. "Is that a challenge?"

"I told you what you wanted to know about my uncle over

dinner. And I'll tell you even more. He's moving large pieces tonight and meeting his partner from New York tomorrow here in Paris. They have something even bigger brewing. They haven't told me all. But they will."

His fingers danced between her legs, rising higher. "You seem very confident. Why turn against your uncle?"

She had been careful over dinner. A lot of general information and nothing he didn't already know. Confirmation of intel she knew he already had about Frank and Victor Fitz-Perkins and their successful business in forgeries and stolen artifacts. Nothing very specific. She was making him work for it.

"I'm not sure I want to play in their sandbox. I may rather play in yours." She shot him a rueful smile that made her hazel eyes sparkle brighter.

"Seems as though you already are." He locked eyes with her and withdrew his hand from her thighs. Focus, Torres. Let her talk herself into this one. Clean. Almost there.

"Well, Uncle Franco has a soft spot for me. And even if he does find out—" She stood tiptoe on five-inch stiletto boots and pressed hard against his pelvis.

Torres didn't move away. His heart and mind screamed "Kikki!" but the chemistry with Natalia was undeniable.

"He will be very unhappy. And it may be dangerous for you."

"You can protect me. I know that you're a professor at the Louvre and a diplomat, *attaché* from the Ministry of Culture, blah blah blah—as far as your committee is concerned, but seriously— you must think I'm stupid."

Her sudden flat tone startled him. How long had she been onto him? *Joder!* She was a fine seductress and very smart. She'd be a terrific asset. If he could turn her.

"I may be able to help you. That's what you want—besides me in your bed—isn't it, Monsieur le Commissaire?" She said, slipping her hand to his thighs, and in-between.

He remained completely still. *Sang froid*, Torres.

"Depending—of course. Nothing is free. At least not in our world." She stepped away.

He waited, using the cold night.

"Gotcha!" she laughed, breaking the moment.

235

He smiled slowly and waited until she came back to him. And when she did, he kissed her hard. He hated being toyed with, but she was right. She had him. For now. Or his plan to reel her in as an asset had succeeded—so far. She was a good match for him. Trust was another issue. It would be a lot harder to get, and there was never a guarantee. And at what cost?

She would have to choose to betray family. Not to mention the treacherous Fitz-Perkins. Torres knew she was their plant—he'd known from the start. Tricky.

His wound began to throb. Drawing away from her, he signaled to a taxi.

"Finally! My hotel? For godsake! I thought you would freeze me to death."

He slipped into the back seat of the taxi next to her, acutely aware of two things: His erection. And a clear desire that Natalia were Kikki.

But in the meantime, and until Kikki said yes to the whole package, he was a free man. This was his job, his mission and life's work. And Natalia had just jumped ranks, he hoped. But he'd be wise to keep her close tonight—what was left of it.

Wednesday had arrived while they were finishing their Armagnac. They were approaching what Kikki would call the witching hour.

"*Vous allez où?*" the woman taxi driver asked.

"Place Vendôme—le Ritz, *s'il vous plait.*" Natalia ordered. "*Et vite!*"

Chapter 55

In the backseat of the taxi, Torres and Natalia took up where they had left off. Arms and legs flew on the leather bench seat. They slid together when the driver made a sharp right onto Pont Royal. The dividing window between the driver and passenger seat muffled some, but not all of the sounds. Insistent thumping against the doors and leather seat jostled the interior of the sedan.

The driver squinted at the two in the rearview mirror and pulled her cap down over her ears. Of two minds, she sped down through the tunnel under the Tuileries. She was curious to know how far they would go. And she also wanted to stop them at all costs.

Her libertine spirit kept her from interfering directly. As they came out of the tunnel alongside the Tuileries and rounded the corner onto rue de Rivoli, their tempo increased.

"Come on, Torres, don't tease," Natalia said in a breathless whisper. I want you."

"Foreplay, Natalia."

She moaned loudly. He covered her mouth.

"Shh."

"Why? Worried about the old woman driving us?"

"No."

"Good. We'll never see her again."

Torres kissed her to quiet her. Clothes were askew. But he waited. Thoughts of Kikki filled his mind. And abruptly, the car screeched to a hard stop, throwing them apart.

"Place Vendôme, le Ritz," the driver said loudly in a deep voice.

"*Joder!* Great timing," he said.

"No shit!" Natalia agreed. "We can take this upstairs. Hold that —" She grinned.

The two quickly arranged their clothes, pulling coats close around them.

"Take your time." Torres said, getting out on the passenger side. "Stay right there while I pay, and then I'll come around for you."

As he stepped out onto the cobblestoned street and into the icy cold, now windy, night, he felt the heat of Natalia mixed with his own. He was feverish, too, because his wound had opened while they had been going at it.

He stopped to light a cigarette to regroup. He took a drag and exhaled, watching the smoke curl up into the darkness. Just then, the driver lowered the front window near him and hissed, "Psst!"

He hurried to her, knowing in his gut that something had gone horribly wrong.

She lowered the window, eyes wide with fear.

"Tía! I didn't know it was you! What's going on? Is Kikki okay?"

"No! And I hope you've had your fill, *sobrino,* because that is the last you are going to see of Natalia Becchina. Carnally speaking, at least."

"*Dime! Que pasa?* Where is Kikki?"

"Victor drugged and kidnapped her from what we've been able to find out."

"Oh my god!" He threw the cigarette on the ground and stepped on it with violence. "*Coño!*" His heart dropped to his stomach. His instinct had been right. He should have left Natalia much earlier. "But JM texted—said she was fine."

"JM was knocked unconscious, and they stole his phone," Tía growled. "If you got a text, it wasn't from him. *Véte!*"

"Where?"

"Upstairs," Tía waved an arm. "The Ritz, Suite Imperial on the fourth floor. *Apúrete!* I pray that she's there and still alive."

Torres spun on one heel and took off at a run, checking for his weapon as he went. Miraculously, it was still holstered against his ribs under his shoulder. Natalia had said nothing about it. But at that moment, Natalia was far from his mind.

Tía had been watching Natalia in the mirror. When Torres ran, she tried to get out of the car. Central locking kept her safely inside. Tía stepped on the gas, rounding Place Vendôme.

"What the hell?" Natalia said angrily, pushing against the door. "You have no right."

Tía lowered the dividing window. "You're not going to the Ritz, Natalia, my dear."

"What the fucking hell is going on, and who the fuck are you?" European manners gone, her voice was pure New York.

Tía chuckled. This one was born for the role she was about to play. Tía was almost looking forward to it—if the stakes weren't so high.

"Inanna welcomes you," she whispered, fingering the eight-pointed ruby and gold pendant around her neck.

Chapter 56

Inside the Ritz in Victor's suite, Kikki stirred restlessly, half in a dream world and half trance. Her heart beat rapidly, and she was feverish and clammy. Slowly, she turned her head to the left and took a deep breath. Near consciousness and terrified.

Holy Goddess! How long had she been out? She slit her eyes open and peered around.

Though the room was dark, she saw that she was in a bedroom not her own. Walls hung with tapestries of royal sixteenth-century hunting parties and gloomy oil paintings by masters. She felt their archaic, haunting energy. The bed was ornate carved wood, a replica of those in Versailles. Memories flooded through her third eye—beds and bedrooms she had known in past lives in the sixteenth and seventeenth centuries—in the Louvre Palace, Versailles, and nearby in the chateâux of the Loire. Château d'Amboise, where Margot had spent many years of her youth.

She became aware that she lay under sheets of soft white Egyptian cotton. Though her eyes were still adjusting to the darkness, she inspected the duvet that covered her. Vermillion embroidered silk satin. Like being covered in blood. Her stomach churned.

Her lungs were congested and pulse erratic. Her parched mouth tasted bitter. Fully awake, eyes wide open, she took stock. She wore only a filmy black lacy negligée. It felt old and evil. She ran a finger across the garment and her finger burned. The negligée felt familiar. As though she had worn it before.

She ran her tongue across swollen lips. They were bruised and hurt. They tasted of her own blood. She gasped and then shut her mouth quickly, flashing on what had happened to her. Events replayed—a sickening, helpless feeling of being kissed by Victor while she was unconscious—effectively paralyzed. Some kind of drug flowing in her system. Bile rose, and she choked it back down.

With a rush, the whole terrifying episode flooded her being. She was in Victor's suite at the Ritz. She ran her tongue around her mouth. That bitter taste and her fuzzy memory. He had drugged her champagne and taken her from La Frégate. She had only realized who he really was and what he'd done to her when it was too late.

Victor was the enemy—the Devil, the head of the Swords. The evil and darkness they sought to vanquish. And she had walked willingly into his trap. She'd had a plan to pry information from him about the Swords. An unexpected and dangerous opportunity that she couldn't pass up. But she had been unable to protect herself from the demonic rage behind his cool façade.

Had she been able to get anything from him? She couldn't focus. Jumbled thoughts and images of hours spent unconscious at his mercy flashed through her mind.

She had not considered his true motive in seeking her out. He wanted personal revenge from her for betraying him—for leaving him and moving to Paris. The negligée in which he had dressed her had once been hers—a gift from him. He had kept it all this time. An obsessed, maniacal man—a monster capable of anything.

Tears of shame and fear welled up. What exactly had he done to her? Had he raped her? Had he done more than kiss her? She checked her body and felt tenderness in her breasts from where he had touched her. Her loins throbbed from his hands. Had he penetrated her womanly temple? She was afraid to feel, afraid to check her body, hideously violated.

She steeled herself and scanned her body energetically. She

picked up no foreign unwanted energy or sensation in her sex. He hadn't raped her. Thank the Goddess.

But where was he now? Was he here in the bedroom or suite? Her instinct told her no. He hadn't tied her up. Her limbs were free. Something had drawn him away—but she knew he would come back for her. That had only been Act One.

But she knew she was not alone. She sensed the enemy. A dense evil male presence. A guard—one of the Swords' soldiers. She had to escape.

And where was Torres? Involuntarily, her mouth opened to cry out for her lover.

She caught a whiff of perfume and heard Margot's distinct voice. *"Silence. Do not move and do not speak. You are in great danger."*

A large well-muscled man wearing a hotel uniform sat in a wing-backed chair a few feet from the bed—keeping vigil. Though the room was dark, he had excellent night vision and was adjusted to his surroundings. He heard the woman stir. And that brought him fully alert.

He had instructions. And he was heavily armed.

Though he had encouraged the great man to tie her securely to the bed, Victor had refused.

"It will go easier if she thinks she can escape. It will mislead her and add to her punishment and increase her fear. We are not finished. The game has only begun. I will return soon to finish it."

He—as Victor's personal bodyguard—had bowed and acquiesced. But now, Victor was not here. The man would take necessary measures—with pleasure. She could not be allowed to leave, though he was certain she would want to.

It was just after 03:30 hours on Wednesday morning. Victor would not be back until 0:600 hours, he had told the guard. He was completely out of reach, off the grid, underground.

The guard held tightly to his weapon, a 9 mm Luger fit with a silencer. He stood, and in seconds, reached the bed.

Kikki stared. She caught the familiar putrid stench. Dank evil permeated the room. The luxurious Aubusson carpet turned into a black pool. And then, a hulking man appeared. She dived across the immense bed to the opposite side.

"Stop, whore!" he yelled, cursing.

Before she could swing her legs off the side of the bed, he was almost on top of her. She felt his sour breath on her skin. Looming over her, he grabbed her roughly by the shoulders and dragged her back across the bed.

She caught a flicker of silver from the steel barrel of a gun. She watched, stunned, as he raised an immense hand and pointed the gun at her, an inch from her temple. She fought the fear and made a bold move. She moved inches away and sat back on her haunches, pulling the duvet with her. She wrapped it around her body to cover herself. The man followed her movement, gun still at her temple.

She took a deep breath and summoned strength and clarity. She found her voice and her anger. A great wrath at the depth of Victor's betrayal, at him and the Swords and those of his kind who defiled women and the Goddess.

"Stop! Who are you and where is Victor?" She demanded in a voice that came from the depths.

He switched on the lamp on the bed stand.

She held his gaze, unblinking.

He snarled and shifted the gun closer so that the barrel touched her temple.

"Answer me." Her voice was ice.

He leered salaciously. "Victor isn't here." He moved closer, towering above her. "Only me."

Her mind raced, and her third eye filled with pictures of her bloody death. How could she escape? Victor's guard dog was mad and dangerous—but not as powerful as Victor. And not a match for an angry Goddess. No equal to Her rightful wrath.

She channeled Athena and Inanna, speaking with authority. "I trust Victor does not want you to harm me. He and I are not finished. I promise I will not leave if you lower your weapon."

"I don't believe you. You are a heathen slut."

He spoke English, though it wasn't native. Not French either. He might be Serb. A people familiar with violence. She thought of the Butcher of Belgrade—Milosevic, one of Victor's heroes.

She calculated quickly. She was thoroughly exposed but for the duvet, "Get me a robe," she demanded imperiously.

He shot her a repulsive look. "All women are sluts. You are unclean, carriers of original sin. The downfall of man. Only Men of God hold rightful power. And I am not stupid."

"Listen, asshole. I am certain that Victor would not want you to treat me this way."

"Victor is not here. And he will never know."

"Are you sure?" she challenged. "Escort me to the closet for the robe."

Without waiting for his answer, she wrapped herself more securely in the heavy duvet and sheet, slinging her legs off the side of the bed. She stood and faced him.

He was surprised, but he stuck with her, tracking her with the Luger aimed still to kill.

"The robes should be there—in the *armoire* behind you." She thrust an arm out, pointing with her hand.

He grabbed her arm and twisted, and then marched her to the antique Louis XV armoire on the far side of the room.

Opening the wooden doors, he yanked a plump white Frette robe from a hanger with one hand, gun in the other, still dangerously close to her head. Then suddenly he backed away and sneered. "Come and get it."

"With pleasure," she said quietly. "Victor will be grateful for your kindness—as am I—"

He grunted, dangling the robe towards her just out of reach, gun pointed at her heart.

"Must you point the gun at me? How could I possibly overpower you?" she said, now all innocence. "You are a very strong man."

He stepped towards her, so close that she smelled his rank body odor. Her stomach turned, and she struggled to keep her *sang froid*.

He smiled, pleased with himself, and looked her up and down.

But she had succeeded in distracting him, lowering his guard. Through the corner of her eyes, she glanced around, scoping out an escape. She remembered this suite that Victor had personally designed to suit his needs. It was a long way through the bedroom and then to the outer salon of the suite—almost the size of her apartment on Quai Voltaire. She would have to be swift and cunning. The duvet and a robe would help. And she needed a few invisible veils to hide her movements. Instantly, she conjured them.

She called silently to Margot. "Margot—no more blood! No sacrifice! Help me if you want me to lift the curse. Now!"

As her words flew through time and space, Kikki became acutely aware of red silk swaddling her body. The duvet, now fluid as blood, seemed to lift from her.

Chapter 57

When the guard leaned forward to hand her the robe, Kikki yanked it from him in one swift movement and threw it over his head.

He reacted like a blinded bull, his hand jerking. The gun fired. She dodged and felt the bullet passing centimeters from her face.

Quickly recovering, he lunged and grabbed her around the waist. She braced herself against the bed and kicked him in the groin. He howled, doubling over, releasing her. As she lunged free, he fired another shot, narrowly missing her again.

She ran out of the bedroom wrapped in the scarlet duvet. She leapt through the open door into the salon. Glancing over her shoulder, she saw him stumbling as he came after her. He had stopped shooting, but still had the Luger aimed at her.

Seconds was all she needed to get to the far side of the suite. She had vague memories from past encounters in the suite with Victor— kinesthetic imprints of the placement of furniture and paintings.

But just as she was almost free, she entered a filmy cloud of red mist, and the Black Queen stepped out of a painting in front of her.

Kikki screamed at the ghost. "Stay away from me! Be gone, demon spirit!" She flung an arm to stop the apparition. Kikki held Athena's sword. The Black Queen retreated.

Kikki summoned all her strength and fled on the balls of her bare feet, missing narrowly sharp edges of gilded glass tables, stuffed sofas, chairs and lamps. Breathing hard, she reached the door leading into the hallway. She yanked down on the bronze handle. It didn't give.

The guard was on her heels, and she could smell his sour sweat. In her mind's eye, in slow motion, she saw a bullet discharge from the 9 mm. She threw a ball of white light behind her to freeze it and him. It worked!

Then she gripped the door handle and pulled hard. Still it didn't open. Panic struck. Was it locked from the outside, and was she captive—like Margot?

She closed her eyes, inhaling deeply, summoning the rightful wrath of the Goddess.

Finally, the handle released, but just as she pushed it open, the guard's hand slammed into her shoulder, jerking her backwards. Steel dug into the back of her neck. She turned to face him, kicking hard.

Suddenly, he froze and released her slightly. He stepped back.

The door opened wide behind her. Someone was there. Victor! Sheer terror paralyzed her.

Her eyes widened as she turned around to look.

"Let her go or I will kill you," Torres commanded, Beretta aimed at the guard.

Chapter 58

❧———•———❧

On Place Vendôme in front of the Ritz, as soon as Torres left for
Kikki, Tía had raced around like a witch on a flying broom. Tía was
a woman on a mission. She drove fast, in a tight circle. First
counterclockwise, and then clockwise, a vital ritual to shift the
energy, to cleanse the old square of as much darkness as she could.
She meant to draw out Victor, who personified it—the darkness. To
defeat him and it—at least hold them at bay.

She knew it would take far more energetic work than she could
summon now, but this might be enough to save Kikki from the
clutches of a monster—and protect Torres.

Natalia Becchina slid from side to side across the back seat,
squawking loudly like a mad raven.

There was no traffic in Place Vendôme at this hour. Only a few
limo drivers parked outside the Ritz standing by for their VIPs—
one of them would be Victor's.

Tía circled once more around the octagonal square—what Tía
and the Daughters knew to be home to the Sword's secret temple—
its Citadel. Appropriate. Its immense phallic Doric bronze pillar in
the center, constructed from melted down cannons and claimed
very clearly by the military powers. Recently refurbished, its green

mosaic carvings stood out as if alive. The tallest mosaic in the world
—all about war.

Place Vendôme was home to the wealth and power that military
might brought. At one time, home to Cartier, Bulgari, Winston and
Van Cleef. It spoke of jewels and riches, aristocracy and splendor,
though the world was at war and the planet in peril. Ever thus,
despite revolutions, reigns of terror, communes and five republics
in France.

At the meeting of the Council of Eight earlier that evening, they
had set the elements of their intentions and strategy. As senior High
Priestess, Tía was carrying out their wishes now. She had promised
to perform a ceremony at their enemy's Citadel to set up protection
for what was to come.

Her breath in the cold air fogged the windows, but she did not
need a clear windshield to see. As she drove, she chanted a blessing
and a curse. "In the name of the Goddess and her Daughter Inanna
—for Marguerite de Valois, her rightful *serviteur*, and her lineage—
and for all who follow.

Through love from Mother Earth, Mother Water and Mother
Universe, the Divine Feminine and Divine Masculine, through the
Goddess, with light and love throughout.

May this accursed Citadel of patriarchal power be razed to the
ground, cleansed of all darkness—past, present and future. In all
time, all dimension and all reality. Of this world and beyond.
Without limit.

She stopped in front of the stately Ministère de la Justice and
gathered her powers. Underneath the building in an underground
labyrinth of tunnels was the Swords' unholy temple. It was secretly
hidden under that respected French edifice, where a select few were
charged with directing and carrying out social laws and rendering
justice in the name of "*Liberté, Égalité et Fraternité.*"

A mockery. Honorable words subverted to cover the dark forces
of patriarchal power.

At the council meeting, Gabrielle Laroche, well versed in Paris's
labyrinthian history and architecture had reminded them of the
history of the square.

Place Vendôme dated back to at least 1677, originally the site of
the Convent of Capucines. Not to mention the townhouse of the

Duke of Vendôme, illegitimate son of Queen Margot's husband King Henri IV and his beloved mistress, Gabrielle d'Estrées. An interesting twist of historical fate and blood ties.

Later, Louis XIV took over the properties to build a haven and showcase for the aristocracy and its institutions—the royal library, mint house, private housing for select high ranking members of French government. He renamed it Place Louis le Grand—naturally.

One neat package. With a perfect palace for the privileged—le Ritz, where Coco Channel had lived but mostly men of great privilege. Now owned by the family of the one-time *amour* of Princess Diana. Not far from where the well-loved woman met her ill-fated death.

The fifty-three meter gigantic central column, the Column of the Grande Armée, was appropriately hollow like those who had built it and continued to claim it. Consumed with their lust for power, they were no more than shells without heart and soul.

Perfect Citadel for the Knights of the Holy Sword of God.

Natalia, who had been banging hard on the window panel divider, cried out, "Listen to me, you crazy old bat! You are holding me against my will. I will have you arrested for this."

Tía laughed and lowered the window. "Try it. How's your phone working?"

Tía had energetically jammed the signal. Natalia would be off the grid for a while.

"How dare you!" Natalia screeched as she inspected her phone —no signal.

"You are safe. All will be revealed in time." The whir of the middle panel closing muffled Natalia's angry retort.

Tía's black eyes pierced the clouds blanketing Place Vendôme. A dark cloud floated low, hovering with menace. Yet, the nearly full moon persisted in shining light through shadow. She homed in on the sculpture of Napoleon Bonaparte dressed as Caesar high atop the towering symbol of military might.

She peered and let out a satisfied sigh. Atop the tall column was a viewing platform accessed by a stairway in the interior. Closed now to the public but accessible to some. At this very moment, a man stood on the small balcony in front of Napoleon's statue.

Tía had prayed to draw him out of their underground temple to the focal point of their Citadel. The Goddess had rewarded her vigil and her homage.

Victor—looking tiny and powerless, just as she hoped he would soon be.

Tía spat out the curse in a Sumerian dialect from Inanna's time. Victor stepped forward to the edge of the balustrade. For a moment he wavered, and then he raised a silver sword and thrust it in Tía's direction. His eyes burned like red coals boring into Tía, and his face transformed into an angry eagle's open beak. She returned the evil look, flooding him with pure white light.

The sword gleamed as if alive in the now fully moonlit sky. Tía smiled. Almost there. She waited for the transformation that she had envisioned.

She saw the sword leave his hand and hover above him like an infinity symbol—or the number eight. His head contorted, glowing red with rage. Tía bowed her head and whispered a prayer of gratitude.

And then she hit the accelerator.

Tires squealed, and Tía's thick braid flew as she circled the monument one more time and then raced south the short distance to rue Saint-Honoré to her next stop.

Natalia had become silent.

Chapter 59

Tía hummed as she drove, pleased with the ritual. Satisfied that she had drawn Victor into the open and prevented him from raping Kikki—or worse. Had he known it was her—the matriarch he had ordered killed in Granada? Or had he just felt the presence of an enemy when he stepped up to the balcony railing and thrust his sword at her?

Tía had been in deep trance, and he had been possessed. He may have recognized the face of his enemy, though she trusted that he did not actually see her as Tía. She would remain hidden, and she knew that Inanna would protect her.

She screeched to a stop in front of the Hotel Regina. Liam stepped out from under the arched entrance on cue. He wore a stylish overcoat and a smart felt brimmed hat. He blended well with the elements, nearly invisible—like any good magician. He hurried to the car.

Tía pressed the button and the window lowered. She smiled slyly, "*Bonsoir.* Are you ready for her?"

Natalia was woodenly still.

"*Bien sûr.* It is good to see you looking well and alive. I am your humble servant, *Señora.*"

"*Por favor*, I've always asked that you call me Tía. I know how close you and Kikki are, and I am grateful we can rely on you during this critical time."

"I have a perfect private penthouse suite ready for her. And I've had her Vuitton luggage, very elegant, I might add, discreetly brought over from the Ritz," he said, evidently pleased.

Ever the Innkeeper, Tía thought. Vital for this important task.

"Let's get her out, then. I must be on my way." Tía started to open the car door, but Liam stopped her.

"Allow me, please. We don't want you exposed."

"*Claro*. But I hope she will go quietly. She's been quite a lot of trouble—loudly protesting."

"Leave her to me," he smiled broadly and winked. "I will charm her out of her resistance."

"*Seguro que sí*." Tía inclined her head.

"If you don't mind, Tía, with respect, you need to get some rest —" Liam studied her carefully in the dim light of the hotel's entrance lamps. "You look exhausted—and more." Thoughtful, he put a finger to his lips, "As though you've seen Hades himself."

She frowned. "I have indeed." Suddenly, weariness crept into her bones. Liam was an excellent alchemist. He had grounded her and allowed her to be fully present in her body. "You are quite right. I need sleep. *Muchísimas gracias. Hasta luego!*"

She watched with amazement as Natalia walked quietly and sedately into the Hotel Regina with Liam. And then Tía sped off.

Chapter 60

As they entered the hotel lobby, Liam whispered to Natalia, "Not a word, and keep your head down. I don't think anyone will be about, but you never know in a hotel."

She had nodded compliantly, looking too tired to object. Quickly under his spell, she had come with him willingly.

Liam's crepe-soled pigskin boots made no sound as he quickly crossed the Regina's marble-floored lobby with Natalia on his arm. They reached the private elevator to the penthouse.

"I will explain it all to you when we get to the Regina Anne de Bretagne Suite on the top floor, the penthouse, very private. You will be comfortable and quite safe." He thought it perfect that she should be in Anne's suite—one of Margot's role models.

As they rode the small elevator to the floor marked PH 1, she studied him curiously. Who was this very handsome man, and why all this drama? Thoughts of Torres had faded completely from her mind—almost as if someone had wiped him from her memory. Probably that witchy old woman. That and the fact that Natalia had known that something was really wrong. Torres's lover was in danger. She'd picked that up from overhearing the brief words the old woman and Torres had exchanged.

And then she'd watched Torres transform as he ran into the Ritz. She got that he was in deep with his girlfriend.

She was wise to the witchy old bat who'd held her hostage. Natalia knew quite a lot about witchcraft. Her mother and uncle had instructed her. She suspected it was in her blood.

In her business, one learned more about superstitions and religion over the centuries than Natalia really cared to know. Her uncle constantly reminded her of the power of talismans. After tonight's adventures, she thought she needed one of her own.

"Mademoiselle Becchina?" Liam interrupted her reverie as the doors opened. "Is everything all right?"

"Not in the least. This has been a very confusing evening. I'm glad to have landed in your kind and capable hands."

"You can count on me." He led her down a thickly carpeted and artfully lit corridor.

"Thank you. I hope so."

"We're here. Your very private suite. It is nearly four a.m.," Liam said as they stopped in front of the door to the suite on its private hallway.

He ushered her into the luxurious living room. He could sense her weariness and confusion, mixed with a *soupçon* of fear. He would have expected her to rave about this very special nest he had personally curated, but she was blind to her surroundings.

"Get some rest. You'll be safe here. I'm sure you will have a very busy day tomorrow."

Her eyes held a worried look. "What in the world is going on?"

Liam was quiet, working to calm her.

"Am I in some kind of danger? I get that feeling. Even though you're not saying."

"Do not worry now. I'll be nearby." He handed her a card with his personal mobile number. "Call me about anything at any time. I trust your phone works now." He used his powers to distract her from the topic, avoiding her question.

She checked it and then smiled curiously at him, "Yes, miraculously so, it would seem." She was right, it had been that witchy old driver. "Are you some kind of psychic?"

He held her eyes. Shrewd woman. He had done his best to cloak his talents. "Perhaps. I dabble in the Tarot."

"Really? It fascinates me. Would you read mine? I need an update."

Honey, you have no idea, Liam thought. "Of course. I'd be pleased to," he said, using his Innkeeper voice. "Why don't we throw a few cards in the late morning, when you've rested? I will have your breakfast served in the room and then come to you."

"Perfect." He was very handsome, she thought, and so kind. For some reason, she felt more at ease with him than she had with anyone else she'd met in Paris on this trip. Almost like being with a brother.

Moments later, she wandered into one of the most beautiful hotel bedrooms she'd ever seen. And she'd slept in the best. It was like a dream—as though she'd imagined it and he had created it.

Stop it Natalia, you are very tired. She donned a brand new La Perla *negligée* that had been laid out on the bed, wrapped and folded in layers of tissue in its expensive box. And then, she climbed into the enormous four poster bed—a bed fit for a Renaissance Queen. Someone like, perhaps, Queen Marguerite de Valois.

Natalia had two thoughts before she drifted off to sleep on plump pillows and pink satin silk sheets. She'd like to spend more time with Véronique, the American woman she had met in the Voltaire. Natalia liked her and felt understood. They had common bonds—women in business. Yes, tomorrow, she'd find her.

The second was a more disturbing omen—a quickening in her belly. Her stomach was a little funny, and she realized she was late with her period. Her breasts were overly sensitive, especially when Torres touched them. Maybe it was PMS. Or lust.

Could she be pregnant? God forbid. Progeny was the last thing her accursed family needed. She wouldn't tell Marco, her lover. She prayed to a god she didn't believe in that it wasn't true.

But as she slipped into dreams, she heard a child's cry.

Chapter 61

Kikki woke with a start at ten a.m. on Wednesday. Church bells chimed loudly, frightening her. Where was she? She opened her eyes, looking around the room. She was in her own bed dressed in a warm flannel gown. Her heart slowed.

She stretched an arm across the bed. He wasn't there. Where was her lover? Her belly tightened in fear. She closed her eyes and focused her third eye, trying to bring up color that would sooth her. A black screen. Breathe, Kikki, she told herself. Don't think.

She rolled carefully from her side onto her back and stretched her legs, breathing in life force. But she couldn't stop them from coming—dark visions flashed:

A black *negligée* and a giant man aiming a gun at her. Victor's lips on her. She was frozen and still. She couldn't stop him. The suite at the Ritz came into focus—the bedroom with the four poster bed. And Victor's special touches. Black tapers in candelabras burned brightly in the luxurious bedroom, illuminating grotesque tapestries of mythical demonic beasts and terrified women being assaulted by soldiers wearing crosses and bearing enormous swords.

Victor rose in *bas relief* out of the scene. He wore a white bathrobe from the Ritz. He was speaking to her, but she could not hear the words. He emanated angry male dominance—a predator— blocking her. He extended his arms wide as he hovered over her body and became an eagle with sharp talons and a raw, hungry beak. She was under his spell. Viscerally, she felt his power over her.

And then, abruptly, his face reappeared covered by a dark veil. He was surrounded by filmy shadows, and his robe turned black as pitch. The insignia over his heart was not the Ritz' trademark but a Tarot card—the Devil.

Kikki opened her eyes to stop the flashes, terrified. She pulled her knees up to her chest and hugged her body. Her eyes filled with tears. What had happened? She knew he hadn't raped her, thank the Goddess, but were the visions real? Or had it been a nightmare? Her mind was still fuzzy.

The scent of lavender and rose hit her nostrils. It came from her own body. And then she remembered a bath. Her bathtub, old-fashioned, claw-footed ivory porcelain. White candles. The scent of roses filled the bathroom. She remembered Torres pouring warm, scented water onto her back.

A primal need flooded her soul and body. Where was her lover? "Torres!"

Chapter 62

Torres was in his office on the phone with his boss, Flo, when he heard Kikki call out.

"*Voy!*" He shouted. He ended his call abruptly and was at her side in seconds.

"I'm right here."

"Please, come back to bed and hold me." Her voice trembled.

"Of course, *mi cielo*. You're going to be fine, Kikki. I promise." He stifled the voice in his head that told him he hadn't been there for her. He had failed to protect her.

He slid under the covers. One arm encircled her waist. The other stroked her hair. "Shh, *mi amor*. I've got you."

His warm belly against her slender back made her relax. She was safe, and they were together. Yet, more salty tears streamed down her cheeks. "I know. I know." She began to sob.

Wiping tears away, she lifted his hand from her waist and turned towards him. "I can't take it all in—I'm overwhelmed."

He kissed her forehead tenderly.

She closed her eyes. "I keep trying to make it go away."

He kissed her softly on the lips. Then, she said, "I should have known."

"It's not your fault, Kikki. You were the victim. If anything—"

"It's not yours either. You're thinking you should have cancelled your dinner and stayed with me. And you should have told me that Victor Fitz-Perkins headed up the Swords," she said, gathering strength as she spoke. "But I know why you didn't. It's okay. And I knew enough—I took a risk."

He held her closer, remaining silent on Fitz-Perkins. "Thank god you're all right."

"Seriously, I am. Just very emotionally shaky. And a bit of a hangover from the drugs he gave me. Look, it's no one's fault. It's just how it goes with us. We try to protect each other in our own way. It's not ever going to be any different."

"I wish you weren't right, damnit, Kikki," he said quietly with a sad gaze. He was rewarded with a smile. Her pale face was beginning to light up, and her eyes to shine with that depth that she possessed. Leaving him defenseless and more—something he couldn't name.

He was careful not to push her. They hadn't talked much yet about exactly what the bastard had done to her. But he knew enough. Fitz-Perkins hadn't been there the entire time, and by the time Torres arrived, she was alone with the bodyguard, who had quickly saved his own life and let Kikki go. Torres wouldn't have hesitated to shoot if the guard had reacted differently.

Torres felt her pain the instant he saw her—and even more when he realized the state she was in. He had gotten her to the safety of their home. She was in shock. Angry, vulnerable and distant. Didn't want him to touch her at first. And then, she relented when they were in the apartment just before he helped her into the bath.

Then she had said quietly, "I can't talk much about it now—it's too soon. But I want you to know that he did not get to do his worst before he left me—he was intending to return."

They didn't talk about it more. She didn't volunteer, and he did not ask.

Now, she stopped his thoughts with a kiss, seeking his tongue, tentatively at first.

He hesitated.

"It's okay, my love. I need you now to erase him."

He helped her out of her nightgown, and he took such care and was so gentle, she almost wept again.

He undressed too, cuddling her. She felt her body respond to his touch. At first tender and then followed by an almost needy possession. Warmth filled her. Her blood ran fast through her veins, and she began to feel alive and strong, erasing visions and nightmares.

Funny how he could do that to her. And he was the only one who had ever been able to go so deep. A remarkable passion—souls touching and bodies joining so perfectly.

Strong fingers tousled her hair. He reached up and found her breasts, cupping and then gently caressed her now erect nipples with his fingers.

Naked bodies pressed against each other. He was hard and hot. Her mind emptying, easing. Mouth on swollen wet mouth, tongues danced fanning desire.

He stopped kissing and held her face close, memorizing it.

Her eyes flew wide open when he parted her legs and thrust his sex deep into her. Her eyes went from dark brown to opaque ebony, matching his own. All urgent passion, climbing to heights to meet the other with undeniable want.

Chapter 63

The lovers stayed for some time wrapped in each other's arms, safe and quiet, in a world where no one else entered. Kikki drifted off to sleep and so did Torres—stealing a moment of time.

When Kikki awoke, she caught a whiff of coffee and fresh bread. It mingled with the rose scent of her skin, now musky, too, from their alchemy.

"Hmm," she whispered softly, settling against the comfort of his body one more time.

"Yes, I smell it too. One more minute."

"Tía?"

"*Sí.*"

"Making breakfast. I have the feeling she wants us to join her."

"*Claro.*" He shifted onto an elbow, arms still around her waist. "In a bit. She also wants to make sure you are all right."

"Of course." Her voice was quiet.

"Are you? *En serio?*"

"I am. Really." Though she knew neither of them had much sleep and she wasn't sure that they would be all right for quite a while. But new energy surged through her body, mind, spirit.

Renewed, she sat up quickly, ready to move forward. "We have to talk, Torres. Get this out in the open."

"I'm sorry—about—" He began, but she interrupted.

She launched straight into it. "Victor? Yeah, me too. I've known him a long time, and he called out of the blue while you were out. I couldn't stand just sitting by idly. I took a calculated risk. I wanted to get information from him. He knows everyone's secrets. He's a power-hungry misogynist. I knew he would be one of the Swords, maybe their leader, but I—I didn't have enough protection. I wasn't smart enough to understand his game until it was too late." His need for personal revenge, she meant but didn't say.

"Don't blame yourself. He drugged you. And you couldn't have known." Because, he thought guiltily, he hadn't told her who and what Fitz-Perkins might be.

"But I should have known, really. I misjudged his intentions. I had no idea that they were so deeply personal until it was too late." She caught her lover's eyes, waited a beat and said, "Yes, absolutely, Torres, you should have told me that he was the archenemy in this conspiracy."

He was again silent. He'd had his reasons, and they were still valid. Too risky for the op. He'd known because she told him months ago that she had once worked for the man, and their intel confirmed that aspect—though not their secret affair. But he had never asked her about him or the work. He had wondered and waited for her to volunteer. The past was one thing, but right now, he had to know more.

Wriggling free, she swung her legs over the bed and grabbed a shawl. "You want to know about him—"

"Yes, but first—" He tipped her chin towards him.

She looked away when she answered his unspoken question. "He toyed with me sexually, but as I said, he did not rape me." Tears formed in her eyes, but her voice was strong, coming from a place of power deep in her soul.

He went to her and wrapped his arms around her. His mind whirled still. *Hijo de puta*! I will kill him, he swore silently.

She gathered her strength and said, "Let's get the elephant out of the room, Torres."

He was still seething. "*Coño*, Kikki! He might have killed you if you hadn't escaped."

"No, that wasn't his plan. At least not last night. It was his night off—and he wanted to humiliate me and get his revenge because I left him. I left his practice in New York—" She caught Torres's eyes, swallowed and then said, "And his bed too."

He held back anger and matched the evenness of her tone. "Tell me about it."

"I was young. I didn't understand what a megalomaniac narcissist he was. He gave me entrée. He mentored me. We had a sexual thing. Friendly, meaningless sex, I thought. By the time I realized that there was a real quid quo pro, that he expected to keep me in his bed. Well, by then, I was in too deep. I was swamped and stressed with work, and honestly, afraid of him. He was getting increasingly possessive."

Torres lit a cigarette, took a deep drag, pushing down anger and jealousy. "Go on."

"I tried to get out. I went out a couple of times with one of our French clients—he was single—at least, I think he was."

"How did Fitz-Perkins react?"

"He went totally crazy—I mean insane." Her stomach curdled as she remembered.

"Did he hurt you? Did he hit you?"

"Mostly sexual and emotional abuse." She couldn't meet her lover's eyes, her own awash with shame.

"You didn't answer my question," he said softly.

"We argued, and he slapped me really hard a couple of times." She took a deep breath.

"*Joder*! *Coño*!"

"That was my wakeup call. I formed an exit strategy—moved to Paris to set up my practice."

"So last night was about personal revenge. And you had no idea?" He worked to keep his tone even, when inside he was furious —at Fitz-Perkins, at Kikki—and mostly at himself.

"Yes. And I missed the signals—he played me well."

"Have you seen him since you came to Paris?"

"You mean did I sleep with him? Yes. Occasionally. I kept my distance though. He sent me a few clients. We were friendly, or so I thought—until now." She paused, reviewing their history. "It stopped after you and I got together, Torres. I turned him down once or twice. He knew about you—and what you do. I guess that really enraged him."

"But he didn't show that to you—he hid his true feelings?"

"Right. He acted a bit like a spoiled child, but he knows how to mask his emotions. And he did. Until last night. Motherfucker!"

Torres took another drag of his cigarette and tapped it on the ashtray, "So he's held this grudge a long time. He felt betrayed."

"Yes. That's how men like that are. I know that now. And I thought I could handle him and maybe get some information out of him last night. But the man is a raving psychopath now."

"Maybe he always has been."

"Don't know. Possible. Someone or something flipped his switch."

"*Joder*, Kikki. I knew you had worked for him, but I—we—didn't know anything about that. If I'd known about your affair, all that you just told me, I would have warned you."

"I know you think I hide old lovers from you, but I don't—at least not intentionally. As for Victor, I totally blocked him out—you can see why now." She swallowed hard, nausea hitting her, reliving his unwanted touches last night. And then, anger swelled as quickly, and she forced the pictures from her mind and focused on Torres. "And also, he didn't matter—not emotionally. Besides, we both have a past, Torres. I don't know everything about yours either."

He felt his anger rise, and crossed the room, pulling on jeans and sweater.

Keep a lid on it, Torres. Back to that. He had been afraid she might step in it or put herself in harm's way if he told her more about Fitz-Perkins—and she did. But he hadn't seen this. *Coño!* The son of a bitch had arrived early. Somebody got bought off in Alexandria.

He should have followed his gut instinct and cancelled dinner. But now, now it was way too late for any of that. Her heated voice interrupted thoughts of regret.

"I still don't understand why you didn't tell me he was central to your op. You've known for months!" She glared at him.

He was intentionally evasive. "*Mira.* I can't discuss it. And there's no point now. But the fact that he was your lover makes it more dangerous than ever for you to be involved in any way."

"Goddesses, you are *insupportable!*" She sighed and searched for clothes in the dresser. "He's the bloody High Priest of the whole thing. He's running your people and his in circles. Believe me, I know." She stubbed her toe on the bed and cried out.

Torres was thinking about his own past. He wasn't blameless, either, he reminded himself—not to mention Natalia. What mattered was now, he told himself. "I'm sorry. I want this to work for us. But I need to trust you."

"You can. But you don't! Not enough. Look, I had a plan and it worked in part. I did get some information from him. He told me he had a deal in the making with the Louvre, that he had a film in process and about his Italian partner. That's all I could get." She had more, but she wanted to go over it with Monique—in particular about the woman she'd met.

Torres nodded and then briefly said, "Okay. Confirms what we know about the film. The guy you are meeting is Fitz-Perkins's guy."

"*Bien sûr!* You knew that, damnit! Don't humor me. And he didn't kill me. If he wanted me dead, I would be. But I am in one piece. Now, you and I are in this together. No more bullshit. No more shutting me out. Consider me a Warrior Queen in battle from now on."

"Were you in love with him?" He couldn't let it go.

"Fucking hell, Torres. No! Are you a hopeless romantic or a jealous macho Spaniard obsessed with my past? I thought you were above this, or that we were beyond it. I was very young and naïve. Sex. That's it! I bet you've been there! *Basta!*"

And now, she felt betrayed by Torres, just as Margot had, by those closest to her. Victor had sought personal revenge against her last night because he couldn't possess her, couldn't keep her in New York. Betrayal. Torres felt betrayed because she hadn't told him she had an affair with Victor.

Was this all some endless karmic circle? When would it end?

Chapter 64

Tía had made breakfast—coffee, a *tortilla española* and a fresh loaf of bread. She was waiting for Torres and Kikki. She was very concerned about Kikki. The wise crone reminded herself that it was all part of the young woman's journey, but her heart ached. But at the time, she and Gabrielle had encouraged Kikki because they needed help urgently and because the Goddess had guided them thusly.

Kikki was strong enough, and she hoped that her nephew was wise enough to know what to do for Kikki, for them, and for their cause.

Still, it was a spiritual, physical and emotional roller coaster.

She set the dining room table with care. She had been happy that they had found each other and seemed committed to holding on to what they had. A loving breakfast amongst the three of them would help to heal wounds. At the very table where she had sat in the dark for so long after escaping from Granada.

It seemed like many moons ago, though it was only two days. She sat down in the same straight ladder-back chair. Selfishly, Tía wanted this time together before they spread to the four directions, each on their own mission.

Kikki walked out of the bedroom into the salon dressed in jeans and a black turtleneck. She rubbed her hands together in front of the roaring cedar fire. A glance at her reflection in the gilded mirror reassured her.

She was feeling strong and confident, surprisingly, and it showed. Despite real feelings about never ending karmic cycles of betrayal and the painful subjects raised, it had been good to talk. To say it out loud dispersed its power. It shed light on darkness. Love did that.

Sex—especially with Torres—always did that. She was in very deep with him—terrified of losing him and equally so of having him. It would come at a cost.

She wrapped a dark purple cape around her shoulders and leaned over to scoop up the tiny bottle of pure rose oil on the edge of the coffee table. Opening it, she held it to her nose and breathed deeply. It raised her vibration immediately. She shook a few drops into each palm and rubbed her hands together before raising her arms in offering to the Goddess. She bowed and put her palms together in a sign of gratitude. And then she crossed to the dining room to greet Tía.

Torres arrived at the dining room table at the same time as Kikki. The lovers sat across from each other.

"So, dearest Tía, we are grateful for this spread and—"

"And can use the fuel. You're a life-saver," Kikki finished. "Quite literally, we know."

Torres took a sip of rich Spanish coffee. "Incredible."

"Nectar of the Goddess," Kikki rejoined sticking her nose into the porcelain cup to inhale the aroma of freshly ground beans that Torres had regularly shipped from Spain.

Tía served each a portion of *tortilla*—rich with eggs, potatoes and onions, and with certain reverence broke a round loaf of country bread, *pain de campagne*, into three parts. Their fingers touched for the briefest moment as each took their share. Three pairs of dark eyes held a moment of gratitude.

They ate in silence.

Kikki spoke first. "Tía, how are you?"

"I am well, thank you, but I should be asking you that question, my dear. Are you somewhat recovered from your ordeal?"

"Yes." She nodded. "I am. Stronger and stronger."

"I am glad to hear, but it will take time."

"I know, Tía. Thank you again for your help." Kikki shifted gears. Not wanting to be the focus of attention, she turned to Torres. "How is your wound? Shouldn't you see a doctor to have it redressed?"

She looked at Tía, who nodded in agreement.

"I'm fine." He sipped coffee and smiled, hiding the pain.

"I don't believe you. You smile, but your eyes betray you," Kikki began.

Tía said quietly, "She's right, nephew.

He sighed and pushed his plate away. "Two against one, I can't win, especially you two. *Joder!* I need a cigarette." With his good shoulder, he reached inside the black leather jacket he had hung on the back of the chair. Truth was, his injury still caused him pain, and he knew that one stop today would be to a friendly doctor to have it redressed.

He shook a cigarette out of a new pack of Ducados, Spanish *tabaco negro*, he'd brought back from Granada, and lit it with the gold lighter Kikki had given him. He inhaled deeply.

Kikki frowned, worried. And wanting a cigarette too. Rose oil was all very nice.

"Want one, *mi amor?*" He offered the pack.

"You know I do, but no. I quit." She frowned. "And don't deflect. What are you going to do—what is next in this treacherous minefield?" She shot serious eyes at each of them.

Torres's voice was more controlled when he spoke. "I have to meet with my people. Got to go soon. Tía can tell you the rest."

Tía had been waiting for this moment, and she jumped in —"Not so fast, nephew. So many cannot be trusted. You know that better than most."

"You're not suggesting that you vet my people. I know what I am doing. *Joder!*"

"Of course, you do. Not vetting." Kikki focused on the practical. "Who do you trust, then? Tia's right."

"Tía is almost always right." He stopped talking.

Tía interjected. "We will take care of the Snake Goddess and the gala event."

He frowned.

"Flo, right?" Kikki knew Torres could count on his boss at Interpol. Flo had his back.

He took a long drag, blowing smoke out in circles. "Right. And, I've got Jean Marc. Look, you do not need to know who is on my team or what we are doing except that it's all set. We have a secure base. We're not storming the Bastille in force."

The two women frowned in complicity.

He sighed in mock surrender. "There are a couple of guys from the committee who can help with the mechanics. A team of Brits from their art & antiquities squad—part of the Prosecutor's Office, the OCP, of the International Criminal Court. Straight up agents. Manuel and Sara. A couple of Interpol cybercrime operatives under Flo. Honestly, this is highly classified—secret, fast and to be swiftly executed—a special tactics team. One of the biggest attempted heists —and coup—in Europe in decades. So get out of my police business, seriously!"

"Right. I won't worry about you getting killed." Kikki smirked. "Who—besides Victor Fitz—" Kikki choked up and then forced herself to continue—"Who else is running their side?"

"His main partner, Pelligrini, from Milan. But you already know that, I bet." He hedged because he was still flushing out the leaders.

"Actually, not specifically. But it fits. He has a beautiful young business associate, his niece, Natalia Becchina, right?" Kikki said as it all clicked. "His niece—she's your mark."

"How—?" Torres was stunned. "Are you reading my mind?"

"Don't be silly!" She couldn't resist winking. Then she told them both about meeting Natalia. "And, you see, I did get useful information after all from Victor last night. Natalia told me they were moving some big pieces, and Victor confirmed that the Louvre is involved. But you must know that since you're a professor on their staff."

"*Claro.*" He frowned. Kikki was formidable when in battle mode.

"But what else? Steal the Snake Goddess," Kikki paused. "If this is an attempt at a coup, there's a lot more, right?"

He sure as hell wasn't going to walk them through months of

painstakingly gathered *humint*, the constant flow of carefully analyzed terrorist chatter, and Interpol and Europol's interplay with the many international intelligence agencies—all leading up to his Operation Sphinx.

"I can help with Victor," Kikki blurted, interrupting his thoughts. "I will do whatever it takes to bring him down. I want my revenge, now!"

Torres and Tía exchanged looks. Tía tipped her head, a sign to stop him from arguing with his lover.

Kikki continued, in lawyer mode now. "I knew he was a collector and also on the board of the Met. I had no idea he was part of this antiquities ring. He's always had a very secretive side." She hesitated for a moment. There was something she wasn't getting.

She blinked at Torres. "He uses Pelligrini, Natalia's Uncle Franco, to do the dirty work."

Torres shook his head, distracted. He couldn't help wondering about Natalia. Had he succeeded in turning her? A job he had to certainly finish, and soon.

Torres said gravely. "And Fitz-Perkins will chew him up and spit him out when he's done—if he gets that far."

"Victor will have his foot soldiers." Like my new client, just as she and Monique had discussed, she thought but did not say. She didn't want another lecture from Torres. She knew what to do.

New energy and excitement filled Kikki. The picture was coming together at last. She had to fight. For Torres, for Tía, for Margot—fight to end this karmic cycle—for the Light and the Goddess.

It was no longer, if it had ever been, only about the Snake Goddess.

Chapter 65

Moments later, in Torres's office, Kikki watched her lover as he gathered his go bag and holstered his weapon. Focused, moving into cop mode.

He checked his phone. A text from Flo: *On t'attends!* Time to go. But he was reluctant to leave Kikki.

"Tell me." She sat on the edge of his desk.

He turned his back to her. "What?"

"Tell me about Natalia. You had dinner with her last night. Have you turned her?"

"I'm working on it." Of course she knew, he thought.

"But she's on your committee representing her uncle and Victor, right? Who selected her?"

"It doesn't matter at this point. She knows exactly who I am—she was sent to work *me*. I always knew that."

"She's very savvy."

"Indeed, she is. That will make her all the more useful to us."

"And sexy. Torres—" Kikki studied him. "How can you be pissed about Victor being a former lover when you're seducing Natalia right under my nose."

She turned away and stood up.

Kikki's thoughts turned to Natalia. Had their encounter at the Voltaire truly been by chance? Did Natalia know who Kikki was? Had she been using Kikki? She didn't think so—but that explained why Kikki had picked up mixed energy signals from her. She mentally replayed their time together, a film on fast rewind.

Margot had pressed her to get to know Natalia. But not because she was Torres's mark. It had to do with Margot's story. In a flash, it was crystal clear—the mission of the Daughters of Inanna. But how?

Torres phone buzzed. A text from Natalia: *Where are u? Must talk!*

Kikki turned to scrutinize him. "Let me divine. A text from her?" And then jealousy gripped her being like a hand around her throat. She shook her head—tried to shake off the destructive emotion. She could not allow herself to go there.

After a deep breath, she said, "You know, Torres. I think that in the end, you and Victor did me a favor. My trial-by-fire last night is proving extremely useful. I am stronger and clearer. And now that Victor has been exposed, I'm not as blocked. I am starting to see the whole picture. I liked Natalia, but you must be careful you don't get burned. That *we* don't get burned."

"Kikki, I swear to you. She means nothing to me." He came around the desk. "She's using me, and I, in turn—"

"Huh!" She moved away.

"Kikki, I've got to go. There's nothing for you to worry about."

"You're right."

"Good. Glad you're being reasonable."

"But I can help you with Victor. He didn't get everything he wanted last night—didn't get to finish his mission of—he'll still be focused on me." She shut out images as rage rose. "I can use his—weakness—turn it back on him, use it to get to him."

"No. Forget it! And now he's a man thwarted."

"Maybe, but what would you have me do? This is for all of us."

"Work with Tía, please. She needs your help. I'm a cop. Let me do my job. I'm armed to fight, and I want to obliterate him for what he did to you. It's personal with me now too." He pulled her into his arms and cupped her chin, holding her gaze.

She narrowed her eyes. "You can't tell me what to do anymore, my love. I'm all the way in." She stepped away from Torres. She was

Athena embodied, ready to engage.

Suddenly, she felt stifled. "Go, Torres. Do your work. Catch your bad guys."

He was surprised by the sudden chill. "*Mi amor*, please."

Her phone chirped, startling her. A text from Monique. *Call me. Are you going to make the meeting at noon? Are you OK?*

He looked at her expectantly. "Who is it? Tell me it isn't him!"

She took a deep breath. "It's Monique."

He sighed with relief and then raised his brows in apprehension. "Good. Why don't you have her come over?"

"Have to go to the office." She wasn't going to tell him all. "It's important. Even if it might be Victor's film, if he's the backer, he won't be there. That's not the way it works. And a little law will be good for me."

It will remind me how and why to fight for justice, she thought. She and Monique had an angle to work to turn this front man, and they were both still committed.

A perfect way to get her own revenge. She knew Tía would back her on this. She had a right to secret battle plans too!

Time to send her lover on his way.

She stood and closed the distance between them. Then she kissed him hard. "Go meet your Flo and tell her hello from me. She'd better watch your back, or she'll have to deal with me!"

He kissed her back, deep and hard. They held each other tightly for a lingering moment.

"Okay, *maître*." He relented because he knew he couldn't stop her. "Promise me you won't go alone. And be careful."

She nodded. "Heed your own advice, *commissaire*. I want you back in one piece."

He hated to leave, afraid for her—and for himself if he lost her.

Chapter 66

As soon as Torres left, Kikki went back to their bedroom and sat at her Art Deco dressing table. She made quick work of makeup and hair—a swipe of mascara, black kohl eyeliner, dark burgundy lipstick and a light foundation. She swept her hair up in a half French twist, fanned her bangs and pulled a few locks to frame her face. A few strategic sprays of perfume. *Prête!*

She looked at herself closely. Still pale. She pinched her cheeks and then applied blush. She selected a pair of favorite large circular handmade silver earrings from Santorini—copies of those worn by the priestesses in prehistoric Akrotiri. Jeans and black turtleneck set off by a short red leather jacket. Perfect for her meeting. She gathered her red vintage Vuitton Saint-Jacques bag and threw in her iPad and phone.

She opened the bedroom door quietly and tiptoed to the fireplace in her low-heeled black suede boots. She hoped Tía wouldn't appear and hover over her.

Before leaving, she wanted a few moments alone to set the protection in the apartment and clear her own energy. She needed vital information. She had no time for the niceties of placing actual crystals in strategic corners.

She sat, closing her eyes. With a deep breath, she summoned grounding from Mother Earth and called light down from the universe. She filled the entire apartment so it glowed with gold light, surrounded it with certainty blue. She placed invisible white marble pillars at each corner of the apartment and expanded the field of protection beyond the actual perimeters. A virtual container of protection—like a ship or a large crystalline bubble.

Satisfied, she opened her eyes. She stood and faced the fire, arms raised, palms up in blessing. Praying for critical information. What was she missing? She eyed her Tarot cards on the mantelpiece.

She picked them up, shuffled once and split them, turning one card up. The Devil—again. A demonic monster sitting upon a throne, a fallen angel that ruled alongside Hades, the underworld. Enslavement to carnal desires, a man and woman in chains, an exchange of gold. An undeniable patriarch, cunning and vicious. Scaling the peaks of power at all costs.

She shuddered. Given the overwhelming darkness of these nights before balance began on the Winter Solstice—when dark and light would equalize—this card was a confirmation. The Knights of the Holy Sword of God were all that the Devil represented—with Victor as Grand Guignol and Devil.

The last card Liam had drawn on Monday—he had said it meant betrayal—that someone would tempt her and test her. Someone from her past who had chosen this karmic path. And it was about the curse too. She flashed on Catherine de Medici appearing in his suite and shuddered.

Victor. Before, she had always seen at least some logic to his ways, even though he was thoroughly Machiavellian and narcissistic. She had been wrong. Or his maniacal side had taken over. He was possessed by the darkness behind a mask that was becoming harder for him to hide.

She felt invisible daggers stab her shoulders. She intended to draw him to her—she intended to take him down. But could she do it without getting drawn into his circle of Hell worse than death?

A buzz! Her phone startling her. She glanced at it, worried it might be Victor.

Relief flooded her. It was Liam, already speaking. "I'm sending a limo. Don't go anywhere until it's there."

"Did Torres call you, or are you just being the Magician?" She laughed.

"Does it matter?"

"I was just about to walk out the door."

"Well, don't be stupid."

She sighed heavily. Liam and Torres were right. She had to be more careful. Cunning and calculating like Margot. Not leave herself exposed.

"Okay. I am going to my office to meet—"

"I know."

"Oh, so it was Monique, then."

He didn't answer her. "Where's Tía?" he asked.

"How do you know that she's alive? *Merde, alors!* Everyone knows everyone and everything. Why am I the last to find out?"

"Calm down, Kikki. I will tell you later."

"I don't know where she is. Torres said she had something for me to do, but she seems to have disappeared."

"Gotta go. Another call. Wait for me!" He disconnected.

She shook her head and crossed the room to the windows. The curtains were open, and the sky was dark and grey. A heavy *grisaille*. The bare branches of trees bordering the Seine swayed angrily on a strong northeast wind. She opened the French paned door a crack. It was bitter cold and it smelled like snow again.

Tía had been sitting quietly at the kitchen table doing her own meditation, veiling her presence. She had to leave soon, but she wanted to stay until Liam came for Kikki. She heard her speaking to him. She smiled and stood, and then moved quietly.

Just as she was about to lay an arm on Kikki's shoulder, Kikki pivoted. "Tía!"

"I didn't mean to alarm you," she said, taking Kikki's hand. "You are going to your office."

"Yes. I have to get out of here. Everyone is trying to protect me. But I—"

They walked arm in arm to the sofa and sat next to each other.

"Remember that you have allies."

"Yes, I do." She thought of Liam and Monique, and Tía. "But I have to lead this battle. I know that. Last night I was—caught off guard." She hesitated.

"Verónica, *querida*, *basta*! That is ridiculous. And you know it. You don't have to play with words with me. I am not your protective lover. Of course, you are going to be front and center. It is your calling and your journey. You will make mistakes—or call them errors in judgment."

"Like last night. Goddesses, how could I have been so naïve not to see behind his mask?"

"It was a rite of passage. And you survived. There are going to be things that you do that you will think later are ill-thought-out or too risky. But don't let that paralyze you."

"I won't. Believe me. It has only motivated me."

"We will bring you into the Daughters of Inanna and we will all support you in this."

"Wonderful! When?" Kikki's heart quickened at the news. About time!

"Later today we will begin. We have been waiting for certain elements to align. And now, it is time for you to join us." Tía stood with Kikki. "But it is important that you go to your meeting today. For many reasons. Don't be afraid."

"Yes, I agree." Kikki felt a renewed empowerment.

"Do not forget we are here too. Call upon the Goddess. And call upon Margot for help. She is your muse and protector. She will guide you through the labyrinth in these dark days."

Chapter 67

Liam arrived to pick up Kikki in a sedan driven by his trustworthy chauffeur, Claude. When she opened the door, she was only mildly surprised to find her friend waiting for her. She hadn't known Liam, himself, would come.

"Your chariot awaits, *mademoiselle!*"

"How perfect!"

"You didn't think I'd let you cross Paris alone?"

"It's hardly a twenty-minute walk to my office. I've been locked up, drowned and—"

"Trust me," he said. Urbane sarcasm, no nonsense. "Better to be safe. Besides, it's freezing outside. Disgusting weather."

"Winter in Paris." She settled into the seat and was glad to let Liam take over.

He directed the driver to head to her office on narrow rue de Valois on the eastern edge of the Palais Royal.

"Nice leather seats. Warm too. Liam—"

"What else? How are the cards playing out?"

"Rather exactly, so far. I expect Tía has filled you in," she said shortly.

He narrowed his eyes behind his fashionably framed glasses,

inspecting her casual *chic* under a long black shearling coat. Brightened only by a flaming red cashmere shawl and oversized Greek handmade silver earrings.

"What? Don't you think I look like a lawyer anymore?"

"Honey, you never did. Live with it." He laughed. "And be glad."

"I guess. You are right, as long as I am Justice personified. Am I?"

"Exactly, Goddess Athena. Have you brought your sword and your all-seeing owl?"

He slipped his Tarot cards from his pocket and drew one: Justice.

"Perfect, and just as we are coming up towards the Palais de Justice," she said. "I fervently wish—"

"So, are you meeting the new client?" He felt her mood slip.

"Yes."

Liam raised his eyebrows. "Again, are you sure it's wise?"

She told him what Victor had said about a new film and the Louvre. "It's all connected, of course. Seriously, Henri IV, Margot's husband? So, have you talked to Monique recently?"

"No, only texts checking up on you. In person, it's been awhile. Luckily, I haven't needed the services of a lawyer in some time. And your fees, darling."

She shrugged. "You know what they say—if you don't charge enough, they won't think you're any good. So, Monique, I expect you told her about what happened last night."

"Yes," Liam said thoughtfully. "She's a very close friend, and she needed to know. She's worried about you. And so am I."

Kikki eyed him a bit suspiciously, "I expect she's a member of the Daughters of Inanna as well as you, correct?"

He tipped his head in a Greek gesture of "yes" and changed the subject. "What do you expect to get out of this man? You really think you can turn him to help you? Do you have enough information on him?"

"I know how Victor operates. He will have blackmailed this man. We'll offer him an alternative to help us. It's clear from the script that he expects push back on the project with such an outrageously sexist and patriarchally slanted storyline. They've even thrown in a scene involving the Black Queen sending bounty hunters after Margot and her baby daughter."

"Hmm. Yes, clearly, they expect to get your ire up. Do you want me to come to the meeting as support?"

"No! Monique and I can handle this."

"Fine. But call me if there's any problem. Everyone is on high alert."

"You mean everyone in the Daughters of Inanna, I suppose." She held his gaze, not letting him off the hook just yet. She wanted to know more.

"Well, of course. Who else?" He reminded himself to tread carefully. She would be hurt.

"Why didn't you tell me about this before? That's how you and Tía know each other."

"I'm sorry. I couldn't. And you had your own bi-continental battles to fight. In Paris, New York and then Spain. You fell in love —for real. Then Santorini, where you built Hotel Atlantis with Cleo. But don't get me started on that. Trust me. You were doing the same thing we do."

"I can't say, Liam. I guess I'll find out very soon, according to Tía."

"Don't be upset, Kikki. You're right in the thick of it now." And he was frightened for her.

"Yes. I am." She crossed her legs and looked out the window. "What else? Tell me about how you came to be involved."

"In typical fashion for my Greek heritage, my connection is very twisted. My mother is quite the witch, but you know that. Well, 'witch' may not be the right word. But she's a Daughter, and of course, she married my father who is all about the Knights and the One True God and their Holy Sword." He rolled his eyes.

Kikki chuckled, "Quite the Greek tragedy. Explains why you're who you are. Nice combination—really." She kissed him on the cheek. "Old World and New World at once, by which I mean Europe and the new continent we fondly call the States. And a gallant *gentilhomme* with amazing otherworldly abilities."

Kikki's third eye was opening along with her crown chakra as they inched across the Pont Neuf to the Rive Droite. On the right was the lovely triangle-shaped Place Dauphine. Through the perfect symmetry of barren chestnut trees was the Palais de Justice. Literally a palace with classic Doric columns, lions guarding the entrance and a peaked roof flanked by enormous eagles.

As she gazed at the courthouse, she relaxed, glad to be with Liam. As much as she loved Torres, she frequently felt that she had to hide her abilities from him—or she consciously did so that he wouldn't worry. Just as he protected her. She understood why. He saw the world from a very different viewpoint. He had to operate in the real world, fighting off bad guys all the time.

As for Liam, she wondered how he had met Tía and become entwined with the Daughters of Inanna, but he was ever enigmatic. Another day, she sighed.

All of a sudden, the driver slammed on the brakes. Liam automatically threw an arm across Kikki as she lurched forward. She covered her head when she heard a loud noise.

Was that a gunshot that she had heard? Holy Goddess! Maybe Torres was right. She should have stayed home. Horns honked loudly, as if affirming her thoughts.

"It's just a car backfiring," Liam said, slowly. "*Perimene*! Wait. Slow down, Claude."

Kikki's heart fluttered as she watched the plume of gray smoke rise from the back end of a sleek black sedan with a flashing blue light. Who was it? A French Minister? An enemy?

Just at that moment, her eyes were drawn to flames shooting from the caldron of a hooded chestnut vendor. He had appeared out of nowhere on the opposite side of the Pont Neuf just in front of the statue of Henri IV on his stallion. The smoke curled high and turned black, contrasting starkly to the *grisaille*. She shivered. The image of the Devil card flashed.

"Not just a car backfiring. Something dark and of another world," Liam said in a haunted voice.

"And not a good omen—" Kikki whispered.

Chapter 68

Tía had left the apartment soon after Kikki. Disguised as an old man this time, long black braids tucked under a wool cap, wearing a white beard, she had taken her taxi and driven herself to Place Colette in front of La Comédie Française and the Palais Royal.

She sat now, sipping a double expresso and smiled at her companion, Monique Dubois. They were in the Café Nemours just on the edge of the square. She loved this café because of the iconic free-spirited, fierce Colette. And also because it favored coffee served in a glass, as it was often served in Spain.

Monique Dubois de Thorigny was nervous, but not about Tía. Even though she only met with Tía on those occasions when she came to Paris for the Daughters of Inanna's meetings of the Council of the Eight, Monique was the Daughters' gatekeeper by right of birth, a maternal descendant of Gillonne de Thorigny, Margot's lady-in-waiting and confidante.

Monique was proud to be a descendant of brave Gillonne, who had been the daughter of the Maréchal of France, Jacques de Matignon de Thorigny. Gillonne had originally been the principal attendant to the Queen Regent, Catherine de Medici. It was Catherine who sent Gillonne to serve her daughter Margot, in order to spy on her. Gillonne had quickly proved completely and ferociously loyal to Margot.

Monique had held the position of gatekeeper of the Daughters of Inanna since she turned eighteen. She had trained for it from the age of thirteen, when children became women. Monique loved the ritual of preparing the Chapelle des Louanges for the council. Lighting the candles, ensuring that the crystal stones for the perimeters were clean and in place—crystals cut into the shape of the eight-pointed star, Inanna's symbol, and that of Aphrodite. A rosette and a star at once.

The secret society had once been based in a convent in Tuscany and earlier in Nîmes, at the Temple of Diane, around the time the Romans led by Julius Caesar conquered Gaul in the First Century AD.

Monique was proud the society was in Paris now. As proud as she was of her own French heritage from the Daughters through her mother. And equally so of lineage through her Greek father, also a member of the Daughters of Inanna.

"The rosette of Inanna, my fair daughter," her father had told her in Greek, "Is that of Aphrodite, the Goddess of Love. Make her shine."

Tía had always been kind and funny, and a strong role model for Monique. She had a lot on her mind, and she wanted to talk a few things over with Tía. Monique was prepared, but it would be helpful to have Tía's counsel. She wanted to do her best for Kikki and for the Daughters of Inanna.

Tía set the glass of coffee onto the table. "Are you ready for your meeting?" Tía smiled fondly, catching the light of the café in Monique's green eyes and honey-golden hair.

"Yes. I've done all I can," Monique said, smoothing unnecessarily her leather skirt. "But I'm nervous. How is she holding up, really? I haven't seen her and barely spoken to her. She only texts." Liam had kept her up to date on what had happened to Kikki over the last couple of days. But they both agreed that it was best not to question Kikki about it.

Tía reached across the table and took Monique's hand in her own. "She's quite tired. But don't worry. She's strong and ready. Very determined."

Monique held Tía's eyes and nodded.

"Just be there to stand by her at this meeting. After it's over, come to me at the chapel, and we will get everything ready for her initiation later tonight."

"I bow to your wisdom, of course. And I will support her in any way I can." Monique sipped her coffee pensively.

"She must find her own way. She will take Inanna's journey to the Underworld, and back, before this is over. We all have a path to walk and a part to play. Yours is to be her right hand."

"*C'est vrai.* I'm worried about missing details. I've been able to find out a bit more since we spoke about this client, Robert Moreno, and the film project. I've been snooping around about the French partner. We haven't had time to work on a strategy since Kikki and I talked Monday, but now we know exactly who is behind the project. We know the enemy: Victor Fitz-Perkins, her old boss. A ruthless and dangerous man. How can I protect her from him?"

"That isn't your job, Monique. Just support her. Use your combined power. She needs to stand on her own and face this challenge. She's furious. As she should be. She is at a crossroads. I trust that you both know exactly how to handle this minion of Victor's."

"Yes, it's not our first rodeo, as Kikki says." Monique smiled.

"Then all you have to do is hold her hand as she walks across the bridge. It's a critical moment for both of you."

"Of course." Monique took a dainty sip of coffee. "I traced the French *aristo*—he's connected to the money through the shells and their off-shore accounts. He has ties to the Medicis and Bourbons, not surprisingly. Certainly, someone at the top of the Swords' hierarchy. Patriarchal stalwarts of France. Some of our worst. They will all be at the gala on Friday night, Tía."

Tía smiled again at Monique, nodding. She knew Monique needed assurance.

"The budget is huge. The director is well-known and has scouted the location—not far from here." Monique warmed to her subject and felt calmer, more competent. "They plan to shoot at Château d'Amboise, with many scenes in and around Paris, Château de Chantilly, perhaps Château Saint-Germain-en-Laye, where Margot was born. And, naturally, the Louvre."

"Margot spent some years of her childhood at the Château d'Amboise with her favorite brother, François Alençon—Hercule they called him. The Black Queen tucked them away there for safety," Tía noted. "Unfortunately, because they were there, they both witnessed one of the most brutally violent events of the religious wars—the *Conjuration*—the Amboise Conspiracy. A rebellion against King Francois II. In retaliation, the Valois Catholics hung more than a thousand Huguenots from the parapets of the château."

"*Tragique!*" Monique said, "But on a brighter note, the Château d'Amboise is famously the home to King François Premier and Leonardo da Vinci, who spent his last days at the Clos de Lucé nearby. He was invited by the king and came from Florence by donkey, carrying with him his most famous painting, the *Mona Lisa.*"

"He was one of us, you know—a member of the Daughters of Inanna." Tía's eyes shone with pride.

"Yes. It is close to my French ancestral home in Blois where the Valois royals spent much time." Monique smiled and settled.

Tía flipped a mini-Cohiba out of a slim silver case and frowned. She couldn't smoke in here. *Mierda!*

"Sorry, do you want to go outside, Tía?"

"No." Tía lifted the cigarillo to her nose and sniffed the pungent tobacco. "Tell me more about the film."

"The opening scene portrays Henri de Navarre, a Bourbon prince, and Margot meeting as young children, overseen by Catherine de Medici. When Henri de Navarre's mother Jeanne d'Albret was still alive. Jeanne d'Albret was an austere and formidable Huguenot leader. Before Cruel Mother Medici handed Jeanne her death with poisoned gloves. Whether or not that is true, or only legend, we know the Medici had a black magic hand in causing the death."

"Madame la Serpente did not tolerate competition from other powerful women."

"Or men, unless she controlled them—" Monique laced elegant fingers around her glass.

"The Swords, and Victor Fitz-Perkins in particular, view the Black Queen as an inspiration and a kingmaker. Beware, Monique.

This client, even though only a minion, will carry her evil energy. I have felt her presence dogging us. Her ghost and those of her actual descendants will join the battle this week." Tía added gravely, "She will do all she can to thwart us." Her voice lowered to a whisper, and she signaled with a finger to her lips that Monique should do the same.

Monique inclined her head in agreement.

Earlier, Tía had scoped out the cafe thoroughly and blasted white light of protection throughout. But they had to constantly be vigilant. They'd brought up a lot of dark topics that may have invited in their enemies.

"We know exactly who's behind the film, and all you have to do is get to this front man. *Como se llama?* Moreno? That should be easy for you two warrior queens." Tía chuckled. "He won't know what hit him by the time the meeting is over."

Monique laughed, "*Bien sûr.* Coming from New York, he is the perfect front for the Swords and Fitz-Perkins, and hence, the antique racketeers. I just need better details on their financial trail— the millions that they have already put into a production account— supposedly for the film. The Swords have excellent people working for them and know how to cover their tracks. But I'm no hacker. I wish we could get that info now."

"*Mira*, Monique, eventually details are important, but you have a handle on the big picture. And if you run into a snag, the Goddess will be with you."

Monique took a sip of her coffee. "Respectfully, Tía, I'm not sure I agree. I'd like to be able to throw some confidential info at this guy, let him know that we know exactly what they're up to, put him in the hot seat. Can Torres help get the info we need?"

"No. He's up to his eyeballs. He's having a hard time letting Kikki out of his sight. I'd rather you and Kikki handled it."

"I guess. I could ask JM—"

"Too risky. He would feel obligated to tell Torres."

"True. Okay. We'll work with what we have. But I still don't like it. It's very dangerous for her." Monique's voice was fiercely protective of Kikki.

"Know your enemy. Use Moreno. He will be vulnerable. I feel it strongly."

"I know. And the enemy of our enemy is our friend. Still, Moreno will insist that she meet with the producers. *Comme d'habitude.*" Monique finished her coffee, anxious to get to the office now. "I just hope he doesn't bring Victor with him."

Tía raised an eyebrow in question. "Highly unlikely. Stay close to her."

The two women stood, kissed each other and then hugged with affection.

"I will see you at the chapel this afternoon, Monique. We will get everything ready for all of our Solstice visitors and for Kikki."

"You can count on me." Monique made her way nimbly, like a dancer, through the circus of tiny tables being set now for the lunch service. She bundled herself in her fur, stepping into the cold.

Chapter 69

In the dark inner corridor on the fifth floor of no. 15 rue de Valois, Kikki turned the skeleton key in the lock. The door opened. She hit the inner panel and light flooded her offices.

Before crossing the threshold, she paused and looked over her shoulder. She saw no one in the hall, but she felt a presence. More ethereal than real. Hopefully one of the friendly ghosts that haunted the old building.

She sniffed the air—heady perfume. Margot would be along soon—especially on rue de Valois. She hadn't told all. Like everyone else, she was dropping pieces of the puzzle one at a time. Life would be so much easier if Kikki had the whole picture to guide her through the maze of twists and turns, with surprises around each corner.

But she knew it didn't work that way—not with Margot or anyone else. Kikki fervently hoped Margot would finish this installment of her memoirs in time.

With a deep sigh, Kikki crossed the threshold and closed the heavy oak door behind her.

"Anyone here?" She hoped not. She wanted a moment alone. Though she would be happy and comforted to see Monique, she wanted to center herself and ground in this other reality she owned. This other world that for so long had been hers. For how much longer, she wondered.

The small reception area was banked by a row of windows overlooking the gardens of the Palais Royal. She pulled the sheers and curtains back and gazed out at the lovely garden. An oasis in the midst of a busy city. It was quiet now—the central stone fountain silent, its waters a frozen pond. In the bleak weather, she only saw a few people huddled in their coats on benches scattered about the garden. A man and woman sat together sharing sections of *Le Monde*, each with a tiny paper cup of coffee.

Soft lights in apartments and offices across the garden on rue de Montpensier comforted her. Veiled figures, most familiar to her, at their stations. It was she who had not been in the office for a while. She glanced at her phone and saw that it was nearly 11:45.

She caught the silhouette of a tall, slim woman directly across from her in an office of the palace. The woman stood and went to the electric kettle on the window ledge and began preparations for her morning tea break. Kikki let out a breath that she hadn't realized she was holding. She moved quietly to an inner room on her right, her office.

On her Italian design rectangular glass table that served as her desk was an enormous bouquet of white roses in a tall crystal vase. Their heady aroma filled the room. She smiled and opened the card. "*Pour toi!*" A thoughtful gift from Monique.

Finally, she sat in her chair at the desk, assuming her rightful throne of justice.

On the leather blotter was the familiar sight of a blue dossier marked with a note from Monique. She opened it and began to read Monique's update about Robert Moreno and his production.

Kikki had been engrossed in the file and was skimming the script again along with her colleague's updates. And then, she heard them outside talking in hushed voices, a man with a very deep baritone and Monique sounding very cheerful. Moreno and Monique arriving together.

Dommage, she thought as she stood and left her office. She had been hoping to have a few minutes alone with Monique so they could go over the new information and strategy. Perhaps it was better this way. No questions about the last few days and the horrors Kikki had lived through. She needed to keep her focus and *sang froid* for the meeting.

Kikki reviewed again Monique's notes and her own information. Victor was behind the film—he'd told her so. They just had to nail that tie down, connect the dots of the conspiracy—connect him and his Italian partner to the shell companies, to the production funding through Swiss, Cypriot and other off-shore accounts. A paper trail— solid proof of fraud and money laundering.

Monique had reached out to her contacts from the Faculté de Droit and her family connections to get info from French and international agencies based in Paris, Lyon, the Hague. She was compiling evidence against dirty officials at the Ministries of Culture, Justice and Interior who were using the Louvre to advance the goals of the Swords' criminal conspiracy.

Kikki thought all were fronts for their war efforts. And undoubtedly dirty money—from the sale of blood antiquities.

They knew that Moreno was being used—blackmailed by Fitz-Perkins. Turning Moreno was key to that.

Kikki took a deep breath and donned Athena's helmet. Resolve to bring them down strengthened. She thought about Torres warning to stay away and smiled with secret satisfaction. She and Monique would help bring that son of a bitch down—it was very personal to Kikki now.

The door opened, and Kikki crossed the short distance to greet them. Kisses and a hug for Monique. She whispered in French, "You look fabulous, as always."

"You look wonderful too," Monique said with affection, though she saw the strained fine lines around her friend's eyes. "Allow me introduce you to Mr. Moreno, Kikki."

"Bob, please, *maître*." He insisted, giving Kikki a very firm handshake.

"*Enchantée*," Kikki said with a smile, letting go of his hand. Very New York. And there was something familiar about him, but what? "And please call me Kikki."

They headed down the corridor past the reception into the small but elegantly furnished conference room. Monique took Moreno's coat.

"Shall I make us some coffee?" Monique suggested. "You can get to know each other."

"That would be divine. I imagine you were here earlier. It is toasty warm. Thank you."

Chapter 70

Kikki studied Moreno as he settled into the comfortable leather chair at their round conference table. He was the epitome of an executive producer for feature film. Turtleneck sweater, leather jacket of softest leather, jeans and motorcycle trimmed boots. All black. He wore his thinning brown hair in a ponytail and sported oversized black framed glasses.

He carried a slim black leather portfolio. He slung it casually onto the table, unzipping it.

"Just let me get out my iPad. It will make it easier if you have visuals—storyboards of what we are doing with this film. It's going to be amazing," he said without looking at her.

"Great. Eventually—Bob?" Kikki drew his attention.

"Yes? Sorry." He looked up. Behind the glasses, Kikki saw big dark circles under his squinty eyes. They were quite bloodshot. I'm a bit jet lagged," he said, sounding chagrined. "Out late last night. Heard some great jazz in Saint-Germain. Didn't know that was possible still—"

"Oh indeed, if you know where to go. Though winter may not be the best season. Coffee will be here soon. Monique makes the strongest coffee." Kikki settled back into a chair across from him.

She shot him her best disarming smile. "So, tell me about the film and what you think we can do for you."

"Right," he said, tapping his screen with a certain frustration. "Oh, fuck it."

"Relax. You're in Paris. I've skimmed your script."

"Right. And we've got a fantastic director. Lined up very A-list actors."

Kikki poured a glass of water for each of them and sipped hers. He was very nervous around her. With Monique, he had seemed relaxed, easy-going. Almost California, rather than New York.

"How do you come to me? Did someone refer you?" She hoped he would mention Victor. Highly unlikely, but perhaps whatever he responded would help her place his familiarity.

"Yes—uh—a well-known French film producer, Gerome Jaoen."

He was lying to her. She could tell from the twitch of his thin upper lip.

At that moment, Monique arrived bearing a silver tray with coffee service for three. "I'll just put it here and let you serve yourselves." She glanced at Kikki long enough to understand that her partner needed a bit more time. "Oops, forgot something. Be right back."

"Tell me more about the production."

"Its working title is *Henry IV: King of Navarre & France.* Our creative team is still tweaking. There have been many films about this fascinating man. Perhaps you'll have a good idea. I understand you are quite a history buff."

"Modestly, yes. Especially that period. I'm sure you'll find the right title—that one is definitely not sexy. But frankly—"

"Excellent." He wasn't listening to her but checking his phone for messages.

A telltale swish of satin skirts caught Kikki's attention. Margot was nearby.

Kikki stood and walked to the window. The scene overlooking the garden shifted. She blinked. The couple sharing the newspaper stood up and looked straight at her. But they weren't the couple who had been there earlier.

Catherine de Medici with Henri de Bourbon, Prince of Navarre on her arm, the small boy, aged about twelve years old.

He looked up to the Medici as she spoke, as if taking her counsel. She nodded solemnly. But the bemused look in his eyes belied his agreement and revealed his independent nature.

Kikki shivered. She closed her eyes and silently pleaded, "If I am to be here in the real world doing work as our lady of justice then you must help me turn this man."

Margot appeared next to her in a voluminous dress of regal red and glimmering pearls. She whispered, "I am here."

"Good. I need you."

"Talk to this man. He is weak. You can use him to your advantage against my mother, the Queen. He is connected."

When Kikki came out of trance, it was Monique who stood next to her.

Kikki gulped. "Where has he gone, Monique? I barely got a thing out of him."

"He stepped out to take a call. I took him into my office."

And now that Kikki was back in the present, she could hear the arguing. He was talking to the film's backer. Was it Victor?

Moreno returned, avoiding eye contact. "You know how they are—the producers."

"Yes. I understand. Sit down, and let's move on." She spoke sternly, all business. "Before you go on, I want you to understand that I am taking on very few, if any, new projects."

"I heard that you've been away. I hope it is nothing serious."

"All is well. But if you wish me to take this on, I have certain conditions."

He fidgeted with his phone, reading text messages, and without looking at her said, "I am sure we can meet any conditions you desire."

And that was always what they said—in the romancing stage, before you agreed. Then you became enslaved to their every want and need. On call day and night. Incessant hand-holding of ego driven child-men.

"We think that you will be especially interested in this film because Marguerite de Valois—La Reine Margot—plays a big role. Rightly so."

"As a film, *La Reine Margot* has been done, and very well, most recently by Patrice Chéreau. But your film—well—let us be blunt. Your script is offensively sexist. It paints a completely negative picture of Marguerite de Valois. Monique and I cannot associate ourselves with such blatant patriarchal propaganda. Not sure you can overcome that hurdle."

"Huh. Well, we might be open to—err—suggestions. Keep in mind that we want to make the film accessible to our wide American audience. But it's also international. It's a huge multinational coproduction. We have French, English and other European partners." His chin lifted slightly, almost challenging, definitely bragging.

She tapped her Dupont fountain pen on her notebook. He had given her a nonresponse response to her objections. Typical.

She pushed further, "Putting our story differences aside for a moment, it's a very ambitious project. And your memo states that you intend to start production in mid-January. That's very soon. You will need me to do your production agreements. Complicated and time-consuming work—and my fees will be substantial. Especially if you are firm on that production start date."

"No big deal. And Monique can do all the agreements." He shot her a crooked smile, showing a row of extremely white teeth. "We need you more as our front person—an ambassador—to represent us and obtain favorable treatment from the French institutions that govern the locations—Versailles, Château d'Amboise, the Ministry of Culture, the Louvre—" He narrowed his eyes. "You will know how to navigate all the French bureaucratic bullshit. We have some very special scenes planned. We need you to streamline things, so we can keep to our schedule."

Of course. The Snake Goddess Exhibition, Victor's vague comment about business with the Louvre, that the museum might be of some help with the film. Confirmation from the source. The film was a perfect façade. A Machiavellian means to the endgame—sets and all.

"It's easy really," Kikki said casually, despite her growing need to pry information from him. "You don't need an expert. Rappers have done scenes with the Mona Lisa, for example. Not to mention *The Da Vinci Code*. Child's play."

"Not in this case, but I can't tell you more until you are retained

—officially."

She remained silent. His eyes were brighter now, she noticed. Had he had some chemical assistance in Monique's office while "taking a call"? Likely.

Sweat beaded on his forehead. He spoke in an overly loud voice, saying, "You have quite a network. And you have a reputation for getting things done." His nervousness increased so he pumped his thigh up and down.

"Thank you." She nodded. He was intimidated by her, she realized.

"It's not necessarily a compliment. Your reputation is well established. You are known as quite a tiger. You should open your own production studio here."

"The last thing I need." She laughed, genuinely amused. Despite the situation, and the fact that her senses were on high alert, she almost liked this awkward, rather timid man.

"I get it. But hey, let me cut to the chase here." He sat back, slightly more relaxed.

"Please." She checked her phone pointedly for the time. "I would appreciate it."

"We have some added benefits that may outweigh your issues with the script."

"Such as?" Here it comes.

"Err. How can I put this? Because of certain connections—uh—relationships—in France and elsewhere, we have access to private collections of the Valois dynasty, Marguerite in particular, the Medicis, and others close to her. These have been kept secret—known of by only our people—secret treasures that have never seen the light of day."

"That is quite a carrot." Was it real, or just a trick? Margot's words came back to her. *"Use him. He is connected."*

"Do you have some personal connection to these families, Robert—Bob? Because that is what it would take. The aristocracy did not die with the revolution or the terror. It is alive and well."

He shot her a childish smile. "You know, I really like you."

So American, she thought, right out there in the open, flattery of the most personal kind, upfront. The strangest thing was that she actually liked him, too, though she felt the shadowy edge of Victor and the Black Queen behind Bob Moreno's mask. His contacts with a secret collection—he was a man beholden to the dark.

"Thank you, it's good to meet you too." Time to push their agenda. "Let me hazard an educated guess. One of your producers must be related to the Medicis or the Bourbons. They were infamous at keeping those kinds of rare *objets* protected and in their hands."

Monique interrupted in her best American English. "Most definitely. So, is that it, Bob?"

"I really cannot say, as much as I would like to," Moreno said, his upper lip ticking nervously.

"Well how can we verify that your so-called advantages are real?" Monique challenged.

"Monique is absolutely correct. And, rare objects notwithstanding—" Kikki glanced at Monique, who shot an affirming smile, "Marguerite de Valois would have been a better ruler than any of the pathetic men who became king, including Henry the Great. If it hadn't been for her monster of a mother, she might have had the chance."

Moreno's eyes widened. Kikki thought he seemed scared that he might be turned down.

"Right," Monique chimed in. "Bob, with respect because I know you're just the front man here, important as an executive producer, but I have to say it. Why the hell would Kikki and I represent you? Your film literally silences one of the most important and interesting feminine voices of the era. And the Black Queen puts a bounty on Margot's child. Seriously?"

"Well, literary license. Anyway, history says Margot was barren," he said. "It's just a plot device to grab the audience."

And to get our attention, Kikki thought, exchanging a knowing look with Monique.

"But we're not doing a bio-pic. So what does it matter anyway?" Moreno said.

The bigger puzzle was coming into focus for Kikki. Her inner psychic radio tuned in. She was beginning to see who he was, where he came from and how he fit.

"It's not important how or why we have them, is it? Look, let's talk more. Can you be available later this evening, at say 8:30 p.m., to meet the producers for dinner?"

Kikki's stomach clenched at his request. Into the lion's den to meet Victor.

"I will have to check my schedule. It is a very busy time."

His hands trembled as he slipped a check from his portfolio and handed it to Kikki. "Perhaps this will be persuasive. A modest retainer."

A check for one hundred thousand euros. Not in the least modest. In fact, such a sum was *gauche*, in the true French sense. But so very American.

The small bronze statue of Athena holding the scales of justice in the middle of the round table began, unaccountably, to move. Balancing the firm's coffers might be a very good idea. If Moreno hadn't been sitting in front of her, she would have placed the check on the scale to see if it did balance or rather, weighted too much to one side, dragging her and Monique down. The feather and heart weighed on the scales by the Egyptian Goddess of Justice Maat.

"Very impressive." She studied the check and learned nothing more than the name of a holding company in Lichtenstein. She thought it matched the information that Monique had included in the file. Monique could probably dig deeper given a bit more time. Kikki hoped they had the time.

"I'll just hold this, shall I—" She said coolly. But her mind raced, dizzy from travel to other realms in search of answers. Goddesses give me answers to the puzzle of this man. He is clearly charged with baiting the trap.

"Of course. If you cash it, we will be more than pleased."

"Yes, I can see that," Kikki said. "But we need to know more, Mr. Moreno—" She paused, held his eyes and it fell into place. "Or is it Mr. Medici?"

She watched his eyes go wide behind the big frames.

Chapter 71

After they had ushered Moreno out of the office, Kikki and Monique sat together again.

"Wow!" Monique sat across the conference table from Kikki. "A Medici? I saw his reaction. But you're certain? How?"

"You know, the way of all good white witches." Kikki chuckled, and so did Monique.

"Psychically, oh High Priestess. Glad to see you haven't lost your touch. You need it."

"Well, Margot gave me a few hints."

"The last time we talked—" Monique paused, swallowing hurt that Kikki hadn't confided in her this week, telling herself to be strong for her friend. "You told me she'd been in your dreams and visions. Was she here today, then? Because I didn't see her or sense her. You know that sometimes I do."

Kikki laughed, "Yes, you are an excellent psychic. If you weren't, I wouldn't be in practice with you. She appeared to me this morning and said that we should use Moreno and that he had a connection to her despicable mother."

"Why am I not surprised?" Monique quipped. "But he does seem malleable, *non*? A Medici—with that lineage, he will be a dark, twisted soul. *Incroyable*. Though given the subject of the film and what's going on this week—"

Kikki felt Monique's hurt and knew she had to say something to her friend.

"Monique, *écoute*, I'm sorry I've been out of touch. It's been difficult. But nothing has changed since we talked on Monday. I'm still determined."

"But are you okay? Holy Athena! What you have gone through," she said quietly with concern, searching her friend's eyes.

"I expect that Tía and Liam filled you in. I'm sorry I couldn't. I hope you're not upset with me—or hurt."

"I understand. You haven't had a minute, from what I hear. Seriously, are you all right?" And, despite what Tía had said, Monique wasn't sure that Kikki should be dealing with this client and his film at all.

"I'm better than a couple of days ago after my near death in the river, though last night was quite a setback. That son of a bitch!"

"You come too close, *ma belle*. I'd hate to lose you." Monique tried to keep emotion out of her voice, but she took her friend's hand and held her gaze.

"Everything that's happened this week has been transformative. Though I'm not sure who I am turning into, *tu sais?*"

"*Ç'est normal.* You don't have to explain it to me."

"Yes, and this week has been an emotional and energetic roller coaster, and we're not half through it." Kikki quieted. She'd said enough about her journey. She knew that Monique got it. She'd taught her a lot, and she came by it naturally. And now that Kikki knew that Monique was a Daughter of Inanna, many things made sense.

"Though, Monique, it feels good to be here in the office, oddly enough. The energy is yours. Very light and clear."

"Thank you—" Though she longed for a good chat, Monique knew that she had to hurry this reunion along. "What do you think, then, Kikki? One hundred thousand euros? We could do quite a lot."

"It's a bribe," Kikki said with spark. "It's dirty money. The Patriarchy. Moreno-Medici. We know the film is backed by that son of a bitch who kidnapped me, Victor Fitz-Perkins. That would include his Florentine partner, as they're in the antiquities racket together. All for the Swords. You must know all about them. And Victor is the Grand Guignol."

"*Sans doute.* So let's nail the bastards to the wall!" Monique said fiercely.

"Right!" Kikki said, raising an arm high into the air. "Strike!"

"You are a total badass, Kikki." Monique loved using that so-American expression that had no real equivalent in French. None as satisfying.

Kikki smiled broadly. "I can be."

Monique was defiant. "We should take back after having given so much. Our retainer agreement says nonrefundable, right?"

"Right," Kikki said, focusing on the strategy. "So, in order to use Moreno effectively, we have to get him to connect all the dots for us. We've got to turn Moreno, and quickly."

Kikki crossed to the window and peered out at the gardens again. This time, no one at all was there. It was early afternoon, lunch hour still. But it was starting to rain. She lay a hand on the radiator under the window, feeling the warmth.

Kikki looked to Monique. "I read the file, but let's take another look. Great work by the way, as always, *ma belle.*"

Monique smiled shyly. "The French production company is Henri the Great Films, SA. The EP, Executive Producer, is this Moreno or Medici. They have an office on Avenue George V, and it's a real office, not a *boîte à lettres.*"

"*Mais, naturellement,*" Kikki said.

"Right—and as I said, I recognize the French partner—a count. A royal in line to the would-be throne, and actually known in the film business. And *trés friqué.* Loaded. Moreno has a residential address and a business in New York for the film company, both on the Upper East Side. But that's all I've been able to dig up about him. They have a Delaware LLC listing only his name. And no track record in the industry. He doesn't show up anywhere in the records. Looks like Moreno has been carefully backstopped—or masked." Monique paused.

"And the money?"

"Well, both companies have substantial financial assets. I'm getting a lot of info that almost completes the conspiracy's paper trail from the other off-shore shells. Missing a couple of pieces that link it all directly to the Swords and the antiquities racket. I'm not a numbers person. I know someone who is, but I didn't want to get him involved without talking to you."

"Right. Keep it close. Too dangerous otherwise. Let's get Moreno to tell us."

"Works for me," Monique said, "But you have to meet with the producers tonight. Do you think Victor will be there in person? Or send some other errand boy?"

"I don't know. Have to think about it."

And then Kikki got a hint of pain in her left temple.

"There's something familiar about this guy Moreno. Maybe I met him before—"

"In New York?"

"Yes, but if it's the same person, then he's changed, and he wasn't running a film business. And then it clicked. "He was a down-and-out lawyer. He was the one who ran Victor's antique business. I had maybe one exchange with him." She paused, running it through her mind. "Yes, I remember. I found some documents he had signed. Victor kept it all separate and secret. I left it alone. Didn't want to get involved."

"Interesting. This guy Moreno has a lot of secrets, a dark past."

"He went by a different name. Stefan something—"

Monique clucked her tongue against her teeth. "Imagine the set and the precious *objets* involved. If they're real, we will have better proof than a paper trail that they're using the film to move them. To steal them."

"Yes—I am very curious about this secret Valois cache. That's enough bait to get me to go along." Kikki was thoughtful, playing out scenarios.

"So, meet with Moreno. Find out more about these never seen precious *objets*. Seems odd to me that after all this time no one has uncovered them." Monique said, "Unless—"

"Unless they aren't real at all and are only a smokescreen." Kikki came back to the table and sat again. Finally, she focused on Monique. "Call Moreno later, but I'm not falling for that ploy— meeting him for dinner with Frank and Victor." Kikki could feel her litigator strategist in full gear, one who had been trained in the art by Victor, the Devil himself.

Monique ran a hand through her honey-colored hair. "Right. We can do this. Fuck the Patriarchy!"

"Move the meeting and select the time and place. Insist that I need one more solo meeting with Moreno. We can persuade him to help us out without them. Let him do his job as EP, keep the producers out of our hair and give us a glimpse at these so-called crown jewels. I know we can turn him, Monique. And Torres can protect him."

She felt the blood of retribution course through her veins.

Monique agreed, raising an eyebrow. "You're right. I'll call in a couple of hours, say?"

"Sooner. Before he can gather his wits or replenish his cocaine." Kikki smiled, enjoying the game now.

"Perfect. Done! Great to have you fully back in the game."

"Don't get comfortable with that idea."

Monique smirked. "*On verra bien.* I have to go. Have to pick up my daughter. *L'au pair* has an appointment *chez le coiffeur.* It's Wednesday. We're going to a film this afternoon." Wednesday, when young children in the *maternelle* were off school for the day. A time usually spent with their mothers.

"Of course. I'm so sorry. I should have—Monique, I don't know how you do it with a daughter and a husband—"

"You do what you have to do. Women run their families, and they should be running the world!" Monique said.

"Indeed! *Va-ton*, Monique. I'll lock up and put this check into the safe."

"Or the bank. And have a chat with Margot?" Monique said, slipping into her white fur coat. "Let me know what she counsels, and then I'll make the call to Moreno to reel him in."

"Very funny. I hope her mother, the evil Queen Catherine, stays away."

"I've burnt cloves and white candles *à la Gréque* to clear the place of negative energy and entities. Don't worry. *Katse ligo*," Stay a bit, Monique said. "Stay and chat with the friendly ghosts of the Palais Royal."

They hugged goodbye.

"See you," Monique said, closing the door quietly behind her.

What a jewel Monique was. Never mind sixteenth-century secrets and crooked filmmakers. Kikki stood for a moment, quiet and at home.

Chapter 72

Kikki hit the *porte* button inside the vaulted stone hallway once meant for horse and carriage. Seeing Monique had lifted her spirits. As had donning the familiar cloak of her business. Mounting a campaign for justice and revenge.

Tant mieux. She was psyched for a battle with Victor. And she intended to win this war.

She covered her head with the hood of her coat and opened the massive wooden carriage door of the building onto rue de Valois. Outside, the freezing rain had picked up a steady rhythm. She pulled her hood closer to her face.

As she stepped off the curb to cross the street, she ran smack into a young man bearing an enormous bouquet of red roses.

"*Excusez-moi, s'il vous plait, madame! Pardon! Pardon!*" he exclaimed.

"*Çe n'est pas grave,*" she said. She felt a prick and reached up to touch her cheek. A thorn had grazed her. Warm liquid on her fingertip. Her blood. And then it stung. "*Merde!*"

"*Ça va?*"

"*Bien sûr,*" she said crisply.

He placed the bouquet into a carrier on his *moto* and slipped a tissue from his jacket. "*Si'l vous plait.* You are bleeding." He reached up and dabbed at her face.

"Really. I'm fine." He was a very handsome man, young, dark hair, refined features, blue eyes.

"Maybe you can help me? I'm looking for 15 rue de Valois, *5eme étage.* Maître Trieste?" He had recovered the roses and held them at a slight distance from her this time.

"Not sure—is that who those roses are for?"

"*Oui. Ç'est vous?* You did just come out of that building, didn't you?"

Kikki said, "I'm not Maître Trieste. I understand she's away."

A black sedan turned onto rue de Valois and rolled to a stop just behind them. Liam stepped out and glared at the young man.

"Give me those," he said sternly in French, motioning for Kikki to get in.

Liam wore a narrow-brimmed hat to shelter him from the rain. He held the young man's eyes, as though staring through his soul. The messenger backed up. Liam took the card from the bouquet, read it, and with a sleight of hand, slipped it into his overcoat.

"*Partez!*" Liam palmed him a bill. "I'll take care of this. I know Maître Trieste."

When he had sped off, Liam threw the roses into the nearest *poubelle.* And then he helped Kikki into the car and got in after her.

"Victor?" she asked.

Liam nodded. "How dare he."

"So like him to make such a grand gesture after what he did— I'm sure the card said that it was all a misunderstanding. Including the 'accidental' prick of the roses." She touched her face again and felt a welt forming. She frowned.

"I bet he was instructed to do that—to prick me. He was cute. You didn't have to be mean to him, Liam."

"*Non?* He's Victor's messenger. You don't think he's some random *moto* guy, do you?"

"You mean Victor sent *him* to me along with the roses?"

"Or perhaps he appeared out of thin air. You, who chose offices in Houdini's former theater on Margot's street. Honestly, Kikki!"

Shrugging, hands out to her sides, palms up, Kikki added,

"Well—they were perfect and available. Fated, you might say."

"Where to?" Liam changed the subject.

"Hasn't Tía given you instructions?"

"Glad to see you're operational. And yes. We're going to Saint-Sulpice. The small café on the square with red awnings. Café de la Place or something banal. Not tarted up yet, miraculously."

Liam directed the driver, who had already turned back towards the Rive Gauche. They headed along rue Saint-Honoré and left, heading south on rue du Louvre.

Through the now descending shroud of icy rain, Kikki peered out the windows as the street became rue de l'Amiral de Coligny, named for the famous Huguenot leader. Coligny was as a father figure and counselor to King Charles IX. And a central figure in the bloody massacre.

The Huguenots had recently assassinated the Catholic leader, François de Lorraine, Duc de Guise, Margot's uncle. Leadership of the extremist Catholic League passed to the son, Henri, Margot's longtime love.

The League plotted revenge. On the eve of Saint-Bartholomew's Day, they shot Coligny, and though the shots failed to kill him, Catherine de Medici, a prime conspirator, had ensured his death with poison bullets with the help of her royal *parfumeur*, René.

Queen Catherine and her cohorts used this event to persuade the king that he was in grave danger. In the name of Saint-Bartholomew, who had been flayed alive, Margot's brother, the king, ordered the blood lust on that Saint-Bartholomew's night.

Kikki shuddered as the sedan inched past the square, Place du Louvre, the royal parish church built in the seventh century, Saint-Germain-l'Auxerrois. A well-known warning bell, the *tocsin* called the *Marie,* had rung to launch the killings—nearly three thousand Parisians on the first day and night—all for the glory of the One True Catholic God.

Eerily, the bells pealed now from the Romanesque belfry. Kikki flashed on a surreal vision—the wide moats that protected the medieval Louvre, where Margot had been locked in her apartments, were afloat with blood.

Kikki gasped. Liam put a supporting arm around her. An

excruciating pain shot through her left temple. She closed her eyes. She felt the car slow to a crawl and heard a muffled whisper. "*Stop the carriage here.*" Her third eye flooded with golden light.

She prayed to the Goddess that, wedged between the thick stone walls of the ancient Louvre and Saint-Germain l'Auxerrois where the curse had begun, she could finally connect the dots. But where it would take her, she knew not.

Trembling, she succumbed fully to the vision.

Chapter 73

The princess's gilded carriage, lined with red velvet trimmed with silver, was led by two fine white stallions.

"Montez, mordi!" Margot leaned out the window, and when she saw her companion, she threw the door open. "Get in, Gillonne! We have to hurry."

In vision, Kikki became the body and soul of Margot's confidante, Gillonne de Thorigny. She stepped up onto the sideboard and swept blue satin skirts with her. She sat across from Margot and drew the curtains.

Margot wore not her usual finery but instead the simple daily frock favored by Gillonne.

"We must hurry to the royal surgeon, Monsieur Paré. I don't have much time." Margot grimaced in pain and held her full belly.

"Are you all right? Can you make it there?" The carriage rumbled over the uneven dirt street, jostling them both. Gillonne feared for her queen.

"It was the only way to get out of the palace. Disguised as you. My wretched mother, the Queen, suspects I am with child, but she has no proof. If she doesn't find the wet sheets—"

Gillonne watched Margot carefully but did not speak. She

smiled with love and placed her hand on Margot's belly. She felt the child move. She hoped Margot's plan would work and that they would get there in time and then be able to escape.

"Be most careful of your mother, my Margot. She will use Henri de Navarre, your husband and his new lover, Madame de Sauve, who spies for the Queen Regent. And her nans—dwarfs—and Flying Squadron of Ladies are everywhere spying on you. The walls of the Louvre have ears."

"Oh Gillonne, you are the only one I can trust. Surely, I cannot trust my brother Charles, the King. He has ordered us imprisoned in our quarters. And my new husband, Henri de Navarre—he is but an ally in arms."

"Would it not be wise to travel through the underground tunnels? A subterranean labyrinth where we could evade those who might follow? Everyone in Paris knows your carriage."

"I am a Valois, daughter of Henri II, and a Queen. I shall not hide myself. A little subterfuge serves—it got us out of the palace, didn't it?" She glanced down at Gillonne's simple, yet fashionable, dress. Over it, she had thrown Gillonne's plain black hooded wool cloak.

"Are you sure this is the right way to do this? Why go to see him?" Gillonne whispered. "How you can trust him? He is the royal doctor to King Charles IX and your mother, the Queen. What makes you think he won't report all to her? Can we really fool him into thinking he is delivering the child of Gillonne, your humble servant, by mere disguise?"

"You know we have greater powers than that, Gillonne. We will make sure, with the Goddesses' help. And I will use a veiling trick my other mother, the kind Diane de Poitiers, taught me. He will see what we want him to see. He will report that I am well and not pregnant. That is the whole point. I want him to report that to my mother."

Gillonne's heart raced, afraid. "Yes, Margot. It is true that we have powers. And Paré is an old man. But—"

"And then, you and I shall take a trip. If per chance my mother, the Queen, learns the truth, it will be too late. I have it all plotted out. Trust me, I was taught by her, but I am more clever."

"As you wish, Margot. I have brought everything." Gillonne

bowed her head.

"And your brother will meet us afterwards with the other carriage for travel?"

"Yes, it is all arranged."

"Do you swear by the Goddesses—by Inanna of Sumer, Isis of Egypt and Athena of Greece, and all that they stand for?" Margot leaned close and took her friend's hand, holding tight.

"My Queen and friend, you know that I am your loyal and trusted confidante and servant. I would never betray you."

"Throw a Tarot card, Gillonne, please?"

"Later. When we are no longer in Paris. The energies here are very dark. Let us not tempt fate, for the cards tell the truth." Gillonne fingered the worn deck of hand-painted Tarot cards in the pocket of Margot's elaborate blue satin gown.

Margot squeezed Gillonne's hand tightly as she experienced another sharp contraction. Her beautiful face was gray and taut with pain.

When it subsided, Gillonne changed the subject to distract Margot.

"How do you ever stand to wear these contraptions around the neck, these ruffs? So fashionable, yet so uncomfortable. And the dress with its impossibly tight corset? Is woman made to suffer for beauty?"

"We do it for love—Eros, Cupido, Amor." Margot paid homage to the triple deities of love and leaned forward and applied some rouge from a small pot to Gillonne's cheeks. "There that's better! Now, let's bring your bosom up so your nipples are showing, a fashion that I invented." She leaned forward and cupped Gillonne's breasts, lifting them so that her porcelain flesh and young, erect nipples showed just above the bodice.

Gillonne blushed, "Margot," she whispered. "Please—not now."

"I said we do it for love, and though I love men—" She kissed Gillonne fervently on the lips and brushed a hand across her nipples. "You know I love you, dear one, even more. We suffer beauty to be admired—perhaps more by women than men."

The next instant, Margot cried out in pain again. The contractions were very close together.

"Deep slow breaths, my dearest Margot," Gillonne breathed

with her, all the while holding her hand tightly.

When the pain passed, Margot shifted in the carriage and smiled weakly.

Her nostrils flared, "Such a sickening smell of blood and excrement in this city. Mordi! Hand me my perfume and handkerchief. Even in this bitter cold weather."

"It is worse near the Seine." Gillonne reached into a pocket and withdrew a white lace kerchief and a small vial of perfume.

Gillonne whispered, "Better?" And then she changed the subject back to what she knew was one of Margot's favorite games. "So, you see? Now you won't need to brighten my breasts with rouge. They are plentiful and rosy enough. Quite so." She smiled shyly at Margot, beautiful Margot. So worried for her.

"No, I see that I have pleasured you. Good! I will save the rouge for just before we arrive."

"I want Monsieur le Médecin to take one look at you with a taper and be certain that you are Marguerite de Valois. You will apply the magic potion I have given you, and he will be certain that it is I. And then, he shall attend to delivering Gillonne de Goyon-Matigon de Thorigny's child. Let him report that to my mother, the Queen!"

"I hope he will think it is only me, Gillonne, and not yourself."

"You worry too much," Margot said, stroking Gillonne's hand. "It is dark. We look alike."

Gillonne watched Margot carefully. Her eyes were adjusted to the carriage's dimness, and her third eye was wide open so that she could see and know without her human eyes. A gift that allowed her to see and feel exactly what Margot felt. Just now Margot's mood plunged into darkness. She heard her violent thoughts and experienced Margot's pain as a knife in her heart.

Margot whispered bitterly.

"It does not matter—we are all cursed by this blood that runs through our veins. This royal blood. Sang real. Cursed by the blood of the massacre that stained the streets and flowed in the river and made the city filthy and wreaking of the stench of rotting flesh."

Gillonne was terrified for her friend and her Queen.

The carriage rumbled over the uneven dirt road along the rue Saint-Germain l'Auxerrois that ran along the River Seine's Right

313

Bank until they reached Châtelet's prisons.

There, they crossed over on the Pont au Change to the Île de la Cité—the ancient island in the river that once was all of Paris.

Chapter 74

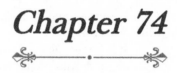

Kikki's eyes opened slowly. She became aware of Liam next to her. They were in a car. She was stifling hot.

"Are you all right?" Liam leaned over her. "Here, drink this."

He lifted a small glass of water to her lips.

"I am burning with fever," she said weakly.

He held the glass for her. "Your lips are stuck together and dusty. Did you travel back to some filthy era of Paris?"

Kikki sipped and blinked.

"Yes. Long before they paved the Quai with cobblestone. Horses and a pretty red and black carriage." She tried to sit up straight but became dizzy. "And a filthy stench."

"God, I hope you didn't catch the Plague."

She laughed wanly. "Not funny."

Liam leaned forward and whispered to Claude, the driver.

"Drive on please."

The driver shifted out of neutral and rolled carefully out of the sequestered Place du Louvre.

He said, "I have to take the Quai, *monsieur.* We'll go to Hotel de Ville, cross at the palais on Île de la Cité."

"No problem, Claude. I trust you to get us there."

"They blocked off the other bridges. Some Russian leader is in Paris—"

"Buying Christmas presents—*rafales*—fighter jets, likely." Liam frowned. "Just drive slowly so you don't upset her."

"What?" Kikki sat up. "I'm perfectly fine now. Kind of nauseous."

"You haven't eaten," he studied her. "What was your vision? Did you get what you needed?"

"I don't know. It's coming back—but I have to be careful not to —"

"Slip back into it. Your pupils are still dilated. Take my hand." He squeezed hers.

The driver turned left onto the Quai de la Mégisserie. Kikki hit the button to roll the window down.

"I need some air. Even if it is miserable freezing rain."

The driver glanced back, and Kikki felt Liam's body tense up next to her, and then he shouted, "Claude, watch out!"

The driver braked abruptly, tossing Kikki and Liam slightly forward in their seats—but he stopped in time to miss an old woman pushing a carriage across the heavy flow of traffic. A baby wailed.

Kikki promptly closed the window and sat back against the seat, eyes closed. She had seen the old woman—and she had seen her face—it was Margot herself, dressed—as in Kikki's recent vision, in a simple black wool hooded cloak. And barely visible at her neck, Kikki saw with x-ray like vision, a necklace of diamonds and sapphires from which hung a faceted ruby pendant in the shape of an eight-pointed star.

In the carriage was a tiny baby girl, a few months old, with curly black hair sticking out from a wool bonnet. Under a bundle of swaddling, she held clutched in tiny hands a leather-bound book of yellowed parchment—waving it about gurgling, smiling with dark eyes.

"What in the hell?" Liam said. "Did you see that, Kikki?"

"I saw something quite incredible, though I doubt it's the same as what you saw."

He moaned.

"Oh god. What now? You are still not in this world!"

"No, not quite yet. And so what? I need to get this—"

"And you also need your earthly wits about you!" he said sternly. "Tía needs you. We all do. You are of no use to anyone in this state. Get over it. Learn to transition quickly."

"No stress, right, Monsieur le Magicien?" She felt herself almost lurch into her body. "Thank the Goddess!" She put both hands over her heart and bowed.

"And you can thank me, too, while you're at it." Liam beamed, happy with his own hand in getting her back to present time.

She flipped her hood back and ran her hand through her hair. "I feel rather ghastly."

"Ghostly, you mean? You look pale." He handed her a makeup bag from her large red handbag. "Here, put a face on as my mom says. Oh, Fifa! Hee hee!"

"You'll want to know what I saw. It's important." And now, fully present, she remembered all of the details of the vision.

"Do tell!" he said, eager to hear.

She told him about the ornate black and red carriage and about travelling to the past in the soul and body of Gillonne, disguised as Margot. And then she linked that vision, that past life, to the old woman crossing the street with the child.

"I am sure they are part of the same story. The old woman crossing the street with the child, wearing the diamond necklace had Margot's face. What do you make of the whole thing?"

"I believe the necklace was a legacy, gifted to Margot from her surrogate mother, Diane de Poitiers, renowned mistress of Margot's father, King Henri II. She helped bring up Margot, along with Henri's consort, as they called queens, the hateful Medici. Margot was very fond of Diane. She taught her much of the ways of nature and the Goddess, of beauty and love. Lessons she would never have learned from her birth mother."

Kikki nodded slowly. "A necklace given to Margot upon Diane de Poitier's death. Perhaps kept for Margot by a friend of Diane's until she was old enough—"

"Yes, that would be most likely," Liam said.

The car stopped just short of the busy Place du Châtelet, now a lovely square flanked by the Théâtre de la Ville and Châtelet theatres. In the middle, there was a sculptured fountain with a sphinx spouting water from its mouth. Place du Châtelet was named for the medieval prison opposite, as dreaded as the Bastille that in Margot's time was at Saint-Ouen, north of Paris.

The car inched forward along the Quai to Hotel de Ville. Just behind that now statuesque building that housed the mayor and City Hall was a desecrated pit of evil—Place de Grève in front of L'Église Saint-Gervais. Since the Middle Ages, an elm tree had been planted on the square. There disputes were adjudged. But it was also on that spot where they burned women as witches and heretics and executed those who threatened the reigning patriarchy. Barbarically drawn and quartered or put on the wheel that stretched their limbs until they died.

As reigning royalty, it was customary to attend such horrors. Margot's mother had insisted she attend the execution of La Mole, the Protestant lover Margot had rescued during the siege of Saint-Bartholomew's Day.

Kikki gripped the seat as they turned the corner onto the Pont au Change, crossed the Seine to the Île de la Cité and stopped just in front of the Palais de la Cité and the medieval prison, the Conciergerie, antechamber to the guillotine. Marie Antoinette spent her last days there. It carried dark energy of wailing prisoners waiting for death.

Bile filled Kikki's mouth.

Chapter 75

As they turned onto the bridge, Liam said quietly, "Almost there."

"Drop me at Saint-Sulpice."

He slid his eyes towards her.

"Why? You're supposed to meet Tía at the café."

"Trust me. I know what I'm doing."

He sighed. "As you wish."

"Of course. I expect no less." She smiled and leaned to kiss him on the cheek.

"Beware of Mother Medici."

"I shall. She has appeared to me on a few occasions, the most terrifying when I was held captive by Victor. He became her incarnated, using her form and wretched soul. In full manipulative evil glory. He had a painting of her in his suite—" She stopped, not wanting to draw the Dark Queen's energy.

"He is using her as a mask. Beware that you are not fooled, not blocked by their combined darkness. Victor may be her present incarnation. *Prothesis!*"

"Stop. Let's not talk about her and invite her in."

"I can't help it. My Greek penchant for drama."

"And superstition. In the end, Margot bested her mother,"

Kikki said with conviction. "I'll just keep following her lead. And my own. So far, we're all intact."

But she shivered, ice-cold, as they drove past the twin gothic towers of Notre-Dame-de- Paris.

Some minutes later, Kikki stood alone under the grand portico of Saint-Sulpice and scanned the magnificent square. She had chills from the weather and her earlier visions of Margot. She took deep breaths in and out to clear her head and raise her vibration.

She drank in the beauty of the monumental fountain that dominated the square. A famed Louis Visconti work of architecture. Homage to religious eloquence. The fountain façades contained four French religious figures of the seventeenth century, the era when Saint-Sulpice and its seminary were built.

Kikki was certain one or more of them must secretly have been fans of the matriarchy. Or been nourished by them. Swords intermarried with the divine feminine Daughters of Inanna.

Memories of this life—of friends loved and some departed, honored by tossing coins into sacred fountains on long summer nights and making wishes—brought a smile and tears.

Now she made a new wish and tossed a virtual coin from the portico. She watched it arc and land, skimming the frozen layer, and then it pierced the ice near one of the stone lions that studded the fountain.

For a moment, she saw a woman on the back of that beautiful lion holding the mane. But it was a new breed of female lion that had crossed gender boundaries—alive and ready to attack to protect its own. Was it Inanna who rode as was legend, riding two lions at once? Perhaps in spirit, but the face was that of an earthly mortal—Kikki's own.

With that vision she felt regenerated, wish granted. She turned to enter the massive front door of her favorite Paris cathedral. The second largest in the City of Light. She was headed for sanctuary during this fated week to light candles in the small chapel of Sainte-Anne, said to be Mary's mother. And a good guardian angel of Kikki's, her own paternal grandmother. Good goddess energy in abundance.

With a full winter solstice moon less than forty-eight hours away, Kikki felt its magnetic pull towards inevitable destiny. These past days, *la lune* had occasionally shed bright light through dark storm clouds.

The Saturnalian Solstice was a pivotal occasion in warring societies like the ancient Romans. They celebrated their God of the Harvest, Saturn, who they believed ruled the land, with a week-long holiday. A decidedly patriarchal view. The Winter Solstice was a dreaded time when the sun stands still—literally in Latin "solstice"—*sol statum.*

In many early cultures, a dark and frightening period lasting two or three days. Shadows lengthen, light is weak and fear sets in. Bonfires are lit—an instinctive Promethean rebellion against what were known throughout Europe until the sixteenth century as the famine months. Foul times, cold darkness, misery, sickness and death. Black chaos.

Kikki felt to her core the light grinding to a halt, leaving a vacuum—or a portal—for all who might come up from the chthonic bowels to snatch the good and living. The societies of peace like her own.

She turned and walked towards the old wooden door. As was often the case, especially in winter, a homeless person had taken shelter under the high arched stone portico. She would be there every day. It was her territory, in fact, her home.

The old woman wrapped in layers of blanket held out her hand, "*Madame, si'l vous plait, aidez-moi—*"

The voice startled her.

"Tía?"

Tía cackled with laugher and rose from her squat.

"You were to meet me at the café across from here, but there is no time."

"And I expect this is a bit safer?"

"Possibly. I will keep vigil while you light your candles."

"How did—never mind." Kikki grinned, feeling cheered by Tía's heartful presence.

"Go, daughter. Make haste. We will meet afterwards at the Chapelle des Louanges. You will receive instructions. The Daughters of Inanna invite you to their celebrations and ceremonies for Winter Solstice—"

She bowed. "I am honored."

"Go now. It is time."

Kikki nodded and pushed open the massive wooden door.

She kept her head down, blonde hair covered with the hood, as she made her way up the right side of the long hall past the famous Delacroix frescos in the first chapel on the right—the Chapel of the Holy Angels—*Jacob Wresting With the Angel, Heliodorus Driven from the Temple* and *Saint-Michael Vanquishing the Dragon*. A few tourists who had braved the inhospitable weather stood in admiration.

The church interior was sparsely scattered with tourists and worshippers who sat in the neatly arranged small straw-seated chairs in the middle of the cathedral.

Kikki tiptoed across the marble floor. She turned as she reached the pulpit, about midway, and allowed a moment to feast her eyes upon the magnificent *Great Organ*, which rose high at the rear of the church. One of Paris's great wonders, immense in size and with exceptional sound—Cliquot's baroque masterpiece, re-built by Cavaillé-Coli.

She often came to listen. Today, she hoped that by some miracle on this quiet winter afternoon, the church's organist might rehearse. Minus the religious trappings of the mass. Just a few resonating notes.

She approached Sainte-Anne's Chapel, just to the right of the central Chapel of Our Lady under its great dome at the front of the church. She fished for a few coins and dropped them into the *troncs* box and drew three long white tapers from worn wooden holders.

She stepped up into the small chapel. To the left was a marble altar, topped by a gold medallion and a painting of biblical figures, arms raised to the heavens, hands in prayer in praise of Mother Anne. To the right was a wooden confessional box. An arched stained glass window depicted a haloed Anne holding a child.

In front of the stained glass window and the altar was the candle stand. One large taper burned brightly. Kikki stepped up, lit her candles from the flame and placed them reverently onto the iron stand. She closed her eyes. Abruptly, she froze.

She wasn't alone. Who or what was in the chapel?

Chapter 76

A woman kneeled on a chair in the corner near the confessionary. She saw Kikki at the same moment and looked up, eyes soulful, mirroring the stained glass painting of Sainte-Anne.

Kikki let out a breath, and her heart dropped back into place.

"Natalia?" She said in a stage whisper.

"Véronique? What in the world? What a small city this is—" Natalia was happy to see Véronique, feeling their initial bond and answering her wish to see her once more.

"Yes, especially this neighborhood. What an interesting coincidence to meet here, in the Chapel of Sainte-Anne—one of my secret sanctuaries—" Kikki watched as Natalia sat up. She was dressed for business in a smart wool pants suit—Chanel, Kikki thought.

"Yes. I thought you were a nun from the sixteenth century with that long black hooded coat. Or I'm seeing ghosts."

"Either," Kikki whispered gently, "And I promise you I am not a nun." She chuckled at the thought. "But I am glad to see you. I was hoping we'd meet again soon."

"Yes, me too," Natalia said.

Kikki mused that the week's events had been very carefully

choreographed by a master puppeteer or two—Grand Master or Mistress. This meeting had Tía and Margot's signature.

But all she said to Natalia was, "I've just come from a meeting, and it looks like you're about to go to one—or have been."

"I am meeting with Gabrielle Laroche again in an hour. Thought I might gather my thoughts."

"You look pale. Are you feeling all right?" She now knew exactly who Natalia was in relationship to Torres and the role he wanted her to play in the secret op. And yet, somehow, she felt more sympathetic than jealous. Suspicious of her ties to known enemies. Whose side was Natalia really on?

But when Kikki tried to read her, she found to her surprise that Natalia was reading Kikki. Did she have a psychic gift, or was she just savvy?

Hesitant to delve deeper, Kikki enhanced her protection and asked, "Did your uncle arrive?"

"Uh. Yes, this morning." Natalia said quietly.

"Well, good. You are probably tired from the moon—" Kikki studied Natalia's face. Her eyes were bright, and she had a moon look about her. Though she was visibly tired, her face was full at the same time. As if—

"Why the moon?"

"It's nearly full. A very intense week—"

"You can say that again!" She relaxed and began to feel comfortable with Kikki. "Would love to have a glass of wine with you again at that lovely Voltaire café."

"That was fun, Natalia." It had been a good beginning to a very disastrous evening. Kikki felt a spike of jealousy and told herself to chill. Far more important matters were at stake.

Kikki's attention shifted, drawn to the door adjacent to them that lead out to the private Chapelle de l'Enfant Jésus and then to the street. Almost as soon as she focused on it, the door creaked open. A bitter wind blew through the tiny chapel. The tall tapers flickered close to the wick, nearly extinguishing the light, leaving both women mesmerized by the fading flames.

On the wind blew an unmistakable perfume. Kikki, catching the whiff of Margot's rich scent, turned away from Natalia and pulled her coat more tightly about her.

Kikki alone could see Margot—Natalia appeared frozen in time and space, while Margot stood earthly real—as though Kikki might touch the queen herself.

She wore formal clothes, reserved for official royal occasions of the Valois court, at her regal best in a red satin dress with stiff wide skirts, a high lace ruff and bellowing sleeves. Luminous pearls encircled her long slender neck and her décolletée revealed porcelain skin. The Queen in full battle regalia.

"You must deliver a message for me."

"Aren't you able to do that—as a being who stretches past time and dimensions?" Kikki insisted.

"I cannot do so. It would be dangerous if my voice were to be heard by any other soul than you. And it is not yet time."

That same frustrating question that had been plaguing Kikki. When would it be time?

"They are closing in. We must be ready."

"How can we fight them? Help me, for the Goddess's sake, in whatever time and place you exist. How am I to save the Snake Goddess, Paris and those I love, to lead the battle, if you don't share all you know. You are Marguerite de Valois!"

"You will know and be guided. You have been so far. But do not show your knowledge. You must plot and be cunning—as I always had to be. I will be with you in spirit, but I cannot expose myself."

Margot whispered, "Hear me now. For this is most urgent. Speak to Natalia for me. She cannot see or hear me. You are my vessel, and I need you to be my medium."

"And what is the message?"

Margot didn't answer.

Just then, a draft flooded the chapel. Margot fled, skirts flying archly behind. Dark stains marred the fabric of her elegant gown— fresh blood that flowed from her like a river onto the floor of the old cathedral.

Kikki gasped, covering her mouth. She took a breath and called forth protection, her heartbeat marking seconds while she waited to see if more dark energy would manifest. But almost as quickly, she felt the air warm slightly in the chapel. She and Natalia were safe for the moment.

How could she begin to tell Natalia about Margot, to relay a message from a ghost? And what was it? She would have to put it into its context of a dark battle against the omnipresent and oppressive patriarchy. To do that, Kikki would have to remove her own mask and share secrets with this young woman she barely knew.

Natalia seemed a very earthly woman, hardly suited for Kikki's ethereal world. She was well educated in history, archaeology and cultural customs. If Kikki remembered their conversation at the Voltaire correctly, she had an MBA. She was a businesswoman. Her uncle had schooled her well—in, among other things, trafficking black market antiquities. Natalia was in league with Victor. She was a plant on Torres's committee—and his mark.

So, how and why should Kikki trust her? But Margot was insistent and urgent. She slipped her hand under her coat, reaching for her talisman. The rose crystals. They were warm.

It was truly time. Kikki took a leap of faith.

"Natalia, listen, I have to talk to you about something—"

"Sure," Natalia said uneasily, worried it might have to do with her faded passion for Torres.

Kikki, watching the other woman closely, said, "It has nothing to do with my lover and your—err—evening with him."

"Oh, well, that's a relief!" Natalia laughed nervously. "Glad we got that elephant out of the room. But are you a mind reader?"

"Something like that. I—how can I put this—I have this other— persona—that is in many ways quite the opposite of being my lawyer 'self' who operates in a logical business world—if one can call it that."

Natalia grinned. "It has its own logic and culture."

"True enough." Spit it out, Kikki told herself. Trust yourself and Margot. "I am able to see in other dimensions and times. They used to call it 'having the gift of sight.'"

"You are psychic? A medium or something?" Natalia met Kikki's dark eyes, sending a message of reassurance. She could tell that Kikki was on edge, and she, Natalia, wanted to hear more from this enigmatic yet bewitching woman.

"Yes, something like that. But more, I am fiercely devoted to the ancient wisdom of the Divine Feminine, the Ancient Goddess in all of her manifestations—a matriarchal worldview."

"I'm with you on that one. So, you are a kind of High Priestess? Makes sense, even as a lawyer, you counsel and keep secrets. I can sense that you are wise."

Kikki felt the tension in her shoulders ease.

"Thank you. And yes, I am a High Priestess, though I thought I had given that up—"

"Fascinating. I can see that in you. Please, don't be nervous. Do go on. We hardly know each other, but it feels as though we were destined to meet."

Natalia realized that she was not at all surprised by what Kikki said and curious to hear more. It resonated with her own deep feelings, ones that she most often stifled for the sake of carrying on, being tough and making a name in her business.

"Natalia, I hope you will not be alarmed when I tell you that I have a message for you from someone not of this world."

Silently, Kikki asked Margot, "*What is it you want to tell her? I beg*—" She was interrupted by Natalia.

"What do you mean? A ghost?" She smiled wryly. "From my mother, I bet. That candle is for her. I really could use her guidance right now."

"Oh?"

Natalia said in a hushed secretive tone, "My mother was a novitiate in a convent. She fell in love with a priest, and they both left their orders—*et voilà*—I was born. My mother never said, but I think they both felt a huge guilt and nearly gave me to the convent so that I could be adopted. I'm not sure I have this story straight, but possibly one of the nuns—a midwife—delivered me when my mother went into early labor. Maybe even in the convent itself—not sure. That might be the romantic version I made up." She giggled nervously.

Natalia wondered why she was telling this woman she hardly knew, whose lover she had coveted and whose priceless Snake Goddess she was meant to steal, about her secret past.

"So, that's why," Natalia said in a shaky voice. "I always come here when I am in Paris and light a candle in this chapel for her, hoping that she will talk to me." Tears filled her eyes. "I shouldn't have told you that. It's my cross to bear. Not that I believe in any of that. But Saint-Sulpice is different, don't you find? It's a haven for all of us."

"What an incredible story." Kikki's lips curved into a smile. "Why wouldn't it be true? Sounds right to me."

And then a searing pain in her left temple caused Kikki to buckle over, holding her head in her hands.

"Are you all right, Kikki?" Natalia stood and hurried to her.

Kikki did not hear Natalia. When she looked up, Margot was there again. Kikki knew that as before, Natalia couldn't see or hear Margot.

This time she was dressed in a nun's robes of the sixteenth century.

Kikki pleaded silently, *"What is the message I am to give her?"*

Margot's head was bowed, and she carried the same baby in her arms that Kikki had seen in her vision on the Quai.

"Don't you see what it is?" she whispered.

Kikki closed her eyes and fell into deep trance. She watched in cinematic flashes a series of frames forming a whole. The tumultuous carriage ride through Rambouillet forest at night fleeing Paris. Exile. The young woman in long dark robes, face hidden, standing before a bonfire in prayer. A rose offering. A tiny little girl held tight in the young woman's arms. The awaiting carriage. Margot.

The scene shifted, and Kikki became Gillonne. The baby cried. Margot was crying. They stood just inside the wooden gate of the stone walls of a convent. Through the window, she saw old vineyards and a potager—a kitchen garden.

When Kikki opened her eyes again, Margot was there, dressed in a nun's robes. She held an infant girl.

Next to them sat Natalia. The likeness was uncanny. Sparkling eyes, elegant nose, oval face and full heart shaped lips.

"What is it?" Natalia whispered urgently. "You're frightening me. Tell me, please."

Kikki focused on the candles. They flickered and their flames rose. Suddenly, the organ sounded deep resonating chords that echoed throughout the cathedral.

Kikki, at last, understood the gravity of Margot's message to Natalia.

She caught Natalia's eyes. In a voice from another time and place, Kikki spoke.

"Natalia, you are a descendant of a very old and royal lineage. The one living heir of Queen Marguerite de Valois. The last of a dynasty thought to have been extinguished centuries ago. Legacy of La Reine Marguerite and her *sang real*. You are the only daughter of the House of Valois."

Kikki took a deep breath and then whispered, "And your life is in great danger."

Chapter 77

Margot vanished. As Kikki spoke the word "danger," the flames on the four candles extinguished at once. The organist abruptly stopped. The *Great Organ's* last note resounded against the cathedral's old stone and slowly died out.

Kikki glanced quickly into the main hall and saw no one. She shivered from a sudden chill in the chapel.

She studied Natalia. Her pupils were dilated, and as Kikki watched, Natalia's face froze, and her aura turned gray. Had she had been energetically slammed by their enemies—darkness in the form of someone from the Swords? Who? And how? The Black Queen? Had she blown in on the cold wind, unseen? Kikki was terrified for Natalia.

Kikki had just lifted a very heavy veil. Even she felt drained and stunned at the information, though it all made sense now.

Finally Natalia whispered, "So, Margot was my mother's great-great-grandmother or something—how many generations ago? Sixteen? Wow."

"Yes, that's about right," Kikki said.

That meant that Natalia carried the curse that Margot bore, passed down through that long lineage.

Margot's battle and her reason for haunting Kikki became crystal clear. A dire message no longer ephemeral. If Kikki couldn't succeed in lifting that curse, the beautiful young woman at her side, Natalia Becchina of the House of Valois, would die very soon.

As the light turned, two days from now. Just as the Swords' threat promised.

Margot's battle and her message were to save her child. The visions clicked into place. Kikki wouldn't succeed in saving anyone if she didn't get Natalia on board. In the eerie silence of Saint-Sulpice, Kikki waited apprehensively. She heard the fall of a footstep. Prickly fingers crept up her spine. Danger was here. Who was it?

Kikki turned to Natalia. As she opened her mouth to speak, the organist resumed. A loud A Minor chord startled both women.

And then, the organist launched into full concert, a dirge by Marais. The same music played by the viola on the Pont des Arts just before Kikki jumped to her near death into the freezing Seine. A very bad omen. She was wracked with terror.

Time to go.

Then she heard the creak of the nearby door open. Her heart constricted. Someone was coming their way. Someone with a heavy step. Someone with a dark purpose. The putrid odor preceded, like rotting flesh and sulfury gas.

Standing flush against the side of the chapel, she risked a glance into the hall. No one. They were right next to the main altar, and she didn't have a view of the grand rotunda at the front of the church.

Her eyes began to sting and tear from an invisible smoke—an invisible darkness. She shouldered her bag and grabbed Natalia by the hand.

"What the—" Natalia pulled back.

"Shh!" Kikki put a finger to her lips and mouthed the words. "We've got to leave. *Viens.*"

"No. I am shaking. And frightened," she said in a hoarse whisper. "Please. A moment."

"We—" Kikki rasped, choking on fumes. Almost like being on the volcano in Santorini.

"I know, you have more to tell me, but—" Natalia leaned in, whispering to Kikki.

"Yes, but it isn't safe here. I will protect you, but we must hurry. Trust me."

And then the sound of footsteps stopped. Kikki turned. A priest dressed in a white linen robe trimmed in gold, wearing a heavy gold crucifix on a chain around his neck, stood at the entrance to the chapel. He blocked their way out.

The priest's eyes were red coals and flames burst from his hair. Half human—half demon. On his old weathered hands, he wore a gold ring with a tiny gold sword.

"Holy Goddess!" Kikki invoked silently. She glanced at Natalia. Had she seen the priest?

She wrapped herself and Natalia in a protective shield.

He smiled malevolently.

"My children, I have come to take you into the fold. We need some new blood in the— parish. And you have strayed."

Kikki stood in front of Natalia, covering her.

"Not on your miserable life."

"Harlots! Heretics! Witches! You will be punished!"

Kikki leaned over slightly so that her heavy handbag slipped down the arm of her coat. She swung it into the priest's face and then stepped forward and kneed him in the groin.

At the same time, Tía appeared behind the priest and shoved him into the chapel's railing.

"*Corren!*"

Chapter 78

Soon after they escaped Saint-Sulpice, Liam had Kikki and Natalia safely ensconced in the front salon of Natalia's suite at the Hotel Regina.

Natalia gulped a fine Bordeaux from a crystal glass.

"You're safe, Natalia," Liam said from his perch by the window seat overlooking the Louvre. "For now," he mouthed to Kikki.

Natalia caught the look, finished the glass and poured another liberal amount of wine.

Kikki was doing her best to sip, though she, too, felt like guzzling. Clarity on all levels was preeminent. She stood and walked to another window, staring out at the winter landscape of the Tuileries. In the distance, La Grande Roue near Place de la Concorde was lit up in the tricolors of the French flag.

She sipped her wine, thoughtful.

"That priest in Saint-Sulpice, I know him," Natalia said finally, setting her empty wine glass onto the adjacent table. "He works for my uncle."

"Seriously?" Kikki returned to the sofa and picked up a finger sandwich from a tray of afternoon tea treats. "I wasn't sure that you had seen him. Thought maybe he was—this will sound funny—only visible to me."

Natalia chuckled and shivered at once.

"I did see him, yeah. He's been helping my uncle with these pieces we've recently acquired, pieces from the sixteenth century. Odd because we don't usually deal in furniture."

Natalia wondered about the wisdom of continuing the work with her Uncle Franco as she flashed on Torres. Her head swirled on overload after what Kikki had told her in Saint-Sulpice. She was confused and halfway to being quite high from wine. She popped a macaroon into her mouth to still her churning stomach.

"The 'priest' seemed to be right out of central casting. Is he a confidante of your uncle, I mean really close—or just an acquaintance?" Kikki asked, wondering about the furniture Natalia had mentioned. It struck a chord. The film? But Natalia was overwhelmed, so she didn't ask her more. She sent her calm, loving energy from the Goddess.

Natalia was a very private person. She was not comfortable sharing her thoughts with Liam and Kikki. She'd only just met them. But maybe they could help her. The landscape of the week and her life had just drastically changed.

Finally, she said, "Yeah, he's very close. Uncle calls him family. But he's no priest."

"Shocking," Liam said, pouring her a glass of Badoit. "You are dehydrated. Drink this."

"*Merci.*" She sipped.

"Anyone can put on the dress." He suppressed a laugh. "Sorry."

Kikki burst out laughing. "Thank you, Liam. I needed some comic relief."

Natalia picked up the wine bottle and refilled both of their glasses. Liam sipped sparkling water.

"Did you see his eyes turn to red hot coals—or his hair on fire?" Kikki asked.

"No—that part I missed," she smiled. "Must be your special vision. But I wish I had. I would have joined you in the attack."

"You'll be seeing more of the likes of him," Liam added sardonically as he tidied the table and discreetly signaled on his phone for more refreshments.

Natalia, with not a little fear, wrapped her arms around herself.

"Reassuring—*not*. But seriously, Liam, weren't you going to read my cards? I could use some guidance with the shocking information I was just given. Holy shit! A Valois, descendant of La Reine Margot, not to mention the whole Medici line. Quite a potent mix. What the hell am I supposed to do with this?"

"Sure. Good idea," he sent her a soothing look. And then, he drew a card from his inner suit pocket. He inspected it and frowned. "Ah. Not surprising. The Hierophant. The High Priest or The Pope in some decks. Male authority and Power."

"Power being key and patriarchal power—" Kikki reached for the bottle of Badoit and poured another glass. Her hand was shaking from the card Liam had drawn. Even though the card would help her get Natalia on board, she'd had enough High Priest energy for one day.

"What does that mean in this context?" Natalia asked, looking to Liam.

Liam lifted a forefinger to his mouth, hesitating for a moment.

At last he said quietly, "It means you had better watch your beautiful back, honey, or make sure you have the right people watching it for you. Because you are going up against the male power structure, whether you want to or not."

"High Priest—sounds like that fixer of my uncle's showing up in robes ready to kill me."

Natalia thought that it must have to do with her uncle and his partner and their nefarious activities, the ones her uncle wouldn't tell her about. And Torres's Operation Sphinx. She was caught in the middle of a dangerous conspiracy in which she was being used a pawn. Just as Margot and her mother had been. She hoped she had the courage of her ancestors to do battle and survive. But on which side?

Chapter 79

The tension in the room was palpable. The three of them remained quiet for a moment.

It was Liam who broke the silence, ever the host.

"It's getting dark."

"That's an understatement. How can you tell the difference at this point in the—err—battle?" Kikki said.

He opened the window an inch and sniffed. "Storm coming. Snowstorm. Could be a blizzard, as predicted."

"Perfect. We'll just get out the skis. If we wear white robes, no one will see us coming."

Natalia interrupted, "Not to change the subject—though you are getting a bit mystical—I have been thinking about the old woman who drove me here last night. Her name is Tía—I heard Liam speaking to her." She had heard Torres talking to her, too, but she thought it best to leave Torres out for the moment. "She is very formidable. I—uh—happened to notice that she wears a necklace with a pendant of an eight-pointed star."

Kikki stared at Natalia. Maybe her job would be easier than she had thought.

"It's the symbol for the Sumerian Goddess Inanna." Natalia

watched Kikki for a reaction.

"Yes, it is," Kikki said quietly, reading Natalia. "I'm surprised you know that."

"I did my master's thesis at Columbia on Inanna before I switched to business."

Liam and Kikki exchanged a look.

Liam began, "Tía is Torres's great-aunt. You may not know that."

"No, I didn't. Makes more sense now." Though the whole picture was pretty complicated, she thought to herself. "Quite a coven you have."

Kikki picked up the thread. They didn't have much time, and Natalia had to be brought into the fold *tout de suite.* "Tía belongs to an ancient secret society named for the Goddess—the Daughters of Inanna."

"Really? Fascinating. I know about them. They are hundreds of years old and a secret matriarchal power base."

Kikki glanced at Liam, who raised his eyebrow. How much did Natalia know about what was going on this week? It was time to put all of the cards on the table.

"Tía is the reigning matriarch?" Natalia asked. "She's old, though still quite spry. Am I wrong?"

"No." Kikki looked curiously at Natalia. "Though being a matriarchal group, it is only a title of respect.

"Well, she gets my vote." Liam said gravely.

"What do you know about Inanna?" Kikki sat across from Natalia, slightly wary.

"She has always fascinated me. Inanna, the Mother Goddess, later known as Ishtar. As has the great Egyptian Goddess Isis and the Greek Athena. Inanna is associated with Athena and Aphrodite. She was a symbol of love and peace and also an indomitable warrior."

Natalia set her glass of wine down and looked from Kikki to Liam. She was glad that her sharp reliable mind was clearing—despite, or because of, the wine. She was beginning to understand what Kikki had not had time to tell her in Saint-Sulpice. Tía, Liam and Kikki must be part of this secret society. Natalia realized that they wanted to recruit her. Perhaps that was the way to watch her back.

Kikki smoothed her jeans. With so much knowledge of Inanna, Natalia was truly Margot's descendant.

"Personally, I've always been partial to Athena—well, partial to the Greeks. Margot admired the Greek Goddesses." Kikki smiled.

Liam turned to the two women and asked, "Margot knew about Inanna, *non?*"

"I'm pretty sure she did. In fact," Kikki began as Margot's visions and words flashed through her third eye, "the Daughters would have been a safe haven for her."

"Naturally," Liam shot her a warning look that meant, *don't frighten Natalia.* "I have always wondered why it was Inanna who was chosen to be titular to this secret society. It existed long before Margot—at least, that is my understanding. Even though I, too, cannot help but be partial to the Greek Goddesses."

"Well, I get it," Kikki said, "She is the most complete and all-encompassing Goddess. Her name literally means 'Queen of Heaven' in Sumerian. I have a statue of her on my altar. Her role was epic, greater than that of any other deity, male or female."

Liam nodded and caught Natalia's eyes.

"Remind me again, Natalia, what time period are we talking about? When were the Sumerians prominent?"

"The land known as Sumer was what is now roughly the southern half of modern Iraq. Between Bagdad and the Persian Gulf." Natalia warmed to her subject. "Settled between 4500 – 1900 BCE. Ancient Sumeria is one of the earliest known civilizations in the world, along with the Egyptians, Minoans, Indus Valley and Ancient China. Sumer's early people were called Ubaidians. They established cities that later became Sumer's great urban centers— Uruk, Ur, Eridu. And Uruk was Inanna's city. The later Semites or Akkadians knew her as Ishtar, as I said. Don't want to bore you—"

"No, please go on," Kikki urged, sipping her Badoit. "So in 3000 BCE. Around the same time that the Pre-Bronze Age Aegean peoples were flourishing in Thera and, as you said, the great Minoan civilization. Fascinating." Kikki felt great kinship with Inanna. "They are linked, not just by common belief systems and humanity. If I remember correctly, linguistic studies have established that Cretan or Eastern Aegean script—hieroglyphics—

338

derived from the Sumerian scribes. We know the two matriarchal societies influenced one another."

"My eyes are glazing over, Kikki," Liam said with playful sarcasm, concerned about the serious mood in the room.

"Get over yourself."

"Yes, Liam," Natalia agreed. "Inanna represented love, wisdom, and was Queen of Heaven and Earth. She was also a fierce warrior who did battle with evil and darkness. She gained wisdom and knowledge through battle by journeying rather quite literally to Hell and back."

"Like the Eleusinian mysteries," Kikki added. "Persephone being captured by Hades and carried off to the Underworld for six months of the year. Her mother, Demeter, wandering the Earth in search of her daughter. Change of seasons, cycles of life and death —"

"Exactly, Kikki," Natalia said, taking a sip of wine. "Inanna had to leave her lover, Dumuzi, the shepherd king, and journey to the underworld to save her sister, Ereshkigal, Queen of the Underworld, who stripped her of her jewels and garments, and hung her naked corpse by meat hooks to rot for her trouble."

Kikki felt her stomach knot. She was uneasy that Natalia knew so much—still, she listened, fascinated.

"Women like Margot and her role models, like Anne de Bretagne, benefited from the secret society," Natalia said, confident on her topic. "They gained protection and strength. All of these women were strong, highly educated and cultured. They were independent spirits who wanted and deserved a voice in a world ruled by men. The Daughters of Inanna was a safe forum."

"Margot's biographers claim she was a devout Catholic," Liam said.

"Hmm. Don't know that I agree," Kikki said. "Anyway, it was for religious correctness. French Catholicism kept a safe distance from the Roman Empire and the Pope. She had to appear to be Catholic. And one did not rule out the other."

"True. Political necessity of the extravagant and decadent French court. But nonetheless," Natalia piped in, "during the time Margot lived, there were more than thirty thousand astrologers in France."

"Margot saw astrologers, seers and worshipped the Goddess," Kikki said.

"Catherine de Medici—" Natalia began, and then stopped, remembering the heated debate she'd had with Kikki in the Voltaire.

Kikki set down her wine glass so abruptly it cracked and red drops seeped out onto the white Damask tablecloth. She felt a pull from the other world. She prayed not that of Catherine de Medici's murderous spirit—to be consumed by the fires of Hell as a sorceress.

She closed her eyes, and she was back in the quaint ornate carriage with Margot. She was Gillonne, and she and Margot were on their way to see the doctor.

Liam was at her side in an instant. He took her limp hand and felt for a pulse.

"Is she all right? What did I say?" Natalia was worried.

"It's not you. It's a very intense time. Just give her a little room."

Natalia retreated to a window seat.

"I hope that's not going to start happening to me. I have a lot of work to do this week."

"So does she," Liam whispered.

Chapter 80

Kikki felt another wave, and she was flooded with golden light. She was floating, and then she became Gillonne in the carriage that rumbled through the forest.

"Gillonne," Margot whispered. "You must never tell anyone what I am about to tell you."

"I promise, my dearest Queen Margot."

"This convent—where we go—I found it through my other mother—my dear Diane de Poitiers. She who loved me more than any mother."

"Yes." Gillonne knew but let Margot tell her story, knowing it would help ease her mind, if only for a few minutes.

"It is not a Catholic order. Not at all. That is but a façade."

"Yes, I know that women or girls have no choice in this man's world. And even those of the most royal blood, such as runs through your veins, are banished to abbeys and convents to hide them—to punish them and to exile them from their beloveds and society."

Tears ran down Margot's cheeks.

"Especially those of le sang real, Gillonne. It has always been so. These women, like us, like me, must leave our children—especially

341

our female children—in a safe place—or they will be killed. Ma
mère would not hesitate if she knew."

"I am sorry poor Margot."

"And some—" She took a deep breath and leaned close to
Gillonne, stroking the sleeping infant's head. "Some would call
these nuns—these women of this convent where we go—witches."

Gillonne stroked Margot's cheek, whispering, "Do not worry,
my beautiful Margot. They are not witches, at least not witches who
practice black magic. But white magic, like my grandmother. They
worship the Mother Goddess and an ancient natural way of life.
And they will teach it to your beautiful daughter so that she may
know a gentler path. And her daughters after her too."

Gillonne cradled the baby girl in her arms, kissing her forehead
as the carriage rumbled over the rough terrain. The earthy smell of
horses' sweat from the strain filled her nose and made her eyes
water. The steady rhythm lulled them all to sleep.

The crack of a whip awoke Gillonne with a start. Men were
shouting. She glanced fearfully across the carriage at the nurse. A
soldier held a dagger at her throat.

Gillonne had the baby in her arms still, both covered with a
dark wool blanket. She looked away and held her breath. Margot
sat on the far side of the coach, head covered and face hidden.
Gillonne prayed to the Goddess that they would not be recognized.
She prayed for a miracle.

In the still night, she heard the sound of coins clanging against
each other. A bribe—a toll. Paid by their trusted driver, Gillonne's
cousin.

The men shouted again, horses neighed, and the carriage
slowly began to move. They had crossed the border into the Grand
Duchy of Tuscany.

The soldier on horseback hung back, watching the carriage at
the border. Ready to follow. There would be no obstacle too great
for a Knight of the Holy Sword of God. "Long live Charles IX,
Queen Catherine and all who serve the One and Only Catholic
God!" he shouted into the cold night, brandishing high his crucifix
hilted sword.

"Certain death to these tainted women—traitors, witches and
heretics!"

Chapter 81

It was nearly six p.m. when Kikki awoke in bed wrapped in a warm duvet, still dressed. She slit her eyes open. Slowly coming to consciousness, she saw that she was in a very luxurious room fit for a queen in the Hotel Regina. She remembered now what had happened. She sat up slowly. She heard footsteps and then a soft knock on her door.

"Are you awake?"

"Liam?"

"*Ç'est moi.*"

"Come in."

He entered quietly to sit in a chair near the bed.

"You look much better. You've been out for a while."

"Natalia?"

"She's gone to her own room to sleep." He had a box in his hand and opened it. "Phones. Encrypted. Sent by messenger."

Kikki looked alarmed.

"Messenger?" She remembered the man with the roses.

"JM himself, again. That good enough?"

"Torres?" She felt panic rise. "Has anyone had word from him?" She longed to speak to her lover, to know that he was safe.

"JM said he was busy but fine. They are all set in a secure location working the op," Liam reassured her. "I'll give you the new phone when you can focus."

Her thoughts on Torres, her heart tumbled in her chest. She sat up to swing her legs over the side of the bed.

"I have a headache, and I am dizzy. Feels like I have the flu, or considering where I've been again, maybe the plague!"

"Don't joke about that. You need fluids. I have a special elixir for you." He lay the back of his hand across Kikki's forehead and frowned. "Slight fever. Let me see your eyes. Open them!"

"They are open, but they're killing me. I think I travelled very far away while I was out."

"Hmm. *Sans doute.*"

Some minutes later, after she had drunk Liam's magic potion, she felt revived.

"Well, that worked, my potion. You're nearly your most Our Lady of Justice self." He chuckled. "*Tant mieux.* Here's your new phone. I think Monique may have left a text. She called me when she couldn't reach you—"

"What an incestuous group this is. What time is it? I have to talk to Monique," she said, smiling. "Thank you for being here. For being you."

"It's nearly six p.m. She arranged a rendezvous for drinks for seven p.m. at Le Meurice. Just you and the EP—Moreno—no producers. Monique's not going because you don't want to double-team him. He wanted to meet at the Ritz, but we vetoed that idea. Then you're supposed to dine at Le Grand Véfour in the Palais Royal—again, *sans* Monique. Or that's their plan. You can get out of that, I hope."

"Absolutely," Kikki said. "Definitely not going to dinner with Victor and Uncle Frank. I hope they don't show up for drinks. I better double-check with Monique."

"Uh. Wait. You're not really clear," Liam said, picking up on something, but he didn't know what it was. "Give yourself a few minutes. Things are out of focus—or something."

"You're stumbling over your words," she joked. "Guess it's been a long day for you too."

"You could say that. You are a handful—not to mention I am

running a five-star sold-out hotel in Paris at Christmas time, no less. It may not be the Ritz—"

"Well, thank the Goddess for that! Sorry." Kikki stood, checked her balance and slowly walked out of the room, Liam behind her.

She picked her phone up from the coffee table in the salon and started to hit the speed dial for Monique, but Liam whisked the phone from her hand.

"You can't use that phone now. Monique is *au courant*. Here." He handed her a brand-new phone. "Use the encrypted one. I programmed your contacts for you."

"This is scary, *non?*" She held Liam's eyes.

"Think of it as an adventure. *Vas-y* call her—but on this number. It's in your phone, but—" Liam jotted a new mobile number on hotel notepaper and handed it to her.

Kikki called Monique's new number and got automated voice mail. She left a message.

"I'll be there to meet with Moreno—19:00 Le Meurice."

The Meurice was nearby, two long blocks away on rue de Rivoli. She gave herself an hour to get ready.

"I've arranged for some fresh clothes. You look a fright." Liam smiled, pleased with himself. "You'll find them in the bedroom's separate dressing room."

She stood on the tiptoes of her bare feet and kissed him on the cheek.

"My prince."

"Right—you've got your prince—well, you've got your very own hunk of real man—a count, no less."

"That's a cover."

"Whatever. Try to hang on to him, will you?"

"Don't get snarky. It's not attractive."

"I've laid out a dress for you." He pulled the door to her room gently closed.

After a luxurious scented bath, she pampered herself with creams, dressing with care.

She opened the door and stepped into the salon, refreshed and wearing the perfect costume Liam had chosen for her. A 1940s vintage black crepe sheath that hugged her body, hemmed just a few inches above the knees.

"You look like a million bucks, *non*? Don't you love the dress? Vintage Dior. I got it from that fabulous boutique in Galerie Vivienne. And the shoes. To die for—vintage Maud Frizon. *Absolutely Fabulous!*"

They both laughed at one of their favorite female British comedy teams.

"I know. I am a prince." He studied her critically. "Can I have someone do your hair?"

"Absolutely not at all. I will wear a hat. It's cold. I'll put it up in a chignon, or I can tuck my blonde locks behind my ears and wear the perfect earrings."

He produced diamond studs.

"I know you don't go in for demure. But think Grace Kelly."

"They're beautiful. Diamonds are always good." She fumbled with the studs.

"Here, let me do it. Stand still and stop fidgeting."

"You're losing me in fashion. I need to mentally prepare. Gird my loins. I cannot afford to be anything other than grounded."

"The diamond studs set in gold will help. And more of my elixir." He offered to refill her diluted green-brown drink. "No more visions."

Kikki drank it and made a face.

"And, as the working ladies of Santiago de Cuba said according to a dear friend, business is business and love is bullshit. But one hundred thousand euros worth of business, just to start us off. I'd love to be able to take it—in good conscience. How can we?"

Liam closed his eyes for a moment. "I don't get anything. Card?"

"Sure. My gut tells me not to cash the check, but financial freedom would go a long way. I get why Natalia works for her slimy uncle."

"You are not Natalia. And Natalia is about to take a—*comment-dit-on?* A transformative voyage. You remember the part about Inanna traveling to the Underworld to save her sister."

"I hope she will be with us and not against us. She would make a formidable enemy."

"*Oui.*" Liam agreed. "It's tricky with her uncle and his—unholy alliance with Victor. There will be a strong pull towards the dark. A place she already knows well."

"True," Kikki said, worry lines etching her forehead. "Torres has been working on her, and he's extremely persuasive. Now, she has even more reason to work with us, knowing who she really is. She's a shrewd woman. But she's maybe twenty-seven. Young. She might think she can handle Victor—like I thought."

Kikki frowned and undid another button on the bodice. She checked her look in the living room mirror that served as a small runway. Then she rebuttoned it, feeling too exposed, even though she usually used her Goddess-given gifts to best advantage. But her world was spinning out of control.

"Margot had something with those ruffs they wore—like Elizabeth I—the so-called Virgin Queen of England, her near contemporary," she said, turning to Liam. "Like some kind of armor around the fifth chakra, neck and collarbone. Show the nipples but keep the critical communication channel protected—that's a fashion Margot either created or embraced."

"Stop thinking about Margot." Liam began to shuffle the cards. "Focus on yourself."

She cloaked her neck with a red cashmere pashmina.

"Closest thing to a *ruff*. They'll never burn me at the stake!"

Liam had been sitting at a table by a window shuffling his deck of tarot cards.

She stood a few feet away and watched him draw a card. He let out a long breath.

"What is it?" She came up quickly behind him.

"The Ten of Swords."

"Ruin. Desolation." Fingers of fear encircled her throat. Victor's face loomed. "Death."

Liam turned. "The Furies call for a sacrifice."

"Look!" Kikki cried suddenly, gazing out the window. "The Ferris wheel at Place de la Concorde is lit up in red—like blood!"

Liam gave her a firm look.

"Don't let it get to you. Be strong. You cannot blow with the wind. It's Christmas. In a minute it will be green. Or the colors of the Russian flag. I think an important Russian Orthodox Bishop is in town with Putin—really. Or maybe it's mad, cruel Mother Medici! Whatever it is, you must see through the veil, the tricks and disguises. Use your gifts!"

"You mean like the Furies? If you don't hear them, they can't scream at you?"

"Exactly." Lost in his private dark thoughts, still in trance, he flipped another card.

"The Three of Swords. Again!" Kikki's heart constricted. "The same card you pulled on the day this all began. A bloodbath."

He didn't respond, but his handsome face was shadowed by gloom.

She steeled herself, straightening her spine, and moved away from the window.

"Put them away. I want a stiff drink before my meeting."

"Last card. You know there's always one more," he said with false cheer, trying to humor his dear friend. "*Et voilà*! Justice! All right, Athena. Looks like you're ready. All will be resolved in our favor. Go balance those scales. And take your sword of truth."

He slipped the cards back into his pocket.

"I'll make you a drink. I may have one too."

She took the crystal whiskey glass filled with a finger of fine single malt and downed it.

"Wow! That clears my head and burns my throat. You're right." She put on her game face. "Robert-Stefan Moreno, *dite* Medici will be very useful. I can turn him—he's vulnerable. He can get us the rest of what we need on Victor and the Swords' endgame. We'll bring them down. We're all in, whatever the risk. Monique and I agreed."

"*C'est ça.* Go forth. And I think you're right. He really is a Medici. Dark bloodlines, and he's not in a favorable position."

"When I've gone, ask Natalia about him. For all I know, he's her cousin."

The phone buzzed. She smiled. A text from Monique: *Bon courage! On my way to meet Liam for a drink at the Regina. See you after your rendez-vous! xo M*

Kikki put on her coat, grabbed her bag, and walked out of the suite. Liam was right behind her. When she walked into the corridor it went dark. Floating on a black cloud of smoke was the pinched and heavily veiled visage of Catherine de Medici. Under the black veil, vipers darted from her open mouth.

Chapter 82

"Liam!"

"What?" he said, worried.

"You don't see her? Madame la Serpente? In a dark cloud spitting vipers? It's a bad omen. Victor—" she choked out the words in a raspy voice.

"No. I don't see her. Vanquish her. She's trying to block you."

"You're right." Kikki closed her eyes. When she opened them a moment later, the corridor was softly lit and the beastly apparition was gone. "She's gone. But—"

"You have to fight." Liam was stern.

She still had a sinking feeling in her stomach.

Liam walked Kikki to the entrance. His bevvy of handsome porters was assisting guests with luggage. Liam motioned for her to wait while he checked the outside entrance under the eaves of the hotel.

Inside, Kikki tapped her heels nervously on the marble floor. The same white marble that had turned into a river of blood on Monday at the behest of the Black Queen, Catherine's hateful, dark soul. Still so vivid. She could almost smell the—stop it, Kikki. She is only a Fury. She cannot hurt you or block you unless you let her.

Kikki took a deep breath and pushed the revolving door open.

Liam looked over his shoulder. Shock and horror marred his face, lips twisted in a grimace.

"What is it?" Kikki felt dizzy and terrified. Her pulse quickened. Pain seared her temples.

He rasped, "Don't look."

He tried to hold her back, but she wriggled free and came towards him.

In the center of the square, the statue of Jeanne d'Arc was illuminated from streetlamps in the area and Christmas decorations elaborately strung across the rue de Rivoli around Place des Pyramides.

A figure in white lay at the base of the statue just below the front hooves of the golden stallion.

Kikki ran the short distance, impervious to traffic. Cars slammed on their brakes. Horns honked. Liam was right behind her.

Her piercing scream carried through the ethers on the cold winter wind of that night.

"No! Please! No! Not Monique!"

Wrapped in her white fur coat, her friend lay on her back in sacrifice below the prancing golden hooves of Jeanne's stallion. Her delicate throat had been sliced, now a gaping bloody wound.

A stream of blood stained the pristine white fur. In death, Monique's beautiful green heavily lashed eyes were open in shock, lips still curved innocently in a smile. A bouquet of red roses lay on the ground near her left hand, now slack in death.

Her lovely honey-colored hair framed her young face.

Kikki closed her eyes and prayed to the Goddess that it was a trick, not real. Not Monique. But even before she opened her tear-filled eyes, she knew this was no vision—no apparition. This was her dear friend, brutally murdered.

A deadly message from very real enemies.

Kikki's chest heaved and bile rose in her throat. She leaned over to touch her friend, to close her eyes, to leave her in peace. Dearest Monique—even in death she smiled—ever fearless, like Jeanne d'Arc.

Liam took Kikki's shoulder.

"Don't. You shouldn't—" He stopped midsentence.

Kikki leaned further over her friend, protective. She growled like a lioness.

Carved into Monique's forehead, painted in her blood, was the single letter *S—Sorcière!*

A cold wind whipped violently around them yet disturbed them not. Protected in the eye of a storm, their world became eerily quiet.

And then, heavy wet snow began to fall in earnest. The wind howled and the blizzard was suddenly upon them. Streetlights and Christmas decorations flickered and then went dark.

Kikki and Liam guarded Monique's lifeless body, shrouded in the cold, black night.

Chapter 83

A sharp metal click made Kikki jerk involuntarily. She shot a look of rage over her shoulder. But it was only Liam, opening a large umbrella to shelter them from the wet snow.

A bevvy of porters bearing similar umbrellas headed towards them. Battling against the wind and snow, they looked like the small army of Thermopylae with shields covering their heads to ward off flying arrows from the two million strong attacking Persian army. At Liam's direction, they formed a protective circle around Monique's body.

Streetlights flashed on and off. Traffic on the rue de Rivoli and flowing up the tunnel under the Tuileries to the Place des Pyramides was at a standstill. Strangely, as if the drivers knew death was nearby, the sound of car horns had ceased in the sea of yellow headlights.

Like the eyes of a pack of wolves, Kikki thought. An image from the start of this nightmare.

Where was Torres? Her need for him was more primal than anything she had ever felt. She caught Liam's eye, and he nodded with understanding.

Numb with shock and loss, she stood in unbearable sadness,

tears streaming down her cheeks. Overwhelmed by grief and devastated for Monique's family, the next minutes were a blur.

And then, Torres was by her side.

"I am so, so sorry, *mi amor*," he said quietly, wrapping his arms around her. She allowed herself to exhale a tiny measure of her grief. She knew he would release her from the comfort of his arms soon. The business of death was her lover's purview. She already felt his grip loosen, and she reached for his hand.

"I've got her, Kikki." He looked into her eyes, dilated and teary. "I will take care of your beloved Monique. She was my friend too."

With great reluctance, she let go of Torres's strong hand.

Without leaving Kikki's side, he leaned over and inspected Monique.

"Garroted or a very sharp blade," he said softly, so Kikki couldn't hear.

He checked automatically for a pulse. As he knew, he found none.

He turned to Kikki, his eyes full of anguish and heartbreak, and whispered, "She didn't suffer. Death was instantaneous. We can be grateful for that. An unspeakably vicious act."

Kikki nodded.

She wrapped her arms tightly around herself, holding it all in, holding herself together. Barring and protecting at once. She was short of breath and began to choke again as her stomach churned sour. She knew she would be sick.

She slipped unseen outside the protective barrier of Liam's men. Then she leaned over and retched.

She moved a few feet away to the far side of the statue's base and Monique's body. Red-hot rage surged through her veins.

She shrieked into the night, "I will have vengeance for Monique! Damn you to the darkest corner of Hades. I am coming for you!"

She felt at one with Gillonne and Margot and the excruciating pain of *les noces vermeilles*—the bloody wedding, so long ago. In oneness with that time, she felt the weight of the curse on Margot, as though it were her own.

She formed the curse into a ball and hurled it with white light through the night at those who were dark enemies of love and all that was sacred. Eyes glazed, she watched it soar through the universe. She shouted as it flew out of the galaxy.

"I curse you! *Tous maudits! Malédiction!*"

Chapter 84

At the pinnacle of La Grande Roue at the far edge of the Tuileries, on the Place de la Concorde, Victor and a Russian man shared a cabin. The Ferris wheel had stopped because of the wind and blizzard.

But neither was concerned. They considered themselves untouchable by mere mortals and the likes of Interpol division chiefs like Torres. The Daughters of Inanna, well, that had never been a question.

Now the message would be clear. Those witches insisted on battle. Then war they would have. Victor was Alexander the Great incarnate, Attila the Hun, Caligula, all great male warriors—victors who wiped the weak from the earth. He laughed at the pun— Victor, a name well chosen for him. He would conquer all.

Through binoculars, Victor had watched the scene at Place des Pyramides, exhilarated.

His companion on the wheel, a highly placed Russian Orthodox Bishop was somber, as befitted his position. Still, Bishop Nicolas Vasilovich felt his heart beating strongly with the righteous power of the One and True God and the Knights of the Holy Sword, his mighty army.

In homage, he stood and raised one arm to the heavens brandishing a twenty-four-carat crucifix with a golden sword affixed to the back. And again, for their powerful leader Putin, another great Knight of the Holy Sword, who was in Paris today signing a weapons deal.

The Bishop sat quickly when the cabin began to sway, and the great wheel moved again. Fitting, he thought, riding the great wheel of fortune and fate. Rasputin, the illustrious prophet, was his inspiration. The Knights of the Holy Sword were sitting at the apex of great destiny, untouchable and far beyond mortal reach.

"Divine justice is ours! The wheel begins to move towards our victory." Victor stood and shouted, even as the Ferris wheel began to pick up speed. "We are protected by God. If it stops again, I'll call my generals. We have the military firmly behind us."

At that same moment, Kikki screamed her curse into the night, and Victor felt a seething pain in his head and heard a strange voice like a wild siren's call. He wavered in his stance. He knew exactly who and what sought to curse him—*that fucking witch who had betrayed him.*

"You dare to curse me. You will pay with your life! All of you, your decrepit Goddess and all who represent her, will burn in the eternal flames of Hell. The French cunt is only the beginning."

Chapter 85

Torres quickly secured the perimeter with Liam's help. The local authorities would arrive any minute, he knew. He worked for Interpol in antiquities trafficking in liaison with the International Criminal Court. A murder in the very upscale First Arrondissement of Paris was certainly not his jurisdiction. But this one was definitely his business. Monique was a friend, and her murder was directly linked to his op. This was his crime scene, and everyone else could go to hell.

He reached Flo, his boss, by phone.

"One of ours—Monique—has been murdered. Get on the phone to our contact and have the local cavalry back off. The blizzard will slow them down but not stop them."

Flo recognized his rage, so she ignored his insubordination.

"*Putain de merde! Qu'est-ce qui s'est passé?*" What happened?

Torres briefed her on what details he had on the murder.

"Monique Dubois was Kikki's partner and a good friend."

"*Quelle horreur!*"

"This is important. I have to be in charge." Torres's voice filled with rage, masking fear. "Do whatever you have to do. No risks and no leaks. Kikki is in great danger!"

"And so are you, *mon grand! Restes vigilant et calme-toi!* You can't afford not to be meticulously rational and by the book at the moment."

"You're right, of course. It's just—" he took a deep breath.

"It's unspeakable. We will deal with it. But you have to keep your focus," she said, her voice deepening. And then she laid it out: "You expected something like this, *non?* And we're prepared. They're ratcheting up their game. But we cannot back off."

"I have no intention of doing so. They will pay for this, those motherfuckers," he said angrily. He took a deep and slow breath, then another, forcing himself to think logically. "Kikki and Monique just took a meeting with an associate of Fitz-Perkins and Pelligrini about a film to be used as a vehicle for money laundering, antiquities trafficking and who knows what else—to get to Kikki, of course."

"Right. I am aware. *Surveille ton dos!*" Flo said. Watch your back!

Torres flipped a cigarette from a pack and flicked a lighter, sheltering it from the high wind and increasing snow.

"*D'accord.* We take charge now. I need some help. We know they have officials high up in the Ministries of Justice and Interior, the Police Judiciare and the Brigade Criminelle. I cannot hold them off alone. They'll be here any second—"

"I'll make the call, and then I'll be right there to back up my words with action."

Torres's next call was to JM. His voice was steely when he briefed JM.

"It's begun in earnest. I was afraid of something like this," JM's voice was grim. "What do you need?"

"Call whomever you think will be most effective. On the inside track—back channel—no leaks. I don't want this crime scene compromised. Otherwise, we won't have the hard proof we need. I wouldn't be surprised if Fitz-Perkins did this one personally. He might have had the arrogance to have left us a morsel of evidence."

"Right. Less than two days and counting," JM said.

"Where is he right now, JM?"

"Place de la Concorde. With a Bishop representing the Russian Orthodox Patriarch. Here with Putin. The two of them took the bloody Ferris wheel!"

"*Joder*! How did they get there, so close to where Monique was assassinated? I thought you had someone on them. Our intel was that Fitz-Perkins was dining in Versailles."

"My fault—I don't know." JM's voice betrayed his guilt even as he continued, always the professional, never casting blame on those he commanded. "They pulled a switch. We lost them in the rush hour—"

"And you had someone on Monique?"

"Yes, fuck, of course! Someone grabbed her in a crowd of people getting out of the Métro at Tuileries. Not a block from the Regina, right in front of the Meurice. With that white fur, she was easy to tail, but they knew it too. When they took her, they covered her with a black coat, and bam, gone—"

Torres was angry, but he was not going to take it out on JM.

"Well, get it together. Don't let those two *cabrónes* out of your sight. Find Frank Pelligrini. Make sure these French bureaucratic morons don't interfere with this crime scene. I have Flo on it too."

Torres disconnected, racked with remorse. Monique—he had been very fond of her. An unnecessary sacrifice.

He looked around for Kikki. Where was she? He had to get her to safety, if it wasn't too late already. His heart crashed against his chest as he scanned in the blinding snow. Just as he was about to search for her, a platoon of dark sedans screeched to a halt in Place des Pyramides, blue emergency lights flashing, sirens bleating.

Liam, who had hovered close by protecting Monique's body, stepped up to Torres.

He laid a hand on Torres's arm.

"What can I do?

"Find Kikki. Get her somewhere safe. I'll deal with them."

The fleet of vehicles brought the nearby Commissariat of Police in full force, along with the Commandante of the Brigade Criminelle, the Médecin Légiste (the coroner), someone high up in the Ministry of Justice and a prosecuting judge. They had all known instantly, just as Torres had suspected. Working together—an otherwise unlikely confederation—the hotline of French connections at its most efficient when real power was at play.

Torres hoped his connections were higher and more solid.

Despite their show of force at the moment, he counted on the notorious French art of evading responsibility. When it came down to it, few would be willing to stick his or her neck out for Fitz-Perkins, Pelligrini and their lot, especially considering that they were foreigners. Always safest in the immense French bureaucracy to keep your head down.

Plus, ritual murder of a beautiful young French woman from a prestigious family in the First Arrondissement would not go down well with the French. She was one of theirs. It was personal and a closed circle. That would be the likely stance of even the Brigade Criminelle. Torres was counting on that.

Later, he could dig more deeply. Now, he only needed enough time to get Monique to their people.

Torres waited as the other men approached. He stood alone in front of the shield of umbrellas that Liam had set up as a barricade, covering Monique.

The entourage reached him. Torres shoved his arms forward, pushing them back.

"*Dégagez! Arretez là!*"

"*Ç'est à nous!*" the Commandante shouted. This is ours!

His arms flew, gesticulating with menace. The others soon joined in, and it turned into a shouting match. Just as they began to stake out their territory, Flo pushed her way through the men to stand shoulder to shoulder with Torres.

"*Assez!*" She commanded. Flo's tall, lanky form loomed commandingly over the assembled *flics*. Her short white hair blew in the wind, mixing with snow, electrified, like an ancient warrior queen's headdress. High cheekbones slashed a narrow face. Her brows furrowed in rage and determination. Smoke from the cigarette dangling between dark red lips swirled around her head, an imposing figure.

"Flo, I've got to find Kikki," Torres hissed.

"*Vas-y.* I've got this."

He broke away.

Madame la Judge, a formidable French woman known for her icy calm and high success rate as a prosecuting judge, *La Proc*, stood elbow to elbow with a Deputy Minister of Justice. They stepped out of the angry group.

Flo spoke sharply, issuing an order.

"*Madame la Proc*, this case is off-limits for you."

La Proc raised her chin in defiance.

"This is our crime scene. Our case."

Flo's steely blue eyes flashed. She held out her phone.

"Take it. The caller on the other end will confirm what I have said."

"*Je vous emmerde!*" *La Proc* shouted, gesticulating at Flo.

But the guy from Justice grabbed the phone.

"*Oui, monsieur. Entendu.*" Understood. He shoved the phone back to Flo, muttering, "We'll see."

Reluctantly, he took a step back and motioned to the others. They did not move.

The blizzard was picking up intensity, and blinding snow flew sideways. Torres could barely see a foot in front of him. To add to the chaos, the cops had left their sirens blaring, lights flashing.

He saw Liam under the eaves of the hotel. Kikki wasn't with him. Where was she? He felt panic rise. Did they have her? He was terrified for his love.

Torres pushed through a crowd of onlookers. They were only just being held off by traffic cops, who were setting up steel barricades around a large perimeter.

Where would she go? Into the Tuileries? But it would be closed. It was dark and late, past 19:00. He hurried through the *flics*, pushing aside those in his way. Finally, he spotted her standing in the blizzard alone, back to him, just at the edge of the Tuileries.

She was wailing, but he couldn't hear the words. He ran to her but then slowed when he was close, approaching her quietly. With a light but firm grip, he put a hand on her shoulder.

"Kikki, it's me! Stop this. It's dangerous."

She turned to look at him. Her eyes were so dilated she couldn't see. Snow pelted her face and her hair was drenched. She wasn't sure who or where she was.

She heard horses' hooves pounding dirt. When she looked down, she was wearing an odd black cloak that was soaked. She was standing in a puddle of blood. She fainted.

Torres caught her and carried her into the Hotel Regina.

Chapter 86

Thursday morning near midday at the apartment on Quai Voltaire, Kikki tossed and turned, tortured by nightmares. Her body felt heavy, almost leaden, and her limbs twitched as though they weren't part of her. Her mind replayed the events of the evening before.

Monique's face appeared in her dream, smiling.

"It will be okay. I wanted to tell you about—" And then she vanished.

Kikki could feel the tears on her face but couldn't lift her eyelids. And she didn't really want to wake up. How could she face a world this cruel? The war had begun. Full darkness of the yearly winter solstice cycle was descending. And it would be darkest in the next hours. Who else would she lose?

Tía sat in the kitchen drinking strong black coffee and plotting. Soon she would wake Kikki.

The evening before, Tía had a healer come to the apartment to help Kikki. Dr. Marie gave her the works. She performed an energetic healing and restored Kikki as much as her spirit would allow. Marie gave Tía a sleeping concoction for Kikki later, ordering rest for fourteen to sixteen hours.

The tragedy of Monique's death weighed heavily on Tía, but they could not allow it to stop them, or even worse, to be in vain. Today, she would put their plan in motion. The Daughters' agenda was unfolding.

She had set crystal rosettes at all corners and windows of the apartment and performed a ceremony invoking Inanna's protection. They must amp protection on Quai Voltaire—and, of course, at the Chapelle des Louanges.

Gabrielle Laroche was taking care of that task. Especially poignant with the loss of their longtime caretaker. Tía fought back tears. There would be time enough for tears and for training Monique's only daughter to take over. She was only seven, but old enough to begin.

With reverence, Tía took a sip of coffee and closed her eyes. When she opened them, she focused on the ceramic object in the middle of the oak table—the small but powerful *Snake Goddess* from circa 1600 BCE, the very one that Kikki uncovered that was to be exhibited.

Our Lady of the Beasts, a mere eight inches in height of all-powerful, ancient earth. Outstretched arms gripping vipers—symbols of retribution and protection. Wearing a beehive skirt of the Queen Bee Cult and a particular crown—a mythical beast, both cat and owl. She was from a Cretan Minoan colony, carried to Thera.

A sister goddess to Sumerian Inanna. Tía smiled.

Last night in her delirium, Tía had heard Kikki cry out for revenge. Though Inanna was a goddess of many things, a warrior goddess, and Marguerite de Valois had a taste for it, revenge was not the way of the Light. Not the way of the Goddess.

Kikki struggled to awaken with sudden urgency. She dug her fingers into the bed and began to focus on her breath. In and out slowly and then deeply. She coughed and her chest ached. She opened her eyes and sat up, dizzy.

She fell back onto the bed, mind swirling with thoughts of Margot's hateful mother—a ruthless manipulator for power. The woman who had played those she considered her enemies like marionettes in order to carry off the Saint-Bartholomew Day's

Massacre. Using Margot as bait to get the Huguenots *en masse* to the wedding celebration. And by taking advantage of her unstable, dying son, King Charles IX.

Kikki fell into a nightmarish vision.

Catherine de Medici appeared in full regal power and stood at the side of Kikki's now floating bed. She wore her widow's costume, a high collared black dress, a single strand of pearls, a black veil that did not mask the pure hate in her eyes.

She was surrounded by a river—the Seine—banks overflowing with blood.

"Kill them all!" King Charles IX cried out in mad delirium.

The Queen's eyes were black tunnels of evil aimed at Kikki. Gauntlet thrown. The Evil Queen—one who never lost. Her ghost, her power, her visceral darkness was at the core of ancient and present enemies.

Kikki donned her battle armor. With her own powers and Athena's helmet and holy sword, she swore to the Goddess, the Daughters of Inanna and to Margot that she would make a worthy and dangerous opponent.

Dauntless, Kikki returned the hideous stare of hate with her own. But hers was one of love and light drawn from within and from her protectors and muse—the greater light that was so powerful that it would extinguish her enemies and their dark well of evil. Darkness could not snuff out light.

The Black Queen opened her mouth and a tiny poisonous viper flew straight at Kikki.

Sword in hand, Kikki sliced the snake in half. It fell writhing into the pool of blood.

Her enemy launched another viper, and Kikki struck anew.

The stench of evil filled the bedroom. A smell she had memorized from Santorini when she had danced with the dark side as the portal swept up lost souls.

Kikki shot one last look at the evil Medici, whose eyes were filled with the flames of Hell.

Kikki stood, raised her sacred silver sword to the heavens and screamed at the apparition.

"Enough! Out! You are banned from this house. It is a sacred

temple of the Goddess. Be gone with you!"
With a hissing noise, the Black Queen vanished.

Kikki sat straight up in bed. Eyes wide, pupils dilated. Still in trance, caught between time and dimensions. Catherine de Medici no longer haunted her bedroom. The parquet floor was not a pond of blood. But there was an apparition.

A marble statue of a sphinx, a raven atop its head. The raven squawked loudly, spreading its wings wide. A message from the raven about the sphinx and her riddle.

Chapter 87

"Torres!" Kikki, fully awake from the vision, shouted for her lover.

The sphinx posed a riddle to be answered on pain of death. Ravens were magic and messengers. Travel beyond the veil. Omens of death in the world of black magic, birds of prey. Thoughts ran together in her unsettled mind.

She stumbled when she climbed out of bed and caught herself, twisting her ankle.

Torres burst in the bedroom door.

"Kikki! What happened?"

She threw herself into his arms.

"I had a vision—"

"Shh—you have been out for a long time." He held her and smoothed her hair and edged her towards the bed. He kissed the top of her head. "Get back to bed. I will bring you some strong coffee."

"I am still very woozy. You won't get much more than 'in bed' out of me."

He squeezed her hand. "I love you no matter what."

She smiled weakly.

"Me too. What a test this is. It's a test for us too."

He nodded and studied her serious expression.

"Tell me about your vision."

He listened to her and then said quietly, "Don't worry, my love. Visions are not my bailiwick, but a dire warning would be one way to look at it. The other is that we will vanquish our enemies and Operation Sphinx will be successful. Be right back with coffee."

"I might need something stronger—" As she spoke, tears flowed unbidden down her cheeks. "I can't believe she's gone."

He climbed into bed next to her and held her, kissing her on the cheek and then tenderly meeting her lips with his mouth. She responded with hungry desperation.

And then she broke away, wracked with sorrow and guilt.

"Go, get the coffee."

Tía was no longer in the kitchen, nor was the Snake Goddess, but she had left coffee and another elixir from Dr. Marie. He poured it into the coffee, grabbed a large bottle of Volvic and hurried back to Kikki.

She was sitting up in a white *peignoir*, wrapped in the duvet.

"It's so cold. Is it still snowing?"

"Yes, but not as hard as it was last night. A steady, heavy wet snow. It's sticking. We've probably had about four inches so far." He set the tray down on the bedside table and then pulled up a chair.

"Torres," she began with a tremor in her voice. "I know that despite Monique, we have to carry on. She would want that."

"*Seguro*. We will. But you must rest more." He chose his words carefully. "You will not be able to help if you are not strong."

"But I know from my vision that you need my help." She swallowed and took a deep breath to steady herself. "If I can't help, they will kill you. That's what it all means—"

"We've got it under control." He checked himself from shutting her out, keeping his voice tender.

"And you really think you can defeat them?" she asked. "Look how easily they got to Monique? How could that happen?"

"There is nothing I can say to excuse it. I am deeply sorry. We're doing everything we can. You have to trust me."

"I do trust you, and I also know that Monique's death was perhaps fated, beyond your control in a karmic way. But on an earthly and very personal plane, I am sick with grief. And I know you won't find out how Monique was murdered because there are certain things that are beyond your team—beyond police work."

He listened and then said evenly, "Maybe—but we can't take psychic visions to court. I need hard proof of murder, criminal conspiracy—trafficking in blood antiquities."

She frowned. "Fine. But the vision I just had made me more worried than ever for the safety of that beautiful archeological treasure and all that she symbolizes. We cannot let her fall into the wrong hands."

The vengeful words of the Swords' threat to Tía stuck in her mind:

"We shall wreak death and fiery vengeance against you and yours. One by one. Your blood shall flow—We come for you before the light turns."

The blood had already begun to flow. She knew the strength of Torres's abilities, his power as a warrior for justice. He and his team were the best. And Natalia was also key.

She gulped coffee and scalded the roof of her mouth.

"*Merde!*" She set the porcelain cup down. "You see. I am right." She began to cry again.

He went to her and took her gently in his arms.

"Cry. Let it out. Allow yourself to grieve. It's important. Let us take care of this. I promise your Snake Goddess will be safe. I understand her significance, and I care about her too. Remember, I'm not just a cop. I'm a digger—an archeologist. That's why I am entrusted with this. We will not fail." He spoke firmly. They could not afford to fail.

"What makes you think you can get them now?"

"Because—I—we—are that good. We have an international mandate with ultimate authority and access to unparalleled resources. We've got the intel. And the timing is perfect." He started to say more and stopped himself. Because she was right, there were great dangers—no guarantee that the op would work, no matter how prepared they were. And the odds were great that someone else would die.

All the power players—the Swords' ringleaders, including Fitz-Perkins and Pellegrini, would be present at the gala. Torres knew they'd be able to see and hear their interchanges and signals.

They'd intercept their "comms" through his team's plant with the Louvre security. They could nail the lot of them—and make sure the Swords' ringleader couldn't slip away or buy his way out.

Based on past bold moves for smaller gains but still important museum heists, Torres's gut told him that the leader would in some way personally initiate the theft of the Snake Goddess.

Torres was counting on Natalia to point the finger when time came for the sting.

Using her best Athena Lady of Justice voice, Kikki spoke calmly, "Thank you."

She sipped the coffee and used his weapon—silence.

"Fitz-Perkins kidnapped you once, and you didn't see it coming —and got away with it. He'll try again. I can't lose you, don't you see that?" He worked to keep desperation out of his voice.

She didn't respond to his need, one she felt just as deeply about him.

"Murdering Monique was meant to get to me—a bloody message. I have to avenge her death. It's become very personal."

Now it was Torres who did not answer.

"My love, we both have our blind spots. But there are things that I can see and know that will fill in the picture."

"I can't take psychic powers to court, and you're in too much danger."

"I'm not just talking about my psychic powers. I can use the film guy, Moreno. Monique and I had a strategy." And that is what got her killed. Monique had agreed to take the risk, yet Kikki felt a heavy burden.

Torres shoved a lock of hair from his eyes.

"Leave it to the cops. Moreno is small potatoes. He's a fall guy."

She insisted. "Don't dismiss him so quickly."

"You know I didn't want you to meet with him at all, but I couldn't stop you."

"Yes, well, I have my work and you have yours, right? That's our deal."

"Huh, yeah, until—" He frowned but held his tongue. She was revving up for a fight.

"Don't go there, Torres. I hope you didn't bug my office! I have to do my work and, as Tía reminded me, make my own mistakes."

She hadn't counted on this mistake costing Monique's life, she thought grimly.

Her psychic powers had been blocked. She hadn't seen that the meeting at the Meurice was a setup. She remembered the vision of the Black Queen she had in the Regina just before leaving. That had been a warning. She had ignored it.

Torres held his tongue, watching her carefully. What she was proposing was true, but dangerous. Now an even more delicate subject with Monique's murder. He understood why she wanted to do her part. But at what cost to her? And to him if he lost her?

"Come on, Torres. I have a huge stake in this. For Monique. I can get you hard proof of money laundering and more from this guy." She hesitated, eyes tearing. "Monique was nailing it down—before. I was on my way to meet him at the Meurice—" Her voice wavered. "Why didn't I call him myself? If I had she might still be alive." She had been completely blocked by the darkness, she realized now—far too late.

"You can't know that. It isn't your fault."

"No? Are you sure? Because I'm not. And now I have a duty, Torres."

"Don't you see that they're trying to get to you? They want to kill you. And Monique was a warning."

"Of course, I get that. They think you'll back off so they don't go after me. Your Achilles' heel. But don't you dare! They are gunning for you one way or the other. And they'll do anything it takes to stop you."

"I know that. It's my job. And also my job to protect you."

"Fine. Protect me, but don't stand in my way. I want you to take them down, for Monique and for me." Her voice was steely. "I don't think Moreno is all that happy to be messenger boy. I can turn him."

Torres thought, but didn't say, that Moreno was now a loose end. He might not make it to any more meetings.

She could see that he was torn and holding in his fury, feeling the futility of trying to stop her and, knowing he couldn't if he wanted to. Their constant dilemma.

"You know I'm right. Trust me, Torres. Let me all the way in, or neither one of us will make it through this alive—and certainly not together. Is that what you want? Are you intentionally trying to sabotage our relationship?"

"No, quite the opposite, in fact."

He caught her eyes and held her gaze.

"Good. Now that we have that settled—Moreno said that they had access to some private archives and secret *objets* belonging to Margot—*objets* that the Swords have stolen—so isn't that hard proof? That was his carrot, that and a hefty check—which will help us follow the money trail. I want to see these jewels, if they're real."

He shook his head. "No."

"For Monique!" she said fiercely, without saying what was on her mind—revenge.

Chapter 88

Torres stood, clenching his thigh to hide his mounting frustration. At least Kikki was sounding more like herself. The elixir and her own strength were pulling her out of the shock and trauma of Monique's murder. For now.

"Why don't you get up and get dressed, *mi amor*. I have to go soon," he said gently. His phone had just buzzed, and when he checked, he'd seen that JM was waiting for him. He didn't want to leave Kikki alone. Tía wouldn't be back for another half an hour.

He wondered about Liam or maybe—Natalia. The last time they spoke, she had been agreeable and ready to do whatever they needed. But that was before Monique was murdered.

Kikki climbed out of bed, taking her lover's hand to help her. She smiled up at him.

"Shall I call Natalia so you can leave? Better not to wait for Tía." She had intentionally shifted her response to her lover.

He stared, and then laughed. "Back to being High Priestess?"

"No—but I can read your mind, lover," she quipped.

"And I can read yours—you're trying to hurry me out."

"Am I?" She feigned innocence. "But, Commissaire—speaking for Athena and Margot—and a soon to be member of the Daughters of Inanna—if you're going after Victor, you had better get out Excalibur. It'll take a stake in his heart to finish him."

"He hasn't had to deal with the likes of me. He won't know what's coming for him. Or what took him down. Trust me."

He took her into his arms and held her tightly. They kissed long and hard. Melted together and hungry for each other. A primal need.

In moments, they were both naked and in bed. His hard cock was inside her sex, open and slippery with desire. His mouth wandered her body, and he bit her nipples. Her hands in his hair gave her purchase to go deeper.

"Torres! Oh Goddesses."

He rode her, and she lifted her hips to meet him. He cupped her and held her still as he drove into her. She let go, arched her back and shuddered. Waves rolled deep inside her sex—entirely consumed. She felt him grow still, and then become even more engorged, filling any emptiness in her soul.

He growled. She felt his warm fountain shoot into her womb and mix with her waves. And she came again. Mixing juices. They held on tight to each other. Fully alive and loved.

Chapter 89

A short time later, Torres left to meet JM just as Tía arrived. Tía had stayed long enough to usher Torres out and provide him assurances that Kikki would be safe with her.

Tía and Kikki had reviewed strategy, and then Tía left for a meeting.

But not before Tía's wise words had comforted Kikki.

"Monique's death was her karma. It wasn't your fault. Even if you hadn't been blocked by the Black Queen, you could not have saved Monique. Sadly, no one could have. Not me, not Liam. No one, my dear," she said gently.

Kikki wiped tears away.

"You are protected. And you are on the rightful path. Trust your instincts. We all have our part to play. I, too, must go. I will see you tonight at the Chapelle des Louanges."

After Tía had gone, Kikki stood at the fireplace in front of a roaring fire. She fingered the rose crystal necklace around her neck. It felt alive. She took a deep breath and inhaled its familiar scents of rose, lavender and old earth.

She had bathed and dressed quickly. Freshly laundered black jeans, soft black cashmere turtleneck and an oversized cardigan.

Black suede boots with sheepskin lining, favorite Uggs. Her favorite battle armor.

Her blonde hair fell loosely against her shoulders, and her eyes almost glowed in the low light, as she took in her reflection in the gilded mirror over the mantle—registering the fierce wildness of her spirit.

Alone again, Kikki smiled grimly to herself, still worried about her lover but determined to take her own initiative and follow her path.

She swept her Tarot cards from the coffee table. As she shuffled, her thoughts went to Monique, and her heart wrenched.

Cards in hand, she crossed to her vigil point at the long French paned doors overlooking her city. It was near midafternoon. The sky's ceiling was low, and it was snowing steadily—just as Torres had said. A blanket of silence. Perhaps a space for her to slip through without being seen, like a large cat on prowl—or a female lion with a ferocious mane.

The Seine was muddy green and turbulent, mirroring her troubled spirit. Only barely could she make out across the river, the dim lights of the Louvre's Pavillon de Flore.

She split the deck and shuffled again. She drew a card and turned it over.

The Emperor: Power, male authority, oppression of women and the end of the Matriarchy. Replaced by angry warring sky gods. A familiar enemy.

Zeus on his throne at Mount Olympus, holding the world and his lightning bolts, an eagle perched upon his shoulder. Complete opposite to the matriarchal Venusian energy of the Goddess. Zeus was Victor, far more powerful than the Zeus who had been her enemy in Santorini.

Ultimate Patriarch. This card was clear and familiar. She knew it was her path. There would be a final confrontation. And she would be on the frontlines.

Kikki fingered the card. Victor's idol and one of the most striking representations of patriarchal power was Alexander the Great—Greek, like Monique and Liam. But so very different. During his twelve-year reign, he had warred and fed his insatiable desire to conquer the entire world.

In the name of civilization, a euphemism for religion, he burnt to the ground the great matriarchal libraries, destroying ancient wisdom—Inanna's heritage and that of so many other peaceful societies.

Victor carried a coin with Alexander the Great's image, which he said was authentic. He also had registered with the heraldic authorities in England, a family crest—a coat of arms of dubious origins reflecting a purported lineage from Alexander the Great.

Why had she not seen the depth of his psychopathy? She knew he had an agenda, that he had mistreated women. But this was far more. She might never know why or what changed, but in hindsight, Kikki realized that he had always used his darkness to hide his true nature, his otherworldly powers of dark heart and soul. Thinking about him now, Victor was capable of projecting a semblance of rationality, while behind that mask was a demonic, possessed being. He was good at dissembling. A specialty of the Black Queen.

As she looked at the Emperor card, the pieces of the puzzle came together with clarity. Victor did not know her, not the woman Kikki had become. He had discounted her and thought only of revenge against the young, naïve woman who had betrayed him.

Looming large in her third eye, Catherine de Medici appeared haloed in blood.

The nightmarish vision in his suite at the Ritz came into focus. In that moment, she now realized, Victor had been Catherine de Medici incarnate. The knowledge hit. Victor had long been using the Black Queen to mask and block. He was her incarnation in present life.

Irreversible steps had been taken. They were pitted against one another. He had murdered Monique. There was no going back. And Kikki was betting heavily that he would underestimate her power.

With mounting fury, she slipped her own phone out of her pocket—not the encrypted one she had promised Torres she would use.

It was time. And it was very personal. She dialed Victor's number from her call list. While she waited for him to answer, she focused on the Seine, and it became a wall of flames. Had she done that? Or had Victor?

The call went to an anonymous voice mail. Enraged, she promptly disconnected.

This time, using her encrypted phone, she called Moreno.

"Robert—Maître Véronique Trieste."

"Oh my god, I'm so sorry about—"

"Thank you," she stopped him abruptly. "Look. I'll cut to the chase. I am very interested in discussing your film and offer further."

"But—" he sounded alarmed and confused. "It can wait. At such a time."

"No. In fact, it is perfect timing. The money will help Monique's family. And for me, it's better to dive into work. Can you meet me, in say, half an hour? Short notice, but—"

"Sure. No problem. You say where. Anything I can do."

"At the Louvre, under the Porte des Lions." An entrance used to access the archives, classes and nearby École du Louvre. Also, a secret entrance used by savvy visitors.

"Uh-huh. I'll find it. I'll ask the concierge—or Google it."

He was jittery.

"The objects of interest about which you spoke—bring them." She heard him draw a breath that sounded like fear, and she said, "Figure it out. We need to seal this deal today."

"Great. Hey, that's terrific! Let me see what I can do. We were all ready for you last night. Just need to talk to the producers again. You understand—might not be possible within that short of a time frame."

He sounded worried, and he was stuttering.

"Make it happen," Kikki snapped.

"Right."

"Let's do it for Monique," she finished softly. "Contact your people, and we'll move."

Chapter 90

Kikki locked the door to the apartment and hurried down the private staircase, out the gate and onto rue de Beaune. The snow had all but stopped traffic. As she rushed by the small grilled window to the kitchen of the Voltaire, she was comforted to see the familiar face of Chef Hervé, busy preparing the evening meal. Almost four-thirty p.m., Paris was nearly dark.

Head covered with the hood of her black shearling coat, she made her way among a few happy tourists. Quickly, she crossed the snow-covered Quai against the light, dodging traffic. She hurried onto the Pont Royal.

She was unmindful to anything but what was going on in her suddenly terrifying world. She slipped her gloved hand into the inside pocket of her coat, feeling for the leather sheath of her Mycenaean jeweled dagger from Santorini that she had removed from its secret place in the apartment. It had been a gift from the new director of the Greek National Museum. After Monique's murder, she had vowed to be prepared.

Halfway across the bridge, she stopped. In moments, she would be at the Porte des Lions, wearing her mask while Robert Moreno or Medici would wear a disguise of his own, though she was not exactly sure what it would be. She was ready to gamble.

She threw her arms, palms up to the sky.

"Athena and Inanna! Give me courage to avenge Monique!"

The low ceiling of gray clouds darkened and thunder sounded —a portent.

In answer, there was a buzz in her ear and then Cleo's voice. Her voice whispered sternly on the ethers.

"*Kikki, be careful. I know you are angry about your friend. You have every right to be. But revenge is not the way. You will be as dark and evil as them.*"

"*It is just ...*"

"*It is a low patriarchal vibration, Kikki. Seek truth and be love and light. Do not allow them to draw you into their shadowy netherworld.*"

"*Cleo, my shadow side is part of me. And this is different.*"

"*It is never different. Remember, we are in the darkest hour before the Solstice. Just like on Santorini, there is a portal. Do you want to be sucked into the vacuum of evil?*"

Still on the Pont Royal, Kikki peered into the swirling icy cold of the river and recalled vividly nearly drowning a few days ago. Cleo's voice disappeared, and all she heard was the noise of cars skidding on ice.

A barge made its way slowly under the bridge. The mountains of earth it carried transformed into a pile of mangled and bloody corpses. The Seine flowed red and stinking, as it had after the Saint-Bartholomew's Day Massacre.

She shuddered and hurried on to the Louvre. As she stepped onto the sidewalk in front of the Pavillon de Flore, she glanced at the sphinx across from herself, still afraid for Torres.

Cautiously, she approached the Porte des Lions, the closest entrance on this end of the long Grande Galerie of the Louvre, once Henri IV's Waterside Gallery.

La Grande Galerie was a long hall in which Henri IV had conducted royal business—a vast arcade originally created by Catherine de Medici to connect the Tuileries and the Louvre's main fortress, providing shelter against weather and a means of retreat and defense. In that era during Margot's time, thousands of soldiers filled the ground floor. Upper floors were for artists' studios.

Kikki felt the ghosts of legions of soldiers and the Black Queen as she got closer to the Porte des Lions. A palpable malevolent presence.

She drew the dagger from its sheath and walked softly flush with the building. When she passed beneath the arched entrance, she cloaked herself with an invisible shroud.

Keen eyes searched for Moreno. He hadn't arrived. From behind a pink marble column, she studied the hallway and security station that she could see clearly behind the Louvre's glass door entrance. In her coat pocket, Kikki carried a special badge for entry into the museum, courtesy of the exhibition committee and Gabrielle Laroche. She touched it, considering whether to go inside and out of the dark cold evening until Moreno arrived. Badge or dagger?

And then, she heard voices—men talking. They were inside and evidently on their way out, not far from the exit. She recognized Victor's voice as it boomed over the more discreet French tones. Kikki heard their conversation clearly.

He was with two other men, whom he addressed formally as Monsieur le Directeur Général and Monsieur le Ministre. Kikki recognized one of the men from the Ministre de la Culture—a colleague of Torres's, a deputy minister linked to his cover committee.

"I am happy to be in a position to make this valuable gift to the world's greatest museum. I know the precious object will finally be in the right hands," Victor crowed.

A priceless donation? So very Victor. Buying his way in. As dear Monique's contacts had revealed. What was this gift? Was it genuine or a fake?

"And, in turn, please consider seriously our offer that you serve on our esteemed international council," one of the men said.

"Of course, Monsieur le Directeur. I am humbled. And I would be honored."

"*Je vous en prie.* We are having a private exhibition tomorrow evening and a small gala. We will unveil a rare piece on loan to us from a sister museum in Greece. What luck you are here for this special occasion, and on nearly the same occasion are bestowing us with such an invaluable relic also of Greek provenance. What an astonishing find from the heroic Alexander the Great. *Formidable, n'est pas, mon chèr collègue?*"

"*Ç'est incroyable, quelle coïncidence, Monsieur le Directeur Général,*" chimed the other man.

"*Très bien!* We will send an invitation to your hotel. The Ritz, I presume? And in the meantime, arrangements can be made for your donation. We will accelerate procedures so that you can attend our board meeting next week. It is a critical one, and we'd benefit from your wise counsel. Especially given your experience on the board of the preeminent Metropolitan Museum. We need to—eh—" the man lowered his voice, "expand our power base."

"Of course. I understand perfectly." Victor sounded triumphant. "I'll have my colleague Frank Pellegrini handle the details. He's tied up at the moment with other business. In fact, perhaps you can help to facilitate this other matter."

"*Mais, bien sûr!*"

"I fear your customs authorities are being—well—perhaps overly zealous," Victor said in a confidential tone.

"Martín, please, see that it is handled at once. Clear the way."

"*Naturellement. Vraiment désolé,* monsieur. If you provide us with details, we shall attend to it *immédiatement,*" Martin, the junior of the two, said obsequiously. "Our apologies."

Victor was buying his way into the Louvre, and easily enough, Kikki thought. Not if she could help it. The idea of revenge tasted sweet. Kikki prepared herself. She crossed to the other side of the archway so she that she would be just next to the exit when they came out. She prayed Victor would be alone.

She drew the double-edged dagger from her coat, ready to strike. For Monique!

Chapter 91

In hushed voices, the men continued talking just inside the museum's door.

She waited. Suddenly, she felt a presence behind her. One of Victor's soldiers? A Knight of the Holy Sword of God?

She whirled, grabbing the man by the shoulder, and catching him at the throat with her dagger.

"Take another step, and I will kill you."

"What the hell?" he gasped in a frightened voice. "It's me, Moreno. You told me to meet you here."

Kikki lowered the dagger but gripped it tightly, on high alert. She didn't speak. Victor was nearby. Suddenly, she was suspicious at this coincidence. Was Moreno here on friendly terms, or was it a trap? He worked for Victor. Moreno might have killed Monique himself.

Suddenly, Margot appeared behind Moreno. She wore a scarlet gown and diamond and sapphire necklace with an eight-pointed ruby star. Unlike other visions, Margot appeared this time as a hologram that lit up the entire archway.

Kikki stared. Time stood still.

"Margot?" she whispered, suspecting a trick—Margot's mother,

Victor's mask. "Is that you?" She didn't smell her rose perfume. "Prove to me you're Margot. What do you want of me? Why are you here now?"

Margot spoke in her now familiar voice.

"Do not seek to avenge what cruelness they have done to me and now to you and Monique. Revenge is not the way. For the love of the child. The Goddess will light our way and shine brightly to vanquish darkness lurking in shadows."

Reassured, but still hypnotized by the hologram, Kikki slipped into trance looking for more answers. She tumbled and swirled through dimensions and time to that carriage ride to the convent in Tuscany.

Horses clip-clopped over the bumpy icy road in the snowy night. Sewn into Gillonne's cloak, which Margot wore, were jewels and precious objects brought to pay their way, to provide for the child, including the diamond necklace from Diane de Poitiers. From her large travel bag, Margot slipped a black leather portfolio, memoires of the love and horrors she had lived these last months.

She offered the leather bound parchment pages to Gillonne.

"I have written it all down in here, Gillonne. From my true love of Henri de Guise to marriage at my treacherous family's insistence. It bears witness to les noces vermeilles—my scarlet wedding—the accursed massacre.

It is also proof in my own words of what my vicious mother did, her beatings and betrayals, the molestations and rape of me as a girl by my own brother Henri d' Anjou's—with my mother's knowledge and consent. She was his favorite. She turned a blind eye. I want you to keep it safe—in case something happens to me. I know you will survive. It should go to my daughter when she is old enough. I have kept it well hidden, knowing there would come a time when I would need it. Keep it safe and use it if you have to. It may save our lives and my daughter's life.

"Of course, ma chère Margot," Gillonne said, tears streaming down her cheeks. "But we will both survive, and so will your daughter. Believe that. You must be strong, as always. The Goddesses are with us. I feel them." Gillonne reached out for the leather bound pages. Her fingers tingled when she touched it. She was afraid for Margot.

Kikki felt her heartbeat slow and her mind clear. The hologram was Margot and not a dark imposter.

And then, she was snapped back into present time. Moreno was still standing inches away, and his eyes were wide with fright.

Over his shoulder, she spotted a Louvre security guard coming her way.

"*Arrêtez-vous!*"

Trembling, she released Moreno and hid the dagger in her coat, hoping the guard hadn't seen it.

She whispered to Moreno in English, "Sorry, I'm jumpy from last night. You understand."

"Is there a problem here, monsieur?" the guard asked.

Moreno stuttered. "Uh—no." He brushed off his coat and cleared his throat. "I'm sorry. I don't speak French. I have a meeting with madame. She had mistaken me for someone else."

He looked up and held Kikki's eyes, nodding with understanding. Almost complicit, Kikki thought. She breathed more easily and shot Moreno a faint smile of appreciation.

Chapter 92

The guard approached but remained in shadows.

"Are you sure, monsieur?"

"Yes, of course. No problem. Come, let's go someplace warmer." He hooked his arm into Kikki's. "I do have something to show you."

The guard remained near, watching.

"Excellent." Her curiosity was piqued. But she was still focused on Victor's near presence, vowing to face him.

Hand in her outer coat pocket, she fingered the dagger—a valuable object with great power. Useful for magic and defense. Both of which she would need against her archenemy.

Kikki stopped Moreno and whispered, "There's someone I need to see. They're about to come out of this entrance."

He grimaced. "I think we should go. I tried to call before but couldn't get you. I found out by chance that my producer has a meeting here. I don't want to run into him."

"For Monique, remember?"

He looked frightened, but Kikki felt him reaching out to her energetically for protection. He was in way over his head.

She and Monique had been right. Moreno would help them.

385

The security guard said quietly to Kikki, "He's right. You must go. It is not safe."

She caught the man's eyes. Liam! He had been using a voice she hadn't recognized and was dressed in the guise of a Louvre security guard. Smoke and mirrors—and very good disguises, she thought. Bravo, Monsieur le Magicien!

"Just a moment, Moreno." She unlinked her arm from his and stepped sideways, still squarely in front of the street exit from the Louvre.

"We have to leave," Liam said. "You're in danger. We have this covered. You showing up now will blow the whole thing."

"What are you talking about? Did Torres send you?"

"No."

Two Frenchmen pushed the door open. Victor was not far behind.

"Come with me, right now! Both of you."

He hurried them out to the inner gardens of the Louvre. They stopped just short of the portal, flanked by two magnificent bronze lions. Teeth bared, frozen in art, they guarded the entrance.

"From here, you'll be able to see. I will cover you. And no one will care about one security guard more or less." He hissed at Kikki in French, "Don't you dare move or say a word!"

Kikki nodded and caught Moreno's eyes. He had obeyed without hesitation. She waited for the men to emerge. First, two well-groomed, sophisticated-looking Frenchmen stepped into the corridor. They spoke in hushed tones. One of them shrugged in classic Gallic manner.

"Liam," Kikki whispered. One of those men is Torres's colleague from the Ministry of Culture. Very highly placed."

"Shh—" Liam insisted. "Listen."

"That went well, don't you think? We've got him."

Both men lit cigarettes the minute they were out the door.

"I don't know. It feels more like he's got us," said Torres's colleague, Martin.

"We'll see. I have a lot of power as Directeur Général of the Louvre. Don't underestimate me, Martin." He took a long drag of the cigarette and blew it out through his nostrils. The smoke hovered in the air—a dark, filmy cloud. "My assistant is helping with the other pieces they are moving. I don't understand how customs got involved. I'll fire the *connasse*. Beautiful Renaissance furniture from a Tuscan convent. The whole lot of it. Long elegant tables and benches—all solid mahogany, desks, prayer stands, choir stalls. Possibly some valuable artwork as well. Fit for a king—or a queen, in this case. The convent sheltered nuns—if they were that—*putains* and *sorcières*, more likely! Still, perhaps you'd be interested for your private collection?"

Martin from the Ministry of Culture frowned and crushed his cigarette with the heel of his shoe.

"We'll see if you're right. I hope I don't have to get the ministre, himself, involved. He won't appreciate it. He has important meetings just now with the Conseil des Ministres. An international summit with a Russian dignitary." He eyed his colleague knowingly.

And then, they walked out towards the Seine to the Quai.

Kikki could just make out the shadow of Victor hovering inside, phone to his ear, behind the glass door. He looked puffed up—bursting. How she longed to puncture his evil and vanities. And then, she heard Margot and Cleo and told herself to be calm and fill herself with light. She shielded herself so he wouldn't see her. Their confrontation would have to wait.

She had gained a lot of information, and information was power.

She watched Victor walk out the exit. He tipped his brimmed hat at an angle on his silver hair. He brushed nonexistent lint from his dark cashmere overcoat and smiled too widely. And then, suddenly, he turned and looked right at them, fixing his eyes on the three of them. His pupils were dilated, and his look was hollow.

Apparently, he saw no danger because the next minute, he actually did puff up his chest and straighten his spine. He slipped his phone from his pocket and flexed a bicep.

"Got you!" he said loudly, voice resounding in the archway. He stabbed a finger at the screen and held the phone to his ear. "Frank! Good news! We're in. All the way."

After the briefest pause, Victor snarled, his mouth a slash.

"Get Natalia. She's up now. She must not fail."

Kikki covered her mouth to keep from crying out. Liam laid a hand across her, blocking any movement.

Victor barked into the phone. "I will see you in exactly one hour in the temple."

And then, he walked out onto the Quai. Watching him from several yards away, Kikki saw not a man but a swirling cloud of black smoke framed in the archway. It lingered a moment and then vanished.

Left behind was a reeking odor and the sound of hissing.

Kikki clutched Liam's arm and fixed her eyes on the lions guarding the gateway. Her mouth gaped when the two lions opened their jaws and roared.

Chapter 93

Liam glared at her, telegraphing that she needed to get a grip and manage Moreno.

Moreno looked at the two of them, puzzled.

Kikki took a deep breath and focused on clarity. Then she turned to Moreno, and in a conspiratorial whisper explained, "Actually, Bob, this man is not a security guard. He's a friend and guard of sorts. We need his help. Good thing he came along."

"Yes, I agree. You nearly slit my throat," he said nervously, "Who is he?"

Kikki shook her head. "Not so loud."

Moreno, typical American, was talking to the back of the room.

"Sorry," he said in a stage whisper. "But great. Very mysterious. Good material. Maybe we can use it in the film."

She nearly laughed. And his comment had the effect of bringing her fully into the present, if rather perilous, reality. Everything was material to filmmakers.

"*Si'l vous plait, les infants!*" Liam hissed.

"*Désolée*, Liam." Kikki stepped back, as if to leave.

"Wait—I want you to see someone else." Liam lay a hand on her arm.

Just then, the glass entrance door to the Louvre under the Porte des Lions opened again. Gabrielle Laroche walked out alone. She wore her staff badge and a discreet smile. She was wrapped in faux fur, and her black chin length hair shone like a helmet. She tipped her head at Liam and started towards them.

"You two stay here. I mean it, Kikki." Liam went to meet Gabrielle.

As Kikki looked on, she watched Gabrielle hold up her phone.

"*Je l'ai—le tout.*"

"Brava!" Liam said quietly.

"*Bien sûr!*" Gabrielle smiled proudly.

"Wow!" Kikki's eyes were bright with excitement. "Gabrielle taped their conversations for evidence? All planned while I was out cold. Perfect!"

"You're fantastic! Send it to Torres, Tía—" Liam looked thoughtful. "Jean Marc and me, of course. All for safekeeping. JM can put it on the private server."

"*D'accord. Tout de suite!*" Gabrielle said. "I am sick to death of corrupt officials and greed in our most sacred institutions—the Louvre—the world's history."

"The most beautiful and comprehensive collection of art in the world," Liam added vehemently in French. "No more. *Á la Bastille!*"

Then he flashed an apologetic smile to Moreno as he took Kikki aside.

"If you'll excuse us just one minute?"

"You're not in this alone, Kikki. You think you can do it alone, but you can't. Your lover is right. And so am I. Tía is willing to give you more leash for some reason." He shook his head. "*Prothesis!* Give me the dagger before you go." He extended a hand.

"I'm surprised you didn't just help yourself."

"And risk my life? *Non, merci.*"

"I want to keep it. In case. And it's got—"

"Power, like Athena's sword?" He arched one well-shaped brow.

"Yes."

"Promise me you will not use it to avenge Monique's death." His eyes bore into hers.

She looked down at the snow-covered ground without answering.

"I know you're angry and hurting about Monique. So am I, Kikki."

She didn't say anything.

"If you think you can play on the dark side and not be taken in by it, think again. You have right and light on your side. If you don't own that, you haven't been paying attention. All these years, all of those challenges that you have met in goodness and light will have been in vain. Don't be tempted. Because you'll lose Torres— lose the love of your life. And more importantly, you'll lose yourself."

"Are you done now, Liam?"

"Yes. Keep your dagger if you must." He hugged her. "But please be careful."

Chapter 94

Vite!" Gabrielle whispered to Kikki. "Follow me. I have a place where you can talk."

Minutes later, she left Kikki and Moreno in a room three floors beneath the *troisième sous-sol* (three floors below ground)—in the Louvre's private archives.

"They have gone for the day," she whispered and turned to go. "When you're ready to leave, just use your badge to open the doors."

"And him?" Kikki pointed to Moreno.

"Here, take this. It's an anonymous visitor's badge." She fished it out of her leather satchel. "If there is a question, tell them I issued it. Madame Laroche. I am well-known and—"

"*Mais oui*, you're the head of the CECOA—the Association of European Experts in Works of Art—the group that certifies experts —like yourself."

"*Oui—ç'est ça! Désolée, je me sauve.*" Gotta go.

The small room smelled of musty old stone and river water, even though Kikki knew that the Louvre would have dehumidified all underground chambers.

They sat across from each other in ultramodern clear Philippe

Starck chairs. Odd juxtaposition to the rest of the room's contents: ancient stone sculptures, heads and arms without bodies, angels without wings, missing pieces. All awaiting restoration so they might be displayed. Like the *Winged Victory of Samothrace*—the Goddess Nike, recently stunningly restored and displayed in her own chamber of the Louvre.

Metal shelving held an array of precious paintings, each shelf labeled with a letter. Only D–E were in this small room.

As Kikki waited for Moreno to start talking, she thought about Leonardo Da Vinci. She wondered if any of his works might be in the room with them. Such a prolific artist—a genius. The Renaissance Man. And he suffered so in love and life. Like Margot.

King François Premier sent for him to live out his days in France at the Château d'Amboise and the Clos de Lucé—the same château that had been home to Margot when she was a young girl. He brought with him, on his long journey from Italy, *La Jocanda* (The Mona Lisa). Upon his death, not long after he arrived in Amboise, it became one of France and the world's finest treasures.

Da Vinci's early benefactor had been the Florentine de Medici family. He would have known the Black Queen. They would have been contemporaries. Catherine's father was Lorenzo de Medici II and her mother, the French Duchess, Madeline de la Tour d'Auvergne, Margot's grandmother and surely a member of the Daughters of Inanna. And Lorenzo, like Catherine, was certainly one of the Swords.

If this man sitting in front of her was really descended from that infamous family, it would explain how he'd fallen prey to Victor and Frank. She had to ask herself again: was Moreno a loyal spy for the Swords? Or was he a man linked by birth to the Swords but now seeking redemption? If he were the latter and he wanted out, he would have to prove his loyalty to her. Starting right now.

Kikki cleared her throat.

"Bob, please, we don't have much time. Do you have something for me? One of your historical treasures?"

"I'm just a bit hesitant." He was fiddling with the buttons on his coat, trying to undo them. And sweating profusely.

"Look, let me help you out. I am well aware of the true identity of the primary financier for your production company."

His eyes widened in surprise and alarm.

"How?"

"It doesn't matter. Victor Fitz-Perkins, right? He had you set up a series of shell companies linked to the film. And his partner is Frank Pelligrini from Florence, in the antique business."

He looked down and nodded.

"There are others, but yes—"

"Right. Look, rest easy, I don't need to know your real name, though I am certain it isn't Robert Moreno. I seem to remember you as Stefan from my time working with Victor.

"Yes." He squirmed in his chair. "You worked for Victor? I don't remember you."

"In New York for a few years. It was a long time ago, and it doesn't matter at the moment. Suffice it to say that I know your boss well. I didn't know about his antique business."

"I see." He still wouldn't hold her gaze.

"And I believe your real name is Stefan de Medici. Correct?"

Let's get it out, Kikki thought. Get him on the right side of the table. It was crucial leverage.

"Eh—well, yes, you asked me about it at our meeting."

"I did. But now, I need to know exactly with whom I am dealing."

"Okay, I think I get it," he said with some reluctance, stumbling over his words, "You're correct. But not many people know, and hardly anyone knows of my—err—lineage. Rather the black sheep. I hope you won't mention it to anyone. It could create huge problems for me. I would prefer to stick to my—uh—pseudonym or my new name, if you don't mind." He looked nervous and scared.

"Why? Surely Victor and Frank know exactly who you are?" Kikki insisted though gently.

"Please?" He begged fearfully.

"Fine." It suited her because she didn't want this man to go back to Victor and tell him that she was onto Moreno/Medici and their likely phony film. At least not until she had what she wanted. "I'm okay with that for the moment. You're caught in the middle—is that right?"

"Blackmail. Keeping my secrets—gambling and other stuff—including my true heritage. But, seriously, I really am into this film.

It's a way for me to work out of this mess." He looked up at her, his face an open plea for help. "To makeup for—"

He was talking about her friend.

"To makeup for Monique? Swear to me that you did not murder Monique. Because if you did—"

He looked alarmed, edging off his chair.

"Certainly not! I have no idea who did. I was waiting in the Meurice, as agreed."

"I thought not, but I have to know."

"I get it. It was barbaric. If Victor had anything to do with it, then all the more reason—" His words trailed off and his eyes teared.

Time to get down to business. But first, she had to see if he was acting in good faith.

"What have you brought then?"

"Will you help me? You and your—uh—influential friends. I do have something, but no one knows. If Victor finds out, I am a dead man."

"I know Victor as well as anyone and how dangerous he can be if you cross him." She chose her words carefully, not knowing exactly what or how much Stefan de Medici knew about Victor's expanding fiefdom.

From the conversation that she had just overheard at the Porte des Lions, Kikki knew that a key aspect of Victor's endgame was to seize power of the Louvre —the most prestigious art institution in the world, beginning with real or counterfeit donations.

"Tell me, Robert, what exactly do you do for him?"

"I—I handle his—how shall we say, unorthodox antique business."

He was getting panicky again.

"Yes, I thought so." Tears welled in her eyes when she thought of Monique. "Monique did some investigation. And his money laundering too? The film's finance. We need the money trail for all of the shell companies and their off-shore accounts—the source that can prove illegal activities. You gave us a check issued from a Lichtenstein account. We need all of the dots connected. You can provide me with that? It's critical."

"Yes, I understand. I promise I will get it for you—if you can protect me." He sighed, "Ahh, Monique! What a tragedy. She must have had a family, and she was so young and vibrant. Do you really think it was him—Victor?"

He was saddened, but not shocked.

Victor or his henchmen, she thought, and then said, "I don't know who else would wish to send a message like that." She reached out and took his limp hand, holding his frightened gaze. "He's ruthless and cruel."

"Your partner is a cop, isn't he?" he said hoarsely.

"Yes. A very important cop."

His face looked pinched. She believed that this man was another victim. Prey for Victor. But could trust him? She closed her eyes for a moment and tuned in psychically. She quickly went deep and saw a garrote around his neck.

She blinked and looked again. It was gone. She made up her mind.

"My partner can protect you if you help us."

Moreno swallowed hard and burst into a coughing/choking fit.

Kikki stood, crossing to him as if to grab him in a Heimlich maneuver.

"I have no water here."

He stopped coughing and wheezed heavily, one hand on his chest.

"It's the dampness."

He pulled an inhaler from his coat pocket and puffed a couple of times.

She sat and waited for him to recover. When she was almost resigned to the fact that he was too scared to betray Victor, Moreno slipped a worn leather sleeve from inside his coat and handed it to her.

"Here—then. For Monique." He smiled sadly. "And her family."

With care, she unzipped the leather sleeve and gingerly took out its contents. She placed them on a small table. Inside a protective plastic folder, a faded red silk ribbon was tied around a worn black leather journal. Peeping through were sheaves of yellowed parchment.

It was exactly what she had seen in vision yesterday on the way to Saint-Sulpice. Margot's child in the carriage, holding a journal.

And again, not an hour ago, in vision when Margot gave it to Gillonne.

"It really is hers? Margot's?"

"Yes. It has been authenticated by European experts—real ones."

Kikki held it reverently without opening it.

"Victor will do to me what he did to Monique if he finds out. I'm scared—" He began to cry. Between sobs, he said quietly, "I'm sorry—for Monique."

"For Monique and for Margot," Kikki said to herself.

"There is more. If I can get it to you before—" he stumbled over his words, "without—"

Kikki heard the sound of a footstep.

"I promise we will do all we can to protect you. But now we must go," she whispered.

He was unresponsive and looked as though he were collapsing. Defeated but redeemed.

"Bob?"

His eyes were glazed, as though any minute his spirit would leave his body.

"Quickly!"

She stood and pulled him out of the chair, grabbing his arm.

Chapter 95

Torres paced the salon of Natalia's penthouse suite at the Hotel Regina. He hoped she would not go back on her agreement to work for Operation Sphinx. After Monique's murder, it could go either way.

In a little less than an hour, he was due to meet with Ian Watson, his British ICC boss from the Office of the Prosecutor (OCP) who was on the Eurostar headed from London's St Pancras Station to Paris Gare du Nord.

After Monique's murder, Torres had succeeded in classic French style, to "unofficially" take charge of the scene. Monique's body was in the hands of a friendly coroner. Evidence was now locked up in their highly secure HQ in the basement of the Musée d'Homme, thanks to Jean Marc.

Now, he needed Ian's gravitas as Prosecutor at the International Criminal Court, the overseeing organization to whom Torres and his team were responsible.

The door opened, and Torres watched Natalia walk into the salon. She was dressed in an elegant pantsuit. Her hair was up in a tight chignon that gave her a serious look.

"Sit, Torres. Please. For heaven's sake," she said slightly

bemused. "I could hear you pacing from behind the closed door of my enormous marble bathroom."

He smiled and sat in a very feminine armchair. Natalia sat on the couch across from him.

"How are you, Natalia?" he began.

"Fine. Look, let's get right to it. I know I said I would help you." She crossed her legs, uneasy. "Even though at the time—well—it was in the heat of passion. But I meant it."

"I'm glad to hear that, Natalia." He caught her eyes. "Your help is critical to us."

"You must know that Monique's murder has shaken me. The stakes are far higher than I had thought."

"Yes." And a lot more than she had bargained for at dinner two nights ago, he knew.

"And my uncle and his partner, Victor, were responsible?"

"It's an ongoing investigation."

"Don't bullshit me. Not if you want me to help, Torres. This is no longer just about fake antiquities. I could meet the same fate as Monique. You're asking me to put my life at risk for your cause—your op."

"They would never hurt you. You are family," he said with some conviction.

"Ha! Families—especially Italian families—are notorious for taking care of their own, no matter the cost—especially when they are betrayed."

She flashed frightened hazel eyes at him.

"You've become very important to their success." Flattery, with a large portion of truth. "You're far cleverer than they are—not just book smart—street smart and you have the advantage of youth. Plus, we will be there to back you up—to protect you."

"I'm not so sure about any of that. I have seen my uncle cut people out of the business. He's just as ruthless as I am sure Victor is."

"It's a lot to take in, I know," he said quietly. "Let's start simple. I assume that you have told them you're playing along—or playing me?"

"Sure. The play was to get intel about your op. And I have a role to play. But your op and their endgame—it's not just their illegal antiquities business, is it? They're planning something far more important—and dangerous—as is clear from Monique's brutal murder. Assuming it was them."

He shot her a challenging look.

"Well I had no knowledge," she insisted. He started to interrupt, and she stopped him with an angry stare. "Look, I'm a big girl, and as you said, I'm no idiot. Fucking hell, Torres! So don't waste my time."

"You're right. I apologize."

"They are going to ask me to cross a very big line. Victor is a scary guy. I have had sleepless hours to think about this. I am honestly overwhelmed."

He nodded.

"Seriously, I'd like to get on the next flight to New York."

"Understandable. But that's not you, Natalia. You don't run from trouble."

"No. It seems I look for it—or it looks for me. And I'm as kick ass as they come underneath the veneer."

She flashed a hard look at him.

Leaning closer to her, he said quietly, "If you want to get on a plane to New York or Hong Kong—anywhere really, I can arrange that. I can help."

She looked skeptically at him, pursing her lips.

"Good, that is reassuring. But I want truth. If you're going to ask me to put my life on the line—" she paused and then said pointedly, "for your op and the Daughters of Inanna, I have to know all about what's going down."

He frowned.

"Yes. I got read in by your—err—Kikki yesterday. I'm sure you know all about it."

"I leave that to Tía and Kikki. Why don't you and I stick to this op?"

"Go on."

He fished in the pocket of his leather jacket for his pack of Ducados. He offered her the pack.

"Cigarette?"

She accepted, and they were silent during the ritual of lighting their cigarettes.

"So, what are you charged with doing for your uncle? And what do you know about the bigger picture? What is on the other side of that line they want you to cross?"

"If I tell you, aren't I agreeing to help you?"

"Not necessarily. It may be information we already have."

He wanted to appeal to the daring and ambitious Natalia he saw beneath the now frightened young woman.

"Hmm. Perhaps." She studied his dark eyes, considering. She still hesitated and then said, "They haven't given me all of the details. The gala event on Friday. I'm to steal the Snake Goddess and replace it with a forgery."

Torres fixed his eyes on hers.

"Have you done this kind of thing before?"

"Does it matter? Maybe someone needs to have a clean profile—relatively anyway. That's why you accepted me on your committee, correct?"

"This is a test? An initiation?"

"Yes. I guess. Uncle Franco is getting older, and I'm the chosen heir."

Torres sat back.

"Chosen but reluctant, if I'm reading you right."

"Maybe," she said. "I know what goes on. I'm not a fool." She took a drag and felt the pleasure of the burn. And then waves of nausea and light headedness hit. Take it easy, Natalia, she told herself. You need your wits about you. "Look. If it were only my uncle. But Fitz-Perkins—"

He tapped his cigarette on the edge of the porcelain ashtray and waited. He was almost sorry for her, getting caught in their trap.

"It's a lot of money to turn down from my uncle. I am already a very rich woman. And I am very fond of my creature comforts." She stalled.

"I know, and expensive champagne requires a healthy income," he tried for a modicum of levity.

She stubbed her cigarette out, half smoked.

"Oh, damn the champagne! I am not totally superficial. Don't treat me like a spoiled child. You want me as an asset. A very dangerous game. Not for children."

Torres went for it.

"I know doing what you are used to seems secure, easier, Natalia. But it isn't. Not anymore. You probably know this, but Giacomo Medici, your uncle's late cousin, traded in some of the finest objects ever produced by the human race. Of enormous cultural, historical, aesthetic and intellectual import—half of the Greek, Etruscan and Roman culture in Italy alone."

Goddamnit, this enraged him.

"Is that supposed to motivate me? I'm quite literally caught between Scylla and Charybdis, mythical sea monsters." Nervously, she reached for the cigarette, realizing she'd stubbed it out. She took a sip of water and set it down. "It's been a successful business. Absolutely no one in the entire world has been able to stop them. So why you?"

He stood and began pacing again.

"I was born for this. I've got the guts and the intel—plus the people to do it."

She smiled, "You've got balls. I'll give you that! Remind me not to piss you off."

"Their time is up. They're making a major power grab—the one that Monique got caught in—the part that scares you."

She grimaced.

"What makes you think they won't take *you* down?"

He stopped and faced her.

"Because I'm that good."

"That may be your Holy Grail, but it isn't mine. She stood up and crossed to the window.

"Think fast and hard, Natalia."

He had to keep the pressure up, but he wanted the choice to be hers. He was asking her to betray everything and everyone she knew—right now. Time was up.

He crossed to stand next to her, a friendly arm on her shoulder.

She was scared out of her wits. She vowed she wouldn't show it. She was, after all, a Valois. Unimaginable! Her life was veering out of control. She stared unseeing out the window at the steady stream of traffic on rue de Rivoli and the ancient stone buildings of the Louvre.

"Your uncle and Fitz-Perkins are using their amassed fortune to make an aggressive play for power through a secret organization called the Knights of the Holy Sword of God. That's who is responsible for Monique's death. They've been dealing in 'blood antiquities' to fill their war chest. Are you okay with that? Are you ready to join them? Because that's what they want from you. To join them in their quest for world dominion—at any cost.'"

As with her conversation yesterday with Liam and Kikki, it once more confirmed Natalia's intuition about her uncle and Fitz—their conspiracy for political power—and they wanted her on board. She swallowed hard. She hoped it wasn't as bad as she feared.

"A rightwing religious group—like the Masons, right?"

"No, far more. They're like the rightwing Christian Dominionists in the US that have long held great sway and power."

He sat down on the coffee table facing her, a grim expression on his face. He briefed her on the full reach of the Swords' conspiracy and its funding. "That's who the Swords are today. Fitz-Perkins is high up in the leadership. We've identified the major players, including prime ministers and a world leader. I'd say that your uncle is in as much danger as the rest of us—maybe more."

"You're frightening me." Natalia felt sick. Torres had confirmed her worst nightmare.

"You should be terrified. If you walk into this with them, you'll never walk out alive." He said quietly, "Now you understand why they killed Monique, Natalia."

Torres liked Natalia—now that they'd gotten lust out of the way. He understood the draw to her uncle's world. But if his gut instinct was right, she had more moral fiber than her uncle or Fitz and their cronies. The Daughters of Inanna should give her double motivation to switch sides. He hoped he was gently reeling her back in with a mix of reason, passion and fear. A lethal cocktail.

"That's exactly why I don't want to get involved." She knew she was arguing with herself.

"It's only going to get worse."

"They want me to meet with them tonight—at their temple. Uncle Franco called earlier."

"They want to use you, make you part of them, and not just to steal the Snake Goddess. Monique's death was a last warning shot to get us to back off—" He spoke in a low voice. "But we're going to stop them. Whether you help us or not."

She thought about her time yesterday with Kikki and Liam, the Daughters of Inanna, being a true descendant of Marguerite de Valois—her realization that she was being used as a pawn by Fitz and her uncle in a dangerous endgame. The Tarot cards and Liam's warning that she had better watch her back. Torres was right. She had to choose sides.

"Natalia, please, you can trust me."

He took her hand again. This time she held fast.

"Can you can really protect me?" Her voice trembled. "You're asking me to risk my life."

He stood directly in front of her and held her gaze firmly.

"Yes, I promise you."

She felt cornered and exhilarated at once. A new start began to appeal. You're a Valois, she told herself. And deep down, for your mother, you belong with the Daughters of Inanna.

"Are you in?"

She took a deep breath. "Let's get started."

Chapter 96

Kikki hurried across the Pont des Arts, head down, crystalline protection up. She shivered at memories of the last time she was here—the near-death experience as she jumped into the icy river to avoid one of the Swords' soldiers. She patted her coat to feel the outline of her dagger.

It was late for a freezing winter night, around 10 p.m. The snow had relented temporarily. The center of Paris and the Seine were in the eye of the storm.

The skies had cleared, but the wind howled, tearing through her shearling coat. Stars winked against the inky sky. She was alone on the romantic bridge, which stood eerily empty and too cold for human souls.

She stopped halfway across and leaned against the railing to take in the spectacular view. The Seine was an elegant black and silver necklace. She could see clearly the twin towers of Notre-Dame Cathédrale in the distance, the Pont Neuf and the Palais de Justice on the Île de la Cité. Just beyond on the Rive Droite, the Hotel de Ville. Showcased with soft lighting so that the City of Light might shine magically for all—hiding its shadowy underbelly.

Her breath caught when the big round moon broke through an

errant storm cloud. Soon, Luna would be in full glory, tomorrow night, not twenty-four hours from now. Now, her light cast luminescent so the Seine, fast-running and turbulent, shimmered like fine pearls.

"To the Moon Goddesses," Kikki whispered, raising her arms to the sky. "May you guide us with your powerful illumination through ancient mysteries and present trials."

She bowed her head and then ran the rest of the way across the footbridge. She floated on air or the light of the moon, all the way across and down the steps that led to rue Bonaparte and the Institut de France—where once Margot's palace had stood. At a time when nearby rue de Seine was not a street but a stream leading from the old Saint-Germain-des-Prés Abbaye to the river.

In her mind's eye, Kikki saw small caiques with huddled passengers, a boatman rowing along steadily.

Kikki thought it odd that Margot hadn't appeared to her as she made her way to the Chapelle des Louanges. As the thought crossed her mind, she caught a familiar scent of perfume.

"Margot?" Kikki saw no person or apparition. "Just as well. Guide me unseen and unheard. I expect you'll make yourself known at the chapel that was once part of your home."

A woman she didn't know stood at the guard's station at L'École Nationale Supérieure des Beaux-Arts at 14 rue Bonaparte. She opened the iron gate and motioned Kikki into the courtyard, closed now even to students.

"Come with me," the woman said in a low voice.

Kikki hesitated. "How do I know to trust you?"

"Tía sent me to guide you," the woman answered. She stopped and flashed green cat eyes at Kikki. "You must trust your intuition. Do you?"

She took a deep breath in the cold night and glanced up at the moon.

"Now would be the time to warn me—"

"*You are on sacred ground. Go forward.*" Margot answered. "*Hurry.*"

Kikki awaited Tía at the entry of the main church of the Couvent des Petits-Augustins. Margot's small hexagonal chapel was tucked away inside. Its dome—the *coupole*—was the first to be built in Paris. Margot was a woman ahead of her time. But, however Italian Renaissance its architecture, tonight it felt entirely gothic.

Now Tía stood before her robed in white, surrounded by an ethereal halo like moonlight.

"My daughter, come forth."

Long white tapers burned brightly the length of the ancient cloister. Each candleholder was encircled with a fresh holly wreath decorated with an eight-pointed crystal star for Inanna. It smelled of fresh rosemary, traditional for the Winter Solstice.

"We are preparing for the Solstice ceremony," Tía whispered.

"They're beautiful. How festive!"

"Yes. We hope so. It shall be very beautiful, indeed, to honor the coming of the Light and all of our Mothers, our female ancestors and the Mother Goddess, as is our tradition."

"Yes," Kikki murmured.

Tía was happy and composed. It brought Kikki solace and relief from the darkness and chaos that had weighed on her the last days.

Chapter 97

Kikki walked slowly hand-in-hand with Tía down the right side of the church, past an elaborately carved spiral marble staircase, wrapped around a Doric column. A stairway to heaven? Inanna's perhaps.

In that moment Kikki was filled with awe at the power of goddess energy.

Tia stopped before the arched entrance to the Chapelle des Louanges and squeezed Kikki's hand. Kikki glanced upward at the cupola admiringly.

On display were sculptures by Michelangelo on raised marble pedestals and on the walls above were gloomy paintings. At the back of the chapel was a framed marble door inlaid with biblical scenes.

Kikki gasped abruptly, frightened.

"Do not worry about the paintings and the rest. They have no energy at all. We neutralized them long ago."

"Good. I cannot imagine Margot choosing this."

The knot that had begun to form in her throat dissolved. But Kikki was hardly listening, eyes on the ceremonial table that Tía and her fellow daughters had prepared.

"How incredible! You have brought all them all here."

A circle of nearly two dozen small marble statues veiled with luminescent white silk graced a wooden ceremonial table. A string of miniature multicolored red, white and green lights made them glow. A goddesses' altar.

"The Queens of the Luxembourg Gardens," Kikki murmured. "All wearing Inanna's horned crown under their veils."

"Yes," Tía's face lit up. Touched by the esteemed assembly of Goddesses. "Queens and saints, and *Les Reines de France et Femmes Illustrées*—twenty of them, unfortunately selected by a patriarch, one of France's last monarchs, King Louis-Phillippe in the mid-nineteenth century. We have added a few, like your Margot, who were left out, her French grandmother, Madeline de la Tour d'Auvergne, Eleanor d'Aquitaine and Jeanne d'Arc. And some who intentionally have not been invited to our inner sanctum. I need not mention their names—"

"I so love them." Kikki's voice was reverent. "Such a tribute."

"For the Solstice Ceremony, we had hoped to use the Luxembourg Gardens, but now it seems unlikely." Tía's black eyes grew serious. "They will be with us in body and spirit. These High Priestesses are all with us."

"How inspiring."

"In the meantime, we need these wise women guarding the flame here in the chapel to help prepare for the coming darkness. To stand strong in the light and to lend us strength. It is a very dangerous time of transition and transformation."

Kikki peered beyond the ceremonial table to a dark purple robe —almost black in color—dressing a life-size statue.

"Come." Tía slipped the robe from the marble statue of the great Egyptian Goddess Isis who represented magic, mother and the moon. Wearing her cow's horns and sun disk, she emanated the power of golden light.

Kikki drank in Isis's power and allowed Tía to dress her in the dark robe with gold trim. She readied to embark on her own journey, her initiation, to the Underworld with Tía as guide. As she had done with Cleo on Santorini, accompanied by Demeter and Persephone.

Tía read her mind.

"It will not be like that. It is Inanna's journey—and of course—

more than that—yours. Search deeply into the shadows and dark corners of your heart and soul. Shine light on the darkness and grief, past and present shadows. Make friends with them and let them go. Embrace those you choose to keep, for they are part of you, as with all of us the ever-present duality of our souls. You will return to us stronger and brighter. Remember—Inanna was a complete Goddess of Love. She was, like Margot, all woman, also a Goddess of lust and prostitutes. All that is feared by the Patriarchy—women who are powerful, independent, freethinkers and spirits. Who strive to be all that they can be."

Kikki nodded.

"Inanna was the bright star Aphrodite, Goddess of Love. To prove herself, she left her people, her protectors and her lover Dumuzi to help her dark sister, Ershkigal. Inanna wanted a throne and a bed—like Margot—to rule *and* have her womanhood. She fully embraced her sexuality."

Kikki smiled.

Tía continued, "The snake, the bird and the Goddess Lilith, who gave form to her earthly fears, her shadows. They embodied the primitive, grasping and human aspects of Inanna. The Goddess Lilith joined with the Anzu-bird and the Snake, a snake that Inanna could not charm, a triad—sexual, lawless creatures that lived outside Inanna's community and sought only power for themselves. Inanna was a woman who laughed. She never cried. But at this, she wept."

"I didn't know that part of her journey."

"Indeed," Tía said, her voice hypnotic. "They are the external representations of her fears and shadows. Once named and let go of, she could realize her wishes—and they held no power over her. She was stripped of all her earthly goods, and she knew she might never come back. She was willing to take that risk. She entered the Underworld naked and was put to torture—flayed. But for her own powerful voice and spirit, she would not have returned from the land of the lost, the dead and the dark. Verónica, you, too, will return to us, brighter and stronger. Trust the Goddess."

Kikki felt shivers run the length of her spine. Soon, her eyes grew heavy and dilated.

Kikki rose at Tía's command and allowed herself to be led to a smaller table at the side of the altar. At her back, she felt the love and light of the assembled queens and goddesses. She felt Margot's presence and was reassured by Ta's voice.

"Open your eyes, my daughter," Tía said. "Behold the table before you."

Three candles in brass holders lit up a collection of fetishes and objects on the table.

A clay frieze of Inanna and her lover, Dumuzi, in their marriage bed. She felt the sacredness of the ancient Sumerian stone and the richness of that lost culture. Next to the frieze, a statue of Inanna mounted on two lions, holding their long manes, riding into battle.

An old parchment map showed the prehistoric world from Sumeria to Egypt and what was now Greece, Thera and the Minoan Cretan colony.

The Goddess Athena was there in battle gear, with helmet and silver sword in hand, all-seeing owl perched upon her shoulder.

Lastly, just slightly in front of the other objects was the *Minoan Snake Goddess.* Her Snake Goddess.

Kikki's heartbeat picked up and she felt herself flush. Searing pain slammed into her left temple, as if she'd been struck by someone. She traveled far back in time, space and dimension.

Tía pressed a piece of bread into her hand and told her to eat.

"You will need your strength for the journey." Then Tía gave her a golden chalice of red wine, and Kikki drank.

It tasted of pomegranate, reminding Kikki of Persephone's journey to Hades.

Kikki reached for her rose crystal necklace, finding it hot to the touch. Familiar odors of lavender and rosemary mixed with rose filled her nostrils.

Before she succumbed to trance on her journey, Tía hung a talisman around Kikki's neck. On a leather cord—an amber rosette. And then she pressed into Kikki's hand a lapis lazuli wand, as Inanna had carried with her to the Underworld.

Not a weapon, not a sword or dagger—a wand.

Tía began to chant the ancient hymn of Inanna. Her sweet voice soothed Kikki as she gave over fully to the journey.

Chapter 98

On the Rive Droite, deep under the Place Vendôme, Victor worked in his private temple. He toiled alone in a state of elation.

His sanctuary was not far from the separate Temple of the Knights of the Holy Sword of God, but his own was a private secret. Hidden off an almost invisible path leading from one of the underground tunnels that ran from the Louvre to Place Vendôme. A mile or more, as the crow flies. A black wooden door bearing a bronze lion's head knocker led to his inner sanctum.

Inside, the walls were exposed stone—ruins of a building that had once been above ground, now one of many underground cities upon which Paris was built.

Victor reveled in this hidden sanctum. It had been here just waiting for him for centuries. Blocked off by an underground cave-in. He had led the excavation himself to renew and ordain the holy spot—a secret endeavor, known only by those few who were crew, all dead now. But for the last one—his friendly concierge from the Ritz. He would be taken care of soon.

He had dug out inner walls in the shape of a pentacle—five sides. Symbol of the wrath of Hades for those who strayed from the way or refused to heed. Five, a number that stood for battle. In each corner a gold sword, a symbol that he won all battles. The upcoming one would be no exception.

Just before descending to his holy ground, he had bathed in his luxurious bathtub at the Ritz—scrubbing himself so clean his skin was bright red. Now he stood naked and ready. A God. He rubbed a gold-based oil over his limbs and felt his power grow.

Primordial force coursed through his veins. His loins grew stronger, his sex engorged. Yes, he was the rightful and supreme authority of this army of God, and they would prevail.

He donned a black robe and walked towards the raised altar in the center. A copper cauldron rested on a rectangular stone tomb.

Six black candles lined the tomb—six, the number of the Devil. With reverence, he lit each one of them. As he did so, he spoke in Latin and Ancient Greek, bringing together the two great Christian civilizations that had conquered heathens.

With each flame, he spoke a name aloud and spat a curse. One for each of those of the Daughters of Inanna who dared to defy the One and Only True God and the chosen Knights of the Holy Sword. Each would die a painful death.

There were so many he wished to see perish, but each of the six candles stood for the most important. Those he would ban to Hades by the time the faint winter sun rose on Saturday—using the dark, the longest night of the year. The depraved dark hearts and souls at that time would aid him. His own black heart would fuel that drive and his rightful supernatural powers.

He poured oil into the large bronze cauldron on the altar and lit it with a long wooden match. The flames roared and so did Victor.

"For Victor and victory!"

Next, he emptied a vial of blood into a small silver bowl. He smiled, remembering the pleasure he had taken in extracting it from her whilst she was unconscious in his bed at the Ritz.

In an identical vial was the blood of a sacrificial animal. A lion escaped from a zoo outside Paris, found roving near Disneyland. One of his lieutenants had the foresight to exsanguinate the animal and preserve its blood. Victor had paid a high price for it with money from the treasury of the Swords.

He poured the lion's blood and watched the two small rivers

swirl into a maelstrom and then join in the silver bowl. He laughed aloud in anticipation of the pleasure of revenge. She who had betrayed him would die first. He could see it in the pattern of the blood.

He touched the golden crucifix around his neck, representative of Christ's suffering and all that was holy in the Church. Then he crossed himself in thanks to his True God. Victor had been chosen by divine right. He was God himself—a Messiah. He laughed—the Antichrist. No one had seen that coming.

But he saw himself more as a type of ubergeneral. An Emperor by divine right. Power, military might, and money were his true gods. He was about to take over the most powerful institutions on the planet, one by one. Tomorrow, the Louvre would be his. All was in motion.

He reminded himself that, at all times, he must remember to wear his unseen mask of loyalty to the Church. The other members of the Swords' council who would be gathering in the next days were not all of his ilk. They may call him a false prophet. Even the Devil himself. He smiled. They must not know his true agenda.

As for Frank—he had played the part of his loyal partner and shared Victor's values. He had kept a tight surveillance on Frank's business and personal life. He could not afford another betrayal. Victor did not trust anyone—certainly not someone who knew so many of his secrets. Frank had been useful. Soon, Victor wouldn't need him. Sacrifices were required for victory.

A different fate awaited Natalia. Young and beautiful, she would become a slave to all of his needs and desires. She wouldn't be able to resist him. He looked forward to it. If she wouldn't bend to his will, she would be thrown onto the pyre with his enemies.

He leaned over and selected a sharp hunting knife from his ceremonial bag. He held his palm over the bowl and sliced it, joining his ferocious blood with the others. He added ancient and powerful herbs, long used to ward off the evil eye. He then began to stir it with a large wooden spoon.

He thought of his forebearers, his inspiration: Alexander the Great; Lucifer—the fallen angel become Hades; Russian Rasputin; Genghis Khan; Catherine de Medici, though a woman in body, a man in mind. He called them to join in his prayers and spells as he chanted in Ancient Greek.

Death would be too good for Véronique Trieste. Too good for all of the Daughters. They would suffer for daring to oppose him.

Victor placed a cheap imitation clay statue of the Snake Goddess next to a similarly ill-made statue of their precious Sumerian whore, Inanna.

His eyes shined like burning coals. He sweated profusely, vowing aloud to destroy anyone or anything standing in his path.

Victor drank a small vial of dark red liquid and heat raced through his veins. He donned a real mask, one he always saw when he looked upon his reflection, and he thrust his genuine battle sword towards the heavens.

"Let the battle begin! Death to the Witches!" He poured cognac into an enormous brandy snifter and lit it with a match. Bright orange flames engulfed the crystal, and it exploded, shards flying.

He threw a virtual sword surrounded by fire high into the air above the Place Vendôme and arced it over the Seine and through the roof of the centuries-old building on Quai Voltaire.

"Vanquish them all this dark night to be condemned souls! I shall take my rightful place on the throne of the True and Righteous God."

Chapter 99

Kikki dove deeper, tumbling in utter darkness down a narrow well. It smelled dank, putrid. Her mouth tasted of blood. She felt filmy, rancid air swirling about her—invading the pores of her skin. She cringed in terror as hungry insects fed on her body.

Tía watched over Kikki in the chapel, raising the energy of light and the Goddess to accompany Kikki on her descent to the Underworld, on the blackest of dark nights. She chanted one of Inanna's hymns.

"My lady abandoned Heaven and Earth to descend to the Underworld.

Inanna abandoned Heaven and Earth to descend to the Underworld.

She abandoned her office of Holy Priestess to descend to the Underworld."

Kikki flew through time, space, dimension and reality. When she landed, bare feet slamming into marble, she stood upright in a throne room.

On the throne sat Hades in black robes and a masked steel helmet. As she watched, Hades removed his mask, and behind it was the head of Catherine de Medici, the Black Queen, wearing a headpiece of hissing serpents—like the Gorgon Medusa of Ancient Greece.

To the left of Hades's throne sat a five-year-old girl dressed in finery on a small throne—the child, Marguerite de Valois.

On the right, sat Margot's brother, treacherous Henri d'Anjou.

At Catherine/Hades's feet a child lay in a miniature coffin. Wrapped in swaddling with stark black eyes, floating in a blanket of blood. Hovering between life and death.

Kikki transmuted into Gillonne.

As Gillonne watched, the young five-year-old Margot transformed to La Reine Margot at age nineteen, at the time the two had been fleeing with the child on the way to the convent.

Margot caught Gillonne's eye and spoke in a raspy whisper, "Save her. There is still time to save her from Hades, my mother, from the Devil. Gillonne, you must save my baby daughter!"

Gillonne blinked, frightened. The scene transformed.

Now Kikki felt herself leave Gillonne's body. Yet, she was still there in spirit, watching a horrible scene unfold. What she saw froze her heart.

Margot was bound to Gillonne. They were being led from the convent in chains back to Paris without Margot's daughter. She heard a shrill and panicked baby wail and the haunting sound of a large iron gate slamming shut.

The soldier on horseback who had followed them the long way to Tuscany led Margot and Gillonne away from the safety of the Daughters' convent. They walked barefoot and bleeding, ankles and hands manacled. He was taking his prisoners back to Paris. He brandished his sword and shouted, "Long Live the One True Catholic God."

A roaring sound made the two women turn. As they watched, the convent burst into flames. The women inside wailed, screaming for help, for their lives. Even over the women's shrieks, Margot and Gillonne heard Margot's baby girl crying.

The two women's desperate pleas and keening sobs filled the cold night. They begged the soldier, but his heart was stone and his soul black.

"These are no women of God. They are traitors—heretics and witches who worship the Devil!" the soldier shouted and whipped *his horse, dragging them along behind.*

As Kikki watched, the vision shifted once more.

Hades as Mother Catherine, the Black Queen, with a face of stone. Her eyes went opaque and turned into hot coals. And then her head became a lion's head—jaws open, teeth bared. Eyes on prey to devour—Gillonne and Margot, who now stood before her in chains. They were enslaved to Hades—to her.

They turned as one, looking for escape. But behind them, a wall of fire barreled down the tunnel of Hell, blocking exit. The fire burned hot, sizzled, and flames rose higher.

The vision shifted. Kikki stepped back into Gillonne's body.

She and Margot were bound together to a large wooden crucifix on a pile of straw. A man set a match to the fire. The flames leapt, threatening to engulf them.

Suddenly, the Black Queen commanded, "Wait! Unbind them. I will allow them to live if they repent. Repent for your sins, heretics, and swear to the one and only true Catholic God."

They were released from the pyre, and Gillonne held Margot's crying daughter protectively in her arms. The coffin with the dead infant had vanished.

A hooded priest led them down a tunnel off the throne room. The narrow tunnel was lit with strategically placed candles, each highlighting a skull. The tunnel wall was stacked with skulls one on top of the other, like the Catacombes of Paris.

The priest led them into a small square room. A raised marble tomb sat in the middle of the room.

The Black Queen appeared.

"My daughter, you must sacrifice your sister and friend Gillonne, along with your child. Then, you may yet save yourself."

Before Margot could speak, Gillonne said, "Gladly, I am ready. Margot, take the child first. You cannot trust her," Gillonne whispered, feeling under her robe for the dagger she always carried. It was gone. They were defenseless.

The Black Queen vanished, the room glowed luminous and the Goddess Hecate appeared with her three-headed hound, Cerberus. Hecate had long silver hair and wore three faces—for each phase of the moon—for each phase of woman. She was crowned with a diadem. Young, middle-aged and wise crone.

She spoke to Gillonne and Margot.

"It is the Winter Solstice, my time in the Underworld. You must make a sacrifice to me in order to feed the darkness so that you may return to the light of the Heavens, out of the Underworld. As keeper of the mysteries, I will help you. You must vanquish our enemies—those who would turn against the Mother Goddess— against women and nourishing, humanistic and peaceful ways."

A fountain with a pool of pure water sprang up in front of the raised tomb.

"Your hearts must be pure. Drink of the water and prepare to make your sacrifice. And then, tell me your choice."

The two women cupped their hands and drank.

Margot bowed to Hecate, giving homage. And then she stepped up and lay on the altar and prayed aloud.

"Take my life—I offer it in love as the sacrifice, Goddess Hecate. But free my sister, Gillonne, and free my daughter. I implore you, Great Moon Goddess."

Hecate's three faces smiled.

"You have made the wise choice. Come with me quickly."

As Hecate spoke, a lapis lazuli wand appeared in Gillone's hand. Gillonne waved it towards the heavens, and the room vanished. Margot carried her infant daughter in her arms, and with Gillonne at her side, they ran.

Hecate herself led them through the tunnel of skeletons to the throne room.

Hades, as the Black Queen, had been turned once more to stone. Margot's brother Henri was in chains—deaf, blind and mute. His handsome face distorted in fright.

Hecate signaled to them to stop. She placed her staff in front of the two women and the child.

"Take Cerberus. He will guide you out of the Underworld." The three-headed hound that hunted men who abused women waited beside Gillonne and Margot.

"But we are freed, are we not?" Margot asked. "We do not need to take Cerberus."

As Margot spoke, a new enemy materialized in front of them, blocking their exit.

Victor. He wore a black robe and was masked by the steel

helmet of Hades. He stood in their path, blocking all light and all energetic ways out.

They were trapped.

In one hand, he held a metal bowl filled with a vile-smelling liquid. He uttered incantations and spells. And then, the bowl vanished, and in his hand, he held a gold-hilted silver sword. He thrust it towards them, and it turned to flame arcing towards the sky over the river Seine.

"Through him," Margot whispered. "He is not real."

"Ride Cerberus!" Hecate shouted.

Gillonne was afraid. She hesitated.

"Gillonne, I'm not leaving without you," Margot insisted sharply, cosseting her baby.

They mounted Cerberus. Victor vanished, and they rode like the wind out through the tunnel on the back of Hecate's protector.

Transformed, Kikki's spirit split off from the vision, and she swirled upward out of the chapel to the sky, like a bright star shooting through the universe.

Chapter 100

In the Chapelle des Louanges, Tía tried to bring Kikki back.

"Verónica!"

She'd been out for a few hours. If she remained out of body any longer, she would be in danger.

Tía snapped her fingers three times. Kikki's eyelids fluttered in the dim candlelight.

Tía stroked Kikki's hair, saying, "Awaken, my daughter. It is time to leave. The morning guard will arrive soon. It is nearly five in the morning."

Kikki opened her eyes, stunned, and whispered, "Tía, I saw Victor doing spells and black magic."

"Yes. We must go."

"He is launching an attack—now."

"Hurry, come with me."

Tía led her behind the ceremonial table and pressed a latch on a panel in the back wall. It opened to reveal a hidden passage and a stairway descending to the tunnels along the Seine.

"We have to stop it, stop him," Kikki said, a flash coming to her. "I saw him—the evil being, in another dimension. But I am sure he was real. He launched fire at the apartment."

Tía took Kikki's hand. "Together it will only take a moment. Ready?"

They stood in the passage, held hands and hurled a ball of white light at the fiery sword flying over the Seine, headed for their home.

"Listen—" Tía whispered. "Done."

Kikki's voice trembled slightly as she said, "Yes, I hear the sound of rushing water. It hit the river just short of Quai Voltaire. Thank the Goddess."

They hurried down the stairs and into the underground tunnel along the Quai. Within minutes, they were safely back inside the living room of Kikki's apartment.

Upon their return home, it was snowing lightly, dark and bitter cold. It was Friday, the morning of the Winter Solstice, the day of the gala and exhibition of the Snake Goddess. Tía had carefully prepared the fireplace in advance and now set the kindling ablaze. The two women sat in sisterly silence, taking in the warmth as they shared a light meal of fruit and yoghurt. They focused on the flames, each meditated, holding space for the Light.

At last Kikki spoke, recounting her vision.

When she had finished, Tía said gently, "Hold it in your unconscious. It will guide you in the next part of your journey. Now, we both must rest for a while. You will need your strength for tonight."

"I am not through my descent to the Underworld?"

"No. The journey is long, as was Inanna's. But you have crossed the threshold into the darkness. You are an initiate and fully one of us, protected by Inanna. As you rest, you will integrate what you learned."

"Will I be able to participate in the Solstice celebration?" Kikki asked, troubled. Before Tía could answer, she spoke, "I understand, my place and my work are at the gala.

"We will be nearby in the Tuileries, the Daughters of Inanna, and many powerful Queens and Goddesses. We will raise the energy and light of the Goddess. Welcoming the growing Light of a new cycle. The energetic defeat of the darkest and longest night will support you in your path as the light begins to build. To assist our work and your journey, we will burn the Swords in effigy, using one of their old power objects we have in our possession."

Kikki raised an eyebrow, curious, but didn't ask.

Tía made a decision to elaborate.

"It's an ancient coat of arms bearing an intertwined crucifix and sword. We've kept it hidden from the Swords in Granada. Now, it is here. And we will set fire to it on the Solstice Eve, taking away any vestiges of its power."

Kikki's eyes went wide.

"Bravo!" Then she rose and stood in front of the fire, poking at it. "When does the full moon peak?"

"At seven p.m. tonight." Tía said quietly, "Now rest, *mi hija*."

Later, Kikki lay in front of the fire, dozing on the couch. Her phone buzzed, waking her.

"Torres! I am glad to hear from you. You didn't come home last night. Are you all right?"

"Perfectly. But how are you, *mi amor*?"

"I'm holding up. I am at home with Tía. I miss you."

"*Yo también*. We will be together soon."

"Goddesses willing."

"Kikki, I've got this."

Her heart ached for fear and love of him. But she forced herself to be pragmatic, like Athena and Inanna.

"Will I see you at the gala later?"

"That depends—" He was grave. "But I will be watching for you, to keep you safe."

"And you have that motherfucker Victor in your sights?"

"Absolutely."

"Good. He'll be at the gala, you know. Front and center."

"Yes. We've got it covered. I have your back."

"Natalia? Is she safe? Is she helping?"

"Kikki—" He quickly turned over in his mind what to tell her. "Yes, and yes. That's all you need to know."

"Torres, I've said this before. You need to drive a stake through Victor's heart to stop him."

"That's my job. Let me do it. We'll take them down."

"I trust." She whispered so he wouldn't hear the trembling in her voice. "I'm scared. If I were to lose you, I don't think I could bear it—"

"*Igualemente.* I love you. Promise me you'll be careful."

"I promise if you do."

He laughed, "I am well protected. They cannot beat us."

"I hope you're right. Don't let them steal the Snake Goddess, I beg you. She means more than you know. And Natalia, keep her—"

"*Basta,* my love. I have to go. Until we see each other. It will be sooner than you think."

"I love you madly, Torres."

Chapter 101

Torres disconnected. He discreetly scrutinized the woman sitting on a metal folding chair across the table from him. Natalia's chin was tipped up, her face tense. She was nervous.

His covert special tactics team was installed at the Musée d'Homme in a closed-off basement section, a safe zone created by Jean Marc. *Quatrième sous-sol* (four levels underground). Surrounding them were sealed glass shelves of the world's human history—thousands of skeletons, bones and skulls from every continent on the planet.

JM had been invaluable as a comforting presence to Natalia Becchina—almost a father figure. It took some pressure off Torres. He scanned the latest intel on a laptop, reviewing all *humint*. With a cyber-mapping system, he and his cousin Sara, his number two on the ground operative, staged the team members placement at the gala and triple-checked the intel from their embedded cyber agent/hacker in the Louvre's security to be sure they'd have access to comms and not be shut out. The Swords' plant they'd allowed to infect the system would give Torres's hacker the perfect back door in, assuring critical access to the Swords' comms at the gala.

Another expert made sure that all weapons and ammunition the team on the ground would wear were in perfect working order. Though, Torres doubted they'd be needed at the gala.

All the while, JM trained his brand-new asset.

She was challenging and highly independent. Torres tended to be too protective of her. A lot could go wrong, especially when family was involved. The real test would be her meeting with her uncle in less than half an hour.

He came out from his makeshift private space to reassure her.

"Is your recording device workable—comfortable?"

"Yes, no problem. In fact, it might be the perfect accessory." She joked and flashed a bright smile that lit up her eyes. Excited and nervous. "Very clever to imbed it into my new earrings."

Torres shot her a brief smile.

"I'm glad it works for you. But it's not a game."

"You don't think I know that?" She twirled a lock of thick red hair. "I'm just using humor—"

"To deflect." He nodded and flipped a cigarette out of a pack onto the square metal table.

Chill, he told himself, flicking his lighter firmly. He took a long drag. Thankfully, JM was not one for enforcing the no-smoking-in-public-buildings rule.

"Don't worry, Torres. I will be fine." She laid a tentative hand on his. "Doing business for my uncle takes raw nerve sometimes. I learned from him. I've got a good poker face."

He tapped his cigarette on a small ashtray.

"Still, I'll be on the comm, and we'll have a man in the bar."

She tucked the lock of hair behind her ear and sat up straight.

"That's reassuring."

"We need an abort or emergency code."

"Okay. Like what?"

"What would your uncle not find unusual for you?"

"Hmm." She crossed her legs and inspected her new boots, over-the-knee purple suede with three-inch stiletto heels. "How about 'boots.' I'll say 'new boots.' Totally true, of course."

"That works. *New boots.*" She shared that love with Kikki and many women he knew. "Nice by the way, Natalia. I hope you won't be hampered by the heel."

"I'm cool," she said, shooting him a wry smile. "I bet I could outrun you. And besides, Uncle Frank would be suspicious if I were wearing anything other than the very height of fashion."

Torres shot her an encouraging smile.

"Yes, I can see that. Let's go over this again, Natalia. We need hard evidence on the recording. His instructions to you about stealing the Snake Goddess."

"Right. I'm to get him to go through it with me, as though I am some kind of initiate—since it's my first time. Or," she paused, "because I'm a little nervous—say, about Fitz-Perkins."

"Yes. Whatever you think he'll buy. You said your uncle plans to give you a forged Snake Goddess at this meeting, correct?"

"The last time I spoke to him, earlier today, he was tense but buzzed about this—err—opportunity. So yes, that's the plan. The Ritz Bar in half an hour."

"Good. I expect you'll have it in your handbag, as small as it is. You're making the swap at the gala?" "Right." She nodded. "Sleight of hand. Catch-a-thief style."

"Let's hope he has no reason to suspect you." Torres clenched his jaw.

She shot him a serious look. "It's not my uncle I'm worried about."

"Fitz-Perkins—and whomever he has tracking your uncle and you." Torres thought about the Serb guard who had held Kikki hostage. "But I'll be close by, and we will have someone in the bar watching you."

"That's good. I can handle it, but if Fitz-Perkins is with my uncle, I'll abort," Natalia said bluntly. "I just managed to dodge that private meeting last night with the two of them at their temple. My uncle said Victor was furious."

"But you handled it?"

"Of course."

Torres stood up and began to pace. It was time for Natalia to move.

"Good luck, Natalia. Be careful, and if you're in trouble, what's the code word?"

"New boots." She smiled, flipping her long red hair out of her coat. Excited by the secrecy and the challenge. "Let's do it."

Chapter 102

❧———•———❧

In a cozy corner of the Ritz's Bar Hemmingway, Michel, Torres's man, sat drinking a fine whiskey from a short glass. He wore a navy wool blazer and gray flannel pants. A colorful blue ascot adorned his neck. Perfect for the French temple of wealth.

Few tables of the small bar were occupied at this hour of the day, between long lunches and cocktail hour. A couple of rich women with expensive designer bags sipped champagne, celebrating their purchases. And Hem's ghost, perhaps.

Over-the-top of the editorial section of *Le Monde*, he glanced across the softly lit, clubby room at Natalia and her infamous Uncle Frank. They, too, sipped champagne, seemingly pleased to be in each other's company. An obsequious male waiter hovered, serving them frequently from the bottle of vintage Dom Pérignon.

Michel wore a comm, so he was also privy to their conversation. So far, Natalia hadn't said much of use. She was dressed head to toe in couture, including an ostentatious Hermes handbag—purple to match her gloves and boots.

Frank was a well-preserved, rather portly man in his sixties. He wore a tweed suit with a red ascot and a beige sweater vest. Dyed blonde hair and large-framed tortoise shell glasses. Quintessential antique dealer, Michel mused.

They were talking about problems with the furniture they had shipped. Frank told Natalia that Fitz-Perkins had arranged the matter—bribes to officials and a slick path from customs.

Natalia sipped champagne and tipped her head back, running her hand through her enviable red locks. Then she turned to her uncle.

"Is everything set for the gala? I'm ready. I just need the *objet*."

"Yes, of course, my dearest niece," Frank cooed. "Voilà! I have a present for you. He handed Natalia a Gucci shopping bag.

"Thanks, Uncle Franco." She took the bag. "Can I peek at it?" She didn't wait for an answer but reached in with one hand and began to unwrap something. Her eyes widened, sparkling. "Wow, it looks amazing. Love my present. It will be perfect for tonight."

"Are you sure can do this?" Frank sounded worried as well as protective. "The actual relic is worth an enormous amount of money. Victor is particularly keen."

"No worries, Uncle Frank." She caught his hand and squeezed it.

"So, you'll choose your moment. Create a small diversion and slip the genuine Snake Goddess into your handbag. Replace it with this forgery. Got it?"

"I don't need to be spoon-fed, damnit!" She finished her champagne. "Don't be insulting, please. I can handle this."

"So, all is going well with your man on the committee, Natalia?"

"Yes, Uncle. Why do you ask now?"

"Just want to make sure. Torres is a very clever and dangerous man—to our—uh—business and our future, Natalia. Don't underestimate him."

She laughed and sipped champagne.

"Really, he's absolutely divine. I'm sure he is completely taken in by my charms."

"Hmm. Who could blame him, but are you sure it's not the other way around?"

"Uncle, are you questioning my talents at seduction? Haven't you seen me work my way through men like him all of my life? I assure you, he means nothing to me. Haven't I always been loyal to you. More champagne?"

Uncle Frank stared hard at her, as if trying to ascertain if she was telling him the truth.

"He's quite smitten with me. I'm good at this. Give me some credit." She signaled for the waiter. "Another bottle, *s'il vous plait.*"

"Really, Natalia, is that a good idea?"

"I have time, and you know I have a hollow leg. What is that silly expression?" She squeezed his hand affectionately. "I need a little Dutch courage for the gala."

Liquid courage for the dual roles she would play.

Natalia hadn't used the code word, but Michel was concerned about the turn of the conversation. Frank was slippery. He wouldn't have missed how quickly Natalia had changed the subject. Natalia might be a natural, but she was still green.

Frank might love his favorite niece, but Frank's life depended on this operation and pleasing his partner. If he had to choose—as that thought ran through Michel's mind, Frank looked directly at him, narrowing his bespectacled eyes.

Natalia took his hand, turning him back to their festivities.

But Michel felt that hard stone in his gut—had she been made?

Chapter 103

Torres was just outside the Ritz, alone in a sedan, listening to the conversation between Natalia and her uncle. It was a tough assignment—fooling the best of the best. But she was doing beautifully. He hadn't underestimated the power of the mentor-protégé relationship. It helped that her uncle doted on her. When he had questioned Natalia about her relationship to Torres, she'd handled it well.

But Torres was still worried about her safety. Her mission was dangerous.

As he sat in the sedan monitoring Natalia, he was also tracking Fitz-Perkins' movements. At 16:00, he had left the Ritz dressed in white tie. Fitz-Perkins had headed into the Ministry of Justice on Place Vendôme. Once in the building, their inside person had lost sight of him. Torres had issued strict instructions not to follow.

They knew that the Swords had a temple under the Ritz. They had noted thermal activity in the area but wouldn't go in until the sting—the last thing they wanted to do was spook their targets.

He needed to let them play it out. For Fitz-Perkins to make his move—and to see who else might try to upstage Fitz-Perkins.

Near the Swords' main temple, Torres also knew that Fitz-

Perkins had his personal sanctum nearby. No one was to go near until Torres gave the order. His gut told him that after the gala, Fitz-Perkins would go to his hidden temple if Torres didn't arrest him first.

But Torres wanted him for something very personal—his kidnapping and molesting of Kikki.

Tonight was the night. Masks would come off. Hubris would be the downfall of this heinous syndicate. Operation Sphinx had to succeed.

As all of this rolled through Torres's mind, he listened attentively to Natalia and her uncle. Waiting for her abort code. So far, so good. When he heard Frank confirm that the switch would go down, he let out a breath, relieved for a moment. He had hard proof.

Minutes later, Michel spoke, "They're heading out of the bar together."

Torres watched them part ways at the Ritz entrance, listening to their parting words—a make-or-break moment.

"Why don't you come up with me, Natalia? We can go to the event together."

"Can't. I have a coiffure lined up for just before. Meet you there."

Torres watched Natalia kiss her uncle and hurry off towards rue Saint-Honoré. Frank stood for a moment, looking after her.

Torres let out a sigh of relief when Frank smiled and headed back inside the hotel.

The whole multiagency op fell onto Torres's shoulders. And he was feeling the weight of the mantel. The ICC, Interpol, Europol, World Customs Organization (WCO), the French antiquities squad (OCB), and his highly classified elite team. Not to mention Tía and the Daughters of Inanna. A lot of coordination to manage, but he was good at it. Adrenaline had been pumping for days. But in the back of his mind, or in his heart, perhaps, he was deeply worried about Kikki's safety.

He pulled out his comm and lit a cigarette to clear his head. He was just starting to feel the focus and strength in his core and mind when the phone buzzed.

JM interrupted, "I've got Flo on the phone for you."

"How's it going, Torres?"

"Good. We're on track."

"*Bon.* A lot of people are counting on you, Torres."

Torres clenched his thigh and said, "Thanks for the extra pressure, Flo."

"I'm just *préoccupée.*"

"That makes two of us." Torres waited a beat and then said what was on his mind. "Flo, don't come to me at the last minute and tell me to shut this down because someone on high and on the take doesn't want to rock boats—We knew that going in, Flo."

"Just tread carefully."

"*Putain de merde!* It's too late to worry about disgruntled politicians."

"Don't be pissed at me," she said curtly, and then she softened. "Torres, I'm telling you that until it goes down, you have options. Keep your eyes open. Make sure this is really the battle you want to choose."

"Goddamn right it is."

"*Bien*, but the continued functioning of this new division is more important than a single op. *Tu comprends?* But whatever you do, I'll back you."

"Thanks, Flo."

He disconnected.

But Torres didn't agree with Flo: If this op was doomed for political reasons, there wouldn't be any point at all in going forward with his division or the international tactics team.

Chapter 104

At around 5:30 p.m., an hour and a half before the gala, Kikki paced back and forth in front of the apartment's French windows that overlooked Quai Voltaire. She drew back the heavy red velvet drapes hoping that a window on the Seine and a view of the Pavillon de Flore would calm her. But on this particular cold, dark winter afternoon, the soft yellow lights in the round portico window failed to soothe.

La Lune shone brightly. Kikki watched her light increase and finally her full glory rising just behind the Louvre. The Full Winter Solstice Moon—appropriately in the sign of Scorpio—death and transformation. During the critical time, they were in dark shadow.

Kikki sat on the *récamier*, maintaining her vigil. The Moon Goddess brought enlightenment and clarity, shining in all the corners. And too, at her height, she spun confusion and delusion. Wiley companions.

She and the Daughters of Inanna needed the clarity of the Full Moon as the Wheel of the Year turned from darkness to light. Swirling the duality of all life together and opening an enormous energetic portal. An opportunity and an ending. A final earthly ending for some. A soul reckoning for others—when the light

434

turned.

Her eyes took in the living room of the home she shared with her lover, Torres—the Count, the Cop—the infuriating, impossible love of her life.

She closed her eyes and prayed: May the Goddess keep him safe.

When she opened them, her gaze landed on Dumas's novel *La Reine Margot*, still on the table where it had been at the beginning of this high-wire week. Courageous Margot fending off an attacking soldier.

A rush of emotion overwhelmed Kikki. She spilled hot tears as she watched a fast rewind vision of all that she had learned. Of what Kikki knew now about that tenacious, brave rebel queen. An inspired and intrepid woman dedicated to education, letters and arts, to having a voice, to love, to humanism and equality for women. Dedicated to the Goddess and to saving her own daughter.

Kikki felt a rush of cool air and looked for her past life companions. Though not visible to her, Kikki felt at one with Gillonne and Marguerite de Valois.

Margot had never faltered despite impossible obstacles. And neither did her faithful confidant and friend Gillonne.

"And neither will I fail," Kikki vowed aloud. "Your death will not be in vain, Monique."

Kikki looked up as Tía entered the room, speaking words that mirrored Kikki's thoughts.

"Indeed. Women were burned for their so-called heretical beliefs in the goodness and wholeness of nature, the Universe, Mother Earth, Humanity and the Goddess," Tía said in a righteous, angry voice. "Branded, burned, drowned and stoned as witches."

Kikki turned to Tía. She was dressed for the evening's events. Most striking of all, she had braided her thick black hair in several coils and wound them around her head like so many snakes, with two small piles accenting the extraordinary headdress. They were entwined with a long string of lapis lazuli beads.

"The horned crown of Inanna," Kikki said with amazement and admiration. "You look like the Radiant Queen of Heaven and Earth."

Tía bowed. Kikki rose and crossed to join Tía in front of the fire.

"I know you are struggling with powerful emotions and visions," Tía said quietly. "It is a natural part of your continuing journey to the Underworld."

"*Xero*," I know, Kikki responded in Greek. She took Tía's proffered hand. "I will not let fear invade."

"Remember that you are not alone. Trust yourself. We will all be there with you—to celebrate the Solstice, sisters and brothers who will dance the Light into prominence. Some of our sisters have already begun."

Kikki felt deeply the comfort of those words.

"Tía, I can't get the Snake Goddess out of my mind. I know she is but a symbol and not a person. After they murdered Monique— well—the people we seek to protect are more important—and yet."

"The Swords are using their dark energy and blocking your love. Do not concern yourself with your Snake Goddess. I promise you she is safe from harm. Do not be distracted by power games of the Swords. Sharp focus and protection are key."

Kikki nodded. "I understand."

"It's a pivotal battle. Natalia is vital. If we lose her to the Swords, it will take centuries, perhaps millennia, before we have another opportunity. And that is why they want to use her, to turn her to their ways."

"I know, Tía, and I see that she carries not only in her bloodline, but in her heart, that same kind of spirit as Margot. She is a symbol more important than the Snake Goddess. They want to make an example of her. Turn her like her ancestor, the Black Queen, or annihilate her, and thus, all women. As they said in their threat to you."

As Kikki remembered the words of the threat, rage and fury surged through her veins. "All because they believe women and their bodies sinful. Threatening our very existence and of those who hold the Goddess and her ways sacred. These men, these Swords, are afraid because they have no control. Fear of their own lust— shame and guilt."

Tía smiled, "You have all the knowledge you need. Allow it to work for you through the Goddess. I must go."

"Go with the Goddess, Tía. I already see you all in your white robes in the Tuileries under the bright light of our Moon Goddess. Music and dancing, linked hand in hand, circling the pool and fountain. And I see a ceremonial bonfire. Not that it's permitted."

Tía chuckled, "Who says we will be asking? I must go to the chapel first, so I bid you a fair and just evening. Call for us if you need."

Tía slipped behind the secret panel next to the fireplace and was gone. As the panel shut softly, Kikki heard the rustle of Margot's satin skirts.

Chapter 105

At 6:30 p.m., Kikki examined herself in the bedroom's full-length mirror. Blonde hair swept up into a chignon. Indigo mascara, liner and eye shadow enhanced her dark brown eyes. She puckered vermillion-tinted lips. Vermillion or blood.

She smoothed her mid-calf length red crepe dress and fluffed the flounced skirt. The deep V-necked bodice sparkled with sequins and showed to advantage her breasts. The dress was vintage Louis Féraud *haute couture*, a gift from a client who owned her favorite boutique in the Palais Royal's Galerie de Valois.

She carefully arranged two necklaces against the pale skin of her neck. The rose quartz lay under a triple strand of pearls, such as Margot herself had worn. Low-heeled black suede boots hugged her calves.

Ready for battle. A modern version of what La Reine Margot had donned for formal occasions in the Valois court. As Kikki looked into the mirror, she caught Margot's reflection in her own— and then she merged with the apparition.

"Regal and perfect for battle. Straighten your spine," Margot whispered.

Head high, prepared for Goddesses' warrior work, Kikki left

her bedroom and crossed to the front windows. La Lune swathed a path on the Seine that sparkled like diamonds. Someday, she thought, I may wear diamonds, but for now, I have my perfect protection. Diamonds are for the likes of Natalia Becchina of the House of Valois.

She banked the fire and then picked up her Tarot cards. She shuffled three times, focusing her intention, and cut the deck.

The Moon Goddess—Hecate and Artemis at once. Perfect. It was her night.

Like the Three Moirai, the Three Fates who spun the Wheel of Life in Greek myth, Hecate ordained and reflected the inevitable changing faces of life.

Ruler of the moon, magic and enchantment and holder of the mysteries of the Underworld. Banished there by Zeus.

Contact with childbirth of a mortal woman had made Hecate impure. Male Gods and mortal men through the patriarchal ages called it original sin.

Margot had to flee with her newborn daughter. In the eyes of the reigning patriarchy, she had become impure by giving birth to a girl. A love child—and a crime of treason for a Queen of France.

Wise Hecate turned to advantage her punishment. As the Invincible Queen of the Underworld, she came out on Solstice to seek out and punish sexual predators. Like Artemis, she demanded sacrifice— Iphigenia, and now Monique. Liam's cards from earlier that week.

Kikki placed the deck on the table and stared into the embers. She felt that presence of Hecate, a powerful ally in battle who would provide her needed strength to reach into the depths of her own unconscious—primal oneness—the great ocean of life from which we are born. No more sacrifices of women, Kikki vowed.

Hecate had been there for Kikki on the first leg of her initiation journey into the Daughters of Inanna last night. She accompanied her again now.

Kikki bowed once and was ready. She donned her black shearling coat and wrapped herself in a protective red cashmere shawl. She slipped Hecate's card into her pocket.

Without a backward glance or a hesitant step, she left the apartment, walked out of the building and marched up rue de

Beaune and across Quai Voltaire onto Pont Royal.
  Headed for a date with destiny at the Pavillon de Flore.

Chapter 106

Kikki was among the first guests to arrive at the gala. In the small VIP room in an upper floor of the Pavillon de Flore, festivities were underway. Expressionless waiters in black tie floated across the room with silver trays holding flutes of champagne. A familiar low buzz of conversation and anticipation.

Guests wore varying degrees of formal dress. Men in white tie. Women in shiny jewels and high heels. There were several couples —important men exuding self-importance with beautiful young women on their arms, wearing them like adornments.

Kikki accepted a flute and sipped, studying the group through crystal and golden colored fine bubbles. A trio of musicians stood in a corner of the room near the window over the Louvre's gardens. They were playing Saint-Saëns *Le Cygne*. The romantic music took Kikki's tightly wound state down a notch.

Among the more than a dozen illustrious guests gathered, Kikki knew some from the Louvre's exhibition's committee. Others were representatives of the Louvre, potential donors. International power brokers—elected by state and church and elevated by class and money. All were people of taste and importance. She recognized several of these important guests, a Russian Oligarch, a

441

French Bourbon Count, and a Vatican Cardinal. She knew they were Swords, but to her, they were all an energetic blur. She knew who would be front and center.

She turned from them and flashed a bright smile at the Commissaire de l'Exposition—curator of the exhibit, who was chatting with Gabrielle Laroche. The curator, Madame de Cirugeda, was a woman Kikki knew. She liked and trusted her, as did Gabrielle.

Gabrielle and Kikki exchanged discreet smiles. The formal unveiling of the pieces to the distinguished gathering was yet to come. It wouldn't be long.

The Snake Goddess was the principle attraction for these connoisseurs of art, anthropology and archaeology. As planned, Kikki knew that the curator had chosen one other piece—a last minute surprise. Knowing who was in charge, Kikki trusted the second piece would be magnificent, equal to her beloved Snake Goddess.

After the gala, the exhibit would be open to the public for one week in another part of the Louvre beginning tomorrow—appropriately in the Salle des Caryatides, where Margot had her debut ball. Kikki took a slow, deep breath. If, she thought, they made it through tonight.

Gliding across the fifty-meter long rectangular room, as though it were a frozen pool, Kikki sipped her champagne slowly. She stopped and stood apart in a strategic spot not far from Gabrielle. She wanted a close view of the unveiling. A discreet podium had been placed in front of a meter high platform that served as a stage over which floor-length, blue-velvet, gold-fringed stage curtains hung. They would be opened ceremoniously when the event began.

Kikki stood not far from the podium and near what was effectively the backstage exit at the south end of the room, towards the Quai and the Seine. From there, she had a view of the entrance. At least two of the servers looked as if they might be more focused on maintaining security—certainly Torres would have his people undercover. She hadn't seen Torres. Her heart hitched just a little —she knew he was close.

And where was Natalia? As the question crossed her mind, the door to the room opened and a flurry of people came in all at once.

Kikki quickly surveyed them.

She spotted Natalia among a small contingency, standing out with her lush red hair. She was a picture of beauty all in purple, worthy of her lineage. For a tiny moment, Kikki was jealous of the younger woman.

Until she saw Natalia's reality. She swept into the center of the room on the arm of Victor Fitz-Perkins. Natalia's face was flushed, and her smile was unnaturally bright. Her aura was gray and flat. Something was horribly wrong.

Masking her anxiety, Kikki smiled at Natalia and then returned Victor's gaze. She met his eyes, narrowing her own in a thinly veiled threat. She did not give him the pleasure of her smile. Bring it on Victor, she swore silently, meeting his phony smile with an unforgiving look—her lips pursed red and hard.

Victor looked the part of The Man, dressed in white tie and tails, a morning coat, British style. Very over-the-top for this event —for the French. His meticulously colored silver mane shone as though it had been sprinkled with glitter, which she expected was the case. She knew that he thought vainly of his hair as a crown that made him look distinguished, elegant and wiser than his real age, early fifties. He wore wire rimmed glasses that revealed sapphire blue eyes, an unbecoming affectation. He'd had a professional makeup job. His mask for this show.

He quickly corralled a waiter and served Natalia and himself each a flute of champagne. He managed to do it without letting go of Natalia, whose arm he was gripping too tightly. Where was Uncle Frank? As if Kikki had beckoned him, he sauntered in accompanied by Robert Moreno. Kikki discreetly sipped champagne as she studied them.

Uncle Frank was a portly, but spry, elderly man with blond hair and seemingly kind eyes behind oversized tortoise shell glasses. He wore a black tux with a flashy chartreuse cummerbund and matching bow tie. He looked exactly as he had been described. A jolly queen. Kikki could see why Natalia was fond of him. He was in his element.

Kikki caught his eyes flicker. He was looking for Natalia, she thought, but Victor strategically kept her out of her uncle's line of sight.

Moreno looked like a frightened rabbit doing his best to hold it together. He wouldn't meet her eyes. But with his right hand, he made a downward gesture that meant stay away.

Had Victor discovered his treachery? Or was Moreno just being cautious?

Kikki felt a presence nearby, and she turned to a waiter who appeared at her side with a chilled champagne bottle wrapped in a serviette. He bowed slightly and refreshed her glass.

"*Merci beaucoup.*"

He offered her a plate of canapés.

"*Non, merci.*"

"It's a lovely night out, don't you think?"

She looked up and found herself staring at Liam.

"What are you doing here?"

"Tía sent me," he whispered *sub rosa*. "I tried to catch you earlier, but no luck."

"I am glad to see you," she whispered. "Just give me some berth —"

"*Bien sûr.* Just know that if you need me, I am here."

"Thank you. I really appreciate it. I'm just—"

"Focused." He turned to serve another guest and then came back to her. "Anything you need?"

"Everything. I'm worried about Natalia. She doesn't look right. Too bright, flushed. And Victor has her in an iron grip. Dangerous."

"I agree. I'll see what I can do to separate them," he said over his shoulder, feigning to flirt with another waiter. "And help her out. See what's going on."

"Thanks. It isn't wise for me to get that close. Find out what's going on with Moreno and Uncle Frank. Moreno looks very frightened. Not good—"

"Got it. No problem." Liam topped off her champagne and caught her gaze with a knowing look. "And?"

"Where's Torres? He should be here." Her fear flashed as anger.

"Calm down," he hissed. "He's backstage, behind the curtains, doing his job."

"*Merci, jeune homme.*" She smiled and dismissed him.

THE FRENCH QUEEN'S CURSE

Mask in place, Kikki swished her scarlet skirt like a magician's cape, and carrying her crystal flute like Athena's sword, she crossed the room to the windows overlooking the gardens.

Chapter 107

Kikki took up a position next to the window and gazed out at the snow-covered lawn and symmetrical rows of hedges in the Women's Garden. Artfully illuminated dark green bronze statues of the female form in varying poses peeked out from between the hedges, frozen in motion. As if in silent play or standing guard. This was a garden for women.

Though from her viewpoint she couldn't see inside the Tuileries, with her other acute senses, she heard singing and saw in her mind's eye the Daughters of Inanna dancing hand in hand in long white robes round the Tuileries's fountain just across the way from the Pavillon de Flore. Dancing to defeat the long, dark night.

A frisson of fear ran up her spine, and she knew without turning that Victor had fixed on her. Using her powers of alchemy, she transformed her champagne flute into a lapis lazuli wand. She lifted her eyes to the gardens again for courage and protection. One of the statues began to move, twirling and dancing amongst the others, up and down the hedges. Tía, wearing a long black cape over white robes.

Tía looked up at the window and their eyes met in silent knowing. It was time.

Her mind sharp and clear, Kikki turned back to face the now crowded room. She brandished in her right hand, her champagne flute as lapis lazuli wand and Athena's sword.

The musicians wound to a close their last dramatic baroque piece, *La Sonnerie de Sainte- Geneviève du Mont-de-Paris* by Marin Marais. Had Margot been alive in 1723, she would have loved this stirring piece by the court's musician at Versailles. Perhaps played it on her own lute for Sainte-Geneviève, whose prayers had saved Paris from the Huns.

Many more guests had joined the *soirée*. Among them, the two men whom she had seen yesterday with Victor at the Louvre—the Directeur Général and Torres's colleague from the Ministry of Culture—were chatting with the curator.

What sort of bribery, what gift had Victor promised that would allow him coveted *entrée* to the council of the world's most famous and elite museum? A focal point of his siege for power. Fury fueled her determination.

Victor was still holding Natalia close, not allowing her to mingle with other guests. Emboldened, Kikki stepped forward to greet them.

Just as she got close, a distinguished, lanky blond-haired man stood in her path. She nearly spilled her champagne, so focused was she on protecting Natalia.

He effortlessly tipped her flute upright.

"*Ma chère.*" He lifted her hand and kissed it. "How very good to see you again," he said in flawless French, though he was thoroughly British. Torres's boss from the International Criminal Court.

"Ian, what a pleasure, to see you again. No need to be so formal." She reached up and kissed him on each cheek. "Are you intentionally keeping me from those two, and if so, why?"

"For your own good, my dear. Trust me."

She nodded and stepped back, allowing Ian to greet Victor, who was quickly closing the distance between them, Natalia in tow.

"Natalia, how absolutely lovely you're here. You look smashing," Ian said in his most posh accent. "Haven't seen you in London recently. Where have you been keeping yourself? You are certainly more beautiful tonight than ever. Small world, *n'est pas?*"

Victor squinted slightly and released his grip on Natalia with a grand gesture.

When had Natalia met Ian? Kikki wondered. As part of Torres's op or before?

"Victor, old man, great to see you on this side of the pond."

"Professor. Wouldn't have missed it for the world." Victor laughed pompously and pumped Ian's hand. "Tell me, how is academia treating you? Are you enjoying heading up the Archaeology Department at Oxford?"

Ian feigned a smile and answered with marked indulgence, "Cambridge. The best in the world, if I do say so myself."

"Yes, of course. I was only pulling your leg. Don't want it to go to your head."

"No, quite," Ian said, sipping his champagne.

They held each other's eyes like men marking their territory, Kikki observed. Unspoken challenge issued in their small and exclusive world.

"I understand you've just made an important donation to the Louvre, Victor. Quite a *coup*—for the Louvre. Look forward to having a closer look." Ian's manner was all charm, but his eyes continued to menace Victor.

"I'm terribly sorry, old man," Victor said, putting on his best British accent.

Sounding, Kikki thought, ridiculous.

"Won't arrive for some time. We're arranging shipment from Alexandria. I'm sending my man Moreno tomorrow morning first thing in my jet." He gestured towards Moreno and Frank, who stood a short distance away, tasting frothy bubbles from champagne flutes.

Moreno smiled timidly, wiping his brow with a crumpled handkerchief. Frank nodded with formal Italian dignity. Neither approached.

Oh Goddesses, Kikki thought, shuddering. Moreno has been found out, and Victor means to sacrifice him.

Natalia, though momentarily free of Victor's physical touch thanks to Ian, seemed tethered to him energetically. Kikki had to break the predator's chain of enslavement. Victor was the Devil incarnate.

Had Natalia fallen prey? Was she possessed or drugged? Or was she acting? Her hazel eyes were dazed.

"Natalia." Kikki stepped up to her and spoke sharply.

Natalia jumped. "Véronique, forgive me. I was lost in thought and—umm."

She was definitely lost, not in her body. Kikki had to act quickly.

"What gorgeous boots! But I bet your heels are killing you." Kikki tried a woman's touch. "Let's sit down for a moment. Leave the men to posture." She motioned towards a tiny red bench seat along one wall.

"I—" Natalia hesitated, not moving, energetically tied to Victor's side, his prisoner.

Natalia gripped her purple evening bag close to her body. In that moment, Kikki realized that in her handbag was the fake Snake Goddess. Goddesses, where was Torres?

Kikki remembered Tía's last words—focus on Natalia. Was it too late to save her?

"Come with me—now!" Kikki hissed and then dug her fingernails into Natalia's arm to break the psychic hold and to bring her back. She yanked her a few feet from Victor.

All of a sudden, Natalia's eyes focused on Kikki.

"Oh god, what is happening?"

"Give me your champagne glass," Kikki whispered urgently, remembering how Victor had drugged her. "Don't drink anymore. Natalia, what has he done?"

Natalia's eyes grew wide and frightened. She didn't answer.

At that very moment, the trio of musicians finished the last movement of Vivaldi's *Four Seasons—Winter*. The assembled guests stepped forward, lowering their voices to a murmur. The curator stepped up to the podium.

The anticipation was palpable.

Chapter 108

Madame de Cirugeda stood at the podium and tapped her flute. The blue curtain behind her shivered ever so slightly, thanks to the careful attention paid to climate control in the room.

"*Si'l vous plait, mesdames et monsieurs.*" She smiled graciously, pausing to allow the guests time to quiet. "*Merci bien. Le moment est venu.*"

There was a murmur of approval and a palpable expectant ambiance.

"We are very happy to have you all here tonight as we unveil truly extraordinary treasures." She paused, pivoting just slightly and gesturing to the curtain—and the treasure behind—before continuing. "We would first like to express our appreciation to Anastasia Simoudis, Director of the Greek National Museum, for her generosity and the rich cultural heritage of the Greek people and for lending us this exquisite recently found *objet*. Unfortunately, she could not be here this evening and has sent her apologies.

"*Alors*, I would like to have a fellow member of our small exhibition committee and an esteemed advisor join me." She motioned towards the wings.

Two people came forward and stood next to the curator.

"First, allow me to present and express gratitude to Madame Gabrielle Laroche." The guests applauded discreetly. Gabrielle bowed slightly and stepped back, so she stood inches from the curtain.

"And, of course, this would never have been possible," she said, before breaking off for a moment, "for so very many reasons, without the generous time and intimate knowledge of our very own Professor Jean Michel Beauregard de Torres. A member of our faculty and a valued advisor at L'École de Conservation du Louvre. One of our very own true royals—in all senses of the word. Monsieur le Comte?"

Torres stepped forward, kissed Madame de Cirugeda and took the podium. He wore a hand tailored black cashmere suit with tie, sober and elegant. His wavy black hair shone, and his dark eyes were bright. A very handsome man.

For an instant, he caught Kikki's eye, and his lips curved a soft smile meant only for her. She knew it well. Her heart quite glowed with love and gratitude that he had appeared in the room at the perfect moment.

He cleared his throat. "*Merci bien, madame.* I must first acknowledge Maître Véronique Trieste, who dug up one of the treasures about to be unveiled—an astonishing Pre-Bronze Age *Minoan Snake Goddess* from circa 1600 BC—only this past summer in Oia, Santorini, on the grounds of her new Hotel Atlantis." He extended a hand to her, inviting her to come forward.

Kikki shook her head and spoke "no" to him with her eyes.

"*Merci.* It was quite a revelation. *S'il vous plait, Monsieur le Comte et mesdames distinguées.* We are all very excited. I understand we are to have the pleasure of another precious artifact to stand beside the *Snake Goddess.* We await revelation." Kikki smiled graciously, even as fear vied with anticipation.

"Curtains, please!" Madame de Cirugeda nodded to the wings and stepped back.

The assembled guests applauded again.

Torres stepped to one side, and a waiter came forward to whisk away the podium. Though her eyes were on her lover, Kikki knew from the panache and grace with which he made the stand disappear that the waiter was Liam.

She looked over her shoulder, scanning the room for Victor and Natalia. But she couldn't spot them among the small crowd that was moving forward in a clump for a good view. Her heart raced, alarmed.

In the next moment, the curtains were slowly drawn back to reveal the alcove behind. But as it happened, Kikki could not see the precious artifacts.

With the whooshing sound of curtains, she was suddenly in the room alone, in trance. She saw only darkness.

She swallowed a rush of air and a suffocating, rank and sulfurous odor. She was consumed by dark energy that swirled up through the Louvre and its many basements, from the tunnels beneath, from the medieval fortress it had once been.

An invisible wind tunnel from the bowels of Paris. Once a peaceful place of nature and the Goddess protected by matriarchal tribes. Before the dark warring of patriarchal powers had ill-used Paris, her magic and river pure, the Seine. Egotistical people used their patriarchal religion as an excuse to wield power. Generals conquered Lutèce for Rome and Roman Catholics. Knights of the Holy Sword of God now guised as admirals and generals. Tarnishing the City of Light.

From the heart of her spirit, from the center of the universe and galaxy, Kikki fought not to be enveloped by the black smoky cloud that rode on the foul wind of lost souls. She coughed and choked as she felt her throat close.

"Stay present. Fight for her," Margot commanded as she appeared by her side. Kikki turned. How strangely alike they looked at that moment, both dressed in Margot's favorite color red —the color of blood.

Desperate for grounding, Kikki dug her boots into the plush red carpet decorated with golden *fleur-de-lis*. It worked, along with a little help from Margot. The smoke dissipated and then evaporated. Kikki could breathe.

She fixed her eyes on the alcove behind the drawn curtains and crept closer. Once more, she moved among the guests gathered to view the ancient artifacts displayed by soft spotlights. She scanned quickly for Victor and Natalia, expecting to see them among the first row. Not there. But before she could check further for their energetic signatures, her eyes were drawn to the prehistoric relics, as though they called out to her.

The tiny *Snake Goddess* of ancient baked earth stood on a marble pedestal.

On a pedestal next to her, was a stunning terracotta plaque with relief from 2,000-1600 BCE, the Old Babylonian period, near the same era as the *Snake Goddess*. The *objet's* central feature was the great Sumerian Goddess Inanna, known also as Ishtar.

Inanna in full regalia with a crown of multiple horns of divinity, wearing a divine garment of flounced fabric. Around her neck, multiple-beaded necklaces, and in her outstretched hand, an emblem composed of mace flanked by heads of lions, her sacred animal.

The guests crowded closer murmuring in awed appreciation. Kikki stood her ground at the forefront, eyes fixated on Inanna, who seemed to be speaking to her. What was she saying?

There was a loud buzzing in Kikki's ears that caused her to shift her gaze to the *Snake Goddess*. Something wasn't right. She knew well the tiny goddess's distinct energy. She had held the precious goddess in her hands. Last evening at the chapel, she beheld it before her.

And then, she knew. The one displayed was not real. It was a fake.

Natalia had stolen the authentic *Snake Goddess*. How? It must have been the evening bag she clutched so tightly. It had held the forgery. And Victor, with his dark magic and shape-shifting ability, could have provided the screen for the switch.

Where was the real *Snake Goddess*? Kikki's rose crystal beads became so hot her neck began to sweat, and then they began to choke her. She tried to turn her head, but her neck was frozen in place—blocked by a dark force that could only be Victor.

As she stared with growing alarm, Kikki thought she saw the floor beneath the two pedestals begin to sink. The walls shifted. Suddenly, with a snap, the curtains closed on the exhibition.

She began to hyperventilate. She searched for her lover and couldn't find him.

A sharp pain slammed into her left temple. She bit her tongue to stop the oncoming vision. Someone behind her was shaking her shoulders. Friend or foe? Her heart crashed against her chest. She was petrified.

At that moment, Madame de Cirugeda spoke in an urgent voice, "*Mesdames et monsieurs, désolée.* For safety reasons, you must evacuate the room. *Immédiatement! Vite, s'il vous plait!*"

Kikki caught only a muffled version of those words. What she heard instead were the deep resonating tones of church bells. The *tocsin* sounding alarm, as it had done nearly five hundred years ago —signaling the Saint-Bartholomew Day's Massacre.

The bells rang out in a near deafening tone. Over their clanging, Kikki heard a distinct voice shout a dire warning. It was the Italian-accented French of Catherine de Medici.

"Death to all who do not follow the One True Catholic God."

The Swords! Shock and terror snapped Kikki out of trance. She summoned Athena and the chokehold on her neck released. Her eyes flicked over the guests filing out. Frantically, she searched for a woman with red hair in a purple dress and a tall man in white tails.

They had vanished.

Chapter 109

In the nearly empty exhibit room, Kikki crossed to a window overlooking the gardens. She closed her eyes, tuned in psychically, and saw clearly what had happened. Victor had taken Natalia as prisoner to his secret lair next to the Swords' official temple. Flashes of her visions in the Chapelle des Louanges flew through her mind. She saw Victor's white tails. Natalia's limp body draped in purple in his arms. Victor stood in front of a black wooden door.

The door opened, and Victor carried Natalia inside before vanishing behind the closed door.

In her third eye, she saw the Place Vendôme, the Citadel of the Swords, and men in robes worshiping in the underground labyrinth of old tunnels. Though she knew not the precise location of Victor's lair, she knew the moon's light and the Goddess Inanna would guide her.

Sinister thoughts of predators' chains filled her mind. As Kikki opened her eyes, a dark cloud shrouded the full moon. Her own black thoughts were the darkness blocking the light. She must save Natalia.

"Be gone! Do not dare to block me with your evil!" she shouted aloud.

Kikki grabbed her coat, ran down the stairs and out the door, taking courage from the fierce lions that guarded the entrance to the Porte des Lions. The lions that had roared only yesterday. She ran through the Women's Garden to the Tuileries—towards those who sang in the light of the new cycle of the Wheel of the Year.

The snow-covered ground was perilous, frozen and slippery with black ice. She lowered her frame and bent her knees, using her hips to give her balance. She skated across a sheet of ice over the ground on which once stood Catherine de Medici's Tuileries Palace —now the edge of the Women's Garden.

The moon lit her path, and she flew down the stairs leading to the park's entrance, dark coat flapping behind her. In a world all her own, she straddled time and dimension. At her side, she felt Margot and Gillonne, silent ghosts with passionate presence. Now three Furies.

Horses' hooves on cobblestone and a carriage rambling fast in the night. A baby cried.

This time, the voice was Natalia's.

"Help!"

And then the sound of a whip on flesh.

Kikki ran faster. The eastern gate to the Tuileries, locked after sunset in winter, was opened by a tall woman in a long white robe wearing a golden cat-eyed mask. Wordlessly, she opened the heavy gate—ornate wrought iron tipped in gold arrows—or swords. Kikki rushed through.

She tipped her chin in gratitude as she flew past the familiar marble statue by Leveque—the robed Goddess Diana, hunting dog at her feet. She had been dressed for the Solstice Celebration, covered in snow and wearing the horned crown of Inanna.

Down the long middle corridor of the palatial gardens, Kikki glided, as if on air, praying for Diana, Artemis, Inanna, Isis, Athena and Hecate to guide her. Her fingers ran over the smooth surface of the Tarot card of Hecate in her pocket—a talisman.

Quickly she reached the central fountain—*Le Grand Bassin.*

Kikki stopped short, flooded with emotion at the Solstice ceremony. So many women and men, white robed, wearing golden masks and diadem crowns—like Hecate and Inanna.

Against the white snowy backdrop that was the Tuileries on this wintry Solstice, they had been invisible until she was right upon them. Those of the dark, she knew, would not see them at all.

To the beat of drums, they sang to welcome in the Light and banish the darkness. Ancient hymns in languages not now spoken—songs of Inanna of Sumer, the Mother Mountain Goddess of Thera and Minoan Crete, and the Great Moon Goddess Isis of Egypt.

Kikki rounded the right side of the fountain, at one with the wind at her back. She was quickly past the fountain and down the middle corridor.

She stopped to catch her breath, as if called to do so. As she turned to watch the ceremony, the frozen fountain turned to flame.

Tía was there now, tending the fire, white robes flying like angel wings. She was chanting in a deep voice. Over her head, high over the fire, she held an oblong stone like a shield. It had barely discernible Greek letters inscribed at its base and a design at its center. As Kikki watched, the moon caught a glint of silver and she saw its inlaid insignia—a single silver sword entwined with a crucifix of gold.

Flames rose high as if to grab the shield from Tía.

Kikki watched, mesmerized. It was just as Tía had said.

She and Tía locked eyes and souls. In that moment, Kikki understood what Tía held to the fire. The shield was an object of immense and old evil—emblematic of the Swords and the full horrible glory of the predators of the Patriarchy through the ages—the black heart of a crumbling empire.

Over a cauldron of fire, under the full moon, the coat of arms sprung a host of wailing demons with spidery legs and web feet. The sword and crucifix danced out of the stone. The shield became an open cavern dripping blood and crying its death scream.

Tía chanted the last words and plunged the coat of arms into the burning cauldron. Kikki heard a roaring growl and then a clap of thunder as the stone shattered into a million shards.

Holy Goddesses! With one last glance at Tía, Kikki turned on her heels and fled through the barren trees, on her way to meet her nemesis—directed by ancient wisdom and fueled by courage. On a sacred mission to recover her sister Natalia from the grasp of the Devil, of Hades, of Victor, in all his guises and madness. Emperor and High Priest of a singularly vile Underworld. General of the

Knights of the Holy Sword of God, his mask and cover. But now without the maleficent power of his shield.

Upon a booming clap of thunder, Kikki ran towards the gates that led out of the Tuileries.

"Save her! Save my child!" Margot screamed in desperation. "Do not let her die at my Mother's hand. She who seeks to destroy me and all that is good and right. Let not her life be as mine! Or we will be forever cursed. Maudites!"

Victor—a reincarnated more demonic version of the Black Queen gathering evil over centuries and lives. Victor was intent that Natalia would carry forward the curse of the lineage.

Forever cursed by blood—by *le sang real.*

Chapter 110

Kikki skidded to a stop, nearly to the exit, at the border of the spindly row of trees that lined a long alley, stretching from the Louvre through the end of the Tuileries to the Jeu de Paume, where in Margot's time, tennis was played.

She glanced to her left towards the garden's large octagonal pond, one that might have been designed with Inanna and her eight-pointed star symbol in mind. She mounted the steps to the iron gate, filled with trepidation. It was closed.

The Black Queen, herself, had designed these royal gardens. Kikki saw a row of silver swords freshly tipped in gold. Poisoned tips.

She was so cold it felt as though her blood had been frozen. Were her psychic senses playing tricks? Or was it a premonition?

She took deep breaths. She had sworn not to falter. Dropping to the ground, she spit up bile. The wind whipped at her like the silver spikes of the fence. The dangerous north wind, Boreas, heralding winter and a storm—a thunder snowstorm.

Cleo's sweet voice penetrated the darkness.

"Bella! It's not real. The swords are not there. You are strong. Be Athena, put on your helmet, let your owl guide you to our sister

Natalia. Her time is running out. Please, Kikki! Hurry!"

Kikki wondered if it was Cleo or a trick? Was she being lured into an impossible trap?

"No, it is not a trick," Cleo whispered. *"You must take the full journey. We need your light, bella. I will hold it here on the island. Go! For Natalia and Monique!"*

Kikki straightened her spine. Expanding her protection, she energetically secured her virtual Athena's helmet.

Despite Cleo's message of love and light, Kikki was driven by a need for revenge for Monique's brutal murder. She advanced to the gate, determined and ruthless. Athena as Warrior Goddess and Atalanta, Amazon Queen, stood at her side, armed and poised to kill.

She reached inside her coat for the Mycenaean dagger. Revenge would be hers.

Her hand met soft fabric. The dagger was gone.

"No!" Margot stood in front of her in her royal red gown. *"Revenge is not the way. Do it for love—if you have darkness in your heart we are doomed."* Her young face was stern. *"You will be just like them."*

Margot vanished. Kikki stood alone and struggled with her dark need. Church bells rang out again, striking midnight at L'Église de la Madeline, Mary Magdalene's place, just behind Place Vendôme.

Kikki felt the distinct whoosh of an energetic portal. It was the exact moment of the Solstice—equality of darkness and light. The long dark night though not over, was turning. The balance would shift.

The stench of the earth's bowels from ancient subterranean tunnels traveled on the harsh wind. It was then that she knew. He was luring her and blocking her light at once. He was working to turn her towards the darkness.

She had to get through the gate. She raised her arms to the heavens, imploring the Goddess for support, and then shouted, "Hear me Victor! Your so-called guardians of the One True God— you and your demonic Holy Swords! You will not defeat the Light. It is coming. Coming to extinguish you."

The sky opened and it began to snow. Thunder boomed and lightning flashed meters away, blinding and electrifying her. In the near distance, a searing bolt struck the centerpiece of the Place Vendôme. The bronze column made of instruments of war.

Instantly, she manifested Athena's holy sword and brandished it at the Tuileries gate. It opened wide, as if by a magical force. And then, she was out.

"Be careful, Kikki!" a voice called out. Her head whipped around.

"Liam?" In a dark coat under heavy clouds, he blended in with the shadows.

He stepped towards her.

"And hurry because she will not hold out much longer."

"How—?"

"You will know the way." He pressed an ornate skeleton key into her hand.

Liam's strong divine male presence brought her added courage.

"Go—you must go alone." Liam pointed towards Place Vendôme.

Chapter 111

She skated on the ice for the short length of rue de Castiglione to Place Vendôme. But her arms and legs were heavy, wrists in heavy cuffs, chains dragging at her ankles. She amped her crystal protection and the bonds fell away.

Beside the massive green bronze column a familiar figure stood erect, not wavering in the blinding snow. Tía.

"You must hurry, my daughter. For all of our sakes. Save her!"

Tía opened a door to a stairway that led inside the column to the platform on top. Kikki saw in her third eye a hidden door, and behind it, stairs leading down. Down through the labyrinth to Victor's hidden temple. His secret cave.

Kikki ran through the door and instantly found the wooden entry door to the tunnels. When she yanked, it stuck. Tugging with a superhuman force, she strained, and it opened.

She stepped down a spiral stone stairway that looked nearly as deep as the column was high. She ran down the musty stone steps spiraling 'round in a tight circle. She ran until she was dizzy and choking on the gaseous smell of the bowels to which she descended.

She reached the bottom step and stopped. A three-forked entrance. Which way?

462

"Left," a voice whispered.

Margot? She couldn't tell. But she took the first step towards the dungeon. The passageway was narrow, and its crumbling stone walls seemed to lead to a dead end.

Dark and fetid, ever deeper into the underbelly of Paris. Oily black water puddled in the narrow path. How far would she have to go?

When she reached what had seemed a dead end, she discovered a sharp turn, and when she took it, the pathway lit up. Gargoyles of mythical demons held oil lit lanterns in gaping mouths. She buckled at the knees and stumbled. But faint sounds drew her upright again.

"Help me! Please!" cried the faint voice of a woman. Natalia. She was his captive—but alive how much longer?

Kikki had to free Natalia from Victor without becoming his prisoner too.

Kikki prayed, "Margot, you promised I would not be alone. Inanna, for your sister, for all of us—lead me to her."

At once, with a force she didn't know she had, she was propelled onto Inanna's twin lions, lapis lazuli wand in her hand. Kikki straddled the two mother beasts, holding fast to manes that empowered the lionesses to protect their own. At one with the holy beasts and Inanna, Kikki rode.

And then, lions gone to another dimension, she found herself standing at the end of the corridor facing a black wooden door centered with a gold knocker—a male lion's head clutching a golden ring in his teeth like captured prey. This Underworld was eerily silent.

With the skeleton key Liam had given her, Kikki took a deep breath and turned it in the lock. The door opened wide.

"I have been expecting you," he growled.

Chapter 112

"Come, join us. But I fear you are too late for Natalia."

The force of Victor's voice threatened to knock Kikki off-balance as she stepped onto the narrow wooden threshold of his cave-like room. She caught the scent of burning candles, and yet, the light dimmed as she stood transfixed, barely able to breathe. Steeling herself, she manifested an invisible shield and called upon her Goddess protectors. Their energy instantly manifested, jolting through her, protecting her heart, mind, spirit and body with a luminous shield.

She took a shuddering breath and faced Victor straight on, now able to see him fully. He held the room's center, his body seemingly taller and more powerful, as defined by his long black robe trimmed in gold. But it was his head that shocked her—he had no human face but instead wore the head of a lion, an alpha male with proud flared nostrils, streaming golden mane, jaws wide showing sharp teeth, incisors bared to devour.

She heard his breath rasping through the open jaws just as a fetid smell hit her. Honing her sight, she stared into dark holes where once there had been eyes.

Quickly, she averted her gaze from those black hollows. The

form she had known as Victor was gone. He was fully possessed by the demonic forces.

Holy Goddesses, he was completely mad.

She stood outside on the threshold. Instantly, she called for Athena's power, and it bolted through her as white light. She formed it into a ball and hurled, freezing the demon she'd known as Victor.

She couldn't hold him for more than seconds, so she scanned the lair.

Natalia, are you here? Are you still alive?

Suddenly darkness shrouded the room, obscuring Kikki's eyes and all her senses until she called Light up from Mother Earth and down from the Universe. The shroud lifted illuminating a raised marble tomb. An altar surrounded the tomb—and a body was laid out atop the stone coffin.

Natalia! Kikki almost doubled over with sudden shooting pain.

Natalia lay resplendent, her red hair streaming over her purple gown, vibrantly beautiful still, even while enveloped in a ghostly glow.

Blindfolded but not gagged—and completely immobile.

Is she even breathing? Am I too late? Thoughts raced through Kikki's mind as the energy in the cave shifted with an audible crack.

He'd broken free from Athena's bonds. Time to engage the Devil!

As if he'd heard her thought, his growl seemed to rise straight from Hell to fill the room.

With all her focus on Victor's demon, she summoned her powers and prepared to enter his darkest of worlds. The threshold acted as a precipice, and Natalia, not yet trained in the power of the Goddess, had fallen. Kikki refused to succumb—but would she have the power to bring Natalia back from this abyss and this Hell Beast?

"Victor," she said slowly. Would he even recognize his human name? "I've come to take Natalia back." She thought she saw his body flinch, but she couldn't read more, not with the lion mask. "Let her go with me now."

"Too late!" he growled, his voice bouncing off stone walls. "It is righteous penance for her betrayal. It is my will that she shall make retribution and pay with her life."

Dear Goddesses, that meant she was still alive.

"That's too high a price," Kikki said, her voice deepening with the power of Light and Gaia.

He seemed to flare his shoulders, drawing in the power of the beast. "I gave her a choice. Be my mistress for life, my possession and my chattel, or die."

For an instant, he almost sounded like a petulant child. Kikki felt his energy shift again, as if his defenses were mustering, as if he must prove himself. Good. Kikki took one step off the threshold but froze when his roar echoed round the cave.

"Regard the magnificence of my work!" He raised his arm, the folds of his cloak shimmering, the gold gleaming—the ultimate showman, Lord of the Underworld. "Another witch!" Now, he focused his wrath on Kikki. "Do you see your fate, slut! Fear for your own life. You cannot save hers."

As he raged, his warring energy slammed into her, and her knees buckled. She strained to stand to her full height, to bounce it back, fighting it off with white light. As she did, she stepped fully into his lair.

He had built a black magic pentagram-shaped temple for his evildoings. Marked by swords in each corner. Finely sharpened steel swords with golden tips. Exactly like those she had seen at the Tuileries gate. The swords were lit with clusters of black candles at their base. She could not see the details—but the dark vibrations were unmistakable—satanical tools of torture.

Her throat began to close, and she summoned strength from Inanna, becoming one with the Goddess. Her throat eased open again, and she drew a deep breath. It was time. She stood with Inanna and all fear vanished. She had entered the deepest realm of Hades, and she was not afraid.

"Come in so that you may witness—and join—"

Kikki stepped carefully, circling him. All the while, she was moving into battle mode. Keep him distracted. She summoned her voice.

"Join what?"

"Become one of us and give your life for our cause. Enter as Natalia entered."

"For your Knights of the Holy Sword of God? For you are the

General of God's army and power on earth are you not? And where are your loyal followers, your soldiers of God's might?" She taunted him, crossing the line as far as she could without being ensnared in his trap along with Natalia. She must shift his maniacal fixation.

Silently, she called in the Goddesses and those who danced and sang the Light nearby. As she did, she moved around him and closer to Natalia, who lay still as death on the tomb.

"You will die with her," he hissed. "You witches and heretics who have forsaken the One True God. It is for the good of all that the righteous take power—and weed out and destroy the weak—like your Daughters of Inanna and all they stand for. They will all burn in Hell tonight, along with your wretched Snake Goddess."

"And who else have you harmed in the name of your so-called righteous cause?"

Summoning Athena and Atalanta, Kikki snapped her fingers. At first, he stiffened, then he inched back, giving her a closer view of Natalia.

"Dear Uncle Frank," he growled. "What can you expect from someone who still carries the Medici name and blood? As does your lovely Natalia, though the last of the Valois bloodline is tainted—cursed—just like your Reine Margot—whore and witch!" He tossed his head back like a lion. "I am the New Order."

As he boasted, she inched towards Natalia and the altar. But his attention shifted, as if he were suddenly aware of Kikki's intentions.

Quickly! She chose words she knew would feed his ego, playing off his bold claim.

"With your other sycophants, other men and women of power —your loyal soldiers? Those from the French Ministry of Justice and Culture, the Louvre. Where else?"

"Ah, the Louvre! Even you must understand by now, the Louvre is mine!"

In an instant of uncertainty, Kikki froze. Her third eye exploded, and she felt her mind begin to fracture. She saw a full spectrum of color through a thin veil. Could his words be true?

But she heard the Goddesses whispering through the eons, *"Stay the course, see with your owl, Athena!"*

A flash of dozens of women burning at the stake rushed through her third eye. Branded and damned—*maudites.*

She committed herself once more to this trial, turning her energy on the Hell Beast, releasing her own unearthly cry.

"Impossible! You will have to survive to have the Louvre or anything at all, and you will not live to see tomorrow. The Justice of the Goddess will prevail."

Kikki now stood close to the raised altar while the beast stood in an opposite corner of the cave. She had a perfect view of Natalia—and the instruments of torture and ceremony that Victor had assembled for his personal Solstice Ceremony.

Black candles at strategic points on the altar. An empty syringe. A tiny stone lion's head and a row of coins minted in the time of Alexander the Great. A bronze cauldron. And the *Snake Goddess*—she prayed not the real one.

The beast snarled, raging, but she shut him out, focusing only on the cauldron in front of her. It was filled with what looked like oil and blood. Exactly as in her vision. She told herself not to flinch. She could not fail. There was far too much at stake. Let this madman take pleasure in his insane vanity while I push him over the edge.

The Hell Beast let out a wild laugh and threw his lion's head back.

"You and your powerless Goddesses, your sacred Inanna—you could not save your Monique!"

Dark energy raced through Kikki, and she might have given in to his taunting trap. But at that moment, she saw the slightest movement of Natalia's fingers. Praise the Goddess! She was still alive.

She looked more closely at the altar and saw another object: a stone shield with sword and crucifix—a miniature of the Swords' coat of arms. Kikki smiled, knowing that Victor could no longer make use of the real object's dark powers. The shield was nothing more than dust.

But Victor did not know. If he tried to draw strength from it, he might tip into the void. It gave her an advantage that would serve her in this ancient battle.

"You cannot betray me," he growled. "You are nothing."

He attacked where he sensed vulnerability, like the lion scenting blood.

But now, his tirade only fueled her resolve. In a rush of Goddess insight, she knew exactly what to do. She saw that his lair was a black magic pentagram with an inherent weak point at the bottom. Well-marked to gather evil.

She knew how to break it.

Slowly, Kikki, step by step.

She began walking the perimeters of the pentagram, knowing it would infuriate him and also break the black spell that held Natalia, and now herself, captive.

His stink gusted over her, and Kikki braced—it was the smell of pure evil, made of the Devil's anointed oils and rot. The beast was feral and hungry for blood.

Now, in the close, small room, the energy grew dense with unseen demonic and angelic entities that crowded them, waging battle on a parallel realm. Kikki felt and saw these otherworldly energetic beings. The beast would discern their presence and suffer their effect for he was only darkness, a walking dead now. The demons would suck out his lifeforce until he fell.

Time to push him over.

"Spare Natalia's life and take mine instead."

As she said those words, his energy shifted, and he grew eager for Kikki's death. But he wasn't ready to give up Natalia, she knew.

Natalia might be Kikki's Achilles heel, but her mission to save Natalia and win this battle had emboldened and enraged her. She took one more step to the bottom point of the pentagram—the breaking point. There!

She stood firm on that point, gripped Inanna's wand, the one that Inanna had to surrender to save her sister, and thus descend further into the Underworld. In Kikki's recent initiation and journey to that Underworld, it mirrored the sacrifice that Margot had offered to Hecate to save Gillonne.

Kikki thrust the invisible wand at him. He bellowed, and a sound wave shook the room and jolted Kikki. Then he yanked a gold tipped sword from the wall to parry, crossing the room, leaving the top two points of the pentagram and the support of their black magic.

"To the rightful power of the One and Only True God!" These familiar words that meant life or death for so many thousands to

Kikki's ear were uttered by a voice from afar—from another time and dimension.

"Never!" Her strong clear voice that spoke for so many reverberated off the stone walls and filled the room. Black candles flickered as the pentagram wavered but didn't give. Millenia of depraved dark souls supported this energetic construct of war and conflict. Sucked from the chthonic bowels of the earth. Black hole of evil at its deepest on this long Winter Solstice night. Darkness clung fast to Light, seeking to extinguish it by any means. Hate not love.

Kikki gasped as Victor with his lion's head transformed into an apparition of the cruel face of Catherine de Medici. Pinched and bitter from hatred, bent on asserting power inbred in the name of her Valois sons. Her head was a pile of hissing snakes. Madame la Serpente.

The stone floor beneath them transformed into a stagnant pool of blood. Kikki cringed in horror but stood in her power, facing off this ghost of the Black Queen. Kikki could feel the presence of Margot and Gillonne and her child, innocent and pure—the daughter. The Queen Mother had sought to kill all three of them.

But she had failed.

Staring down the ghost of Catherine de Medici, Kikki rose above the floor so she was floating as she cried out.

"Too much blood has been spilled. Men, women and children, oppressed, tortured and murdered. Crusading terrorists waging an unholy war of power and revenge—lost souls. The blood curse ends now!"

The Black Queen let out an inhuman sound and lunged for her. Kikki dove to safety at the foot of Natalia's deathbed.

"It is our turn," Kikki chanted, using her voice as channel. "It is time to return to a society of peace, of nurturing and love. Where we are at one with Mother Earth and nature, practicing the Goddess's way. Before it is too late for the planet. You have despoiled our sacred Goddess's groves on Gaia for too long."

Catherine de Medici's ghost approached, and Kikki brandished the wand at her. The apparition crumbled to dust, a high keening sound seemed to dart up and away, and the pool of blood transformed to bracken oily water.

Chapter 113

In the next moments, the real claustrophobia of the dark cave became overpowering—omnipresent and menacing like a living hungry predator. Kikki felt Natalia's vital energy slipping away. Time was running out.

Kikki watched the beast that had once been Victor. He had backed into a corner, and now he roared like a wounded lion. His vacant black eyes burned red coals. He clutched at a wooden box she hadn't seen. What new depravity was this?

"You cannot defeat me, for I am protected by God and greatness, you accursed witch!" He opened the mosaic wooden box and thrust it at her.

"What is that, more spoils of your war for power?"

"The bones of Alexander the Great! Recovered by me in Egypt. Look on the altar, a tiny stone lion he carried as talisman, along with coins he minted. Men have done great things in the name of the One and True God! As will I. You will help me. Your death will aid the cause."

Kikki let his fury build to breaking.

"Those bones are not real, and if they were, they would hold no power over me. You think you can kill me? You cannot. I will not

471

fall."

Kikki faced him fearlessly. She wore her red dress as armor and her long black coat as protection. For black was but the complete absorption of the light. At this moment, she embodied the love and light of the Goddess.

She held the energy of all light on the Solstice night, standing firmly at the base of the pentagram. She closed her eyes, and with a deep breath, she envisioned the collapse of Victor's depraved darkness—a weakened structure—and acting as alchemist, willed its destruction and collapse. She envisioned the pentagram-shaped room in ashes.

Donning her powers as High Priestess, she summoned the Tarot card, the Five of Swords of the accursed House of Atreus. The five elements, each in turn destroyed by another. The last card was for Victor, who thought himself Emperor and High Priest.

She reached behind her, and with a well-cloaked sleight of hand, took one of the five swords from the wall, hiding it behind her back.

He crossed the room towards her, lion mask still in place, and shoved the box in her face.

"This is my gift to the Louvre. A sacred place that belongs to God and men, rational men of law and order—and yes, power, wealth and the privilege of those of royal blood. Not to Snake Goddesses and weak matriarchal history. Certainly not to your decrepit Goddess Inanna. Your Tía and her band of witches will burn tonight in the Tuileries."

Kikki stared into his hollow eyes.

"You thought I didn't know that she is still alive?" he barked. "And Natalia—that ancient whore, Margot's only descendant. Natalia is my holy grail—my *sang real* to do with as I wish. She refused to be my slave. And I vow to destroy all of her lineage—to wipe the world of her bloodline forever."

Kikki waited, gripping the sword.

He shouted at her. "You think that saving Natalia, the last of the Valois line, will change the world? Give the power over to you? To the pathetic Goddess? How naive you still are."

Kikki's wrath spiked. Margot whispered to her, and at once, she remembered—Victor, the man—was deathly afraid of snakes. She envisioned the snakes of retribution in the hands of her Snake Goddess and called them. She repeated a mantra in her mind: Snakes for retribution and transformation. Snakes are lightning. Snakes hunted down mountain lions. Serpents were Eve's. Bring me deadly vipers.

The rough stone floor transformed to a pit of writhing vipers.

The beast stared horrified.

"Whore!"

As the beast stood frozen in terror, Kikki stepped through the vipers untouched and grabbed Natalia, pulling her limp, drugged body off the altar. She removed the blindfold and shook her, but Natalia didn't stir.

Kikki slapped her once, sharply. "Natalia!"

Natalia's eyes blinked half open.

Kikki took her hand, arms around Natalia's slim waist for support.

"Can you stand?"

Natalia murmured, "I think so."

"Quickly," Kikki hissed. "Behind me."

The beast stood where he'd frozen, terrified of the vipers.

Instantly, Kikki manifested a ball of white light. She hurled it at his black, hollow eyes.

He screamed and tried to rip off the lion's head.

"You fucking cunt-bitch! What have you done? I cannot see. I am blinded." He roared when the mane stuck to his fingers, tugging at the remains of the lion's head, now melded with the man, the possessed Hell Beast.

The two women began to back out of the room.

"Slowly," Kikki whispered. "Stay close. Do not look at him."

The beast lurched towards them, thrusting his sword wildly. Kikki still wielded the sword she'd taken from his wall. It was now hers and Athena's. She thrust it at him, holding its sharpened point to his chest.

He stumbled backwards, hitting the altar, knocking over the cauldron of oil and blood.

Kikki backed out the open door with Natalia safely behind her.

As they crossed the threshold, the snakes vanished. The beast rose up. Black robes flapping, sword leading, he lunged at Kikki and held it at her throat. She parried. Swords clashed. Life or death for one of them.

Kikki expanded her energy and stepped back, waiting out the beast's rage. Calling in the calm and love of the light and the Goddess.

He screamed. "Your life for Natalia's? Isn't that what you said?"

"So I did."

She lowered her sword and fearlessly edged forward so that the tip of his sword threatened the soft skin of her throat. A throat protected by a necklace he could not see.

"No!" Natalia cried. "Don't!"

"It is right." Kikki stepped close to the beast and dropped her sword. "I am defenseless," she said, her voice calm. "Would you really kill me?"

"You betrayed me." His eyes were red coals, and they burned into hers. But he hesitated.

"As you betrayed me and all of humanity." She returned the look, her own dark eyes completely dilated. "The Divine Wrath of the Goddess be upon you!"

He made a guttural sound and stepped closer, pressing the sword harder into the skin of her neck. It pierced her skin yet did not bleed. She remained still, calling forth a host of goddesses and white light.

He stared. Shock and terror registered at the bloodless wound.

Still, Kikki refused to break her gaze from his dark form. He struggled to remove the lion's head, failing again. He began to back away, tripping on the skirts of his black robe. He stumbled backward, barely recovering.

Kikki waited. She had seen what was to come.

The cauldron's contents spilled onto the altar and flowed around the flames of the black candles that encircled the stone tomb.

Kikki stared intently, willfully at the altar. Fire sparked and roared into flames. The flames leapt to the floor and caught a tail of Victor's robe. But he hadn't seen it.

Still, she didn't move. She faced down all the darkness before her, all that this possessed demonic being now held.

She and Natalia stood on the threshold in a protected vortex.

The room began to shake. A thunderous sound filled the tunnels behind her.

A flash of lightning descended through many layers of earth and struck. In slow motion, the electric bolt from the heavens connected with the silver and gold sword in Victor's hand. It traveled up his arm and through the pathways of his earthly body to the depths of his blackened, heartless soul, felling him.

His robes caught fire, and flames engulfed his entire body—a peculiar dark red-orange flame laced with blackness so opaque it completely shrouded his tattered lion's head.

The lightning sparked the fire, and the room instantly became a wall of flames.

Over the fire's roar and the howling wind of the vortex surrounding her and Natalia, Kikki heard a familiar voice calling her name from the tunnel.

Torres!

Kikki took one last horrified glance at the beast engulfed by flames, and for an instant, Victor returned—but only long enough to melt to viscera in the raging inferno. Leaving behind the stink of Hell.

Kikki grabbed Natalia's hand.

"Run for your life!"

Chapter 114

"Hurry!" Torres shouted, reaching for the two fleeing women. "The fire will fill this tunnel with a raging back blast." He flicked his eyes towards the gargoyles. "When it hits the oil lamps—" An explosion was likely, but he didn't want to frighten them more. "Victor?"

Kikki shook her head. "Dead."

He pushed the women forward, shielding their bodies with his own. "Run! *Corren!*"

Torres tore off his jacket and sweater.

He shouted, "Cover yourselves—your faces!" He threw clothes over them from behind. He pulled his own shirt up over his head, leaving a thin T-shirt and an exposed wound.

They careened through the tunnel's crumbling stone walls already scorched by fire. When they reached the fork at the bottom of the spiral staircase, the flames roared and rushed high and hot at their backs.

Instantly, fire filled the small contained space of the tunnels, sucking oxygen from the air. Black smoke rose mixed with flames. A raging inferno.

Natalia began to falter and cough. Kikki too.

"Keep moving." Torres grabbed Natalia.

"Carry her, Torres. She's weak. I can make it."

How would they survive, Kikki wondered? They had escaped Victor, but now Hell was chasing them. As she ran, she called up white light from deep within Gaia, mixed it with virtual water from the nearby river, beseeching Mélusine, the River Goddess. An alchemist's fire extinguisher.

It would take a miracle. She prayed it would work.

The roar and flames abated the tiniest amount—Light against Dark.

"Margot, *aidez-nous!*" Kikki shouted, her voice unearthly in its power.

They reached the spiral staircase, and Kikki raced up the steps with Torres right behind her, carrying Natalia in his arms.

At the top, the door to the tunnel was already open, and the trio stumbled out.

The Citadel of the Swords had been breached. Victor's private temple destroyed, and the Hell Beast vanquished.

Outside, Place Vendôme was a full-on emergency scene manned by Les Sapeurs et Pompiers de Paris, city ambulances and a fleet of cop cars from the various jurisdictions.

As flames receded, the suited and helmeted *pompiers* entered, advancing like an army on its enemies—time, fire, smoke and gas. A fight to extinguish the fire. A lot of expensive real estate, and many lives were at stake.

Four enormous fire trucks with flashing lights and blaring sirens filled the square, lit up now with high-powered lights, like a stage set.

Torres hurried the women aside towards teams of waiting *sapeurs*. As soon as they were clear of the entry, a squadron of *pompiers* bearing enormous hoses charged in—powerful rivers of water shot into the tunnel, beating the fire back.

A vast tent, complete with refreshments, waiters, and heaters had been set up on the far side of the column to shelter the crowd. The Ritz guests had all been evacuated, as well as occupants from all adjacent high-value real estate at risk. People stood in varying degrees of disarray, most of them dragged from their beds. Dogs barked, straining on their owners' leashes. All stood humbled on the elegant square in their nightclothes and overcoats.

A separate smaller tent was attached to three ambulances.

Torres delivered Natalia, barely conscious, to the awaiting team. He pulled Kikki into his arms and held her tightly.

"I nearly lost you," he whispered. "I love you." He kissed her and then released her. "I've got to help. The medics will take good care of you. Be back soon."

He grabbed a jacket from one of the medics and took off in search of his team.

Natalia had become fully conscious but was coughing and wheezing. Medics fitted both women with oxygen masks and checked their vitals. A few minutes later, waiters from the Ritz appeared and offered each of them water and brandy on a silver tray. With a nod to the medics, they pushed up their oxygen masks to drink.

"Oh my god!" Natalia whispered hoarsely to Kikki. "What a nightmare! How did you know where to find me? I am in shock. It's hard to breathe."

"Me too, Natalia." With shaking hands, Kikki quickly drank the glass of water and then gulped brandy. She was still pumping adrenaline, and her mind raced, feverish. "I could see what was going on at the gala. What he had done to you. He did the same thing to me."

"But how did you find me—?"

"I saw you there—" Kikki said in a shaking voice as visions of Victor and her descent to Hell flashed once more. She fought back tears and sipped brandy.

"You were so right about this—about him." Natalia began to cry. "I thought I could handle it—handle him. I knew he was a horrid man, but—"

"Don't think about it now. You are safe." Kikki reached for her hand, squeezing it.

"But you risked your life for me. How will I ever—" Natalia tried to smile gratefully, but her face felt paralyzed.

"It was for me to do. Take it easy, Natalia. You're still affected by the drugs, and you're in shock. Focus on breathing. Finish the brandy and put the oxygen mask back on."

Now that Natalia was safe, Kikki needed Torres. He had run off before she could speak to him. Where was he now? Was he with the *pompiers*?

She caught Natalia's eyes and said, "Listen, I'm sorry, but I have to go. You'll be safe now."

She stood, still a bit shaky. She drained the snifter and hurried away.

"Torres! Where are you?" She scanned the crowds in the square.

Snow was falling. Standing there in the bitterly cold night, Kikki began to cry. Her heart hurt, and her body was numb. She feared for her lover's safety. And then, she saw him walk out from around the column. He saw her at the same time.

They ran to each other's arms and held on. After a few moments—and a long very fervent kiss—he broke their embrace.

He studied her to make sure she was all right. Eyes were dilated and still in shock. But she was safe.

"Thank God—Kikki!"

"Thank the Goddesses. I'm dazed and numb—but I did it. I fucking did it!"

"And then some! You fucking did. And he's dead." He shook his head, angry and relieved at once. "*Joder!* You scared me to death. I didn't know where you were, where you had gone." His dark eyes clouded. His heart clenched, and he felt a visceral mix of rage and fear. "I thought he'd taken you again. Bad enough that he had Natalia. I ran out into the reception just as they were evacuating, and you were gone. I left the team at the Louvre."

She held his worried look. Tears began to stream down her face.

"I'm sorry—I had to save her. How did you know—" Her words faltered.

"We had this area under surveillance, their temple—which was close to his private chapel. We thought he'd come here. Eventually. But you got here before we could. How did you—I am so sorry I didn't get here in time to save Natalia and you. That I let him leave the fucking reception at all—"

"Stop—you arrived just in time." She finally said softly, "I had to go to her. And it had to be me to—take him down." She reached up and touched his cheek. "Tía? And the others?"

His anger receded, and he melted inside.

"They're fine—safe."

Kikki said evenly. "He killed himself with his madness. He created the fire that took him." She swallowed hard and bowed her head, remembering. "It was surreal and horrible."

He took her tenderly in his arms, kissed her hair and her forehead. She leaned into him, letting go of terror. They held each other tightly.

Kikki whispered into his ear, "I love you so much. I swear I would die if I lost you. Promise me you'll never leave me."

"I will if you do."

"Hot sex and hot love, then." She shot him a shy but certain smile.

Chapter 115

It was snowing hard when Kikki and Torres left Place Vendôme, which was still chaotic but now looked more elegant with a blanket of snow. The cacophony of sirens and people muted. In the back of a sedan, they sat close and held hands. Both lost in thought.

Just as they were about to leave the square, Kikki spoke to the driver.

"Wait. Stop the car, please. Just for a moment."

She ran her hand across the fogged window and peered out. Amongst the crowd of people, fire trucks, emergency vehicles, tall ladders and helmeted *sapeurs* and *pompiers*, Kikki caught a glimpse of another world.

Place Vendôme cleared of its present state, peace and calm restored.

A black and red satin carriage from another century drawn by handsome black stallions.

Inside, two women sat opposite each other holding hands and gazing out the window. Margot and Gillonne smiled.

The carriage paraded slowly round a splendid Place Vendôme filled with joyful onlookers from the sixteenth century.

Margot smiled regally and held up for all to see an infant girl.

481

Her daughter. The baby was dressed in lacy finery only fitting for a princess of Valois. Perhaps a future Queen of France.

Kikki smiled at the joyful scene and felt the tension within her begin to dissolve. And then, the vision faded.

"Thank you. Drive on."

Torres looked at her curiously and then drew her close and kissed her.

As they passed through Place de la Concorde, Kikki opened the window on the left side of the sedan and leaned her head out.

The snow had suddenly eased and was coming down in soft flakes. Just behind the western gate to the Tuileries, behind La Grande Roue, surrounding the octagonal pool, Kikki spotted the white-robed flock of the Daughters of Inanna. The group had grown larger. They danced around the pool in their white robes with golden diadem crowns, their singing louder and more joyful.

In the moonlit snowy sky above hovered an ephemeral host of Goddesses, Queens and heroines of France— Marguerite de Valois, the Queens from the Luxembourg Gardens and Eleanor d'Aquitaine, Anne de Bretagne, Jeanne d'Arc, Inanna, Isis, Hecate, Artemis, Athena and Aphrodite.

They were joined by those starry newly freed spirits who had entered the light—many thousands of brave women who had been burned, drowned or stoned as witches and heretics by the ruling patriarchal powers over centuries and millennia. Kikki saw clearly their faces illuminated against the backdrop of snow and moonlight.

Front and center, Monique's beautiful face smiled, at peace.

Tía watched over Monique, glowing and still wearing Inanna's horned crown headdress—her wizened face at once beatific and fierce, like Inanna.

Floating high above, further east, towards the center of the Louvre, Kikki saw her own face. She floated serenely hand in hand with a woman who looked like Natalia.

In the east, in the predawn, dark storm clouds began to lift and give way to a faint light. Not the sun, not yet, but the day of December 22 was dawning with a bright new light.

She shivered with excitement and hope, and at last, closed the window.

But still she couldn't take her eyes away. She remained in

trance, and the tinted dark glass of the sedan's window became a stained glass painting, one that looked so very familiar.

Its beveled iron lines replicated Kikki's dream—women in white robes standing in the Tuileries with Margot at the center.

The painting shifted frames, and Kikki saw Margot put a finger to her lips, as if to silence the gathering. Natalia Becchina of the House of Valois came forward, dressed as an initiate, to stand before her in the center of the circle.

Chapter 116

"We're home, *mi amor*," Torres said quietly.

Kikki looked up at her lover, dazed.

"Did I fall asleep?"

"I think you were in one of your High Priestess worlds." He smiled ruefully as the car pulled up in front of the blue gate on rue de Beaune.

She took his hand as he helped her out of the car.

"I guess that's something I'm going to have to live with," he said.

She looked up at him and smiled enigmatically.

Upstairs, they collapsed together into the plush cushions of a sofa in front of a blazing fire. Tía must have been there.

"I'm so tired," she murmured. "But I don't think I can sleep."

"Me either."

He was unwilling to leave her, but he had business to deal with that couldn't wait. There were many important matters that needed urgent attending. Thankfully, Fitz-Perkins himself would not be one of them.

"Don't tell me," she said, placing a hand on his taut thigh. "You've got to go."

"*Desolé.* We've got to sweep this up so your superwoman efforts will not have been in vain. Many international tentacles of darkness —*ténèbres.* One head of the hydra has been chopped off, but two grow back and the beast still rumbles and roars."

"I know—" she nodded. "And Natalia?"

"I got a text that she's recovering at the Hotel Regina. Tía and Liam are with her. Dr. Marie is checking her out. I hope she will be able to rest. I hate to think what might have happened to her if you hadn't—"

"But I did. And if I hadn't, you would have, my love." She squeezed his hand tightly. "Maybe I should have some of that potion to make me sleep," Kikki joked, and then she grabbed him and kissed him hard. "Or—

"*Ojalá!* I so want to make love to you, really—" He kissed her out of an insatiable need for her.

"Yes," she whispered. "I need you."

Deftly pushing clothes aside, he held her tightly. She dug her fingers into his back as they joined. They moved in rhythm, and in moments, they came together, breathing heavily. Then kissed once more, as if to seal their love and begin anew.

When they broke free, he said, "I'll make you a coffee and brandy."

"If that's all I can get for now—" She stood up and pulled him with her.

In the kitchen, they both smiled at the layout on the round oak table. Fresh *pâtisseries*—still warm—*croissants, pain au chocolate* and Kikki's favorite baguette—*un monge*—as well as fresh butter and homemade jam. A feast.

"Thank the Goddess and her messenger. Suddenly, I'm starving!"

She sat down and bit into a *pain au chocolate* as he prepared coffee. He turned to her, and she held his gaze, feeling slightly giddy. "I'm surprised there aren't fresh Spanish *churros* too."

"Hard to find in this part of Paris. And I don't think Tía has had much time to bake—" He handed her a crystal snifter with a good amount of Spanish brandy. "Here, brandy first. Or did they give you that at the Ritz."

"They offered, but I only had time for a sip. I had to find you."

485

His heartbeat increased. Fighting the urge to make love to her again on the kitchen table.

"Torres, I have no idea what actually happened at the gala. Can you tell me now about your op if I promise not to—" she caught his dark eyes—filled with desire like her own. "Touch you."

As she said those words, she felt naked and totally open. She knew that he felt the same. Walls disintegrated, hearts open. Both vulnerable.

He held her gaze for a moment, completely open and intimate.

She smiled shyly. He kissed her softly.

And then, he sat at the table with her and sighed.

"So—the *Snake Goddess* is safe.

Kikki shook her head. "But how? He had it in his—"

"That would have been a forgery." Torres said. "In the *mêlée* as the curtains came down, before anyone knew what was happening, including me apparently, Gabrielle switched them again. Or so Tía told me not long ago."

Kikki smiled enigmatically.

"Sounds about right." She raised her snifter. "Well, thank the Goddess. And you, Tía and Gabrielle, of course. Torres, you have a great team, and you carried off a brilliant op—as I knew you would."

"It sure as hell didn't go as planned." He shook his head, still pissed that he'd let Fitz-Perkins slip away, kidnapping Natalia. "There was no sting. It was you who brought him down. You chopped off the head—so to speak."

He clinked with his coffee and took a seat at the table across from her. He flipped a cigarette out of his nearly empty pack of Ducados and lit it.

"And Natalia?" Kikki asked. "What was going on with her at the exhibition? I had the feeling that she actually made the switch for the Swords. For Victor, even though she agreed to be your asset. A lot of smoke and mirrors."

"In those few moments before we closed the curtains, she did make the switch. Though I'm sure Fitz-Perkins left her no choice."

"He drugged her, like he did me. I spoke to her and tried to help her at the reception, but she was possessed by him." Kikki's voice was sad.

"I'll have to arrest her."

Kikki frowned. "Really? I don't like that. And neither would Margot or Tía."

"For her own safety. And I don't answer to Margot, or for that matter, Tía." His voice was serious. "Don't worry. You'll have time to get to know her. Sooner rather than later. She will be working with us. Voluntarily, arrest or not. She's got a big job to do."

"Her Uncle Frank?" Kikki sipped brandy and bit hungrily into a well-buttered *tartine*.

"Locked up and pleading for mercy. Lucky to be alive. We arrested the major French player, too, the Bourbon Count related to the would-be King Louis XX, as it turns out, and a Russian oligarch, a Vatican Cardinal and the other ringleaders—and uncovered a major stash of tens of thousands of blood antiquities and a dark web sales presence, thanks to Pelligrini. We're playing them against each other to get intel to bring down the entire network."

Kikki was afraid to ask the next question.

"Moreno, the film guy?

"Believe it or not, he managed to escape the fray at the reception."

"Hmm. Then he had help."

"You're right. Gabrielle and Madame de Cirugeda whisked him backstage when it went down," Torres confirmed.

"You know, he gave me Margot's journal and promised access to a private collection. I'd still like to see that. What's his situation?"

"We have him in protective custody here, safe house. He's been arrested. But you'll have to wait for the dust to settle. There will be plenty of time later, Kikki—when you're rested." He smiled gently, debating. Finally, he said, "He asked me to tell you that he still wants to do the film."

"Well, that's interesting. But more than I can take in right now."

"*Claro.*"

She cleared her throat.

"Back to the gala. What exactly did happen?"

In truth, she hardly remembered because, at the time, she had been sucked into a parallel universe. Perhaps it would come back to her. She sipped more brandy.

"On my orders, the Louvre shut it down. It was very strange—" He eyed her. "Just at the moment that we were about to carry out the sting and take him down, right after Natalia made the switch with Victor at her back, there was something like an earthquake or an underground explosion. So he got away in the chaos. Interesting timing. We're still trying to figure out what happened—" He shot her a quizzical look. "Maybe you or Tía will have a better idea."

"Honestly, my love, I don't remember it very well. I was in trance in my High Priestess world." It was beginning to come back to her. "But I know there was some kind of earth movement or collapsing of something underground."

"Like what specifically? And how?" He asked, voice tight. "*En serio*. It's how Fitz-Perkins escaped."

Kikki tapped Torres on his nose.

"But together we got him, destroyed his lair and the Swords' Citadel. It was meant to play out that way. Ironically, I couldn't have done what I did if you hadn't set up your sting. So take credit my supercop and savior of sacred relics. And, hey, when it comes to causing portals to open and blow darkness out of the water, I am not in charge. I only do my part. I am a vessel for the Goddess."

"Right." He raised an eyebrow and suppressed a frown.

"What? You're wrong if you think that me or one of the Daughters of Inanna set up an underground charge to go off at that moment to save the sacred feminine artifacts?"

"No. Let's just say that your call to the Goddess was answered."

"The Snake Goddess is very powerful—whether real or forged. She helped—whether through the quick hands of Gabrielle or perhaps Margot. But you can't see that kind of energy. That is, normal eyes cannot."

"Go on—"

"The Snake Goddess carries darkness of retribution and punishment. We all carry darkness. At that moment, it was released from ancient clay or her forged image. It literally rose up to battle the light and caused a shaking up of matter—of energy. Consider the possibility."

He smiled. "So Goddess magic, then?"

"Truly. Along with the combined light and strength of those in the room—Gabrielle, the curator, you, me—" She stopped and swished the heady brandy around her mouth and swallowed, feeling the fire from head to toe. "You see what I am getting at—"

"Yes, I get it. It's a bit hard for a cop to swallow, but I've been hearing it from Tía all my life. And before her, my grandmother, my mother."

Kikki eyed him seriously. "As a cultural archeologist you know —symbols and artifacts carry power—and magic."

"*Vale*—"

"Wait!" She interrupted as the moment flashed through her third eye. "I remember now that when it happened, I saw smoke and smelled the sulfurous stink of sewer mixed with river water and blood. Really. As happens sometimes to effect a cleansing—a healing."

He took a drag of his cigarette and met her eyes. Oddly, or not, it made sense. He thought that he remembered a foul smell.

"You might just find one of Margot's pearls from the night of the massacre floating on a rancid puddle under the Louvre. Rational explanation, Torres." She grinned brightly, pleased with herself.

He stood up.

"*Basta*. Plenty of time to talk about this later," she said, shooting him a smile. "You have to go. Debrief later."

"*Lo siento, mi amor*. Truly. I hate to leave you, but Ian and the team are at the HQ, and we've got to stay on this."

"I know. I'm glad you succeeded—even though I was genuinely pissed that you used the Snake Goddess as bait for Operation Sphinx."

"Couldn't be avoided. I know you understand that now."

"Yes, and the danger—the sphinx's riddle to be solved on pain of death—solved by my magical ravens. You were given rite of passage to enter and save Paris granted by the sphinx, herself."

"Hmm. Perhaps." He took one last long drag of his cigarette and stubbed it out in a souvenir ashtray from Granada engraved with the words: "*Dale Limosna Mujer, Que No Hay En La Vida Nada Como La Pena de Ser Ciego en Granada*." Give alms, woman, for there is nothing more painful in life than to be blind in Granada.

An old and very chipped souvenir from the Alhambra that Torres bought for Kikki so many years ago. He couldn't get her out of his head or this frustrating, primal, yet futile need to stop her. To keep her safe. But he held his tongue.

"Spit it out, Torres. You've got something on your mind."

"Goddamnit, Kikki. I hate that you can read my mind. What if you *hadn't* been able to save Natalia and yourself? What if he had killed you both? *Joder*! Why do you have to walk the knife's edge of danger?"

"Live with it. Didn't you say that you would have to just now?"

"How can I protect you? I don't know what to do. It's in our genes, the male species."

He sounded angry, more at himself than her, she thought.

She stood up and went to him.

"I thought you were my neomacho man," she said catching his eyes.

He evaded her look and was silent.

When she spoke again, the words tumbled out with emotion. "Think about this from my point of view. I have a need as a woman to nurture and protect you. How do I know you'll be safe running ops at greater and greater risk? And what if you don't come home to me?"

He studied her for a moment and then wrapped his arms around her. He kissed her long and hard, and she matched his passion.

Hot sex and hot love. A beautiful but terrifying combination for Kikki.

When at last they stepped away, both breathless, she braved a response.

"I guess we will both have to learn to—live with those fears—that ever-present dilemma—if we want to take this to the next level."

"Do *you*?" He asked softly. "Do you really want to take that step? Make sure you do."

She reached up and touched his face. "I do." She smiled.

I'll be back—" He blew her a kiss, eyes dark and full of love.

Her heart fluttered wildly as she watched him walk out the door.

EPILOGUE

In the late afternoon of the 24th of December, Tía and Kikki prepared a celebration. The front rooms of the apartment on Quai Voltaire were festive. Kikki and Tía both wore their finery, Kikki in a long golden silk gown and Tía in her best black velvet bodice and pleated skirt.

"It's so beautiful, Tía." Kikki glowed with happiness.

The front salons were wreathed in pine boughs and fat red candles tied with red bows. Crystal hearts hung on ribbons from the red velvet curtained windows. The apartment's three chandeliers had been newly polished and emanated light.

The fire blazed and crackled in the fireplace, emitting the heavenly scent of cedar, frankincense and evergreen. A pine wreath hung above the gilded mirror—an ancient Yule decoration symbolizing life everlasting. In the dining room, crystal and porcelain bowls filled with fruits and nuts were laid out on the table.

On the long buffet several bottles of Ruinart champagne, delivered that afternoon by the Voltaire, nestled in ice-filled heavy silver champagne buckets. Crystal flutes lined up, waiting to be filled.

Natalia came out of the guest bedroom to join them.

"How gorgeous! The room's perfect!"

The two women crossed to each other and kissed. Natalia wore a long white silk satin gown. Her red hair swept up into a chignon, shimmered. She wore no jewelry.

"You look more beautiful and radiant than ever, Natalia."

"Do you think so? I'm very nervous," she said shyly, ignoring her queasiness. "Are you ready for me now?"

Tía motioned the two women towards fireplace.

"Of course, my daughter."

"Do you feel Margot's presence," Kikki asked quietly, holding Natalia's hand. "I do."

"I'm not sure. I have a lot to learn about these ephemeral things that you and Tía so easily attune to."

"It is in your blood. It runs in your veins because you are of her, Marguerite de Valois, and one of us too. Now that you are here and safe, you will come to know her," Kikki said.

"No convent—promise me."

Kikki led her to the sofas. Tía had already taken her place on the sofa with her back to the window. Kikki laughed softly, thinking of Cleo and how on the eve of her initiation as High Priestess on Santorini she had been so hesitant and asked the same question.

"*Au contraire*, Natalia. And certainly not on account of Margot. She was a lusty woman, and so was Inanna."

"Besides," Tía said, smiling, "we are not here to initiate you. That will come later, after you have spent some time with me in Granada—as part of your 'house arrest.'"

"Then what are we doing?" Natalia suddenly alarmed, stepped back.

"Careful!" Kikki motioned to the open bottle of wine on the table. "Do you remember this wine? We drank it when we met at the Voltaire. Château Beycheville Saint-Julien Grand Cru 2010."

"Of course. What a great idea, though I have to admit I have been feeling rather light-headed and queasy."

Tía nodded knowingly. She ceremoniously poured the velvety red liquid into three golden glass chalices. Then she chanted a blessing and drew the infinity sign in the air.

"Smells heavenly!" Natalia raised her glass to her lips to sip.

"Not yet," Kikki said. "Wait until she appears—Margot."

Natalia set her glass down, with an anxious look.

At the same moment, Natalia and Kikki both stared wide-eyed, seeing for the first time the small precious objects that Tía had placed on the table: the *Snake Goddess*, the terracotta plaque of Inanna/Ishtar from the gala and a millennia-old clay statue of the Egyptian Goddess Isis.

"Appropriate that they join us, *que no?*" Tía said, pleased with her idea. "They are authentic—not replicas."

"I can feel that," Kikki said. "Wow—"

Tía held a finger to her lips, gesturing for them to be quiet.

It was dusk, a liminal time. The veil between the worlds was most thin—an easy time for spirits to cross over. They waited in silence for the ghost of Marguerite de Valois. Dumas's book *La Reine Margot*, with her image on the cover, had been placed prominently on the coffee table, not far from the goddesses.

Finally Tía caught Kikki's eyes.

"Yes?"

"Yes, but I cannot see her." Kikki sniffed the air. "I smell her rose perfume. Should we not pour her a glass? I know this is not wine of her century, but she was quite fond of wine."

Tía poured a fourth chalice, placing it opposite them.

The fire crackled and flames rose. And then, Kikki saw Margot in her regal red dress with high ruff and low-cut bodice. Trademark pearls set off her luminous dark hair and porcelain skin. Face flushed and gay smile. So young, Kikki thought.

Margot smiled and spoke softly—"I am eternally grateful to you."

"She is here," Kikki whispered.

The women raised their chalices as Margot spoke only to Kikki.

"You heroically saved my child—her descendant. I am released at last from the curse on me and on my lineage. Free to love and be loved. No longer cursed by blood, my sang real. My bloodline can now serve the higher purpose it was always meant to—that I always wanted. By the divine right of the Goddess."

Kikki looked Margot directly in her sparkling black eyes and spoke softly aloud, so that Natalia and Tía would hear.

"We did it for Love and Light. For you and your long suffering.

493

You, who were punished and oppressed. Your voice silenced. You held the dark energy of the curse in your spirit—the brutally destructive emotion for all women who have chosen our ways throughout these thousands of years and were burned, stoned, drowned and subjected to pillory as heretics. Their voices silenced. But now they, too, may speak and be seen once more. I am honored that you came to me. You pushed me to be stronger."

Margot smiled, "Gillonne, you were always the brave one! Do not forget that in the coming time. You accompanied me on that terrifying journey, escaping with my newborn daughter to the convent that worshipped the Goddess. Teach the ways of women. And remember—love passionately and fearlessly. You can have what I could not. Speak truth and fight for justice and the way of the Goddess, the way of peace and nurturing.

Do not let power hungry men and women rule and desecrate our Mother Earth. Protect her as a mother should a child. She is the Goddess. She is our only Gaia."

And then Margot was gone.

At the same moment, as night fell on that wintry evening, the small colorful lights throughout the room came on at once.

"I—I felt her presence," Natalia said with wonder. "It's true, then, I am descended from her, from the Valois line?"

"Your mother knew, but she kept it from you for your protection, Natalia," Tía said.

Kikki raised her glass, and Tía and Natalia joined her.

"To us, to Margot, to Monique and Inanna!"

The three women stood and clinked glasses before sipping the velvety wine that tasted of Mother Earth. Kikki and Tía savored a drop in their mouths. Standing in front of the fire, they spat.

"Be gone, cruel patriarchs!" Natalia imitated.

At that moment, a Tarot card blew off the mantelpiece from Kikki's deck—the Three of Cups—a celebration of a beginning, an initiation and a marriage. Eros, the God of Love and Psyche, the bridegroom. Surrounded by three water nymphs dancing in a circle, golden chalices raised.

When they saw the card, the three women laughed and cried at once. Tía poured more wine, and they sat.

"Look, look!" Natalia cried. "The fourth glass. It's gone."

On cue, Tía and Kikki nodded to each other and rose simultaneously. They crossed the room to a side table and drew out two wooden boxes.

Kikki was anxious. Torres would be here soon. And then, the others for the evening's festivities.

"Hurry, Tía."

"You have eternity. That is the message of the Lost Women of Yule, whom we celebrate today. The Wheel has turned and light is returning. An eternity of Light and Love. Danger has passed for now. We have won the battle. The war—well, the war may never be over."

"Is there more wine?" Natalia asked, nervously. She watched Kikki and Tía as they returned to the sofas and placed the boxes on the table.

Kikki smiled and poured the last of the bottle into their glasses.

With long slender fingers, trembling slightly, Natalia picked up the box that Tía had placed on the table and handed it to Kikki.

"Open it. It is for you, in appreciation."

Kikki gave Natalia a curious look. She opened the box, and her eyes widened. A silver braided bracelet in an open circle—two lions' heads faced each other. A very old Greek design. The lions' eyes were made of rubies.

"Oh my Goddesses, how absolutely stunning, Natalia! How—where?"

"It was my mother's. She gave it to me when I was very young—a girl. I have always kept it with me but never worn it."

Kikki stared at Natalia.

"Oh, but I couldn't—it is too precious."

"I insist, and so does Margot." Natalia winked and raised her glass. "*Santé*, sister! To Margot! To my mother! To all of us!"

With tears in her eyes, Kikki slipped it onto her wrist. "It fits perfectly. I'll always think of you when I wear it. I am grateful."

"Now," Tía said, "It's your turn, Natalia."

Tía opened the second box on the table and turned it towards Natalia, revealing an extraordinary diamond and sapphire necklace, from which hung a faceted ruby pendant in the shape of an eight-pointed star.

Kikki cried out.

"Oh my Goddess! That is the necklace that Margot and Gillonne smuggled out of the Louvre for their trip to the convent. I saw it in my visions. It was Margot's gift from Diane de Poitiers."

Tía smiled beatifically. "All true."

"How did you—" Kikki turned to Tía.

"Let's just say that Natalia's Uncle Franco intended to keep it for himself," Tía said slyly.

Kikki looked puzzled. "I don't understand."

Tía continued, a satisfied grin on her wizened face.

"It was in the furniture from the Tuscan convent. Part of their planned antiquities heist this week. Victor stole the collection from the Metropolitan Museum of Art and was going to sell them on the black market. Fortunately, this week, Gabrielle appraised them again at the behest of the Louvre. She recognized the pieces at once since she had authenticated them for the private collector in Paris holding them on behalf of the Met. The necklace was hidden in a secret compartment."

"Really? And—" Kikki was puzzled. Something was missing in the story. What?

"Yes. Torres knew all about their plan and recovered the furniture as well," Tía added, flipping her braid behind one shoulder. "The furniture dated back to—"

Natalia interrupted, "I saw a part of the same collection at Gabrielle's boutique. They did feel familiar. Lovely pieces." She was wide-eyed. "I wondered why my uncle was interested in furniture."

Kikki's left temple seared, and she was whipped into vision.

She closed her eyes, bowed her head and spoke in a trance-like voice.

"Margot's time. It was from the same convent in Tuscany where Margot and Gillonne fled with her child. And centuries later, at that convent, Natalia's mother was a novice and there, Natalia was born."

"How do you know that?" Natalia asked incredulously.

"I *see* it clearly." Kikki was buzzing from wine and still in trance. She barely made out a blurry image. "If we had not defeated Victor, he wouldn't have sold it to the Louvre. No."

Kikki saw a huge wall of flames and swayed. Tía reached for her hand and tapped her firmly on the forehead—her third eye. "Come out of it now, my daughter. Open your eyes."

Slowly, she came back to a still dreamy present. As she stared into the blazing fire, the rest came to her. She sipped wine, and after a moment, she spoke. "He meant to burn it to wipe out the powerful goddess energy the pieces held. That beautiful furniture. And all that it meant. Its entire history—Margot's, her daughters, Natalia's and all the women who sat around those familial tables, protected from patriarchal powers. Raised and nurtured in the Goddess's natural ways."

"Holy shit!" Natalia cried. "You know, I believe you're right. Now that you mention it, I overheard my uncle talking to someone about a surprise aspect of the endgame. Maybe Fitz. I only heard part of that conversation, so I didn't make the connection."

"It doesn't matter now," Tía spoke with finality. "We are all here, and the furniture has been saved. Gabrielle is taking care of it. You can thank Torres too."

The women were thoughtful, sipping wine and at peace for a few moments.

After a moment, and with a sleight of hand, Kikki gingerly lifted the diamond and sapphire necklace from the box on the table. Tía nodded in encouragement. The necklace glowed in Kikki's hands. Natalia watched, wide-eyed.

"It's time, Natalia, for you to don your famous ancestor's necklace," Kikki said.

She stepped behind Natalia and clasped the diamonds firmly around her slender neck. Kikki's fingertips tingled. She blinked and felt that she touched Margot's delicate royal skin.

"Stand up and look at yourself in the mirror. A Valois Goddess."

Natalia rose and stood in front of the mirror over the fireplace.

"It's too beautiful. How will I ever dare to wear it? I will have to keep it in a bank vault, and even then—" She stuttered, marveling at the sparkling jewels that lit up her face.

"Close your eyes and look again," Kikki urged.

Natalia closed her eyes and opened them. When she looked once more, she saw only her bare neck.

"Where did it go?"

"It's there. Protecting you—your sacred jewels and talisman—as

497

it did Margot. Visible to you alone."

Natalia slipped her fingers up to her neck and felt the necklace. "It's true!"

Tía stood behind Natalia and said very quietly, "And you may pass it on to your own daughter when the time comes."

Natalia turned to her and stared.

"How—I don't even," she stammered. 'I'm not sure I'm pregnant. I've been feeling queasy, but I thought perhaps it was nerves."

"Trust Tía," Kikki said with a wink. "It explains why you are so radiant. I hope the father is worthy—"

"And," Tía added ruefully, "of course, this wine has been especially blessed by the council of the Daughters of Inanna. It will fortify your child, your bloodline and your happiness."

Kikki smiled to herself when she heard Margot's high gay laughter echo throughout the room.

A few minutes later, the three women separated. Natalia went to nap in the guest bedroom, and Kikki headed to her bedroom.

Alone in the salon, Tía cleared the coffee table and reverently adorned it anew for the evening. A purple silk veil covered the small statues of ancient goddesses for a secret offering.

In her bedroom, Kikki refreshed herself. She peered into her mirror and swept her hair up. Thoughts of Monique suddenly flooded her mind and tears welled.

"I'm so sorry, Monique. I miss you so much, and I wish you could have been here with us to celebrate," she whispered as tears spilled down her cheeks.

"I am here with you always," Monique whispered. *"It was as it should be. Now, dry your eyes and fix your makeup. You have a big evening ahead of you. Allez, ma belle! He's on his way. Be brave!"*

Kikki put a hand over her heart.

"Thank you, Monique. For everything."

When she returned to the salon, she eyed Tía's handiwork, wondering why she had covered the goddesses.

Tía caught Kikki's eye, looking her up and down.

"Verónica, you are beautiful in that dress."

"Thank you, Tía."

Then she heard her lover's step and the click of his key in the lock.

She turned and watched him walk in the front door and take off his coat. He was dressed in a dark blue suit, sky blue shirt unbuttoned. Long, wavy black hair curled in his collar and a stray lock shading his forehead.

He was tired, she could see as she crossed the room to greet him. She hadn't seen much of him in the last couple of days. It had been a long week.

But his eyes were all smiles when he looked up at her.

"You are a vision in gold, my very own Goddess."

He took her in his arms, kissing her. She was barefoot in her long golden gown of spun silk. She stood on her toes to meet him.

She took his hand and led him to join Tía. Whispering a prayer, Tía lifted the veil, revealing the three priceless goddesses.

Kikki smiled knowingly at Torres and said, "Aren't they amazing?"

"*Sí*! And now I know who's been stealing artifacts from the Louvre."

Kikki pulled him onto the couch beside her, facing the window. The curtains had been drawn to reveal a perfect view of the Louvre and the Pavillon de Flore, softly lit with yellow lights on that Christmas Eve.

"On official loan," Tía said. "Thought you might like to have them here tonight."

"What a marvelous idea, Tía." As Kikki beheld the precious artifacts, they exuded a tangible power—miniature *objets* thousands of years old, now festively encircled by fragrant candles that smelled of roses.

Kikki's voice was a whisper. "They are truly one and the same. They are all our Mother Goddess, Gaia."

The Goddesses spoke to Kikki in silent chorus. They seemed to vibrate and a soft golden light surrounded them. Kikki wondered if Tía could see. Kikki looked across at her and saw a glimmer in her eyes.

"Such perfect harmony, and not a little divine synchronicity," Torres said, quietly. "You discovered the Snake Goddess, worshipped by the Pre-Bronze Aegean peoples on your island and nearby Minoan Crete. You know that archeologists now posit that the Minoans existed long before was originally thought. The *Minoan Snake Goddess* and the culture from whence she came was contemporaneous with Inanna and Isis."

Kikki leaned closer to inspect them.

"A continuing flow of time and goddess energy."

Tía took Kikki's hand and said, "I have brought them here to your home. To fully take in the power, peace and love that the Goddess and Divine Feminine hold and always have throughout time. There are many others who represent our Mother Goddess from other corners of the world. The goddesses before you come from your power place in the Eastern Mediterranean basin. They, and we, all are grateful for your courage and sacrifice. You took a perilous journey, guided by your rebel Queen Margot here in your beloved City of Light and Love. With the highest of stakes."

"I am truly awestruck and feel such love." Tears filled Kikki's eyes. "And the gala and exhibit—the showing of my cherished Snake Goddess, about which I was so worried and protective, she was the link—for me to come to full understanding. She was the catalyst to join them harmoniously as one to enhance the power of the Goddess, helping us to win this battle. Now I know why I had to let go of my attachment and worry. It was the only real way to protect her and all of us. To offer her up as sacrifice for Natalia, for Margot, for the Daughters of Inanna."

"And for beloved Monique and your Paris," Torres added.

Kikki's eyes teared at Monique's name. "Yes, for Monique. Perhaps the sacrifice Hecate demanded to honor her on the Winter Solstice." She saw the vivid Tarot cards. The Moon Goddess and the Three of Swords. "And innocent Iphigenia sacrificed on her wedding day cursed, like Margot."

There was a hush in the room, as if the powerful icons had demanded reverent silence.

"We are all one with the Great Goddess Mother Earth," Kikki heard the clay objets whisper.

The small lights that lit the wreaths in the room flashed on and off. The candles flickered, and the flames in the fireplace leapt. The ancient goddesses grew larger, surrounded by a golden light.

In the unearthly calm, Tía crept silently out of the room.

Torres left to have a word with Tía.

Moments later, Kikki rose from the sofa and crossed the room to her place of vigil at the French paned windows overlooking the Seine. It was calm and quiet on this cold winter night. The still full moon was bright on a cloudless evening in an inky winter sky. Venus and Jupiter aligned to form a triangle with the moon. A mystical omen.

She gazed at her reflection in the window. Who had she become in this last week? She was paler than usual and had dark circles under her eyes, but they shimmered. Her soft blonde hair framed her face. Deep crimson lips, lapis eye makeup and a long golden gown that softly framed her breasts.

She looked different—of course. But what was it?

Lighter, yet stronger. Transformed and empowered.

Inspired by brave Margot, she had become one with Athena and found deep within herself a strength and courage she hadn't known she possessed—not fully. She had faced true evil to save the City of Light.

She had reclaimed a part of her soul that had been lost—even cursed—for four hundred years, though her heart ached with loss for Monique's sacrifice.

Blood curse lifted, karmic debts paid, past life circles closed. Full of love, Kikki was ready to walk forward hand in hand with Torres. She glanced at her reflection in the window again and smiled.

Just then, her lover came up behind her and put his arms around her waist. He nuzzled her bare back.

"You are luminescent tonight, *mi cielo.*"

She turned to him. They stood a foot apart, holding hands, memorizing each other's faces.

"I want to remember you always as you are this night, Kikki," he whispered.

"And I you."

She reached up and traced the contours of his cheekbones, his nose, his lips. She ran her fingers through his hair, brushing it from his forehead.

She wanted to kiss him, but a voice told her not to. Not yet.

She closed her eyes and saw the Ten of Cups—the Goddess

501

Aphrodite blessing the union of Eros and Psyche. A union of great passion. She thought of Margot's words. Her heart thumped loudly in her ears. Margot was right about loving fearlessly and passionately.

"Have you thought about it—about us? I am back for my answer."

"I haven't stopped thinking, feeling—"

"Shh." He took her in his arms. "I've got you."

"You do, don't you," she said shyly, heart racing.

"So then, Véronique—do you—take me, this man?'"

"Will I?" She was terrified and yet racing towards him.

"Yes, will you, do you want me? Us. Will you promise? I love you Kikki more than life itself. I would never leave you."

"I told you before. Yes, I will, and I do take you."

"I want to hear you say it again."

She smiled, "I promise. I love you madly, wildly, passionately, Torres. You're so infuriating, but—" She caught his soulful dark eyes and said, "I know, I'm quite a lot to handle. And I'm not going to stop being who I am. Nor are you. But we can do this together."

"Yes, *mi amor"* He kissed her tenderly, wonderment filling his heart. And not a little fear too. How would he handle her—and her him? Together they would learn and figure it out.

They held each other's eyes in promise.

"Hot sex and hot love, then?" They both spoke at once and laughed.

"Well then," Torres whispered, drawing her closer. "*Mi amor?*"

She had stopped breathing, and all she could feel was love.

Nervous, Kikki stuttered, "Aren't Liam and Tía and the others —Cleo is coming from Greece, and—"

"You mean are we going to have a ceremony? I know you love ceremonies." He teased, arms around her waist.

"Well, yes, but—do we really need witnesses and a group, however dear they are? Can we keep the intimacy of the moment to ourselves—please?"

He pointed to the three goddess statues. "Good enough for me."

"Goddesses, I love you Torres."

He drew her onto the *récamier*, and they kissed deeply, tongues entwined, vital juices flowed. Hands touching bodies, clothes askew.

They were nearly joined when a discreet cough interrupted their passion.

"What?" Kikki asked hoarsely, voice full of sex.

Liam spoke quietly, but his voice carried across the room.

"Thought you might want champagne to celebrate. To toast a very long road!"

They sat up together, arranging their clothes.

Kikki blushed and then caught Liam's eye.

"Very funny! *Bien sûr!* Champagne!"

Liam, Tía, Natalia and a joyful Cleo, just in from Santorini, joined them.

"Just one toast, and then we'll leave you. Or rather, you'll leave us—" Liam winked at Kikki.

"Oh Cleo! I'm so glad to see you. You came!" Kikki hugged her friend, overwhelmed with emotion. "You'll stay for a while, then?"

Cleo laughed, "Of course, *bella!*"

Liam lifted his glass, "To the two of you! Finally!"

They clinked and drank.

"And to all of us for winning this battle and living to tell the story." Kikki lifted her glass and flashed a radiant smile.

In the moment of silence after the toast, Kikki heard Monique whisper again, "*Stini yiamas!* Be happy, Kikki!"

Silently Kikki answered, "*Merci, ma belle. You'll always be here with me, in my heart.*"

As they stood in their small circle, laughing and drinking, Kikki felt Torres's heat. She finished her champagne and set the flute on the table.

She took Liam's hand and said, "You'll take care of our guests, Liam? Tell them—" she looked to Torres for help.

"To have a good time, Liam. Thanks." Torres held fast to her hand. "We might join you later—very much later. Say, tomorrow— for a late breakfast." He guided Kikki through the doorway and followed, closing the door behind them.

They were happy to be alone and on their way to a very private party in La Reine Margot Suite at the Hotel Regina. After a long, passionate kiss, as they waited for the private elevator, Torres released her and said, "*Mira.* There's one more thing—"

"Oh Goddesses, not more business. Not now. I will kill you!"

"I just thought you might want to know that you just joined the aristocracy—in a manner of speaking."

"What the hell are you talking about?"

"Comte Jean Michel Beauregard de Torres—my cover—"

"No." She caught his chin. "The story is real?"

"Indeed, Madame la Comtesse." He smiled mischievously, enjoying her reaction. But he eyed her closely to see if she was truly surprised. Had she already known? Very likely, knowing Kikki.

She flashed a mock-angry glance. "Distantly related to Margot, I suppose? And Natalia too. I might be jealous."

He caught her chin, kissed her and then said, "Most probably."

She laughed. Kikki had known for a long time that his legend was actually true. Her heart knew, and if that wasn't enough, she had seen the proof that Tía had prepared. After all, thanks to Gabrielle, she had a key to the secret compartment in the Spanish Renaissance desk she had gifted him.

She didn't know yet how she felt about being part of royalty. Margot might have a lot more to teach her now that the curse had been lifted. She looked forward to that. She wondered what and where he had his domain. She might like to retire to a more tranquil life in the country. Perhaps give up her legal practice—or fight for selected causes. Still, wherever she resided and whatever she did with her business, she knew now that she would always be the High Priestess—and Athena—a calling.

"We'll talk about all that. Later, much later, *mi amor*—Madame la Comtesse Beauregard de Torres." He laughed.

"I'm going to get you for this one, Torres, I swear by the Goddess!"

"I look forward to it!"

"You will pay for a long time to come."

She smiled and stepped into his arms.

"I am counting on it." His dark eyes held hers.

The elevator door opened. One long stemmed red rose lay on the floor.

Kikki whispered, "Thank you, Margot."

Kikki and Torres crossed the threshold. Lips met and they embraced, all hot passion and love. Joined together, moving in rhythm.

A perfect fit.

FIN

Acknowledgments

I am grateful and fortunate to so many people who have supported, inspired and kept me going during the long years of bringing this book to the light—who have been there for me when I was on the verge; read early drafts and encouraged with praise and notes. A huge amount of gratitude:

~ to my extraordinary publishers, Indies United Publishing House and their authors, especially Lisa Orban and Lisa Towles;

~ to Sarah Lovett, my brilliant editor, amazing author and dear friend, who midwifed this book through many drafts while also keeping me relatively sane;

~ to my family: my beloved parents, Ferd and Eileen, who continue to inspire; to my sister and brothers and their beautiful families for believing in, and supporting me always;

~to John Simoudis for friendship and a gorgeous cover design; Jack Arnold for a beautiful website; Nick Zellinger for brilliant final cover production; and, Jennifer Marshall for her excellent proofing.

Merci infiniment to wonderful friends on both sides of the Atlantic who have enriched my life with their love, friendship and company, so important in the solitary life of a novelist, and more so during a pandemic. Enormous thanks:

~to Stephen Thomas, Cynthia Miller, Barbara Grygutis, Paula Van Ness, Alán Huerta and the late wonderful Minnette Burgess, Heather Jones, John Jannetto and Eleni Sakeller of New Zealand, each of whom have been singularly steadfast friends from Tucson, who stood by me and cheered me on;

~to Katia Davis, muse and priestess, Lynn Perry, who brought me Greek goddesses, Ana Matiella, a constant positive and inspiring author, Muriel Fariello, Barbara Seiler, who share my love of Paris, Jess, Ryan and Rob for taking me in at the Bobcat Inn, Santa Fe, Kim Pentecost and Bobbie Martin, extraordinary healers who literally kept the darkness at bay, Stephanie Jourdan, brilliant astrologer, Dovie Wingard who read the first draft, Lola Lorber, lovely goddess daughter, James Egan, for generous advice and support, Johanna Baldwin, Guadalupe goddess, Russ Stratton, Stephanie Denkowicz, for all things archeological and about Egypt, Liliana Morales, Claire Chinoy, Karen Fischer for Spain and flamenco, Laurie Robinson, for travel and France, Kat King who read first pages; to friends re-found, Becky, Jill, Carole, Kathy and the gang.

In Paris:

~to NC Heikin, film goddess, for excellent notes and abiding friendship, Robert Pepin for his support and faith in books, Christophe Vessier, Merlin of magical forests, who always believed, Judith Weber, Hotel des Marronniers, Marie-José, Hotel de Lille, Malek & Abdel at Proxi, rue de Beaune, Mohamet "Nicolas" Chaid, Gabrielle Laroche for her friendship and boutiques of beautiful antiques featured in the novel, Amélie Laroche, a shining light, Kim Coston for always encouraging, Brigitte de Cirugeda for our long friendship, for dear David Fischer who inspired, Rob Watson for early reads; the owners and staff at Les Antiquaires, rue du Bac, the Ricards, Éric and Flora, the Voltaire, Catherine, Thierry, Pascal and Regis, the Picots and new owners;

And to the inspiring Carré des Antiquaires where I have been privileged to live.

In Oia, Santorini:

~to Alexis Zervas, the late Takis at Ether Sunset everyone at Ammoudi, especially Katina's, Katina and Vangelis, Sunset Taverna, Mary Kay and Niko at Gassapiko, Maria "Baba Vida", Mihales of Santorini Mou.

Finally, my humble gratitude to the Mother Goddess and to my muse, Margot, for this incredible journey through her life and times.

Author's Note

In Queen Margot's Garden

This novel is a labor of love. It's been my passion, borne of my romance with Paris and her history, the City of Light and Love, with Marguerite de Valois as my spirited and insistent muse.

Having lived for many years in Europe, mostly Paris, in 1993 I found myself living in the 17th century gardens of La Reine Margot's one-time Rive-Gauche palace. Much like my alter ego, Kikki Trieste, I was literally haunted by the spirit of Queen Margot who compelled me to share her untold story. She put her quill in my hand. She came up time and again through the old tunnels under the 17th century building where I lived and insisted that I listen and give her voice.

She spurred me to do intense research. A student of history, thanks to my father, I read all I could about her life, France, Europe, Paris and the Valois Court in the tumultuous 16th century.

I studied Margot's *Memoires,* written while she was imprisoned. Not only was she a female author in a man's world, she was one of the inventors of the genre of memoir.

She haunted and inspired me to re-envision a story that has not been told about the complex, iconic woman that was Marguerite de Valois.

She was with me, haunting, yet somehow comforting, when wandering Saint-Germain along storied streets—rue de Seine, rue de Buci, rue Jacob, rue Bonaparte, the Institut de France, the Pont des Arts, Pont Neuf and the Palais des Beaux-Arts. There, where were once her palace with its extensive gardens and inside, the Chapelle des Louanges.

While I was sipping a glass of wine in the *quartier* at the Voltaire, Bar Bac or Les Antiquaires, she whispered in my ear.

Walking along the Seine near the Pont Royal, at the bottom of rue de Beaune, rue du Bac and Quai Voltaire, she accompanied me, as I gazed at the ever-changing river, the Louvre and Pavillon de Flore. I felt her tap me on the shoulder, whispering urgently. Her scent enveloped me – a peculiarly strong musky rose.

Ever the *flânneuse*, when I wandered the Jardin des Tuileries or the Jardin du Palais Royal, she took my hand. As I strolled the courtyards of the Louvre, her ephemeral presence was often visible to me in the Cour Carrée, as I gazed at the *Salle des Caryatides* and *Venus de Milos* through tall windows in the crepuscule of dusk—the magical liminal time. The *Salle des Caryatides* where a 16 year old Marguerite de Valois had her debut ball.

Her spirit accompanied me when I strolled through the Jardin du Luxembourg to pay homage to the queens, *Les Reines et Femmes Illustrées*, behind the Luxembourg Palace.

And she demanded, *"Why am I not among these queens of France at Marie de Medici's palace? I was a Queen of France. And godmother to her son, King Louis XIII."*

Even when I was swimming in the silky waters of the caldera with the Sea Priestesses in the Aegean, Santorini, she followed me, urging me not to stop writing until I had told her story.

And so finally I did—so that her voice might be heard anew in our pivotal time when women seek agency, as she did 400 years ago —as did her contemporary, Elizabeth I, a queen who fought to rule without a husband or a male heir, defying patriarchal boundaries of the High Renaissance.

Though Margot wished to be a fair and just voice as Queen of France, she was doomed by the era's patriarchal structure, a time of eight long religious wars. Voltaire thought her one of the greatest queens of France. Yet, she was blocked: cursed by blood, *le sang royal* of her family.

She was damned by the Saint-Bartholomew's Day Massacre—a bloody slaughter on the eve of her wedding to Huguenot, Henri de Bourbon, King of Navarre—instigated by her treacherous mother, Catherine de Medici, the Black Queen, and her elder brother, Henri. The streets of Paris flowed with blood for weeks, the Seine turned scarlet. Her wedding earned the sobriquet: *Les noces vermillion*. Scarlet wedding. And she was branded Bloody Margot.

At only 19 years old the beautiful, brilliant Margot was condemned—held prisoner in the Louvre and exiled from court. Ultimately exiled to desolate Usson, imprisoned in a medieval fortress perched on a volcano. She remained a threat and understandably plotted against her jailers. They sent assassins to kill her.

In her *Memoires,* written in prison, she gave a reflective account, referencing celebrated minds with whom she regularly corresponded. Her writings responded to poet *Abbé de Brantôme.* To paraphrase: *Mother Nature created a perfect work in Marguerite de Valois, such a rare and perfect beauty that one sees her as a goddess, rather than an earthly princess.*

In 1605, Henri IV obtained a "royal divorce." After nearly twenty years in exile, Margot finally returned to her beloved Paris. She built a palatial estate across from the Louvre on the Left Bank, then considered insalubrious. Margot was the first to make it fashionable. She invented the renowned *salons* of Saint-Germain that brought together artists, intellectuals, and aristocrats.

Historians, mostly male, claim that Margot had no children and was sterile. The same historians label her whore, heretic, nymphomaniac and witch. As a woman of the 21st century, aided by Margot's whisperings, I uncovered a different story.

She bore a son who became a key agent in the conspiracy which resulted in King Henri IV's death by the assassin Ravaillac in 1610.

Queen Margot outlived him and her treacherous family. She died in 1615 at the age of 61.

But she was not *the last daughter of the Valois.* That story is written in *The French Queen's Curse.* Will her ghost now leave me in peace? If she does, I may miss her, however I hope I have done her justice as she sought.

Among my original inspirations were Alexander Dumas's wonderful novel, *La Reine Margot,* and the exquisite film adaptation by Patrice Chéreau. Though this novel is a work of fiction, I have endeavored to be accurate with historical facts, anecdotes and present day detail. Any errors are my own. It is not my intention to provide here a thorough historical note of my muse, the complex, fascinating Marguerite de Valois and the times in which she lived. I will delve into that in newsletters and blogs in the future on my website. Juliettelauber.com.

Made in the USA
Monee, IL
05 May 2022

95959952R00301